A Puhaka Books Selection

puhakabooks.com

A Jack Wesley Novel

Pleasure Smiles

W. B Martin

Also by W. B. Martin

The Jack Wesley Series

Trouble Leaves Too Slow
Shoving Back the Shadows
Only Pretty Lies
Forever Now
Chasing the Blackbird
Just Empty Every Pocket
Shaking Off Futility
Be Prepared To Bleed
Too Stupid To Survive

Other Novels

German Golfers Who Changed the World
Sweetness in the Dark
Endangered Species
Cubo Zoan
Vincent van Gogh Likes Cats

Pleasure Smiles

#8 in the Jack Wesley Thriller Series

Printed by permission of
Puhaka Publishing

Printed in the United States of America

Edited by Timothy Johns

Cover Layout by Morwenna Rakestraw

Print - ISBN 13-9781940554181
eBook - ISBN 13-9781940554198

Version 3.1

First Edition October 15, 2018

To Larry S.
Marine, State Police, writer, friend

Chapter 1

Boston, Massachusetts

The fall leaves of New England were at their peak as Boston sat under perfect weather. A continuing dry spell only enhanced the brilliant leaf color. The dryness almost made the yellows too bright to look at without sunglasses.

The reds and oranges bust in color from the dry summer end. Fall had just arrived but the days continued to be warm followed by cold nights. An old-fashioned Indian summer had been pronounced by the local television news pundits and the populace seemed to be out in force to enjoy every minute.

After the winter that had hit Massachusetts hard, no one was looking forward to any repeat. The entire East Coast had suffered under relentless cold weather and snow as the 'polar vortex' had announced itself numerous times.

Old timers in New England guffawed at the young and their labels for everything. Polar vortex was a new one that didn't sit well with them. They knew a good nor'easter came every winter and sometimes more than once. In the old days, snow would accumulate in inches per hour as a nor'easter blew mounds of snow onto the land as the storm came in off the Gulf of Maine. Nothing new to those folks.

Jack Wesley stared out the shop's windows at the color displayed across the street. Boston Common lay before him and the sight was none he had ever seen. Raised in the Pacific Northwest, nice fall colors there amounted to a few small vine maple trees high in the mountains that turned bright red. The trees around his hometown would turn a tepid yellow and sometimes orange to be almost immediately pounded to the ground by the sideways rain that showed up about the same time. The color display was typically dull and brief only to be followed with local flooding as all the fallen leaves proceeded to clog all the catch basins.

No, this was something else, he thought. *When I'm done today I need to rent a car and drive out of the city. I'm sure the countryside around Boston is spectacular.*

"Good afternoon Mr. Wesley," a customer said. "It's an honor to have you here today. Can you sign my book?"

Jack looked up at a teenager holding his book. This was a new experience and he still hadn't gotten used to being a celebrity. *Not that one book makes a celebrity,* he thought. But his numbers were moving up the sales chart that his agent emailed him each week. And now with the German edition out last month, things could get interesting.

"Thank you," Jack said. "Who should I dedicate it to?" This part made him nervous. Even after years of writing police reports, getting people's names spelled right made him nervous.

"Could you make it out to Brad?" came the answer. "He's my boyfriend. He really wanted to be here today to meet you. He's a huge fan."

Brad, thank God. I can handle that, Jack thought. In the three weeks of his first ever book tour he had heard some beauties. And he was amazed at how often

'Mackalah' showed up. He actually was remembering how that one went.

Jack took his pen and inscribed the inside title page on the hardcover book as instructed. He added a little personal note to Brad, closed it and handed it back to the young woman. She immediately opened and read the inscription.

"He'll love that, thank you."

"No, thank you for purchasing my book. And tell Brad I'll expect to hear from him on my website." The price of the limited amount of fame Jack was experiencing was that he now had numerous emails to answer on a daily basis. *I'm not sure how the big authors handled this part of celebrity,* he thought. *At some point they must hire staff to do it.*

With all the social media sites he kept up with since his book was picked up by a major publisher, his time for living was slowly disappearing. With a blog to write each week, he didn't see how authors had time to write their books.

And Jack was determined to move along on his second book. He had no intention of being a one-book wonder. Each winter had been dedicated to writing and his second book was progressing. He was just amazed at how much editing and rewriting the publisher had required before his first book came out.

But summers were reserved for adventures. Jack would have to figure out what would happen to all his book promotional duties when the nice weather returned. But until then, he had books to sell and signings to attend.

Jack was distracted as he thought of all the things the publisher had scheduled for him.

"Please sir, could you sign my book?" The voice was of an old cranky man. Jack looked up to the big white grin staring out from a large black face.

"LaMarcus, you old war dog," Jack said. "I thought I might see you."

"Still have time for us little people, Mr. Celebrity?" LaMarcus teased.

"Hey, knock it off. This fame stuff isn't all it's cracked up to be," Jack said. "And I'm not even on the Times bestseller list. I can only imagine."

"Yeah, fame, big money, fast cars and large breasted women," LaMarcus offered. "Those are all hard to take."

Jack looked around and luckily no one else was in earshot of his Marine Corps buddy's comments. He had noticed the folks that ran the book store here on Beacon Street were a little snooty. *The big tit comment wouldn't have gone down well with them, even if spoken by a minority type*, Jack thought.

Decorum had its limits, and Sergeant Lewis, as he would always know him, was a bit rough around the edges. Not that he couldn't shine it on when he had to. His making captain on the City of Cambridge Police Department across the Charles River was evidence of that.

"So, what brings you in, if I have to ask?"

"To buy a book and get it signed by my famous writer friend," LaMarcus said.

"You didn't have to buy one, you know that."

"Well, I didn't want to steal the book from the store. Besides, you probably need the money, knowing you," LaMarcus said.

Jack took LaMarcus's book and wrote a long dedication in the front when he saw another customer walk up behind his friend. Handing it back, Jack asked, "Can we get together after this? I'm done in an hour."

"There's an Irish pub to the left and up the hill. Just past the Statehouse on the right," LaMarcus said. "I'll meet you there in an hour."

Jack finished with his signing duties and thanked the shop proprietor. Picking up his bag, he slung it over his shoulder and shoved it onto his back. As he opened the door to leave, the cool early evening wind coming in off Boston Harbor made him turn up his collar. *Boy, it drops in temperature fast when the sun goes down,* he thought.

Walking into the pub, he saw LaMarcus waving from a booth on the side. The Celtic music blared and the afternoon crowd of Statehouse workers mixed it up. The twenty-somethings who worked the political end of the Bay State looked to be maneuvering for companionship. Jack slid in across from LaMarcus and dropped his bag on the seat.

"Kind of noisy, don't you think," Jack almost yelled across to his friend.

"But so much to look at."

Jack scanned the crowd more closely and noticed that the female-to-male ratio was decidedly in favor of the males. In favor that they had more to choose from as the women outnumbered the men. Many of the young women were decidedly good-looking and appeared loose enough from alcohol to be easy marks.

Turning to his friend, Jack commented, "Yeah, but even us old war horses would have a hard time finding love here. Too young and too liberal for the likes of us."

"Speak for yourself, you Wyoming redneck," LaMarcus said. "I for one, know how to entice the finer sex into just that."

"So retirement has freed up your time, I see."

LaMarcus's attitude changed at the mention of his retirement. Jack knew his friend had risen up through the ranks, finally obtaining his cherished captain posting. He had earned it largely on Jack's help in cracking the case of a school shooter. Tipped off on an impending attack on a Massachusetts grade school, LaMarcus just happened to be there at the right time to stop the attack. Hailed a hero by the media and his superiors, LaMarcus was soon promoted to captain.

But a change in the political winds in city government had brought a less-then-reputable mayor to power. When corruption charges were leveled, LaMarcus was expected to blunt the State Police investigation. When he failed to pursue a cover-up to the charges with the enthusiasm thought necessary by the police commissioner, he was offered retirement or a demotion. LaMarcus had taken retirement.

"Sorry politics caught up with you my friend," Jack offered.

"I guess it was bound to happen," LaMarcus said. "The Marine Corps oath I took wouldn't have it go any other way."

14

Jack lifted his wine glass and proposed a toast. LaMarcus raised his beer mug and held it aloft.

"To all enemies, foreign and domestic," Jack toasted.

"To all enemies," LaMarcus retorted.

A period of silence followed as the two comrades-in-arms reflected on the enemies they had fought over the years. And the comrades-in-arms that they had lost in those struggles.

After a few more rounds and much conversation, they were fully caught up with each other's lives. The crowd slowly drifted off to other locations for other activities as the two warriors talked.

Chapter 2

Boston, Massachusetts

"Jack, I need your help," LaMarcus finally said.

"You've got it. What's up?"

"It's my uncle. You remember. My Dad's younger brother."

"Sure, fought in Korea with the 1st Marine Division. Survived Chosin. The Chosin Few they call themselves. How could I forget," Jack said. "Oorah."

"Oorah," LaMarcus added. "I think he's in trouble."

"What kind?"

"He's missing. His wife hasn't heard from him in over six months," LaMarcus said. "And two months after he left, he changed where his pension and Social Security check got deposited."

"Why did he leave? And didn't she have a say in where his checks went?" Jack asked.

"They've been legally separated for a couple years now," LaMarcus said. "He was too cheap to move out totally so he was living in their basement. They have a house out in Mattapan. Been living there since I was a little kid."

"So he up and bolted and no one knows where?" Jack asked.

"Well, sort of. She got letters postmarked from Las Vegas about once a month up until the time when he changed deposits. Then nothing. So we know he was alive and living in Nevada. But since then, no news."

"Any other family members in touch with your uncle? Did you ask them?"

"I'm the only one left. Besides my aunt," LaMarcus said.

"Did you check with the VA? Those checks have to have a live body to receive them."

"They confirm that his VA checks still are sent out each month. Social Security won't release any information other than he would appear to be still alive. The check is deposited electronically in a bank account in Nevada. That is all they offer. Same with his pension."

"So how much are we talking? Does your aunt know how much he gets each month?" Jack asked.

"She got half his pension and half his SSI. But even at that, he's taking home about three thousand a month."

"What do you have in mind then?"

"I want to head out to Vegas and see what I can track down," LaMarcus said.

"Have you considered that maybe your uncle doesn't want to be found? He had a reason he left," Jack said.

"And knowing my aunt, I would have left years ago. I always enjoyed my time with my uncle," LaMarcus said. "After my Dad left the family, he was my male role model for me. He's why I joined the Corps. But his wife was never a happy person. They couldn't have kids and I think she took it out on everyone. My uncle put up with a lot while he was there."

"Then be careful what you go looking for. You sure don't want to lead your aunt to him, from the sounds of it."

"I need to know," LaMarcus said. His voice cracked as he spoke by the emotion it brought up. "I need to know if he's OK."

"Then let's go make sure," Jack offered. "My only problem is I have a book signing tour set for Germany. My book has just been released over there and they're expecting me next week. Any chance you can get started in Las Vegas and I catch up to you there? If you need any immediate help, I can break off the tour. But it sounds like routine police work to me."

"I guess you're right. I sure don't want you messing up your tour on account of some old timer hiding out in Vegas," LaMarcus said.

Jack looked at him sharply and tried to determine if what he had just said was sarcasm or not.

"Look LaMarcus, we go way back. You come first over any book tour," Jack said. "If you need me now, I'm there for you. Just spit it out."

"Relax, Jack," LaMarcus said, "I'm just messin' with you. Just making sure it all hasn't gone to your head."

The two friends laughed at each other as they finished their drinks and paid their tab. Pulling on his jacket for the cold he knew awaited, Jack walked with LaMarcus to the door.

"Where you staying?" LaMarcus asked.

"The Lenox House on Exeter near Copley Square."

"Well, if you're taking the 'T', we better hurry. Some stop running at midnight."

Jack checked his watch and realized how long they had been visiting. The cold bit into them as they walked briskly down Park Street toward the Park Street Station. The MBTA subway would get him back out to his hotel in no time, if they got in before the last train.

"Where are you headed, Cambridge?" Jack said. He wasn't sure if LaMarcus had kept his house in the city that had retired him. With his divorce a few years back, Jack knew that LaMarcus was known to step out with the ladies. Where he took them back to, Jack had no clue.

"I'm out in Newton now. Expensive, but the rich divorcee rate is sky high out there. So, it's the good old Green Line for me too," LaMarcus said.

They reached the Park Street subway station just before Jack thought his ears and nose would break off. The cold was biting and it was a huge contrast from the warm sunny days he had experienced walking to the book shop.

Paying the fare, they descended the steps and followed the Green Line signs for outbound. Other riders scrambled through the labyrinth of pedestrian tunnels as they sought out other lines. The Red Line took people north to Cambridge or south towards Braintree. The green line headed west from Park Street station and forked into multiple lines.

Since Jack was going just a short distance, he could take any one of the Green Line trains. Since the line split into multiple routes after Copley, LaMarcus could only take the Riverside train unless he wanted to walk a long way on the other end. Luckily, a Riverside bound train pulled in and they climbed on board together.

Not a true subway line but a street car, Jack had to step up into the car, LaMarcus right behind him. As Jack turned to find a seat, he realized that they had picked the wrong train. He moved a short distance but did not sit down.

Jack glanced as LaMarcus came around him looking for a seat. His friend stopped and stood next to him as they stared at the back of the train.

"Shit," was all LaMarcus got out.

"Hey, you need to stop right now," Jack bellowed.

The five teenagers who had been beating some unfortunate rider stopped and turned at the intrusion. The five thugs were minorities and their victim wasn't. *Great, just what I need*, Jack thought.

"Who you yelling at?" one of the teens challenged. His glare matched his partners threatening poise.

"You, shithead. Let the guy up now," Jack commanded.

He glanced and LaMarcus stood with his best cop threaten mode. But they weren't cops anymore. At least LaMarcus wasn't a cop. Jack carried a badge and gun, courtesy of the Teton County, Wyoming Sheriff. Even after his thirty years of police work, this appointment was more an honorary thing that his politically connected brother had worked out. Jack was a real deputy sheriff in official terms but, from past experience with East Coast law enforcement, knew that fact carried less than full weight.

Because of trouble he had had in New York State and the subsequent pissing match between Wyoming and New York, he was reluctant to identify himself. And even more reluctant to draw his weapon which was safely tucked in his small-of-the-back holster.

"Watch your mouth or I'll rip it out of your head, honkey," came the answer.

The foot holding down their victim prevented him from getting off the train's floor. The teen holding him down pushed his fist into his opposite palm in defiance.

LaMarcus finally spoke, "You boys need to simmer down and let that boy up now."

"Look Uncle Tom. Just 'cuz you hangin' out with whitey there don't make you somethin' special." the leader said. "Now, you two go crawl away and we won't hurt you."

"Not going to happen," Jack said. His hand lifted his jacket in the back and waited close to his weapon.

Four of the teens started to move forward. The fifth kicked the downed teen and stood guard over him, preventing his escape. Jack and LaMarcus moved apart so they had more room for what was coming.

Because of the closeness of the train's empty seats, only two teens could approach them at a time. The first two lunged, one being met with a baton that suddenly appeared in LaMarcus's hand. The metal rod-shape weapon struck one teen across the neck and he fell in pain, screaming.

Jack met the other teen with a high booted kick to the chest, sending him crashing back into the other two charging teens. They stumbled for a minute, then regrouped. At the change in dynamics and with two of their cohorts on the floor, they each drew a weapon.

A knife appeared in the hand of the teen in front of LaMarcus. The baton immediately swung with a blow on his wrist as the knife flew across the train. Grabbing his now broken wrist, he stood as LaMarcus applied the baton to side of his knee, dropping him hard onto the floor.

But the fourth thug pulled a gun. A small caliber semi-auto, it held seven shots that could kill or maim. As he raised the weapon to fire, Jack grabbed the thug's gun hand and forced it down. The gun went off with an echoing blast. With Jack's other hand, he smashed the perpetrator in the side of the head. The teen staggered and attempted to raise his gun again.

LaMarcus ended the struggle with a baton across the back of his legs. Dropping the gun as he fell, he clutched his knees in agony. Jack took the gun, ejected the magazine onto the floor and cleared the round in the chamber. He slipped it into his coat pocket.

The fifth and final teen quickly took his foot off the downed teen and offered to help him up.

"Hey man, we was just funnin' with you." He held the injured youth steady and pretended to brush off any dirt from the floor. "We do this all the time, don't we?"

The victim broke free and walked behind Jack. Everyone staggered as the train pulled into the Copley Square Station. The train driver ran off the train and soon two uniformed transit police ran onto the train. Their guns drawn, they motioned everyone to place hands on the side of the car and spread their legs.

Jack and LaMarcus joined the teen thug and the victim in complying. *No time to identify myself,* Jack thought. *Things will get sorted out in a minute.*

With one cop holding his gun on everyone, the other started searching each person. Feeling LaMarcus's sleeve, he reached in and retrieved a now compact baton from where LaMarcus had returned it. The officer threw it toward his buddy.

After the victim, the cop searched Jack. He hit the small handgun in Jack's pocket first. The cop retrieved the gun and after making sure it was empty, threw it on the floor away from everyone.

"You're in trouble carrying a gun in this state. I don't suppose you have a permit for that, do you?" the cop asked.

"No, I don't. I have something better," Jack answered.

"What's that?"

"Can I lift the front of my jacket up?" Jack asked.

"No, you just stand right there grabbing the wall."

The cop reached around and felt along the front of Jack's coat. Feeling hard metal, he reached up under the fabric and retrieved Jack's sheriff badge.

"What's this?" the cop asked. "Deputy Sheriff, Teton County. Where the hell is that?"

"Wyoming," Jack answered.

"Well, you're a long way from home, cowboy," the officer still holding the gun finally said. "That don't carry much weight in this here town."

"Well, be careful on my back for what my sheriff asks me to carry with his badge," Jack said.

The cop conducting the search moved to Jack's back and located his Glock 9mm. He pulled it from its holster and held it up for his buddy to see.

"That, my friend is worth twenty years in this state," the second cop said.

The first cop finished his searches of all eight people as his partner called for back-up. With LaMarcus and Jack in handcuffs, they were lead away first while the new crew took over the teens.

"Nice welcome for your out-of-town guest, Lewis," Jack said.

"It will get straightened out once we get to the station. Should be someone I know there," LaMarcus said. "Thirty years of policing in Cambridge should help."

LaMarcus was partially right. They ran into someone LaMarcus knew almost right away. It took another three hours before the right people were contacted that got LaMarcus freed and his baton returned.

Meanwhile Jack sat in lock-up waiting. A desk sergeant finally showed up and opened the cell door.

"Wesley, let's go."

Jack stood and headed in the direction the sergeant indicated. A police lieutenant was waiting in his office as Jack was shown in. A chair was offered as the lieutenant continued reading a paper he held. The sergeant returned to his duties.

"Mr. Wesley, you seem to have stepped in it," the lieutenant said. "We've checked your credentials and they are legit. We get a lot of people in here with some flim-flam ID from some two bit law enforcement office somewhere out west. All so they can carry in our state."

"So I'm free to go after you return my weapon and badge?" Jack offered.

"Not so fast, Deputy Wesley. As I said, your credentials check out, but we still have a problem. You had a small semi-auto in your pocket we took off you. We're running ballistics on it but it matches the description of a gun used in a drive-by shooting over in East Boston one hour before we picked you up."

"And the fact I took it off the perpetrator instead of letting him keep it adds nothing to the story," Jack said.

"The teen said he'd never seen that gun before."

"And they hand out gold shields to idiots in this city," Jack said, his irritation growing. "Did you think he'd say, 'sure,-man, that was my gun and I just pumped off a few shots at some home-boy for the fun of it'."

"Simmer down, cowboy, or you'll find your ass in my jail."

Just as Jack was about to add insult to injury in the case of the dimwitted lieutenant, LaMarcus walked in with a uniformed officer. Jack could tell by the captain's rank on his shoulder that LaMarcus had moved up the food chain of the Boston Police Department.

"That will be all, lieutenant. If you'll excuse us," the captain said. He waited for his red-faced officer to leave the room, the door closing with extra force. "Now Deputy Wesley, a word before you go. Captain Lewis has personally vouched for you and informs me that you did thirty years in Oregon as a police detective. He also has informed me that you are leaving my jurisdiction forthwith. Make that so and think twice before returning. You may not have your friend to cover your ass next time."

"And my Teton County issued equipment . . ." Jack started to ask.

"Will be returned to you at the front desk," the captain stood up and without acknowledging either, walked out the door.

"Well, thanks I guess," Jack said as they walked to the desk sergeant. Putting his Glock back in his holster and clipping his badge on his belt, he asked, "I suppose I have to walk back to my hotel now?"

Chapter 3

The man lay in his bed and listened to the rustle of the palm fronds outside his open window. The sea breeze had picked up during the night so that sleep was finally possible. While the humidity still hung in the air from the all-day rain that had fallen, the fall weather was at least tolerable.

Not that the seasons mattered much when one lived ten degrees north of the equator. Even after six months of living in this setting, the man still had not fully acclimated. His bungalow partner keep telling him that at least eighteen months was the standard time people took to fully adjust. And that was an average.

Another year to go, he thought. He opened his eyes to sun streaming in his window. Barely above the horizon, the sun glittered off the placid sea a short distance away. From the elevated spot that held his home, the man had an expansive view over a large area.

But he wasn't so high that he couldn't just make out the small swells as they broke on the nearby beach. As his new friend had announced, they were high enough to keep out any tsunamis but low enough to easily walk to the beach.

The place he was in had avoided the great catastrophic waves that had hit this part of the world after the 2004 Indonesian earthquake. The man drew some comfort at least that he wouldn't be swept out to sea in any future events. And they seemed to happen often if one believed the locals.

The person next to him moved and the soft feel of her body rubbed on the man. Before he could say anything, she was out of bed and had disappeared into the bungalow. He scanned the doorway but saw no one moving.

As he was looking, a man's face appeared in the doorway. A smile announced itself.

"Looks to be a sunny day today," the intruder said. "The beach will be crowded."

The man in bed acknowledged the weather and entertainment report. The rain for the past three days had kept everyone inside. He had noticed that everyone seemed to get cranky the longer they were confined indoors.

"So, L.C., you really survived Chosin?" the man in the doorway asked. "Hell of deal. You still get problems sleeping from it?"

L.C., which was short for Lance Corporal, was his new nickname. When he had arrived, the people who managed things suggested he adopt a new name since his old life was now officially over. So, Joe Lewis disappeared and L.C. was born. And that's all he knew people by now, short nicknames.

Gunny seemed to ask the question at least once per week. At first it had been annoying, but L.C. had finally resigned himself that Gunny was just impressed that someone who had survived the battle of Chosin Reservoir had landed as his bungalow mate.

L.C. had learned over the past six months that Gunny had been a Gunnery Sergeant in the U.S. Marine Corps. Although younger, Gunny had managed to be too young for Korea but too old for Vietnam. So Gunny had seen the normal peacetime duties of any Marine. Consequently, his nights seemed more settled than L.C.'s nights.

But last night had been better: cooler, less humid, and with female company. Yes, the combination helped ease his nightmares from long ago. L.C. climbed out of bed, threw on some pajama pant bottoms and joined Gunny in the small kitchen they shared.

Food was already on the stove cooking as L.C. moved to the pot of coffee. Taking a cup off the rack, he poured it full. No need to leave room for anything else, L.C. had learned to drink it black.

Sitting at the table, L.C. considered the facts that the person he shared his cabin with had so many similarities. Both were Marine Corps veterans, both were of similar age, both shared a common ethnicity and both had grown up and lived in the New England part of the United States.

"Hey, there's a mandatory meeting today over at the amphitheater at ten this morning," Gunny reminded.

"What's up? We haven't had one for a month," L.C. said.

"I think it may be about that guy who snuck out two days ago. They get very touchy about leaving here, you know."

L.C. knew from experience that leaving wasn't an option. The walls that surrounded him kept the outside world out but also stopped anyone leaving. Not that it wasn't difficult. The wall didn't extend into the ocean and one could easily swim around the barrier if one wanted.

But the consequences were severe. L.C. considered what had happened to those who had chosen a little time away and their fate afterward. *No, it's not worth leaving here for what would happen to me*, L.C. thought. *Even for a night of whatever those that tried considered worth it.*

L.C. had no intention on screwing anything up to be forced to return to the white man's world and the white man's rules. As a black man he had done fine maneuvering through those rules an had set himself up financially for a good retirement income. But he had chosen a different route now. One that so far didn't care what color he was and where he had grown up.

Sipping his coffee, a scantily clad young petite woman scampered by on the way to the bathroom. *No, I'm liking things just the way they are*, he thought.

Chapter 4

Amsterdam, The Netherlands

Jack sat patiently as the line stretched across the small book shop. He had been signing books for three hours now and was struggling to keep up. His hand and fingers were sore as they wrote for the fifth day in a row. Amsterdam was the fifth city in a row for his book tour and already his book was on both the German and Dutch bestseller lists.

A story on which he had been the chief detective led to his first writing project. Published initially in English, he had seen respectable sales. Having the book translated into German set sales on a rocket ship. His tour had started in Vienna where there was less interest. Munich and Frankfurt had seen large numbers of people show up. When he had hit Cologne, the word had spread.

With Berlin next on the schedule, his agent was pushing him to add more cities to his tour. But Jack remembered his promise to LaMarcus that he would help locate his uncle for him as soon as his European trip was completed. That he hadn't heard anything from his friend bothered him. *But, I take that as no news is good news*, he thought.

"Goedemiddag," the middle-aged woman in front of him said. Her friend next to her smiled as they both handed a copy of his true crime saga to him.

Jack looked at them as to say what name they wanted inscribed in the front. His German or Dutch fluency was limited to saying good morning and thank you and he was frustrated that the publicist hadn't offered to help with the translation duties.

Each woman rambled off something in Dutch and he attempted to match what they had told him. As he handed each book back, the smile he received made him content that he had come close.

"Dank u voor het kopen van mijn boek" he prattled off from memory as he thanked them for their purchase.

Two middle-aged woman stepped forward and Jack repeated his attempt at Dutch as he scribbled what he wrote in almost all the books. He had one of the store clerks write something in Dutch before he had started and he had memorized it. He received his smile and 'Danke' in return. He thanked them both for their support.

A man stepped forward next and rattled a long spiel in Dutch at Jack. Not having a clue what was being said, Jack reached for the copy of the book the man held. The man pulled it back, not allowing Jack to sign.

As Jack was at a loss to the problem, a young woman poked her head around the man.

"If I may translate, he asked you to say something about Mary Zweip. The Dutch victim was his niece. He drove all the way from outside The Hague to thank you for capturing the man who murdered her."

"Thank you," Jack said toward the young woman. "I had no idea what he had said. I would be honored to write a little something about his niece."

A quick exchange between the young woman and the man ensued. She translated again.

"He thanks you again. He understands that it will be in English. That would be fine."

Jack asked for the man's name and then added a lengthy comment about the woman from the Netherlands who had been one of the victims. He handed it back and noticed tears in the man's eyes. Jack attempted an understanding look in support as the man vigorously shook Jack's hand. The Dutchman finally wandered off.

The young woman who had translated stepped forward and handed Jack her German edition of the book. Asking what inscription she'd like, the woman inserted, "It is for my mother. Her name is Marijke."

At Jack's stare as to how to spell the name, the young woman spelled it out. Jack wrote the name and then his standard Dutch inscription, signing the bottom of the page with a flourish.

"Thank you," the young woman said. "They don't provide you with anyone to translate. That is terrible of them." She opened the book and read what Jack had written in Dutch. She smiled and something registered inside Jack's memory.

But before he could place the thought, she asked, "Would you like me to assist you?"

"Thank you, that would be very kind," Jack said. His relief was noticeable and any further thought that the smile had conjured was forgotten.

Another person in line was already placing a book down and Jack took up his pen once more. The young woman volunteer leaned close after a quick conversation in Dutch and told Jack how to spell the woman's name. *I can only imagine how badly I mangled them before this,* he thought.

The line continued to extend across the shop as Jack checked the clock on the wall. He had one more hour before the shop closed and he noticed the owner already talking to late comers. *Hopefully informing them that they didn't have time to stand in line for a signing*, he thought.

That seemed to be the case as the line gradually shortened as Jack and his new assistant moved into high gear getting books signed. With just ten or so people left in line and the shop keeper looking at the wall clock, Jack was startled when the young woman assisting leaned close and whispered in his ear.

"What!" he exclaimed, which startled the people remaining in line and drew the shop keeper's attention.

Whispering again, the young woman said, "I really didn't want to bring it up with so few people left."

Jack turned away from the person holding a book for signing and leaned in close to his assistant's ear. "You mean I've been spelling the word wrong all this time?"

"It's OK. I shouldn't have brought it up. I'm sorry," she whispered again.

Jack turned back to his signing and received his new instructions from the woman. He wrote his basic Dutch inscription and attempted to change the spelling on the word she had commented on.

"Better?" he asked.

"Yes, that's the right way now," she answered.

Jack sighed a limited relief as he finished with the customers. The shop owner escorted the last ones to the door and locked at as they left. Jack gathered his belongings and turned to the young woman.

"Thank you again. May I offer dinner to you for your help?" Jack asked.

Jack waited as the young woman seemed to consider the offer. He didn't think it was going to be accepted from the long delay between asking. Finally, that smile again appeared.

"Yes, I accept," she said.

Stepping out onto the sidewalk, Jack was stopped by the shop owner. Some Dutch and a cane was handed over to Jack. Embarrassed from almost forgetting his cane, he thanked the owner. Seeing the young woman look down at his cane, Jack felt stupid that he had brought it along on his trip. *Not a way to impress a woman,* he thought. *Unless I'm going for the mature set.*

The woman who stood before him was certainly not mature, in a matronly way. Jack estimated her to be middle twenties. *Nice to have a translator but for someone like me at fifty seven, way out of my league,* he thought. *Oh well, a nice dinner and a thank you is better than eating alone.*

That had been his fate each night on this book tour. With the number of people interested in his book, his nights had been lonely as he traveled from city to city. He had hoped that someone would have offered some personal time on the tour, but it hadn't worked out.

"So, I'm assuming you know Amsterdam," Jack offered. "I'll let you pick our restaurant. And money isn't a problem as the trip is paid for by the publisher." Which was partially true. He did have an expense-paid trip but each meal and overnight stay did have a limit. *No need to toss that in though,* he thought. Then Jack added, "You know my name, but I'm afraid we haven't been introduced."

"I'm sorry, my name is Katarina," the young woman offered.

"Well, Katarina, lead on."

The two wound their way through the streets of Amsterdam, crossing several canals. The early evening held numerous people walking or riding their bicycles as they made their way home from work. Car traffic was surprisingly light inside the city and many side streets only held parked cars.

Walking along a canal, Katarina stopped at a moored canal boat. She led Jack across the narrow gangway and down the steps into a small salon. Several tables and chairs were arranged and Katarina sat down at one. Jack took off his coat and hung it on the back of his chair. The smell hit him as he sat down.

"Is this a restaurant?" he asked.

"Yes, you like Indonesian food I hope?"

"I don't know, I've never had it," Jack said.

"That's right, you're from Wyoming, but originally from Oregon. Eugene, right?" she said.

Jack sat a little dumbfounded at the information the woman had just rattled off. Before he could say anything, she added, "Maybe I should have taken us to a barbecue place. There is one now in Amsterdam. My friends tell me it's quite popular."

"No, this is fine. But I may need help ordering," Jack said. He was still rather put off by this woman's knowledge of his life. He knew that becoming a successful author would open up his life to the public, but there were some things he definitely didn't want out.

"I'll assume you like meat, being from Wyoming. I'll just make sure they keep the hot sauce toned down," Katarina said. Jack noticed her staring at him and she brought that smile out again. While he struggled with why the smile triggered something in him, his thoughts were interrupted.

A waiter arrived and Katarina translated. Finding out he could get a glass of wine, Jack mentioned that red would be preferable. Some Dutch was spoken and Katarina refocused her smile back on Jack.

Finally she said, "You don't remember, do you?"

Jack's mind raced. *Is she is saying she knows me? I don't have a clue*, he thought. As he searched his memory as to who was sitting across from him, Katarina sat back and removed her coat. She had left her coat on the entire time in the shop and it was Jack's first glimpse at what was underneath.

Then he remembered. "Oregon Coast, about two years ago. At Heceta Head Lighthouse Overlook. You and your family."

"You do remember." The smile grew bigger.

I knew I'd seen that smile before. It was the kind of smile not easily forgotten, Jack thought. He and a friend had been traveling down the coast in a two-seat sports car when he had stopped at an overlook. Just before pulling in, he had passed four long-distance cyclists in the Heceta Tunnel.

Jack had followed along in the car giving the cyclists time and room to clear the narrow tunnel. Having

37

been a long-distance bicycler just before meeting them, he knew bikers appreciated a car's courtesy.

But it was when the four had soon grabbed the small turnout that Jack had realized it was a family. As they pulled in, he had first focused on the older daughter who wore a tight long-sleeve shirt stretched over well endowed breasts. Talking to them, he found out they were Dutch cyclists riding the Pacific Coast bicycle route.

Jack remembered that he had been amazed that a gaggle of young male riders weren't right behind them considering the looks of the daughter. And then she had smiled, and it had knocked him over. While she was good-looking, Katarina would never have been mistaken for a super model. She didn't have the stunning good looks that required.

While models required ten out of ten looks, Katarina rated up there as a nine certainly. With her athletic body shaped by cycling and nature, definitely a nine, he thought. He remembered back to a brief conversation with all four and then he had gotten in his car and left.

"But how did you ever remember me?" Jack asked. *I was just another middle-aged guy stopping for a brief chat with the foreigners,* he thought.

"It was a couple of things. The woman who was with you was very beautiful. Your girlfriend?" she asked.

"At the time, yes."

"And the setting. That turnout was one of the most beautiful spots on the entire trip. Steep cliffs, a lighthouse, sea lions barking below and a narrow road with a tunnel,"

Katarina said. "You had said you had just finished the Trans Am with your girlfriend when we talked."

"Part of the Trans Am," Jack said. "And you remember all that? I'm amazed."

"Actually, I have to give credit to my mother."

"She remembered that stop out of all the stops you must have made?" Jack asked.

"If you remember, your girlfriend offered to take a family photo with the lighthouse in the background. We insisted you step into the photo with us. When she bought your book and remembered your face from the picture on the jacket liner, we searched our trip photos and found you," Katarina said.

"Then it wasn't a coincidence that you were at my book signing today?"

"Oh no. I've been waiting all week for you to finally get to Amsterdam. My mother will be so excited that not only did I get a book signed, but I had dinner with you."

Chapter 5

Amsterdam, the Netherlands

Dinner was ordered by Katarina as Jack was content to swirl his wine and sip. The evening was turning out splendidly, and when the food finally arrived, Jack discovered that he liked Indonesian food. At least what Katarina had ordered for him. He had tried her dish and noticed the beads of sweat that immediately rose on his forehead.

With the bottle of red wine consumed, the two finally noticed that they were the only two diners left on the boat. Jack asked for the check and they made ready to leave.

"Where are you staying?" Katarina asked.

Jack retrieved the hotel business card he had grabbed when he dropped off his luggage and read the name.

"Oh, that is quite close. I can walk you there."

Turning to leave, the Indonesian proprietor stopped Jack. "Excuse me sir, you forgot this."

Jack looked down at his almost forgotten cane. He thanked the man as he took it in his right hand. Turning, he noticed Katarina staring down at his hand. *This cane isn't lending itself to the situation,* Jack thought.

Stepping spryly up the steps and across the gangway, Jack made sure his movements belied any infirmity. As they reached the sidewalk, Katarina placed her arm under Jack's elbow and led the way to his hotel.

They talked the entire time of bicycles and cars and camping out and of the western United States. Katarina and her family had spent a month riding from Seattle to Los Angeles, following the coastal highway the entire distance, and she had many interesting observations on America.

As she related a story of the family's time passing through San Francisco, her route to Jack's hotel took them down a narrow street lined with unoccupied buildings. Where before they had been on streets lined with people's homes and the resulting human activity even at the late hour, this street was different.

Noticing the signs on the buildings, Jack surmised that these where some sort of government buildings, only busy during weekday hours. Katarina kept her hold on his arm as she led him forward. Halfway down the city block she suddenly slowed. Jack had already noticed the change in atmosphere.

Up ahead two men had appeared out of a darkened doorway. Jack turned his head to the right and saw that two more men were walking two-hundred feet behind. The two groups were moving confidently and swiftly to meet where he and Katarina were now slowing to a stop.

But Katarina made the decision to change direction and Jack felt the pull on his arm as she took them through the parked cars and across the street. The two ahead adjusted their bead and moved to intercept. Jack turned slightly and saw the two following had also made the adjustment.

Jack quickly scanned the area and no exits offered escape. Only darkened buildings and an empty street. *At least this side of the street didn't have parked cars. There's more room for what's coming,* he thought.

Finally Katarina slowed as they reached the sidewalk on the other side. "Jack, this is not good."

It hadn't take Jack's thirty years of police work to reach the same conclusion. Without saying a word, he moved Katarina into a doorway that was set back from the sidewalk. With walls on three sides, she was reasonably safe from the attack that was coming.

Taking up a position on the sidewalk with his back to her, Jack could see both groups approaching by staring straight ahead.

"Katarina," Jack said softly. "Stay right there and don't move."

"Yes," she said, "I'm dialing the police right now."

"No, do not call the police," Jack said. "They'll arrive too late to do anything."

"If you say so," Katarina said.

Jack stood still clutching his cane as the four men closed on his position. Finally, the dim street light offered more details as to who his adversaries were. With dark complexions, each had a slight build and stood no taller than five foot eight inches tall.

From behind him came a loud explosion in Dutch as Katarina seemed to be warning off the four. A return challenge in Dutch seemed to confirm that a verbal warning wasn't about to change anything.

The four moved slowly forward as Jack scanned their hands for weapons. *So far, nothing showing,* he thought. Still too far away for him to act, he grew frustrated at the slowness of it all. "Come on assholes, come and get the shit kicked out of you."

"Oh, an American. This will be so much better," the one on the left said.

The leader, Jack thought. Then from his peripheral vision he saw the leader reach into his pocket for something.

Katarina spoke first, "Knife, Jack. Guy on your left. The police said they would be here," she lied.

Good, she's keeping her cool through this, he thought. *I don't need her doing anything that will get in the way.*

But the mention of the police being called moved the four ahead slightly faster. As the one man furthest to Jack's right stepped a little closer, Jack responded. From holding his cane in two hands in front of his body, he swung the notched wooden device with his right arm full force, landing the heavy curved end across the man's throat. The man staggered, grasping for breath. Jack leaped at him, landing with his boot on the front of his knee. The cracking of tendons and cartilage followed as he fell to the ground in screams of pain.

Jack landed and swung immediately around to catch the next man coming straight at him, while the other two adjusted their movement to where Jack was now. But Jack didn't wait for the three to meet up as he went for the nearest one. One-on-one was preferable to three-on-one and he moved fast to even up the odds.

Lunging at the next closest assailant, Jack swung his cane up with as much force as he could and caught the man in the balls, actually lifting him off the ground. The guy fell to the street, clutching his male parts, screaming.

The other two stopped, hesitating at their diminishing odds. The one with a knife threw a verbal threat at Jack, but Jack wasn't waiting for a pissing match of words. At six feet tall and over two hundred and twenty pounds, he knew his only advantage was massive force applied quickly.

Stepping over their writhing buddy, Jack faked an attack left toward the leader with the knife. While the man flinched and turned slightly to blunt the expected blow, Jack dinked to his right, the cane coming in a roundhouse to the man's left ear. The man staggered as he bent over in pain, clutching his ear.

Jack left him dazed and continued forward toward the now retreating man with the knife. Stopping in front, Jack studied the ten feet separating them. Before Jack could react, the man screamed something in Dutch and ran full speed at Jack, the knife leading the charge.

Well, thank you, Jack thought. With a black belt in Taekwondo, he had practiced this move repeatedly with his son Carl. Both had reached the highest level in their martial arts and now, once again, that experience was about to pay off.

As the knife sped toward Jack's torso, he quickly jumped aside, the knife grazing his jacket. With a swift elbow swing, Jack clocked the attacker in the side of the head with enough force to drop the man to his knees. A round house with the cane to the back of his head put him down flat on the street. He didn't move.

Noticing that the man with the severe ear pain was recovering slightly and not wanting him to run from the scene, Jack wound up and chopped the back of his knees with the cane. The thug pitched forward and collapsed on the ground. Making sure all four were down and immobile, Jack walked back into the doorway and retrieved a stunned Katarina.

"We better move on before anyone comes along," Jack said. He took her elbow and guided her past the four bodies, three still moving and whimpering.

Reaching the end of the street, Jack turned left. The residential neighborhood returned and was joined by a canal running along beside the street. He kept the pair moving even though he didn't have a clue where his hotel was located.

After three more turns, Katarina finally regained her composure and stopped them. Noting where they were, she moved Jack off in the opposite direction. In the background, the two-toned horn announced that police were racing somewhere close by. Katarina redoubled her steps.

When Jack recognized the street in front of his hotel, he stopped her. Still wide-eyed, she faced Jack.

"What just happened back there?"

"Just some boys acting up, is all," Jack said. He tried to keep it as low-key as possible.

"But, what you did. Those were bad men intent on hurting us," Katarina said. The trembling in her voice announced the adrenaline still running through her.

"I thought European cities were safe. I'd expect that in some American cities," Jack said.

"Is that normal where you come from? You're so calm."

"Ah, no, trust me, where I come from, that never happens," Jack offered. "Maybe in the cities on the east coast of America, but Wyoming, never."

"Well, in some neighborhoods here in Amsterdam, it is very unsafe. Like Paris or Stockholm, certain elements have taken over and it is very dangerous for others to go there."

"So, this isn't an everyday occurrence in Amsterdam?" Jack asked.

"Not in the downtown area, almost never."

The police sirens had stopped not far from where they were standing. "Well, no harm," Jack said. "I recognize my hotel over there. Thank you for walking me back. I've had an interesting evening."

Chapter 6

Amsterdam, The Netherlands

As they stood across the street from Jack's hotel, he noticed a certain hesitation on Katarina's part. Finally she asked, "Jack, do you have the time? I'm afraid I might have messed up."

Jack pulled his watch from his pocket. "If we're still on Cologne time, then it is one-fifteen. I'm sorry I've kept you out so late."

"Oh," was all she said.

"What is it?"

"The trams stop at one."

"Where do you live? I'll have the hotel call a taxi," Jack offered.

"My parents live out by Hilversum. A taxi would be much to0 expensive, even for your publisher," Katarina said.

"Then what can we do?" Jack asked.

"I don't want to impose on you. Dinner was special."

"Impose away. After your help today, you just name it," Jack said.

"Does your room have a couch or settee? I could sleep there. I won't be a bother."

Jack listened to what had just been proposed. *Have her sleep in my room when we've just met?* he thought. A certain hesitation slowed Jack's answer.

"It's not like we're strangers. Remember, you know my family. And we've known each other for at least two years."

Jack considered what she had said but continued his hesitation. Amsterdam had a certain reputation for libertine behavior. He was on a book-signing tour and maybe he needed to be careful not to get into any entanglements. Then she smiled. That electric smile that made Jack go weak in the knees

"Let's go see what we can do," Jack offered. "I haven't even seen my room to know what's in it. I arrived by train today and only had time to drop off my luggage."

They stepped into the lobby of the small hotel where an exchange was taking place between the proprietor and an elderly couple. Jack and Katarina took up a position behind them and waited.

"But we had a reservation and now you tell me there is no room available," the elderly man said.

"Yes, you had a reservation, but it was for last night, not tonight, I'm afraid," the attendant said.

"That's because the airlines kept us in Istanbul waiting. We missed our connection in Zurich. My wife and I have been traveling now for twenty-six hours and we're tired. And you have no rooms?"

"As I told you, I have made inquiries and all of Amsterdam is quite full tonight. I only have our suite available."

"Like you said," the elderly woman said. "And at three-hundred and fifty euros, I don't think so."

Jack heard that and broke into the conversation. "Excuse me, but I might have a solution."

"Ah, Mr. Wesley," the attendant said. "You have returned. Your bag is in your room waiting. I have the key right here."

"Wait, could I change my room to the suite and these fine folks could have my room?" Jack asked.

The attendant looked at Jack and then shifted his gaze to Katarina. He smiled slightly. "If you would prefer, Mr. Wesley, of course. And the rate is fine?"

"Just add it to my bill," Jack offered.

"But of course." Then turning to the elderly couple, he said, "Good news, an opening has come open. We have a delightful room for you in keeping with your budget. Just sign here and I'll take you all up."

The elderly couple stared at Jack and Katarina in the elevator as they rode to the third floor. As the front desk clerk opened the door to the room, Jack retrieved his bag. He thanked the attendant and stepped around the elderly couple. Taking the key to the suite, Katarina slipped her arm under Jack's elbow as they headed back to the elevator. As Jack left, he thought he heard the woman say, "That type of thing never happens in Omaha."

As the doors closed and the lift engaged, Katarina said, "Those people didn't even thank you for changing rooms."

"Well, Katarina, they looked like they have never been to Amsterdam before. Your city does have a few things that might take time getting used to."

"Like the Porno Museum by the Main Train Station?" Katarina said. "I'm not sure those two would ever get used to my city."

As Jack opened the door to the suite, he was happy to see he'd made a good decision. While he wasn't sure what the other room held for accommodations, this suite had two separate bedrooms off a small living area. *Perfect,* he thought.

"Looks like you get your own bedroom tonight. Which one would you like?" Jack asked.

The smile was gone as Katarina chose the room to the right. She disappeared after saying good night, the door closing quietly. Jack heard the lock latch.

Jack moved to his bedroom and opened his travel bag, retrieving his nighttime things. He grabbed his Big Dog shorts as he figured he'd better avoid his usual naked sleeping style. After getting ready for bed, he swung the door shut but did not latch it. He climbed into bed where the lateness and wine helped him fall right to sleep.

Jack's dream was of bicycles and open roads. He was working hard to avoid the cars that repeatedly came at him, trying to run him down. A massive semi with two trailers loomed out of a fog coming straight at him. Jack lunged toward the side of the road and just avoided the tandem rear wheels as they flashed by close to his face.

"I think we'll have sex," a voice carried to his swerving bicycle. Jack tried to focus as to where the offer of carnal pleasure was emanating from. All the cars were fading as the voice again announced itself.

"Yes, we need to have sex."

Jack opened his eyes in a start. In the darkness he saw a figure sitting in the easy chair at the foot of his bed.

"What? What's going on?" Jacks mumbled, half asleep.

"I've decided that we need to have sex," Katarina said.

Now fully awake, Jack sat up and stared in the dim light provided by a table light in the living room.

"Right now?"

"Seems like a perfectly good time."

Jack's pause at the bluntness opened up doubts.

"Don't you like sex?" Katsrina asked.

"Well, yes," Jack stammered.

"Good," Katarina offered. "And you do like sex with girls?"

More awake than ever, Jack answered. "Its always been my preference."

"OK, then we can have sex." This stated in a matter-of-fact way.

Again, Jack hesitated to respond. He definitely wasn't sure what he was involved with. While he enjoyed physical pleasure like most, this was very sudden and with someone that he barely knew. But being in a foreign land, he stalled for time.

"Does all your equipment work properly?" Katarina asked.

"Last time I tried it out, it sure did," Jack said.

"Then we can have sex."

"Do all the Dutch women act like this? Because I don't want to appear culturally insensitive."

"What do you mean by that? Sex is sex."

"Yes, I know sex is sex. But where I come from, things happen a little bit differently," Jack said.

"No they don't. When we were cycling the Pacific Coast, I was asked to have sex all the time."

I bet you were, Jack thought. *And I'm not sure why I'm resisting so much to this offer.* Sitting across from him in just her top that barely covered her panties, Jack's control was being severely tested.

But Jack continued his evasiveness. "And did you ever take any offers on that trip that came your way?"

"No, I didn't take up any of them."

"Because your parents were with you?" Jack asked.

"You obviously don't know Dutch parents, but no, not because of them," Katarina said.

"Then why?"

"Because those that asked didn't appeal to me," Katarina said.

That helps, Jack thought. *She does have some scruples.* Again, Jack's non response elicited one from Katarina.

"Oh, I understand now," she said. "I don't appeal to you."

On no, let's not go there yet, Jack thought. *It was too early to close out any options.* "No, that's not it."

"Then what is it?" Katarina asked. "I find you very appealing. And if you're worried, I don't say that to just anyone."

"I find you very appealing also."

"Then we can have sex now."

Jack was beside himself. This woman seemed to have a one-track mind and he was dead in line with the train that was bearing down on him. He had to think of something to change the direction things were headed.

"Katarina, so you remember the wine we had for dinner tonight?"

"Yes."

"Did we pull the cork and pass the bottle around taking gulps?" Jack was hoping this might work.

"No." A certain hesitance told Jack that he wasn't there yet.

"No, no gulping wine," Jack explained. "We poured into our wine glasses and then what? We swirled it around and gazed at the clarity. Then stuck our noses into the glass to smell the bouquet."

"OK . . ." Still a certain tone in her voice indicated she was processing things.

Good, Jack thought, he continued. "Then with two senses involved, sight and smell, we took a sip. But only a sip which we then let linger in our mouths. Not swallowing, but swishing it around to get the full flavor"

"I remember."

Jack saw some awareness come over Katarina's face in the dark. "Our fourth sense was satisfied by the loud swishing our mouths made, and our final sense, touch was involved with our tongues moving the wine around in our mouths. So before we ever swallowed, all five of our senses were involved in making the act of drinking wine as pleasurable as possible."

"And not just to get drunk," Katarina added.

"Yes, we didn't drink to get drink. We experienced a sensuous act that wine provides and as a reward, we felt the buzz the alcohol gave us after the fact."

Katarina was now the one who sat quietly. Jack sensed that his attempted analogy would slow the train down.

"And maybe unlike your young friends who might buy a jug of wine to get drunk with, some, like me, savor the process, not the end result."

Jack let that settle as the room went quiet for a long time. Jack was nodding off when a voice finally broke the silence.

"Then could I still sleep in here tonight?" Katarina asked. She stood up and started to remove her shirt.

"Nien. What is Dutch for 'with clothes?'" Jack asked.

"Met kieren," she offered.

"Then yes, but met kieren," Jack answered. He pulled the covers back on one side of the bed.

Katarina pulled her shirt down, covering her panties and climbed in next to Jack. He directed her onto her side facing away from him. Moving into a position behind her, Jack reached around Katarina and placed his arm on her stomach, avoiding any sensitive zones.

"Lekker ist gut," Katarina said.

"I'm sorry, I'm not up on that one."

"I said, snuggling, it is good."

Chapter 7

Amsterdam, The Netherlands

Jack woke easily as the morning light filtered in the window through the drapes. With eyes still closed, he remembered what had happened the night before with Katarina announcing that they should have sex. He had dodged that request but he could feel the issue was still with him.

Now laying on his back, his arm was wrapped around a sleeping woman who had moved into the crutch of his arm to snuggle. With her breasts pressing against his side and her leg on top of his thigh, she sleep contentedly.

Opening his eyes, he looked down at the woman in his arms. She moved slightly and her right breast moved. Her left breast was squashed against his rib cage. *It feels wonderful,* he thought. It had been some time since he had been this close to one so young and beautiful. His thoughts raced.

Why was she so intent on sleeping with me? Jack thought. *And I had to negotiate hard to just get her sleeping. She had wanted more last night. Not that I wasn't interested.*

But Jack had never been a jump-into-bed-with-anyone kind of guy before. Even after his marriage had failed, he had resisted the set-ups people had attempted. He had preferred spending time with his son to try and make up for the damage the divorce had caused.

Some nice relationships had come his way over the past few years, but never as fast or as young as this one. One relationship had been similar to this one in age and speed, but not that close. *There was something else going on here,* he thought. His police antennae went up at the thought.

A movement next to him broke his daydreaming. Katarina opened her eyes and drew back slightly. Her right breast dragged itself across Jack's bare chest, and even with soft cotton in between, the feeling moved through him. He focused to control himself.

Her leg retreated down his leg and Jack worked harder at self-control. *She might have been interested last night but who knows what today will bring?* he thought. *I'm not about to assume anything.*

"Goedemorgen," Jack said.

A sleepy Katarina half sat up. "Morning. Was last night a dream? Did all of that really happen?"

Which part was she referring to? Jack thought. "It wasn't a dream. It really happened. Are you all right?"

"Yes, I'm fine, thanks to you."

"Good," Jack said. "I don't know about you, but I'm hungry. I think we get breakfast with our room."

Katarina looked back with a quizzical look. Jack noticed that something seemed to be bothering her.

"What is it, Katarina?"

"Do you think that man is dead that you hit last night, the one with the knife?"

"Don't know," Jack offered. "And don't much care. In the big scheme of life, we could have been the ones back there lying in the street. You do know that, don't you?"

"Is this what Americans are like?"

"This American, anyway," Jack said. "And many more, at least those who live in the more rural parts of the country. The big city folk seem to think everyone needs respect of some sort."

Jack noticed the long thought that the statement caused in his bedroom guest. He moved aside, grabbed some clothes and headed to his bathroom to shower and dress. When he emerged, Katarina was gone.

He threw his old clothes into his bag and gathered up the rest of his belongings. He figured he would eat breakfast and catch an early train to Berlin. No need to hang around Amsterdam with police looking for the culprit in an attack on four men last night.

Glancing in the second bedroom and checking the bathroom, he made sure that Katarina was really gone. *Oh well, it was nice not sleeping alone one night of my book tour,* he thought. Berlin would be his last stop and he had an extra day to kill there. He promised himself that he would see the sights in the German capital.

Taking the elevator down to the first floor breakfast room, he stepped out into the hallway. A familiar face sat just inside the room holding a cup of coffee. Katarina waved him over.

"I didn't wait for you. I hope that was OK?" she said as Jack sat down.

"Fine," Jack said. "But I don't understand."

"I debated about leaving. But what you said intrigued me," Katarina said. "I heard the same attitude many times in our bicycle travels down your West Coast. And you are correct, most of the rural people had a similar attitude to yours."

"I'm sure the rural people of Europe might express some of the same thoughts."

"Yes, but there is little of any rural areas left in Europe. And practically none in Holland," Katarina said.

Jack moved over to the buffet line and served himself breakfast. He took a cup and added hot water, grabbing tea bags as he went. Returning to their table, Katarina sat white-faced. He looked around the room and noticed that the attendant had just brought in the morning paper. Katarina had grabbed a copy and stared at the headlines.

"What is it?" Jack asked, the Dutch text resisting his scrutiny.

"The front page. We made the front page."

"Shhh, not too loud," Jack said.

"The paper says four men were assaulted last night in the government section of Amsterdam," Katarina read. "One is in a coma from head injuries. The other three have described a man and a woman attacking them, the woman Dutch and the man American. No description of the woman is provided but the man fits your description quite well. The cane is even mentioned."

Jack ate his breakfast as he added milk and sugar to his English Breakfast tea. Katarina stopped reading and looked up. Jack stared back as he chewed his food. He broke the staring contest by looking down for his tea. Lifting it to his lips, he blew slowly before sipping. His gaze locked on his table mate.

A long silence followed as the two sat and stared at each other. Jack continued his tea sipping the entire time.

"It's true," Katarina said.

"What's true?"

"What they say about you."

"Who says?"

"The internet. The websites," Katarina's eyes grew bigger. "I wasn't sure I believed them. That's why I came to your book signing yesterday. I wanted to see the real Jack Wesley."

"And the real Jack Wesley is who according to these websites?" Jack asked. He wasn't sure he liked where the conversation was going. People had told him a little bit of what was on the web about him. But he had tried to ignore it. *Maybe I shouldn't be ignoring social media so much*, he thought.

The publishing company that had picked up his book had pushed him to be involved with all sorts of internet stuff. He had tried at first, but had quickly moved on, finding the whole experience much too intrusive on his life. *And much too impersonal,* he thought. *It seemed as if people were forgetting how to socialize in person, dependent on the impersonal separation the internet provided*

Jack wanted life to be real and personal. He wanted to feel things and experience life without the wall the digital age provided. *Even when it got messy, like last night,* he thought.

"The reports that have been posted. Stopping a school shooting, that was really you," Katarina said.

That was headline news at the time, Jack thought. Jack had stopped a school shooting in New York, though not before kids and staff were killed. At least he had limited the damage a psychotic killer had attempted.

"Yes, just in the right place and the right time, I'm afraid. Pure luck."

"But you did it," Katarina's eyes grew bigger as she spoke. "And you were there when that woman shot the deputy sheriff in Oregon. I remember reading about that. We were just down the road on the Oregon Coast at the same time. And she was the same woman that was with you when I first met you, her picture had been in the paper."

Jack wasn't sure he was liking this. Too much information about himself. And if Katarina had discovered this information on the internet, who else was out there with this knowledge? And what else did people know about his life?

A chill came over him as he ran through the events of the past few years of his life. There were some things that he would not want posted on the internet. Things that had happened that could lock him up in prison for a long time. He decided he needed to tread carefully.

"And now that you know about the real Jack Wesley, what have you decided?" Jack asked. He wasn't sure if he was going to like the answer.

Katarina's lack of an answer stymied the conversation. She was staring at Jack as he returned the look.

"Jack, last night. What should we do?" Katarina asked.

"Relax and eat our breakfast, to start," Jack answered "I'm headed to Berlin and life will move on. With the life those bad boys were leading, we probably spared some poor innocent people as they all recover a good long time."

A look of calmness came over Katarina's face. Slowly, a small smile appeared. "Whatever you say, Jack."

Expecting a different reaction, Jack was frozen in response. The woman that a short while ago was panicking over four hospitalized thugs just switched gears on him. *What is going on?* he thought. His police antennae continued scanning for information. The response he had just received didn't fit with the conversation they had just had.

But he decided to let things be for now. That was when Katarina really changed the dynamics.

"Jack, I was wondering."

"Yes, about what?" Jack said, his police training screamed in warning.

"Your next stop is Berlin, correct?"

"Berlin, then I head home. What about Berlin?" Jack asked.

"I know German fluently. You could use a translator there. To help with the book signing."

"And are you volunteering for the job?"

"Yes," Katarina said.

"In spite of the trail of bodies I'm leaving in Amsterdam?" Jack said quietly as he glanced to make sure no one was in earshot.

"Oh, yes." Almost cooing as she said it.

61

Jack knew he had to be careful with this woman. She could call the Dutch police right now and turn him in. They could probably extract DNA of the victims off his cane that would prove his involvement. *Yes, I need to be very careful right now*, he thought. *And the way she had said yes makes me more nervous.*

"You can get away from whatever you do?" Jack asked. "I have tomorrow off before I have to do my signing."

"Then we have time," she said. Her smile grew. "My mother would love to meet you again. She's the one who I had you sign the book to, remember. And she's the one who recalled meeting you on the roadside that day."

"I don't know," Jack hesitated.

"Oh please, they live close by, and we can catch a train from there right to Berlin when we're done."

Jack thought through meeting the family. He also considered the police waiting for a tip to the assault last night. Things were a little delicate and he knew discretion was called for.

"I guess that would be fine. Let me get my bag."

Chapter 8

Hilversum, The Netherlands

The train ride from the Central Train Station in Amsterdam was brief. But the trip seemed to last an eternity for Jack. Boarding the train with Katarina, he had no knowledge of their destination. He saw the reader board on the platform that announced the train's stops and a chill went up his spine.

As the train pulled into Hilversum, things were much too familiar. Jack had been here before in much different circumstances. And circumstances that he sure didn't want posted to the internet. With a friend, they had wreaked revenge on someone in the small nearby village of Loosdrecht. Hilversum had been their spot to wait out until their strike.

Jack hesitated as the doors opened to step off the train. An arm under his forced the issue. Carrying his bag with his cane buried inside under his clothes, they took the stairs down to the taxi stand. Katarina told the driver in Dutch where to take them as Jack climbed in the back. Katarina slid in beside him.

"You're suddenly very quiet." The conversation had been going strong between the two until Jack realized where they were headed. As Hilversum station loomed into view, he had grown very quiet.

Now he was dreading the visit with the parents. This was much too close to things he didn't want to return to. He prayed the taxi would head anywhere but south.

The driver swung through the center of Hilversum, bicycle riders parting to let the cab pass. They closed into the ebb as the car passed. Jack stared at the number of bicyclists dominating the traffic and pushed other thoughts away.

Jack realized the driver was heading east out of town and relaxed. Katarina noticed the tension ease from her arm hold on Jack's elbow.

"You don't have to be so nervous about meeting my family," she said. "They already know you, sort of."

Jack sat silently and attempted a weak smile. He was content to let Katarina assume his nerves were the result of a family meeting. *If she only knew*, he thought.

The taxi stopped on a street of brick two-story homes. Short, brick walls denoted each yard in the quiet residential neighborhood. Jack reached for his wallet to pay the driver but Katarina stopped him.

"My suggestion, I pay," she said.

Jack grabbed his bag and waited on the sidewalk until the taxi drove off. Katarina was back hooking her arm through his and pulling it tight against her breast. She smiled at him, the electric smile returning.

"Mama, Papa, I'm home," Katarina announced as she swung the heavy wooden door open. "And I bring a guest."

"Wat is dat?" Came the voice in Dutch from the back of the house. A quick exchange in Dutch ensued between the invisible voice and Katarina. Soon, a slight-framed fit middle-aged woman appeared in the hallway. "Ahh, you do have a guest."

Katarina provided introductions as her father and sister soon showed up. Soon, all five were sitting around the dining room table rejoining their previous meeting.

"Well, Mrs. Zender, I'm am still amazed at your memory," Jack said. "All this time and you recall our brief visit on the Oregon Coast."

"Mr. Wesley, you must call me Marijke. We met many wonderful people on that trip, but excuse me, none wrote a Dutch bestseller. A sad story, but an important one, none the less."

"You must call me Jack, Marijke," Jack offered. "But I'm grateful that you did recall me. Katarina showing up yesterday helped out greatly."

"I almost forgot," interjected Katarina. "I got Jack to sign a book for you. It's in my shoulder bag. Let me get it."

"So, how did you find Amsterdam?" the father asked. "I hope the news of last night's trouble didn't bother you."

Jack decided to act the dumb tourist. "Trouble, what happened?"

"It's on the front page of today's paper," the father continued. "Seems that a gang fight broke out very close to downtown. It's bad enough when they ruin the places outside of town, but now it seems they are bringing it into the city itself."

"Bringing what in the city, Papa?" Katarina asked as she returned to the table. She dug through her large bag and pulled out the book.

"Oh nothing," the father said, changing the subject.

"Mr. Zender," Jack said. "I was only briefly in Amsterdam. My book tour keeps me moving right along. But I found the people very friendly and I'd love to return when I have more time." He looked at Katarina as he said it. He received the smile he was learning to love in return.

"Oh my," the mother said as she read the inscription in the front. Everyone at the table sat up and looked at her in surprise, her tone announcing a certain shock.

While her mother stared at the inscription, a rapid exchange in Dutch flew through the room. Katarina finalized whatever had been said and her mother's mood changed. A broad smile broke out as the rest of the family quickly read the front of the book. Each broke out smiling after reading.

"What? I'm the subject of something here, I think?" Jack asked.

"I'll explain later," Katarina said as she smiled.

"You must be hungry. I'll throw a lunch together so you can eat before you take your train to Berlin," Marijke said. "Papa, take Jack and show him your garden while we women get the food ready."

Jack followed as instructed and stepped outside after Piers. Although narrow, the yard stretched back a long distance to a brick wall in the back. The fall detritus of a large garden lay scattered about the space.

The two men walked along the cultivated ground where Piers had laid compost for the winter. Reaching the four-foot high wall on the back, they stopped. A canal lay on the other side and a pleasure craft motored by. A slight breeze rustled the remaining leaves, stubborn to drop to the ground.

Staring at the pastoral scene, Jack realized it just needed a windmill to make it perfect. Piers startled him from his day dream.

"Katarina seems quite intrigued with you."

Jack was startled by such a statement coming from a father. And a father who appeared to be five years younger than himself.

"Yes, I believe she used those exact words herself."

"Did you two have sex?" Piers asked. His look was one of mild interest considering the topic of his question.

Jack wasn't sure how to answer the question. He knew attitudes were different in many parts of Europe, especially northern Europe. Not that such things didn't happen back in America, but Jack was sure American dads didn't ask older men about sleeping with their daughters.

"No, Sir," Jack answered.

"Oh, that's too bad," the father said. "She needs a steady hand at her age. She is much too frivolous at times. She treats life too casually."

I can't believe I'm having this conversation, Jack thought. *I never even had this kind of talk with my father-in-law after I married his daughter.*

"Yes, youth can be superficial these days," Jack added. He tried to keep the conversation on a general nature.

"Katarina lacks purpose. Someone older could give insights into what life really holds," Piers said, as he zeroed in on keeping it very personal.

"I've seen it many times. My book puts in detail the downside of a life without purpose."

"Exactly. I don't typically read those kinds of books, but my wife insisted. And since we knew you," Piers offered, "I found it very enlightening to the problem with youth these days."

"Yes, investigating that crime led me into a very sordid world," Jack said. "I know that's the main appeal of my book, but I hope my readers get more than titillation from it. There is more to life than immediate gratification."

"Yes, Jack," Peirs said. "Pleasure comes in many forms over one's lifetime. Too bad it's all about vaginas and penises at my daughter's age."

Jack was holding back, absorbing his talk with Katarina's father when a voice asked, "Whose vagina's and penises are we talking about."

Jack turned to see Katarina walk up. Piers turned to leave, "Good talking to you, Jack. Remember what I said." He headed toward the house.

"What have you two been discussing?"

"Life and the nature of things," Jack offered.

"Well, lunch is ready." She grabbed Jack's arm and shoved her large breast tight against his side. He felt it flatten out and knew it was all natural.

As they finished lunch, Katarina stood and began to clear the table, her sister right beside her.

"So, Jack, Katarina says you're off to Berlin now," Marijke said.

He hesitated at the information being common talk around the family table. Piers smiled at him.

68

"Yes, Berlin is the last stop on my book-signing tour. Katarina has offered to translate for me."

The little sister piped up from the nearby kitchen, "Good, you need a good translator."

With the comment, all four broke into laughter, leaving the ignorant American the obvious butt of their little joke.

Soon, Katarina disappeared upstairs to return with a packed bag. Jack stood a little self-consciously. *Waiting for their young daughter to return so I could take her across state lines*, he thought. He still wasn't sure about the whole arrangement and having her family standing there didn't help his conscience, no matter what the father had said.

Just as they were walking out the front door, Marijke ran back into the kitchen and returned with a large manila envelope. Handing it to Katarina, she added, "I almost forgot. This came for you yesterday."

Katarina took it without opening it and stuffed it into her bag, zipping it closed. Catching a ride to the station from Piers, they were comfortably seated on their train when Jack found out the joke.

"Remember when I whispered for you to change slightly the inscription you'd been writing?" Katarina said.

"Yes," Jack said. "What had I been writing before? The shop owner had written it down for me beforehand."

"Well, something got lost in the translation or the shop owner was a jokester," Katarina said.

"What did I sign in all those books Katarina?"

"Lets just say that a lot of women are looking forward to more than your next book. And their husbands

69

might be a little jealous the next time you come to town." Katarina said, her smile growing as she spoke.

"And I signed that to your mother?"

"Well, it made her day, at least until I told her the truth of what happened," she said.

"Good thing I have a German translator along. I wonder what I wrote in all those other German cities I visited?" Jack said.

"I'll have to think about that for a while," Katarina teased. She leaned her head onto Jack's shoulder as she reached her arm across to hold him tight. She was still there as the train pulled into Berlin. It had given Jack time to think about the woman who seemed to be part of his life all of a sudden. *But one more day of signing and I'll be winging my way back to Wyoming*, he thought.

Chapter 9

Berlin, Germany

The next day, Jack and Katarina took in the sights of Berlin. The night had gone smoothly with just the 'lekker' taking place. After his talk with Katarina's father, Jack was more confused. At least the talk of immediate sex hadn't broken out in the night. Jack was comfortable with snuggling. Any idea of more than that only brought up an image of her father standing in the room watching.

A second night passed with what now was their routine. The book signing that day came off without any embarrassing moments as all the women seemed content with whatever Katarina had provided for an inscription. No irate husbands materialized and Jack figured his plane reservations the next day would be uneventful.

After dinner following the book event, Jack excused himself and sought out a telephone. Inserting his calling card, he dialed and waited for an answer. He glanced in the restaurant window and saw Katarina sitting patiently for his return. Tomorrow he would head back home and she would return to whatever it was she did. *I still don't know much about her,* he thought.

The phone connected and a familiar voice came on. "LaMarcus, is that you?"

"Jack, no wonder I didn't recognize the number on my screen," his friend answered. "Where the hell are you?"

"Berlin, I've just finished up. How's it going?"

"Great. I've been in Las Vegas for a week now," LaMarcus said. "It's a long-ass drive out here from Boston, you know."

"Yes, I live out there, remember. But how's the search for your uncle going."

"Interesting. It seems his trail leads right to the Nevada brothels. Did you know this shit's legal out here? Man, these guys know how to live in this state."

"Yes, like I said, I live out there," Jack said again. "But any news on your uncle's whereabouts?"

"Ah no," a sheepish sounding LaMarcus said. "But I've been looking real hard. I've been interviewing some of the women to see if they've seen my uncle."

"And I'll assume you've been interviewing them at their work place?" Jack asked, but already knew the answer.

"Hell yes, but I'm willing to interview them any place. They just seem to be more responsive where they work."

Jack pictured how responsive they would be at about two-hundred dollars every fifteen minutes. He wasn't sure how long his friend could take conducting his interviews.

"So, they holding out on you?" Jack asked.

"Me? No way. Man do they know how to put out," LaMarcus said.

"That's not what I meant. Have you gotten them to talk?"

"No, good buddy, not a lot of talking going on. But I'm on the case. I'm sure one will crack soon."

"So, I'm getting the feeling you don't need me immediately?" Jack asked.

"No, I've got a handle on it just fine," LaMarcus said. "But if you want to join me, I'm sure we can make accommodations."

"No, I'm good for now," Jack said. "I'll call you in a week and see how you're coming."

"A week then. And I'll be coming just fine."

Jack smiled as he ended the call. His randy friend was certainly wrapped up in his work, which left Jack free for the moment. He would be able to fly back to Salt Lake City and check up on his project. He hadn't heard how it was progressing, assuming no new was good news.

Katarina looked up as Jack reentered the restaurant. She could tell by his smile that he'd gotten good news.

"Life is good back home?" she asked.

"Fine as a fiddle." Jack noticed Katarina wrinkle her nose to understand the American colloquiums. "An American phrase to say 'zur gut'." Jack wasn't sure if his attempt at a little local lingo made it across the language barrier.

But his comment hit her understanding and she smiled. "So nothing pressing to get home to?"

"Just the regular stuff," Jack said. "I have a friend with a major problem, but he seems to be dealing with it just fine."

"Then maybe you don't have to rush home tomorrow?" Katarina asked. "You could linger here in Europe and maybe see some things you haven't had time for because of the book thing."

Chapter 10

Las Vegas, Nevada

LaMarcus rolled off his latest interview subject and collapsed on the bed. He knew he was getting too old for this type of physical interview. The dreaded sixty years old birthday was just around the corner and he was determined to show he could still hold his own when it came to the ladies.

But he had never conducted this type of police work before. At least not officially. Over the years there had been plenty of opportunities that landed in his lap, literally.

He was always amazed at how many women would do just about anything to get out of a ticket. And while he was a patrolman, he hadn't minded one bit looking the other way on small infractions if things came his way.

But as he moved up the ladder to officer rank, things had changed. While opportunities still presented themselves, the attitude had changed. Cops were getting arrested and going to jail for having sex on the job. LaMarcus adjusted his place and time for receiving favors so he was off duty. That gave him cover as long as his fingerprints weren't on any cases that affected the women. *The old days were easier,* he thought.

The woman he had just been with got up to leave but LaMarcus stopped her. He pulled out a picture of his uncle to show her.

"Have you seen this man?" he asked. "Please look carefully. He would have been in here about five or six months ago."

The woman feigned interest as she threw on a robe. The twenty-dollar bill that LaMarcus held in his hand made her stop and examine the photo closely. She had already been paid her agreed-upon rate before they had started, so this was extra.

"No, I don't think so," the woman said. She handed the photo back to LaMarcus.

"OK, thanks," LaMarcus said. His disappointment showed at once again striking out on any information. While this method of investigating was superior to any he had experienced, at the rate the women charged, he was quickly going broke.

LaMarcus was on the second week of his search through the brothels of Las Vegas. Actually, they were the brothels of nearby Pahrump. Located about an hour's drive west of Las Vegas, Pahrump was were prostitution was legal. Unlike the populous Clark County where Las Vegas sat, rural Nye County with the community of Pahrump was the closest town with legal prostitution.

Not that it didn't happened in Las Vegas. But sex for money was illegal in Clark County. Only the rural counties of Nevada were allowed to have legal prostitution, Reno and Las Vegas had been excluded under state law.

Which left little Pahrump LaMarcus's main area of research. The last known address for his uncle had been Las Vegas. While Nye County held other brothels, they were more distant from Vegas. LaMarcus would work his way through the sex workers in Pahrump before he ventured further.

Not leaving, the woman stood as she thought through something. LaMarcus didn't interrupt, waiting naked on the bed.

"If he was here about five months ago, you could be missing some workers," she offered. "There is a fairly high turnover rate of those of us working. Some save up for tuition and then return to college. Your uncle, if he was a regular for a couple of months, could have settled on one girl. Many of our regulars request a certain girl."

"Really?" LaMarcus exclaimed. "With all the choices, why would someone stick with the same one?"

"Lots of reasons," she said. "I don't try to figure out the psychological make-up of the men that use our services. Trust me, it covers a wide spectrum. I've even had clients that just want to lie in bed and cuddle."

"No shit," LaMarcus said. "At your rates."

"Yeah, go figure. Men look for pleasure in all sorts of ways."

"These women that do this part time, they go to college nearby?" LaMarcus asked.

"You might run an ad in the UNLV college newspaper with a picture of your uncle," she offered. "A reward-type request if anyone has seen this man, you know. Also, run the same thing at College of Southern Nevada. It's the community college and probably most of the girls attend there."

"Hey thanks," LaMarcus said as she turned to leave, two additional twenties stuffed in her robe's pocket.

76

Chapter 11

Berlin, Germany

Jack looked carefully across the table at the woman who seemed to be proposing something. His thoughts switched to her father's comments and Jack worked to bury that image. The smile across from him had intrigued him from the day they had met back in Oregon. *Should I?* he thought.

"What did you have in mind?" he asked carefully. A certain trepidation hung over his words.

"Well, before coming here with you, I had a diving trip planned."

"Then you should keep your plans," Jack said. "When does the trip start?"

"It started yesterday, in Greece."

"What are you doing here then? You should have been on your trip."

"But we got together, and that seemed more important to me," Katarina said. Jack noticed her smile disappear and her eyes tear up slightly.

"I'm sorry. I do appreciate you helping me. And I'm sure German men all over the city are content tonight because of you." That brought a smile back to Katarina's face.

"Would you consider joining me on my trip? It sounds like you have the time now."

"What kind of trip is it? Usually the guides are not excited about anyone just dropping in at a late date," Jack said.

"Oh no. These are friends of mine, not a commercial trip. We do this two or three times a year, so it wouldn't be a problem."

"So there's room if I wanted to go?" Jack asked.

"Of course. I have a stateroom for myself. You can certainly stay with me if you choose."

"And could we catch up to them tomorrow?"

"I have their itinerary," Katarina said. "They'll be in Santorini for the next two days. Then they head north to dive off Ios."

"This is a diving trip, as in scuba diving?" Jack asked.

"Yes, my friend has a boat that he keeps in Greece and a bunch of us fly down as often as we can. It's marvelous this time of year. Warm water and nice weather, the fall is the best."

"I don't know how to scuba dive. I've never done it. I've snorkeled, some. Don't you need to be certified or something?"

"That's not a problem. I'm a certified instructor. Have been since I was twenty years old. I can teach you everything you need to know. And I'll stick with you on every dive so you won't get into trouble," Katarina said as her excitement rose. "Please, Jack. You'll enjoy the others on the trip. It's very relaxing."

"I suppose I could change my ticket home. I've never been to Greece. Seen lots of pictures. And movies," Jack said.

"Good, let's get back to our hotel right away and get on their computer," Katarina said. "We'll change your flight and book both of us to Thira."

Heading back to their hotel, Jack could barely keep up with Katarina. She was bounding down the street like a child with a new toy. Realizing that a week of sharing a stateroom on a boat might test his resolve, he started to wonder if the resolve was worth having.

Katarina swooped in to his side from her dance on the sidewalk and grabbed his arm. Jack steadied himself from the exuberance displayed to keep the two from bumping into others walking with them.

Katarina nuzzled her face into Jack's neck. He felt her heavy breathing from her exertions on his skin. His heart took a leap as his body reacted to the overt sensuous moves.

"Jack, there is one other little thing," Katarina whispered in his ear.

He felt his loins heat as the warm breath mixed with the inviting whisper. His resolve lowered significantly as he awaited the answer.

"The boat is a clothing optional trip," Katarina continued. "Maybe I should have told you first, but I was afraid you would have said no."

Jack's resolve fled completely at the mention of clothing optional. The image of Piers loomed in his mind.

Landing the next afternoon at Santorini Airport, Katarina made a quick cell phone call to locate her friend's boat. A short taxi ride south on the small island delivered them to Vichada Harbor. Once on the docks, Katarina followed the directions she'd been given and found their boat on the outside finger. A small party was taking place.

Jack quickly counted eight people on the rear fantail. The boat itself was about fifty feet long and had a center cockpit. An awning had been installed for comfort from the sun. With the twilight and the lights of the harbor, it just added a welcoming touch.

The party stopped and greeted the newcomers. Jack was introduced all around and managed to catch a couple of names. He'd have Katarina fill him on each person but he did manage to catch that Roland and his wife Griet owned the boat and he expressed gratitude that he could show up on short notice.

"Not a problem," offered Roland. From his accent and Katarina's quick intro, he believed Roland was a German, his wife Dutch. "We're an easy going bunch here, you'll find out."

At least they have their clothes on, Jack thought. He had been pondering since Katarina had mentioned the clothing optional aspect of the trip. While dress was required in any populated areas, Jack assumed that tomorrow would find them out diving au natural.

"We left so suddenly, I'm afraid all my personal gear is in Amsterdam," Katarina said.

"You know we have plenty of extra on board. Griet, take them both down below and see what we have," Roland suggested. "Otherwise, you can make a quick trip to the dive shop and rent what you need."

Jack followed the two women below into the main salon. Katarina led him forward while Griet stopped in the salon. Following close behind, Jack stepped into the V-Berth and Katarina threw her bag onto the bunk.

"We're last onboard, so we get the least favorite stateroom, except for the two singles who get to sleep out in the salon."

"This looks fine," Jack said.

"Until we're under way and the boat is pounding through the waves. It can get pretty bouncy up front here." Katarina smiled a mischievous smile as she said.

Jack joined in and added, "Bouncy sounds fine."

After dropping their bags, they both walked back to Griet who had spread the extra gear out on the settee. Katarina grabbed a mask and handed it to Jack. He tried it on, pulled it off and adjusted the strap. One more attempt and he announced, "This will do."

Katarina had performed the same and placed her mask on the table. Snorkels were added to the masks. Both sat down and tried on flippers. After adjustments, each had a set ready for tomorrow.

Two regulators were selected and set aside. Weight belts were pulled on as Katarina judged Jack's weight and made adjustments. She pulled a weight off her belt and announced they were ready.

"I'll get the cleaner. You probably want to scrub everything before you use it," Griet said.

Katarina found a bucket and filled it with fresh water. Handing Jack a brush, she poured the cleaning solution into the bucket and helped Jack go through everything, at least all the things that would come in contact with their face and mouths. Satisfied, she rinsed everything and placed them in the cockpit to dry.

Taking Jack's hand, she led him back to the party that had resumed in their absense. Someone handed Jack a bottle of beer as he took a seat. Katarina sat down right beside him and accepted a bottle.

Beer wasn't Jack's favorite drink but had learned in social settings to tolerate it. Working as a policeman for thirty years, he had certainly learned to nurse a drink for most of a night. Soon the conversation turned to the new couple.

"Jack was on a book tour when I rescued him from certain embarrassment," Katarina started. She proceeded to explain what the shop owner in Amsterdam had perpetrated on the unsuspecting American. The group roared with laughter. Jack's face turned red until Katarina shook him back to the fun.

At least she left out the part about her mother reading what I had written, Jack thought. *That was a little too uncomfortable for public discourse.*

"So, Jack, what book is it that you wrote?" Griet asked.

Before he got a word out, a blaze of Dutch flew from Katarina as she explained Jack's turning out what was a German and Dutch bestseller.

There was a decided change in the attitude of everyone when they realized that they actually had a celebrity on board. The quiet was noticeable before Jack spoke up.

"I'm not sure what Katarina said, but I'm not up there with Gunter Grass."

Everyone absorbed the fact that Jack knew the famous German author of 'The Tin Drum', not a familiar book or author to most non-Germans.

Katarina would have none of it and added, "Not yet, anyway."

That got the group all chatting again as they discussed Jack's book. One of the women had already read it and asked if Jack would sign it for her. She had brought it on the trip because she thought one of the other woman would enjoy it.

Suddenly, her copy of the book was the most sought after item on the boat. With the author in their presence, each wanted to read it so as to be conversant with the subject.

Jack looked on as Katarina beamed with her newfound status of having the most interesting person on the boat. Jack received the electric smile in return from her.

More beers were passed around while Jack held up his half-drunk bottle. He was passed by on this round and the talk on the boat continued. One of the couples announced they were done in for the day with the dives and were heading to bed. Soon after, Katarina gently tugged on Jack's arm with little head flips indicating she wanted to leave also.

Making apologies and promises to see them in the morning, they stood up to leave. The smiles of the six people remaining was a little unnerving to Jack. He had just met them but was feeling a conspiratorial attitude forming.

Once in their stateroom, Katarina said, "Jack, there's only two heads on board. We share one with the other two forward staterooms. The two single people share the rear head with the owners."

"Katarina, it may have missed the social media, but I have been on extended voyages on small boats before," Jack offered. "I've sailed part of the Pacific and I've circumnavigated the eastern U. S."

Jack noticed her taking his statement as a slight admonishment. He hadn't meant it that way. It was just that he was still frustrated at his privacy being broken with his newfound celebrity status. He knew he needed to switch tacks. "I'm sorry. Thank you for the heads up." They both laughed at Jack's small joke.

"So you know the trick with toilet paper?"

"All sailors know about toilet paper," Jack said. Her smile quickly returned. Then he added, "I do need to know about the clothing optional thing, though."

Jack knew that tomorrow would find them out in a quiet area for diving. And any clothing would be gone. Katarina's smile broadened.

Chapter 12

Thira, Greece

Jack slept through the first easy motions of the boat as it got underway early the next morning. Tired from his whirlwind book tour through Europe, his sleep continued as the sailboat raised its sails and leaned over with the wind. With the diesel engine stopped, the quiet of the morning was only interrupted by the whoosh sound of water under the hull.

But as the big boat came out from behind a protective headland, the wave motion increased. The boat began to pound into the waves, causing a noticeable increase in the discomfort of the V-berth. Jack was rudely shaken awake as his body slid across the berth into the inside of the hull.

Now fully awake, he looked around to see that Katarina was already up. And from her nighttime attire lying on the berth, she was opting out of wearing anything. Jack had continued his weakened resolve by insisting on clothing at night at a minimum. *Things might be naked in the daytime, but I need that thin layer of cloth between me and my berth mate,* he thought.

Noticeable nighttime activity had announced itself through the boats thin walls as the other two staterooms were occupied by lusty couples. It seemed to take forever before both pairs settled into slumber after their physical workout.

It had gotten so bad that Jack and Katarina could barely hold in their whispered comments as each new groan and thump reverberated through the walls. At least the humor had lessened the erotic noises from enticing them to further action. *At least for me,* Jack thought. *Just the idea of others on board listening to my love-making holds me back.* He wasn't sure how Katarina was handling the situation. She hadn't attacked Jack from frustration.

As Jack climbed out of the berth, he steadied himself against the bulkhead. The boat was lively in its motions as it sailed along, heeled over. He walked carefully across the slanted deck and found the head. Sitting down to avoid spills, he relieved himself.

Pulling up his nylon shorts, he remembered what Katarina had told him the night before. Clothing optional meant what it said. Each person was free to choose how they would be dressed or not. No pressure would be applied to join in being naked. Some people were comfortable right off and some never get comfortable. She had passed on the info that some women only went topless, leaving a swim suit bottom on.

But everyone followed some basic rules; no staring, sit on a towel if naked and have a good time. Seeing no one in the salon, Jack considered all of what Katarina had said as he made his way to the cockpit where everyone seemed to be gathered. He stepped up the stairs and got his first eyeful of the trip. He tried to look casual while not staring.

All were naked except the single woman who wore only her bikini bottoms. Jack stepped into the cockpit and sat down.

"Good morning," came the refrain from everyone.

As Jack returned the greeting, Katarina moved form her spot next to Michael and sat down next to Jack.

"You were tired," she said.

With a naked Katarina next to him, Jack had glanced at the twenty-four-year-old who had become his companion. Trying hard not to stare, the body he had been feeling beside him each night for the past few days was exposed in every part. *And it is every bit as stunning without clothes,* he thought.

Again she grabbed his arm and pulled herself close, smashing her breast onto his chest. With no cloth between each, the sensation caused Jack to twitch slightly. He looked around to see if anyone had noticed, but the group was busy discussing the day's dive.

"Can I get you some breakfast?" Katarina asked. "We've all eaten."

"Maybe a cup of tea. I'm not feeling too hungry right now," Jack answered.

Katarina was gone in a flash, her bare bottom moving by his face much to close as she stood, turned and descended into the salon. Jack leaned back and tried to put his mind to other things.

"So Jack, Katarina says that you've never scuba dived before," Roland said.

"Just snorkeled some," Jack said.

"You couldn't have a better instructor than Katarina. That's how most of us met each other. We took classes from her over the years and found we enjoyed each other's company."

"I'm looking forward to it. Will we be there soon?" Jack asked.

"Another twenty minutes," Roland offered. "If we're first in the small bay, we establish it as clothing optional."

Jack looked confused so Roland explained. The rule of thumb was whoever got to a secluded site first, set the rules. If textiled swimmers were there first, then everyone wore clothes. If they left, then the order could change. Or if they arrived first, then the bay would be clothing optional until they left.

Jack nodded he understood. Katarina soon returned with a cup of English Breakfast tea and a Greek yogurt container. Jack took both, setting the yogurt against the boat so it wouldn't slide off.

"I made the tea as you like it, milk and sugar," Katarina said. "And the yogurt might help with your stomach. You'll need some energy for diving."

Jack thanked her and sipped his tea. It helped settle his stomach from the noticeable motion of the sailboat. He had been on ocean crossings before, but knew it took his stomach awhile to adjust. As he nibbled at the strawberry-flavored yogurt, he felt its affect.

Sails were soon dropped as the diesel auxiliary fired up. A solitary bay announced itself as the boat came around a headline. No other boat was present, and with no other sign of human habitation, Jack knew it would be a naturalist kind of day.

Dropping the anchor, the sailboat slid to a stop. The engine was killed as the boat swung into facing the slight wind coming out of the south. With the headland for protection, the bay was smooth with only slight riffles.

"Looks perfect," Katarina said. "Jack, let's get below and get suited up."

Not sure what suited up meant to a naturalist, he followed her below. Most of the party was right behind as each moved to make ready for the first dive. Jack soon found out that suiting up only included putting on diving gear, although two of the women slipped into shorty wet suits.

Katarina sat with Jack and explained the operation of his equipment. While the instruction continued, the others all drifted out and soon Jack could hear splashes from their dropping into the sea.

Now alone, Katarina continued her instruction. Satisfied that her pupil was ready, she helped him into the dive equipment. As Jack pulled the tank and harness on his upper body, he stopped. Reaching down, he pulled his shorts off and threw them into their stateroom.

Katarina smiled as she stared at him standing naked. With her tank and harness on, Jack looked back at her, keeping his gaze at eye level.

"Hey, no staring, you said," Jack said.

Katarina raised her gaze up to meet Jack's as she laughed. She added, "Well, it's not a hard and fast rule."

"Then if that's the case," he said as he lowered his stare. The tank harness accentuated her breasts as the straps pulled in on her upper body. She slowly pulled her weight belt on and cinched it tight. Jack watched the entire motion with interest. She wiggled her hips for added emphasis as she adjusted the weight belt.

She reached down onto the deck and grabbed Jack's weight belt. She moved in close to reach it around him, pulling the two ends to the front. She watched his reaction as she tightened it, the belt hanging from his hips. Her hands lingered on his waist with her mouth just inches from his.

"We better get in the water," Jack said in defense of what seemed to be happening.

"Oh yes, let's get wet," Katarina offered.

They stepped into the cockpit and then over the side to a secured rubber dinghy. They sat down on the outside tube and rolled backwards into the Aegean Sea. Dropping into the warm ocean, Jack's immediate sensation was that he was glad he had left his suit on the boat. Once he was comfortable with the regulator controlled air, he and his personal instructor dropped below the surface. The feeling of freedom as he swam was marvelous.

His second sensation was he was glad that Katarina had left her suit on board. *That is, if she even had a suit*, Jack thought. With her leading their foray into the natural wonders, Jack was more fixated on her swimming just in front of him. As her legs stroked back and forth as she swam, her muscles rippled in her legs and butt as they worked in rhythm. Jack barely noticed the brilliant color of the coral and fish.

Katarina stopped and raised up, slowly moving her arms back and forth to hold her position. She pointed at Jack and made a thumbs-up motion to make sure he was doing fine. Jack returned the hand signal to indicate he was OK as he stopped and joined her in a vertical position. Even through the blockage caused by the mask and regulator, Jack could see her smile. Coupled with her eyes, her expression spoke pure joy.

She took Jack's hand in hers and bent to swimming forward. Jack swam next to her, now enjoying the things she pointed out. Fish scattered as they approached and each one was highlighted by her.

As they swam, occasionally some of the other divers would loom up. Hand waves of recognition would ensue as each pair would carry on their search of the bottom of the bay. Jack pulled Katarina's wrist in front of his mask and checked her depth gauge. It indicated twenty feet as they floated along about ten feet off the bottom.

Soon, Katarina motioned it was time to return to the boat. They slowly rose to the surface as Katarina checked her depth gauge against her watch. As they swam, Jack could see the boat hull ahead in the water as they neared the surface. Breaking out above the water, Jack saw that the others were already climbing the ladder back aboard.

Bare bottoms protruded with each climber while the male swimmers exhibited more than the women. Always a gentleman, Jack waited to allow Katarina to climb onboard first. He forgot the staring rule as she stepped up the ladder. Joining the others, he unstrapped his weight belt and tank, placing them on the deck.

"Jack, was that your first bare naked dive?" Roland asked. "How was it?"

"The diving with air was great. And the naked part was even better," Jack explained. "You may have made a convert."

"It usually does. Now, if we could just find water warm enough so some people didn't have to wear wetsuits, life would be grand," Griet said as she stepped out of her shorty wetsuit.

Roland rolled his eyes at Jack in recognition of his wife's complaint. Then Roland nodded his head in Katarina's direction. She had avoided a wetsuit and the effects were noticeable now. Her nipples stood rigid from the breeze moving across the wet skin. Not wanting to stare, Jack looked back to Roland who gave him a smile in answer.

Yes, there's more staring going on than people will admit to, Jack thought. After using a towel to dry off, he folded it as he saw the others and sat down. The warm air soon returned everyone's tight skin to normal and the group settled into conversation.

Chapter 13

Thira, Greece

"We usually take lunch on the beach Jack," Griet said. "If you and Michael could take the dinghy and set up the sun protection for us."

Jack offered that whatever needed doing he was ready to pitch in. Joining Michael in the small hard shell dinghy, they were quickly motoring to shore. This was an obvious frequent event by how fast everything was made ready.

When finished raising the large nylon wing, they placed folding chairs from the dinghy underneath in the shade. Sitting down to wait for the others, Michael struck up a conversation.

"So, how long have you and Katarina been together?"

"We just met last week. She was a big help translating on my book tour," Jack said. "Too bad she didn't find me at the beginning. I could have used the help."

The discussion halted for the moment as both men stared at the sailboat lying just offshore. Each one seemed to be considering their next statement.

Jack went first. "So how long have you known Katarina?"

"Oh. Let me think," Michael said. "I took her diving class almost three years ago. She invited me along about six months after that."

Jack sized up the man next to him. He appeared about thirty years old, about the same height but a slighter build than Jack, in good physical shape and spoke with a slight accent.

"You don't sound Dutch, from your accent," Jack said. "But don't trust an American on judging accents."

"No, I'm Danish. My company has offices in Amsterdam."

"Oh, you don't look Danish."

"Why, no blonde hair? Not all Danes are blonde," Michael said with a laugh.

"No, I didn't imply anything by that," Jack said. Again, a stall in the conversation ensued. Each man continued to stare ahead.

"Katarina seems very interested in you," Michael said. Then after a pause, "She needs someone that cares about her."

Jack heard again the concern people had for Katarina and their hope that someone would be kind to her. Jack hadn't found being kind to her difficult, just the level of kindness.

"She is very considerate. I enjoy being around her," Jack offered.

"Too bad her husband didn't think the same," Michael said.

Husband, Jack thought. *No one had mentioned a husband before.* Jack sat stunned at the revelation that Katarina was married. Michael seemed to sense the awkward moment.

"But he never sees her. They have a very distant relationship. I don't think they've slept together in over a year," Michael added.

"Why is that?" Jack asked. He was intrigued why someone like Katarina wouldn't be desirable to any man.

Michael began the story of Katarina. She had been named after the great German figure skater, Katarina Witt ,who won two Olympic Gold Medals in 1984 and 198. Katarina's own mother, upon having a baby daughter soon after, was intent on seeing her become a great figure skater.

Michael explained the obsession with skating in the Netherlands. The Dutch were the acknowledged dominant force in long-distance racing and it was this obsession with ice skating that drove her parents. From the earliest age, Katarina had studied to become a figure skater. At the age of sixteen, she was ranked in the world when an injury forced a long recovery.

When she returned to practice a year later, Katarina discovered that her power for her jumps had been compromised. After much discussion, she and her parents had decided to switch venues. Her body still had the power for long-distance speed skating, so she began training for her new event.

That was where she had met her husband. One of the top Dutch men in long-distance racing, the two had become close. Often competing at the same events, their lives seemed to draw closer and closer.

"It was about then that I met Katarina. She was losing interest in the hard work that was required for racing," Michael said. "On one of the diving trips she confided to me that her old injury caused her pain when she skated. The harder she worked, the more it hurt. She didn't want to disappoint her parents after all they had provided for her."

"But she was still involved with this guy?" Jack asked.

"Yes, they were quite an item," Michael said. "But her diving offered her an escape from the pain and the pressure. She told me how much she wanted to please her parents but didn't think she could do it anymore. The next thing I know, she's getting married. And her diving trips stopped for a while."

"What happened?" Jack asked, his curiosity growing.

"About six months after her wedding she showed up on our dive trip again," Michael said. "But she was a very different person. She had quit her skating, which was good for her. Her husband had just won the World Championship in the ten-thousand meters and suddenly was a superstar in the Netherlands."

"And fame got to him?"

"Big time," Michael offered. "According to Katarina, he suddenly never came home. He would typically stay out with his skating mates. Or with others. And according to Katarina, the others were groupies intent on scoring with the famous."

"The Dutch have skating groupies?" Jack asked. " I thought that was a rock and roll music thing."

"Not for the Dutch," Michael said. "The guy was in the paper all the time attending events with any number of young women hanging on him. Katarina was devastated."

"I see," Jack offered. *Maybe I understand her needs a little better now*, he thought.

"But you're the first one she has shown this kind of interest in since," Michael said. "And you can be sure that others have tried. All the single men that run with our group were interested before and after she was married. Even some of the married ones would have been available if their had been an opening."

The conversation halted for a while as Jack digested all that he'd been told. He offered a comment.

"Even you?" Jack asked.

"I could only dream," Michael answered. "Yes, I've had long talks with her. And I've shown my interest, but we've always kept things on the friend level. Never anything more."

Jack could hear the disappointment in his voice at the statement. There was longing there, but obviously never acted on.

"And no one else?" Jack asked.

"Not as far as I know. And we talk regularly in Amsterdam. She moved into my building when things went bad with her husband. We see each other often," Michael said. "And for the last year, if her husband shows up, she slips out and comes down to my place to stay 'til he's gone."

"How does that go?" Jack asked. He suddenly remembered the first night he and Katarina had been together. *She was ready for sex with me after knowing me just a few hours,* he thought. *I wonder how sleepovers at Michael's go.*

"She takes my couch," Michael said, stone faced.

"That must be hard to take. And you say it happens often," Jack said.

"Her husband probably brings his buddies home a couple of times a month, usually with women tagging along," Michael said. "And yes, it is very hard having her run around my apartment in only her shirt. She has a body that will drive you crazy."

"Yes, I've noticed," Jack said.

"Well, at least you get close to it. It's amazing actually," Michael said. "I've met her family and no one else has the physical attributes that Katarina has. It was almost like naming her after Katarina Witt assured her of having a body like the German."

"What do you mean?"

"You never saw Playboy's shots of Katarina Witt.? She posed nude after her Olympic wins. Beside the Marilyn Monroe issue, it's only the other issue that ever sold out in Playboy's history. Compare those photos sometime with our Katarina. The resemblance is remarkable."

Jack made a mental note to do a comparison, not that it mattered a great deal to him. As he thought about the two women, the one who was interested in him, came out on deck. She placed a cooler in the cockpit and sat down. The other woman came out and sat down with her.

"Do we need to go get them now?" Jack asked.

"Yes, why don't you take the dinghy, I'll watch the wing."

Jack figured out the outboard motor and after shoving the little boat into the water, he was soon at the big boat. He loaded up the gear and took four women with him to shore. Making a second trip for the remaining men, soon everyone was enjoying lunch under the shade on the beach.

Chapter 14

Thira, Greece

The five men stood in neck-deep water and bobbed with the small swell. Lunch had been eaten and the women were busy talking under the shade in their chairs. The men escaped for a cool swim nearby.

From the distance, the men couldn't make out what the topic of conversation was on the beach. Assuming that their voices wouldn't carry inland, the discussion soon turned to male-oriented talk. The five men's heads were all aligned and staring at shore and the women.

"I'm constantly amazed at the different shapes women's tits take," Roland said.

Jack waited for the others to join in the discussion. This seemed to be out of the rules of naturalist behavior and he didn't want to make any social mistakes.

One of the married men spoke first. "Yes, just look at the collection that we have on the beach. My wife's tits are the small but handy variety. They go with her tall lanky frame."

Jack glanced at the man's wife. He would agree that from his previous glances, the woman's smaller tits fit her size. As tall as Jack, she stood a couple of inches taller than her husband.

"Yes, they're similar to my wife's tits," Roland said.

Jack again scanned shore at Griet sitting under the shade. Her tits were slightly bigger than the other man's wife's tits, but were on a shorter frame. Consequently, they seemed bigger in comparison.

Then Roland made reference to the other married woman, her husband nearby. "Now there we have ski jump tits."

Looking again toward shore, Jack agreed with the ski jump analogy. Her breast were large, in a 'D' size way, hung down and angled outward - perfect ski jumps. The husband didn't seem to mind the comment and added that he liked them large and pointed.

The single woman was next in the conversation and the husband with the ski jump tit spouse added, "Now there we have ones that have needed support and didn't get it."

The other men all nodded agreement. The woman's tits sagged noticeably from what once were probably nice perky tits. But too many years of braless liberation had taken a toll. They were now a victim of gravity and the middle-aged woman's slight weight gain. Jack figured they would be down to her belly button in a few years, especially if she kept the clothing optional routine going.

"But she's a nice person," Roland added to take any criticism away from her. "She's fun to have aboard."

The other men all nodded in agreement. She was the life of the party in spite of her sagging boobs.

Which left one person to evaluate. The discussion stopped in silence as all five men floated in the surf staring at the beach. Jack felt all eyes on Katarina as the silence grew more pronounced.

It was Michael that finally spoke. "What can you say? Probably the most stunning pair ever to cross our decks."

"Hear, hear," came the refrain from all but Jack. He had no comparison to know how good the competition was for the boat's best. With what he was seeing right now, he would agree.

The married man added, "I may like them large and pointy, but large and rounded sure fills the bill also."

Again, agreement flowed from each. Jack was amazed with the topic of conversation that nudist engaged in. Not that men everywhere didn't talk about women's tits, it just that a lot of that talk was hypothetical. Here, they had the evidence arrayed before them. No guesswork was required to determine real and fake, enhanced or natural.

"Katarina Witt would be proud," Roland said. This from a fellow German.

The other four men all turned toward Jack. A look overcame them as they projected their thoughts that Jack had won the jackpot of life. *If they only knew,* Jack thought.

The group returned to quiet contemplation as the male float continued. Jack looked at the women on shore busily talking. Hand gestures all around animated their topic. *I wonder what they talk about,* he thought.

As he was contemplating that thought, all five women stopped their talk and stared out at the men. Jack seemed to feel their eyes boring into him where he floated, his head just above water. A slight wave from Katarina seemed to end their stare as they turned back to whatever they had been discussing. A feeling of discomfort rose up in him.

Stepping back onto the slowly rocking sailboat, Jack felt his stomach return to its previous state. Lunch on land had been fine, but the added motion now caught up to him. As the others made ready for their afternoon dive, Jack headed below to lie down.

Katarina found him in their bunk. She opened the overhead hatch and fresh air flowed in. The change helped, but not enough.

"Are you going to take it easy this afternoon?" Katarina asked.

"I think I'd better," Jack said. "But I heard the others talking about a deeper dive just outside the bay. I wouldn't feel comfortable doing that, so you join the others."

"I can stay and take care of you if you want."

"No, I just need to lie horizontal 'til my stomach catches up. You go have fun."

Katarina smiled as she bent down and kissed Jack on the forehead. Even with his stomach revolting, it was all he could do not to sweep her into his arms.

Jack heard the splashes of the divers leaving as he drifted off. He awoke needing a trip to the head from the water he had drunk at lunch. Returning to the V-berth, he moved past the small shelf that held Katarina's travel bag, the one she had packed back in Hilversum

A rogue wave hit the boat and a combination of Jack stumbling and the boat leaning caused her bag to tumble to the deck. With the top unzipped, half of the contents spilled out. Jack bent down to shove things back into the bag and as he lifted it back to its place, noticed the manila envelope.

He had seen Katarina's mother hand her the envelop, but had not seen her open it. Now open, Jack, the retired police detective, looked over the outside of the envelope. *She had read what was inside sometime without me around*, he thought.

Jack opened the top and peeked inside. A thick ream of papers took his interest up a level. Without pulling anything out, he turned the envelope over and noticed the return address. His interest redoubled.

The envelope had come from a private investigator with an Amsterdam address. Knowing the state of her marriage, Jack assumed that the contents related to her husband's activities. *Women often hire an investigator when they know they have a wayward husband*, Jack thought. *Information that would be used in any divorce proceedings.*

Placing the envelope back into her bag, Jack sat down on the edge of the berth. He stared at the bag and its contents. The police detective won out in his battle of moral choices as he reached in and retrieved the envelope.

Jack pulled out the bound report and saw the company's logo on the front. *Very professional*, he thought. He flipped the cover sheet open and froze. It was not a report on Katarina's husband.

* * *

The nine divers stayed in close proximity to each other as they reached their dept. Katarina checked her gauge and it registered eighty feet. *Yes, this would have been too deep for Jack to try on his first day,* she thought. Michael came over and motioned her toward a large fan-shaped coral. The fronds gently waved in the sea current. A Red Scorpionfish swam away at the diver's approach.

Katarina pointed out an octopus and both swimmers stopped, floating suspended over it. The other divers moved in for the view and each waved as they headed off to find more. Katarina almost wished that she had worn a wetsuit like the other women. The deeper water was not as comfortable to dive naked. But she so enjoyed the felling of freedom so she put up with the discomfort.

Finally, the cold got to her and she motioned to Michael that she was heading to the surface. As her designated partner for the dive, he was obligated to surface with her. The two made the slow ascent. Soon, they broke the surface, the sailboat a distance away.

Spitting out her mouthpiece, Katarina offered her excuse, "Too cold down there. I should have worn a wetsuit."

"That's OK. It was a little cold for me too," Michael said.

Katarina knew it was a lie and that Michael was being nice. *He was always doing such things*, she thought.

"I'll remember tomorrow, I promise."

"You think Jack will be ready for a deeper dive tomorrow?" Michael asked.

"I don't know. I think the stress of his book tour took a lot out of him. It's hard to dive twice a day at first if you're not used to it."

"Not only the stress of his book tour. Meeting you probably added to his being tired," Michael offered.

"Michael, you're a dear friend. And you've been there for me during some difficult times," Katarina spoke as they slowly made their way back to the boat. "But Jack and I haven't done what you're thinking."

The two stopped moving and Michael gave his friend a long hard look before speaking. "You mean, no sex?"

"No sex, no naked sleeping together, no kissing." Katarina's expression at admitting the state of the relationship gave itself away.

"Your choice or his?"

"His."

"You seem to like him very much, I can see that," Michael said. "So what's wrong? He's not a pretty boy, is he?"

"He says not. I just don't know," Katarina said. "He is an American. They think differently about these things, don't they?"

"Not all of them," Michael said. "Not that I know that from personal experience."

That brought a slight smile out of both of them as the two friends continued their swim.

Just before they climbed up the ladder onto the boat, Michael asked, "What are you going to do?"

"I don't know, Michael."

Chapter 15

Thira, Greece

Jack had heard the noise of returning divers as he rested in his bunk. He had to think. What he had read changed everything. But how should he deal with it? Things had moved into very delicate matters and a wrong decision could cost him.

The chatter of nine people drifted to the front of the boat as he stared through the open hatch above his head. From his vantage point, he could see up the main mast. The rest was blue sky.

As he watched the lines swing and clank against the mast in a rhythm matched with the wave action, his small window filled. A familiar face was looking down on him where Katarina lay on the deck above.

"How are you doing?" she asked.

"Better," Jack answered. "I was just watching the lines tap out its tune above you."

Katarina rolled over to look at the mast. She returned to her spot in the hatch. Her smile withered at the expression she was receiving from Jack.

"What is it?' she asked.

"Can you come down here?"

Katarina sat up and dropped her legs through the hatch. Still naked, she lowered herself down, being careful not to catch anything. She sat down on the edge of the berth and looked at Jack. Her expression had switched to concern at the tone in Jack's voice.

"Please, could you put this on?" Jack said. He held up her T-shirt from the night before. Having put his Big Dog shorts on previously, they each now had some covering. Katarina's expression was stone faced.

Jack moved past her and reached into her bag. Pulling out the manila envelope, he held it in front of her face.

"Can you explain this?" he asked.

Katarina's expression turned white. The two stared at each other before Katarina lowered her gaze. Jack saw a tear form in her eye and roll down her cheek. The two sat together in silence as the boat continued to rock on the swell.

Jack saw Michael approach their stateroom through the open door, assuming that he was looking for the two of them to join the others. As soon as he saw them both, Michael turned and retreated.

"Jack, I was going to tell you about that, honest," Katarina said. "If you remember, I started to once."

"And when was that, because I don't recall."

"You became so upset when I mentioned things, I didn't dare bring up anything else," she said.

"Again, when did you talk about what's in this envelope?"

"That first night. Remember," Katarina said. "I said I knew you lived in Wyoming and had grown up in Oregon. And that you had been in that school shooting where you saved all those lives."

"OK, I do remember you bringing those things up," Jack admitted.

The answer brought a slight smile to Katarina. But Jack's attitude ended any further smiles.

"But there's a lot more than that in here," Jack said. He moved the envelope for emphasis.

"Yes, but my mother didn't give me that 'til after we had talked about the other things. And you seemed so upset by that first conversation, I didn't know how to talk to you about what was in here. It's all new information to me"

"Well, not to me. It's all old information. And most of it I'd prefer be left in the past," Jack said.

"But Jack, I didn't want to hurt you with any of this. You are special to me. I just want to know you better," Katarina said the words but her eyes spoke more. The tears flowed again, this time in large rivulets down her cheeks.

Jack was feeling slightly intimidating at his interrogation of the young woman. When the tears showed up, his will broke and he reached for his shirt nearby. He dabbed at her tears and changed his tone.

"Katarina, it's just that you have dug up some very sensitive items in my past."

"I know, Jack. But not to make you sad or angry. I did it so I could understand you. You are a special man, and the report confirms that."

Sitting and not knowing what to do next, Jack averted his stare from Katarina toward the gangway leading to the salon.

"When my mother brought up that we had met you, I became intrigued. I started researching you on the internet. The more I searched, the more questions I came up with," Katarina said.

"But to hire a private investigator?" Jack said. "That costs a lot of money and says obsession to me. Remember, I was a police detective for all those years. I saw women who went over the edge."

"I'm not over the edge," Katarina pleaded. "And the cost is nothing. My husband made two million dollars in endorsements last year. He gives me a monthly allowance that easily covers the cost. I just had to know more about you."

Jack sat quiet as he digested her ice skating husband pulling in two million a year.

"Please, Jack, please understand. You are like one of those men you see in the movies," Katarina said. Her voice trembled as she spoke. "The kind that can withstand all that comes at them and win. I've never known anyone like you. And then to see you take out those four in Amsterdam. You did that to protect me. Me. No one has ever done that before."

That's when it hit him like a two by four between the eyes. Why hadn't he thought of it before? He was just too naive in the world of young people to have seen it before. But his talk with Michael had set the kernel in his brain. And that kernel of a thought had just hatched into a full blow idea.

She's an adrenaline junkie. An action figure groupie, if they even existed, Jack thought. *If you watched James Bond movies, those women certainly existed. But me, the recipient of such adulation? It doesn't make sense.*

Jack continued to digest everything when a voice in the companionway announced dinner as Jack heard Michael pass on the news that dinner was ready. Jack caught Katarina glancing in Michael's direction. She turned back to Jack, hope in her eyes.

"You can go eat if you want," Jack offered.

"I'm not going anywhere." Katarina said softly, her eyes still holding back tears. "If you'd like, we can row ashore and burn that report. I don't want it."

That could work but the investigator still had all that information, Jack thought. *All neatly filed on their computer. It would keep what Katarina had from getting out though. Yes, a little bonfire tonight might be in order.*

The other shipmates watched quizzically as Jack and Katarina loaded into the dinghy. Jack threw a small bag in before climbing down the ladder without saying a word. The dinghy fired right up and they were on the beach a short time later.

The nylon wing for shade as well as the folding chairs were long gone. The darkness was only broken by the lights on the sailboat lying at anchor. Jack helped Katarina from the boat and grabbed the bag.

He retrieved the investigator's report and placed it on the dry sand. Pulling out some starter fluid from the boat's grill, he squirted the liquid. Once the fluid was safely away, he struck a wooden match and threw it on the report.

The koroom noise of the liquid igniting broke the slow clanking noise of lines on mast. The two sat down on the sand and watched Jack's life go up in flames. Katarina's placed her arm under Jack's and pulled herself close.

"Jack, was it all true?" she asked.

Jack didn't answer. He was still trying to deal with the fact that he had this young woman beside him who now knew too much about him. What he was going to do about it escaped him.

He withdrew his arm from Katarina's grasp and swung it around her back. She took the move as a good sign and moved in tighter. With the cool evening air, they had pulled fleece tops on before leaving the boat ands Jack was glad for the insulation.

That night, the sleeping arrangement were a little strained. No more talk of the report had taken place. Jack and Katarina had lingered on the beach long after the report had disintegrated in ash and blown away. Little was said when they returned to the boat and they quickly headed to the stateroom.

Clothes for sleeping continued and even snuggling was a little stiff between the two. Much had happened and Jack still didn't know how to respond.

The morning dive went off without a hitch but the others sensed that something was up between their friend and her celebrity guest. Breakfast had been a little tense as each tried to avoid any sensitive topics.

It was at lunch that things changed. Jack and Michael had again set things up ashore in anticipation of lunch. But today, Michael was quiet as the situation grew tense. Forgotten was the idle chit chat of yesterday that the two men had engaged in.

Jack sat in his chair and waited for the sign to retrieve everyone. Michael sat beside him, mute. Griet finally gave the sign to come collect them and Michael jumped up in response.

Jack watched the dinghy run out to the boat and retrieve everyone. Before they returned, Jack walked down the beach and climbed the rocks at the end. Scrambling over to the headland, he caught the full force of the wind.

Naked for the morning dive, Jack had grabbed a long sleeve shirt for protection from the sun. With two buttons clasped to hold it closed in the wind, he stood bare bottomed as the wind snapped at the shirt, the tails fluttering.

From his vantage point, he saw that everyone was under the shade presumably enjoying their lunch. Jack knew he was causing stress in everyone's life by his attitude, but Katarina's envelope had laid out much information.

Besides the basics of his life in Oregon and Wyoming, which Katarina already knew from her internet searches, the report held much more sensitive information. The New York State school shooting that he had stopped had been known to her before also.

And Kotone, his old girlfriend's run-in with the deputy sheriff in Oregon. That was public knowledge also, even though she had been found not guilty on a claim of self-defense. But that was two deaths that had been associated with him in the papers that added to the total.

The whole affair in Hawaii when he had rescued Kotone's sister from the kidnapper had been reported. While no public prosecution had ever happened to the perpetrator, he had ended up missing a short while later. And the kidnapper's father's bank had all those problems. Nothing connected to Jack, but when you start considering all the coincidences, there was only one conclusion to reach.

Then to see the report on Kotone and Jack's wedding. Nothing nefarious about that. Small weddings in small towns in Nevada happened all the time. But then Kotone was arrested for drug smuggling while on their honeymoon. And on a Dutch island in the Caribbean at that.

When the rich owner of that same small island ended up permanently indisposed, that was one more coincidence. That the report couldn't account for Mr. Wesley's whereabouts at the time of the man's demise added to the mystery. Out of communication, sailing, the report had said. *That was partially true*, Jack thought.

But it was London where the Dutch investigator had done good work. Jack was even impressed at the level of sleuthing. He had been very careful to stay under the radar on his visit to London as what had happened there had caused international headlines.

Jack had been one third of a team that prevented further destruction and along with one other, had avoided all credit. Jack knew the lone Australian on the team who received the lone credit was a good retired cop who knew how to keep his mouth shut.

But the investigator had dug up passport control dates and times. That he had been in France enjoying a canal boat trip was common knowledge. That he and two others had slipped into London was not. But the Private investigator had placed Jack in the vicinity at the time.

At least the whole affair outside Washington D.C. had been missed by the investigator. That had been messy and an old friend had taken the attention on that one. Unfortunately, he hadn't survived.

And now Katarina had kicked the rock off most of it. *At least not all of it,* he thought. *But it didn't take a rocket scientist to put the pieces of his life together and conclude some nasty conclusions.* Jack didn't consider them nasty. Taking out bad guys was a necessary duty to him.

Now Katarina seemed to want to be part of it all. To be the Pussy Galore to his James Bond. But he wasn't James Bond. Writing one German bestseller was as good as it got. The rest was just chance encounters in his life that he never knew when or if it would happen again. That the last few years had been full of excitement guaranteed nothing that the next years would bring the same.

The youthful mystery he represented to her could be all in his past. *A relationship based on what had been in the report would lead where?* he thought. As he tried to answer his own questions, Jack heard footsteps on the rock behind him. He turned to see Michael walk up.

"Hi, Jack," Michael said.

Jack nodded acknowledgement. He turned to face the wind as Michael sat down on a rock beside him.

"I guess I was elected by the group to come and talk to you."

"I'm sorry for ruining everyone's trip," Jack said. "I guess if Roland is willing to run me back to Santorini, I can catch a flight out. You can get back to your diving."

"Katarina already asked. She wants to go home."

Jack let the news die without an answer. *Considering what has happened, I'm sure she wants out of here*, he thought.

Michael added, "I don't know what's up between you two, but I think its a shame. You seem like a good guy and I know Katarina is special. You two just can't seem to see that."

No response from Jack as he sat staring straight ahead. But something in Michael's words hit home. *Yes, it was a shame,* Jack thought. *Katarina had been special and who was he to reject that? She already knows who I am, why am I concerned about the future?*

Jack turned to Michael and asked, "Where's Katarina?"

Michael pointed toward the other end of the beach. On a rock, a solitary figure in a long-sleeved shirt sat. Jack thanked Michael and made his way toward the other end of the beach. He walked briskly by the others sitting under the shade. No words were spoken as he passed. Never shifting his eyes from his intended target, Jack climbed the small rocky promontory and came up behind Katarina.

Sliding in behind her, she didn't even move at the intrusion. Jack wrapped his arms around her and gathered her in. She offered no resistance. But she also didn't respond directly to Jack's advancements.

Sitting, staring out to sea, Katarina continued her pose. Jack stared straight ahead, looking where she was fixated on. A blank sea looked back.

"I hear that you want to head home," Jack said.

A pause and then a reply, "No point in making my friend's life miserable." From behind, Jack spotted a single tear flow down her cheek.

"I was thinking the same thing a minute ago," Jack said. "But then I changed my mind."

That got Katarina's attention. She shifted slightly but continued staring straight ahead.

"What changed your mind?"

"You did," Jack said. "I've been thinking and I need to apologize to you."

"Why should you apologize?" Katarina said. "I'm the one who invaded your privacy. You had every right to be upset with me."

"I guess I never realized what my life entailed until someone had written it all down in one place. I lived it, but didn't put much stock in all of it," Jack said. A long pause followed. "Except for one."

"Kotone, the woman I met on the Oregon Coast?" Katarina asked.

"Yes, that is a loss I'm profoundly sad about," Jack said.

The two held each other. Out of the corner of his eye, Jack saw the others load up the dingy and make two trips to the boat. Although they were facing away from the boat, Jack assumed the others were getting their diving gear on to move underwater. Jack continued to hold Katarina.

Katarina said, "I'm sorry for you. Life and marriage sometimes doesn't work out as we hoped."

Jack let that lie for awhile, then added, "I guess we both are looking for someone special. If I'm that someone for you still, then I need to accept that. I know you are special to me and hope we can be together."

"You mean that?" Katarina asked. "And in every way?"

Jack knew the reference and agreed that they could be together in every way. Katarina turned and gazed at Jack. Jack reached to cradle her head in his hand as he kissed her. She put her hand behind his head and the kiss intensified.

With their shirts flapping in the breeze but wearing nothing else, the two embraced on their rock. Jack felt a surge in him that had been holding back. A warm soothing surge that Katarina caressed.

Jack reached into Katarina's shirt and took one breast in his hand. She responded with a deeper kiss. As he slid his hand down, she moaned in anticipation. Reaching her freely exposed vagina, he caressed her.

Katarina's hand slid down Jack's shirt and found a willing partner. She pulled him closer as she turned and climbed onto his lap. She carefully guided the two parts together and sat quietly enjoying the moment. Jack barely noticed the rock he was sitting on as Katarina took her weight on her bended knees. Keeping their attachment, she gently moved up and down in a slow rhythm as Jack's two hands held onto the best breasts ever to float on Roland's boat. He couldn't agree more. And the rest was just as spectacular.

Chapter 16

Thira, Greece

The wall between Jack and Katarina removed, the days blended into one sensuous experience after another. Diving each morning was followed by a communal lunch on whatever beach they were near. Each day the naturalists soaked in the sea and the sun as the magic only intensified.

Jack and Katarina skipped the afternoon dives, instead, taking the motorized dinghy to a secluded spot for intense love-making. The others hadn't minded their absence, happy that their friend was once again enjoying life. They would gather each evening in the cockpit to enjoy dinner as a group.

"I think we need a round of applause for our cooks tonight," Roland said. "I think that was the best grilled calamari yet."

The group all joined in their display of appreciation to Michael and the single woman for their effort at dinner. Everyone took turns with dinner and the results were sometimes less then wonderful.

"Jack, you eat octopus much?" Roland asked as he turned to the newest member of the buff diver's club.

"No, can't say that I have. I might have tried it once in a restaurant a long time back," Jack offered. "All I can remember was that it was rather chewy."

"But not Michael's. His has always been the best, but I think he out-did himself tonight," Griet said.

The group continued on with the discussion on the attributes of well-prepared octopus versus the results of badly prepared calamari. The Retsina wine was passed around as Michael and his partner finished with their clean-up duties. With the anchored sailboat gently rocking on the evening swells, the group had the small bay all to themselves. Their anchor light hanging off the mast spreader offered a homey feeing to their sparse anchorage. As the light of the evening faded, Roland directed the evening entertainment.

"I guess we can get back to our music festival. Tonight is Katarina's and Jack's turns," Roland said.

Everyone turned to Katarina in anticipation of her music selections. This had been an ongoing event each evening and Jack had learned it was a boat tradition.

Each person was responsible for selecting five songs that best expressed their personality or mood. They were played one at a time and people could comment or ask questions in between each song. The others had each done their evening stint over the week and only Jack and Katarina were left. With the trouble between the two, they had been pushed off to the last evening on board.

Katarina's smile grew as she plugged her smart phone into the boat's sound system. Jack had been nonplused by the others selections. Most had chosen either current popular music that he wasn't familiar with or old rock and roll hits that were never his favorites. The single woman with the saggy tits had been the worst. It was one suck ass Beatle song after another: *Michelle*, *Hey Jude*, *Yesterday*, *All You Need is Love* and another one Jack chose not to remember. *All sung by Paul McCartney,* Jack thought. *Give me John Lennon and his kick-ass Beatle songs anytime instead.*

Jack's daydream of the songs he'd been forced to listen to all week was broken by a guitar riff that he recognized immediately. Katarina had offered no introduction, but had just started. Jack knew the song immediately, *Don't Take Me Alive* by Steely Dan. He looked over at Katarina, whose smile had grown even bigger.

"How do you know this song?" he asked as Donald Fagen wailed about death in Oregon, Walter Becker hitting the refrain with his guitar work for emphasis.

"My dad listened to them all the time," Katarina said. "It's the only song I knew of with Oregon in it."

I can believe that, Jack thought. *This could be interesting.* The second song changed the tone.

Not waiting for comments about death and dying in Oregon, Katarina jumped right into Phil Collins song *In the Air Tonight*. The drums and and organ oozed out the opening. Again, the tune was very familiar to Jack. As Phil worked his way through the opening, Jack waited for the crescendo in the middle when the drums hit. He thought back to the Miami Vice television show episode he had seen with the same song. He closed his eyes and envisioned the song playing on the soundtrack. The palm trees and speeding cars flashed by on the screen.

Again, moving right to the third song, Katarina kept the new theme moving as Peter Gabriel's *In Your Eyes* came out over the speakers. Jack knew the tune from the movie that it was so prominent in. Except for the dying in Oregon thing, Katarina was upping the sensuous tone in her music. As Peter's vocals died, the group wouldn't let Katarina move on to the fourth selection without a comment.

"Katarina, these aren't like anything you've picked on our past trips," Griet said.

"I know," Katarina said. She looked straight at Jack. "I've never felt like this before."

"Well, except for that first selection, I like the change," Roland said.

"Well, we'll see if you like the next one," Katarina said.

After two slow ditties about love, the guitar introduction of the next song knocked them over. Jack smiled when *You Might Think* by the Cars hit with its pounding pulse. He loved this song and had almost put it in his selections. That Katarina had selected it made him smile. His partner's smile only grew in return.

People were about to comment on the sudden change to more forceful, emotionally exuding music when they were stopped cold by the next song. *Any Way You Want It* by Journey blasted out over the bay as the in-your face beat hit everyone. Jack laughed to himself at the blatant sexual message declared in front of everyone. Jack looked at Michael who appeared not enjoying the evening.

Roland jumped in as the song ended. "Those were a change from the other two. I can't wait for the last one." He looked at Jack and winked. He didn't have to wait long for his answer.

From the brash in-your-face song, Katarina switched to possibly the most erotic song ever recorded. At the first beats from the bass guitar, everyone sat wide-eyed as Berlin wailed out *Take My Breath Away*. Katarina's expression switched to total seductress as her smile turned into a taunting, tongue-moistened, sexual enticement.

Sitting sans clothing, Jack had trouble controlling himself. He noticed a shift or two from the other males on the boat. Thankfully the song finally ended.

"Wow. Double wow," Griet said. "Katarina my dear, I think you outdid yourself on that."

"Maybe we should take a break before Jack finishes out the evening entertainment," Roland said. "I'm not sure I'd want to follow up that performance."

People went below to get fresh drinks as Katarina moved over and took up snuggling against Jack. He worked on his public self-control as her breast smashed into his side.

"How was that?" Katarina whispered in Jack's ear.

Jack stammered slightly before croaking out, "Fine," his voice a little high pitched.

"I can't wait to hear your songs."

Jack suddenly was feeling a little unprepared. Although he had heard the entertainment requirement the first night he had been aboard, with the stress of Katarina added to scuba diving, he had been unfocused on his selections. Jack had grabbed some songs that had always been his favorites, at least the ones that had spoken to him in personal ways. Luckily he had added a couple songs when things between him and Katarina had worked out. But after Katarina's in-your-face display, Jack knew his songs might come up a bit wanting.

Once everyone was settled, Katarina scuttled back across the cockpit from Jack. He would be on display as he played his songs.

"As Roland said, I have a tough act to follow," Jack said, looking at a smiling Katarina. He smiled back at her. "My selections are songs that have always spoken to who I am. Since this is my first time with you, they might explain things."

He looked straight at Katarina as he spoke. He knew his songs would set a different tone than hers had.

He hit the select button on his iTouch and Eric Burden and the Animals came out singing *It's My Life*. The oldie blared out with the pulsating bass guitar while Eric sang of women with no regrets. Jack checked how his first declaration of independence was settling with everyone.

As the song ended Roland was the first to speak, "A definite change from our previous participant."

Small laughing followed his comment as Jack looked at Katarina. She appeared unfazed by the sentiment Eric had just blasted out. He moved to the second song.

A quiet guitar opened before a steady thump of horns and drums announced Savoy Brown's *I'm Tired*. The singer went into his lyrics of again independence from anyone else. Jack loved the song and considered it the best unknown rock and roll song in existence. As Kim Simmons did his blues riff, Jack looked at the group for response. It appeared his theme for the night wasn't going over well.

He hit the third song before anyone could comment. Jimmy Cliff singing *The Harder They Come* blasted out with its reggae beat. *This is a huge mistake,*

Jack thought. *But they wanted to get to know me, and these songs sure say it.*

As the song ended, Roland spoke right up, "Jack, I'm seeing a pattern here."

"You wanted to know me. These will tell you a lot," Jack said. He glanced at Katarina who seemed to holding up. *She hasn't heard much in the way of love songs, but if she wants to know who I am . . .* Jack thought. He gave her a quick smile and got one in return. He pressed ahead.

A fourth pulsating rock song thumped out as Tom Petty blasted out of the speakers with *I Won't Back Down*. Jack sat back and waited as he questioned his song selection.

At the end of the song, Griet asked, "Gates of hell?"

Jack shrugged and moved onto the fifth song. *No turning back now*, he thought.

A familiar guitar and drum intro hit everyone as Roland smiled at the Rolling Stones standard, *Beast of Burden*. Jack looked at Katarina and got a forced smile in return. Five songs, five blatant statements of independence. Fierce defiance to anyone interfering in his life was Jack's message as Mick pleaded his case.

"Well, those were certainly enlightening, Jack," Griet said.

" I liked them," Katarina said, jumping in to defend Jack. "We asked him to pick songs to help us get to know him. I think he did a great job at what we asked."

Michael spoke up for the first time, "I know I have few doubts about Jack's view of life now." Michael glanced at Katarina as he spoke. Jack noticed the slight dig, or at least what he felt was a put down.

"I'm not done," Jack said. "You said five songs, but you didn't say we could offer more."

"Well, if you've left something unsaid about yourself, please continue," Michael said, an air of sarcasm mixed in. Again Jack noticed it was said for Katarina's benefit more than anyone else's.

"Yes, please continue," Roland said. "The night's young."

Jack thought twice and decided why not. He hit the play button and a piano introduction led straight into Bruce Springsteen screaming out *For You.* As Bruce ripped through the lyrics, Jack noticed everyone's eyes getting bigger. He sat and looked at Katarina who seemed to be taking it well. *It's not your standard love song, that's for sure, but it has passion,* Jack thought. By the end of the song, people's mouths were open and Jack waited for the reaction.

"What's with the sores?" Griet asked. Everyone nodded in agreement. As the silence grew from the stunned reaction to Jack's choice for a love song, Jack knew he needed to offer something.

"Maybe that was a little over the top. But I always loved the passion Springsteen gave it." He let everyone digest his comment before offering, "Actually, I just wanted that song for affect after my other five songs. Maybe the next one will express how I'm feeling right now."

He winked at Katarina who sat up at the gesture. *I'm sure she's more than ready for the next song*, Jack thought.

Horns and guitar in a slow steady beat brought smiles all around as the jazz rendition of *Days Like This* by Van Morrison filtered out the speakers. The reaction was immediate as Katarina moved over and took up her position at Jack's side. Holding a tight grip on his arm, she leaned in and kissed him on the ear.

"Thank you," she whispered.

A sigh of relief settled over the boat as the entire group reacted to Jack finally offering up a song worthy of their friend. After the song ended, the talk stayed on Van Morrison, ignoring Jack's other selections.

The evening wound down and everyone headed to their berths for the last night on the sailboat. Snuggling in their bunk, Jack pulled Katarina to his side as they lay on their backs and stared at the stars through the hatch in the deck.

"About that Springsteen song and the 'sores'," Jack finally said. "I've been thinking about that line a lot."

"It was a little gross," Katarina offered.

"I thought so at first too, but then I thought metaphorically," Jack said. "I do have sores, or issues as some would say. I've been hesitant to get you involved with you because of them."

"But that's what attracts me to you, Jack Wesley. And from the songs you selected, I'm even more interested."

"You are?" Jack asked.

"Sores and all. You're a take-charge kind of man. I like that. I saw it when those thugs were going to do something bad to us in Amsterdam. You handled it," Katarina said.

The two lay quiet, holding each other as the conversation ceased. Jack caressed Katarina's back with his hand.

"I did have one more song but didn't want to play it in front of everyone," Jack said. "As you might gather from my song selections, I'm not a very open person."

"Will you play it now?"

Taking earbuds, they moved their heads together and each shared one bud. Jack found his last selection and hit the start button. Van Morrison came back on, but singing *Someone Like You* this time. As the slow tune carried through, the piano solo set a different tone. Katarina listened and pulled closer as the song continued. As the song wrapped up, she lifted up and leaned on one elbow to look into Jack's eyes.

"Do you really mean that?" Katarina asked.

"Yes," Jack said.

A passionate kiss as Katarina moved on top of Jack. He pulled her close as he returned the kiss. The warm ocean breeze swept into the cabin from the open hatch as the two enjoyed the last night of their naturalist vacation.

Chapter 17

Salt Lake City, Utah

The Wasatch Mountains were white with a late fall snow as the plane made its approach to Salt Lake City Airport. That Katarina sat beside him on the plane still had Jack dazed. After his resolve had finally disappeared totally on that rocky promontory in the Greek Islands, the days had whwirled past.

When the trip ended in Piraeus Harbor near Athens, goodbyes to everyone left Jack in a hotel wondering what was going to happen next. He had avoided talking of the future with Katarina, content to enjoy the moment.

But after making his phone call to LaMarcus as to the search for his uncle, it was Katarina's expression that turned to a sheepish grin. Asking about the search, she became more and more inquisitive with each bit of news. Soon, she was proposing they head to America together to help Jack's friend. Two quick plane reservations later and they were boarding their plane the next morning. Fully clothed for the first time in a week, and after a transfer in Paris, they were about to land in Salt Lake City fifteen hours since leaving Greece.

"Why are we landing in Salt Lake City? Do we catch another flight to Las Vegas?" Katarina asked.

Jack knew her understanding of America geography was limited to the Pacific Coast and New York City. Both had been on their itinerary when she and her family had visited.

"No, we get off here," Jack said.

"So Las Vegas is close?"

"Err, no. But I'm hoping we can drive the rest of the way," Jack said. "It'll be most of a day's drive."

Katarina accepted Jack's explanation and turned to look out the plane's window. The plane lurched as it hit the runaway, the engines reversing thrust. Both felt the pull of the seatbelt as the big plane slowed.

Retrieving their luggage, Jack found a taxi. They were soon pulling up to the front of a four-bay garage located in the industrial section of the city close to the airport. Jack paid the driver after gathering their bags.

Katarina followed him as he dropped both bags at the office door and stepped inside. A man looked up from his paper work.

"Jack Wesley, returning to America," he said. "How was Europe?"

As he said it, Katarina stepped around Jack. The man directed his attention away from Jack.

"Yes, ma'am, may I help you?" the man asked, his gaze roaming up and down.

"Goedenmorgen," Katarina said, making the most of her Dutch. She scanned the shop office, taking in the automotive decor.

"Oh, good morning to you," he stammered.

"It's OK, Roger. She's with me."

Roger smiled at his friend. "So your trip to Europe was good, I see."

Jack smiled back, knowing his buddy was conjuring up all sorts of images for himself. *He'd be shocked to know that most of them were real*, Jack thought.

"Ready to pick up your truck. It's been ready for a week now," Roger said. "Right on schedule like we promised."

"Oh, we travel by truck?" Katarina asked.

Roger jumped right in. "Let's show you your ride."

Stepping around the counter, he took Katarina by the arm and walked her out into the shop. As soon as he entered, his mechanics all stopped work. Walking with their boss was a woman in a short dress and high heels. Well-tanned and with her female attributes plain to see, Roger escorted Katarina toward the back of the garage gathering a following of men.

Jack scurried to keep up as they walked to a cloth-covered vehicle. Two of the mechanics pulled the cloth drape off, revealing Jack's truck.

"Oh my," Katarina said, emphasizing her Dutch accent for the benefit of her audience.

"Just like you wanted, Jack," Roger said. "Actually better."

Roger directed Katarina to the passenger's door and helped her climb in. As Jack climbed in the driver's seat, Roger leaned in the passenger window and pointed to the ignition key. Katarina leaned back to give the man room. With his head inside the cab, Roger laid out the work the shop had done.

"Just as you had bought out of North Dakota, a 1947 Ford one-and-a-half ton flatbed truck with dually wheels. But as you knew, the engine was blown, so we knew we had to find a new one," Roger said. He directed one of the mechanics to open one of the large doors. Then he showed Jack the sequence to start the truck.

After the glow plug light went out, he turned the key. The four-cylinder diesel engine fired up with a blue cloud. Jack shifted into first and with Roger riding the stepped running board, he pulled it into the sunshine.

"Diesel, that's better than I planned," Jack said.

"You said to try and we lucked out," Roger explained. "It seems an overnight delivery truck missed its deadline on a delivery to Alta Ski Area, just east of the city. They have an annual contest for the vehicle that gets carried the furthest down the mountain by an avalanche. Seems the truck and its driver came close last winter."

"Hoe vreslijk," Katarina said, her Dutch kicking in at the news.

With his head still inside the cab, Roger turned from his conversation with Jack to look at the passenger inches away. "Yes, whatever it is you said." He smiled at her, then turned back to the driver. "But your lucky day. They rescued the driver but the truck sat buried 'til last spring. When they drug the rig back to the road in the spring, it was totaled. The body was scrap, but the engine and drive train were fine."

"So I have new innards?" Jack asked.

"Less than a year old. We had to adjust the drive shaft to the length of the old Ford, but otherwise it's a new chassis with a 1947 body. As you can tell, we buffed up the body from its North Dakota days."

Switching to English, Katarina added, "It looks and smells brand new."

"We've used it for some parts runs to make sure it runs fine, but otherwise it's like new," Roger said.

"And it fit in my budget?" Jack finally asked.

"Taken care of," was all Roger said.'

Jack knew what that meant. The restored truck was more Jack's brother's idea. His brother collected cars in a small way, but had accumulated some fun vehicles to drive. Jack could attest to that. But Jack felt a little pressure as his brother had let him stay in his house in Jackson, Wyoming for the past few years rent free. The truck was a sort of substitute for paying rent.

Jack had a newer pickup truck that was his daily driver. But now the two Wesley brothers had one more thing in common. They could each drive a classic vehicle to car shows. Not that a diesel 1947 Ford was a classic. It might look like a classic, but anyone seeing it operate would run him out of any classic car show.

Obviously, the newer diesel drive train had gone over Jack's budget. Roger had called Jack's brother and gotten the go-ahead and the extra financing to cover the conversion. *That's fine, my brother can afford it,* Jack thought. *I know if I ever leave Wyoming, this truck will become part of Ed's collection.*

"So, we're good to go?" Jack asked. "No problems driving it to Vegas?"

"Vegas, I'd trust this all the way to . . ." Roger never finished with his destination as Katarina swiveled in her seat. The look Roger gave her as her dress tightened across her chest stopped any vocal remarks.

Looking toward the rear she asked, "But where do we put our bags?" She turned to face forward and almost put her breasts into Roger's gaping mouth. "There is so little room in here."

Jack looked around the cab. In 1947, Ford hadn't designed the truck as a road cruiser for vacations. The cab was barely wide enough for two, which in the old days would be two farmers working hard.

Roger retreated from the personal space slightly. "Ah, we added an aluminum box on the flat bed for storage. It's got a couple of five gallon water jugs in there along with emergency road stuff; flares, jack, tow strap, that sort of thing. Totally water tight."

Jack left the truck idling as he checked the box on the back. Roger threw their bags up to him and then pointed out the fuel tanks.

"We installed two saddle tanks under here," Roger said. He kicked the side of one tank located just behind the cab. "We made sure they matched the 1947 vintage look, but you have enough fuel on board to make it to Vegas non-stop."

Latching the storage box, Jack thanked Roger for the work his shop had done. The Ford rattled off the lot as Jack swung west onto the highway. They would be taking the back road to Las Vegas as he wanted to show some of the scenery to his Dutch visitor. From previous trips, he knew the freeway from Salt Lake City wasn't the prettiest route.

The drive took them west past Bonneville Salt Flats. Jack explained its significance to Katarina. She stared out the Ford's window at the brilliant white landscape as the natural formation extended for miles to the north. Known for its land speed records, each year car enthusiasts would descend on the dry salt beds for fast thrills.

Jack took a left after entering Nevada onto Route U.S. Alternate 93 heading south. The highway would take them along the eastern border of Nevada and pass through Ely which was about the only inhabited spot on the trip. If they were going to stop for the night, Ely was the only choice.

Katarina sat the entire time tight against Jack's side. The first part of the trip she had asked questions and was interested in the scenery. As the hours wore on, she dozed against Jack's shoulder, the Nevada high desert taking its toll.

The truck drove better than Jack expected, the new parts underneath belying themselves from the old body on top. Jack played with the controls and discovered he had not only air conditioning but cruise control. *This farmers sure didn't enjoy such fancy accessories*, he thought.

Cresting a small rise in the road as the highway seemed to transition from one long valley to another, he spotted a car on the side of the road up ahead. The hood was raised and steam billowed out. Jack down shifted.

Katarina awoke at the change in motion. Blinking at the bright sunlight, she asked, "Trouble?"

"Looks like a distressed motorist," Jack offered. "In this country, we never pass anyone by."

Katarina examined the surrounding emptiness and agreed. As Jack pulled in behind the car, an older woman stepped from the driver's seat. Stepping down, Jack walked and greeted the woman.

"Hi, Jack Wesley ma'am. Having car trouble, I see."

"Mr. Wesley, thank you for stopping," she said. "I think a hose let go."

"Well, from the looks of its age, I can believe it," Jack said.

Katarina stepped out to look at the damage, greeting the elderly lady. She joined Jack as he surveyed the damage under the hood.

"Mr. Wesley, I believe my car is newer than your truck."

"What year is it? Looks like a 1948 to me."

"Correct, 1948 Chevrolet Fleetmaster. I bought it new. Only has fifty-two thousand miles on it,'" the woman said.

"Well, you beat me by one year," Jack said, not letting on that he really had a one-year-old truck hidden underneath.

"Does anyone drive new cars round here?" Katarina finally asked.

The two Americans chuckled at the Dutch observer's comment. Jack lowered the car's hood until it latched.

"We'd be happy to give you a lift to where you were going," Jack said.

"And leave my prize out here? No thank you. If you could call a tow truck when you get to the next town, I'd appreciate it."

"And leave you out here by yourself?" Katarina interjected.

The three stood and considered the options. Finally, Jack asked, "Katarina, you think you could drive the truck? I've got a strap. We could tow you to the next town."

Katarina jumped at the chance to help. "Oh yes, standard transmissions are common in the Netherlands and lots of cars are gasoil."

The woman looked at Katarina. Jack offered a translation, "That would be diesel cars."

The car was soon strapped to the back of the Ford, Katarina and the woman in the ecab. Jack sat at the steering wheel and motioned Katarina to move out. *It will be a slow trip to Ely at twenty miles an hour,* Jack thought.

Chapter 18

Another person going outside the walls meant another meeting at the amphitheater. While L.C. enjoyed the view, with its location on the front of the rocky promontory overlooking the ocean, the lecture that everyone received got old.

Everyone already knew the penalty for being caught outside the walls. Management hadn't varied once from removing the individual and sending him away. The thought gave L.C. the shivers.

More adjusted to life inside the walls, he remembered what lay outside -- at least if he was sent back to where he had come. That would mean cold Boston winters shoveling snow and chipping ice. The last couple of winters had been brutal.

He remembered as a child growing up with New England winters and how much he looked forward to winter. It meant school days missed coupled with fun time in the snow with his buddies. But life changed and the cold bothered him now.

His ex-wife complained about the cold but was never willing to do anything about it. *Gripe and moan and sit on her ass*, he thought. *That was her routine.*

For forty long years she had been doing it. *Hell, she's probably still doing it,* he thought. *Thank God I'm just not around to hear it.*

After no children, her demeanor grew worse. Somehow blaming him for the lack of a complete family,

L.C. would escape to work to find peace. A second job enabled him to squirrel away more money that she never knew about.

With a divorce finally, he had made his plans. From the basement of their home, he searched the internet for somewhere a seventy-year-old could find companionship. And not the kind his buddies had found. Marrying local divorcees was not a solution to L.C.

His first answer had come from a website announcing one solution. Six months ago, he had sold off most of his possessions, the ones he had managed to get in the divorce. That was added to his nest egg. Next, he sold off his car and his pot took a bigger jump.

Then with half his retirement check and half his social security, he headed west, first stop, Las Vegas. He found a co-worker who had retired to Las Vegas and had been taken in. That had worked long enough for L.C. to find the real deal.

"Listen up, everyone," the man at the microphone announced.

L.C. snapped out of his reminiscing on how he had landed in the amphitheater. Gunny's jab in the ribs added to his focus.

"Last night, Pacman slipped over the wall and went into Haad Rin."

"Oh shit, it was Pacman," Gunny said.

L.C. remarked with surprise at one of his close friends being tagged for leaving. L.C. had become a regular with the group that hung out with Gunny. His roommate had more time inside than he had and had an established group. And Pacman was one of their gang.

A fellow Marine, Pacman was OK, for a white guy, L.C. thought. Race still carried itself, even inside the walls. The perpetual problem of America wasn't erased so far from its shores. L.C. was happy that it was much less a factor, but it still showed itself.

Among his fellow retirees were plenty of rednecks. They seemed to carry on over race in spite of their location. *Hey, these locals don't even know what the Civil War was*, L.C. thought.

Pacman stared at the ground as the man spoke. L.C. knew that Pacman knew his fate. Management had never strayed from the rule against going outside the walls. Some of the rules had flexibility, but not that one. Pacman would be among the missing within the hour of this little chat.

"And I repeat, there is no deviation allowed where the wall is concerned," the man emphasized. "Anyone outside the walls will be summarily purged from our midsts. No exceptions."

L.C. scanned the crowd of over four hundred. All hung their heads at the fate that awaited one of their own. That one of them had risked it all to taste whatever called to them outside the walls, L.C. couldn't imagine what lie outside the walls that justified such danger.

"Gunny, why do they do it?" he finally asked. It wasn't the first time he'd asked his friend, and it probably wouldn't be the last.

"Dun know, L.C.," Gunny said. "Just plan crazy in my mind."

"But we knew Pacman. We were his closest friends. Why didn't we stop him?" L.C. asked.

"Some fellows just gots to see what's on the other side. Don't make sense to us, but something calls to them."

The man at the microphone ended his spiel and two security guards walked onto the stage. From past experiences, L.C. knew they would escort Pacman to his bungalow so he could retrieve his personal effects.

Gunny and L.C. scrambled out of the amphitheater to be the first at Pacman's cabin. They wanted to say goodbye to their friend, but they had to be careful.

Management allowed no interaction with those caught outside the walls. They could only take what they could personally carry from their belongings, the rest remained to be divided among his friends. And no talking was allowed during the whole affair.

L.C. reached the outside of Pacman's bungalow as he finished gathering his belongings. With his arms loaded, Pacman emerged to a somber, silent crowd. As he stepped down the couple steps to the gravel walkway, he stopped to look at Gunny and L.C.. As he stared at his friends, Pacman's eyes teared up.

A framed picture fell off the stack of things in his arms. L.C. bent to retrieve it when a security guard stepped in the way.

"Leave it, you know the rules," the guard barked.

L.C. clenched his fist in anger as Gunny placed his hand on L.C.'s back. The pressure of Gunny's strength kept L.C. from getting into trouble. As L.C. stood up, Pacman mouthed a thank you to his friend. He shuffled off toward the administration building with the two guards following.

Gunny stood next to L.C. for a long time. The others who had gathered to witness the punishment all dispersed. Still, the two stood sentinel.

"Damn shame," Gunny finally said.

"God be with you Pacman, wherever you may be," L.C. added.

The two friends turned and headed toward their bungalow. Today would be a day to just sit.

Chapter 19

Preston, Nevada

The tow to Ely had been slow and tedious. With just a yellow nylon strap between the old Ford flatbed and the old Chevy sedan, each driver had to be careful. Too much speed and the towed car could lose control or not stop in time in an emergency. Too slow, and they would die of boredom.

Jack had stated that twenty miles an hour would be a happy compromise. Katarina had been instructed to be very cautious with anything that would require them to stop fast. She had scanned the empty country and had asked what in the world could make them stop.

But she had done as she was told and had checked her mirror often for any hand signals from Jack. None came her way as he let the Chevy drift out over the yellow line most of the time so he could see down the road.

At least Katarina had the elderly woman for company. Upon discovering that she was Mrs. Dietrich and knew German, Katarina was enthralled that she could have a conversation in a tongue that was more familiar to her, although Mrs. Dietrich's skill at German was rather rusty.

"I'm sorry my dear," Mrs. Dietrich confessed in German. "I'ts been a long time since I spoke in German. My father used his native language when I was growing up. Since he died, I've had little use of it."

Katarina stated that she didn't mind and the rest of the trip was spent half in German and half in English whenever Mrs. Dietrich was lost for the right words. Through it all, Katarina helped her as a three-hour German language lesson ensued. By the time Ely's city limits came into view, Katarina had noticed a marked improvement in her companion's skill level.

Mrs. Dietrich directed Katarina where to turn to find the garage that she used for her automobile. Almost closing time when they unstrapped the car, the shop owner and Jack pushed the Chevy inside. It would be repaired tomorrow contingent that a hose could be found. Otherwise, it would be the following day after the hose arrived from the warehouse in Salt Lake City.

With the late hour, Mrs. Dietrich offered her rescuers a night's stay at her home. A short twenty minute drive brought them to the sign announcing Preston. More a wide spot on Highway 318 than a town, Mrs. Dietrich's ranch sat right off the road.

Shutting down the engine, Katarina stepped out of the driver's seat. Jack helped their elderly passenger out and headed into the house. A typical ranch style house, the single story small home had wrap-around porches to block the summer sun. Jack looked up at the mountains to the west, a light snow dusting showing on the higher elevation.

"Currant Mountain," Mrs. Dietrich said, noting Jack's interest. "Eleven-thousand five-hundred feet and change. Climbed it a few time in my younger years."

Katarina stepped over to Jack and gazed up at the wooded high country. "Trees. I haven't seen trees for a long time."

"Bristlecone pines at the top," Mrs. Dietrich offered. "Just beautiful, the old ones."

Once inside, they noticed the light blinking on the answering machine. Hitting the retrieval button, they heard from the garage that a hose was on its way from Salt Lake. The Chevy would be finished the day after tomorrow, the message said.

"We can give you a ride back into town then," Jack offered.

"Don't be silly. You folks want to be on your way tomorrow," Mrs. Dietrich said.

"Actually, I think Jack and I want to climb your mountain," Katarina said. Her smile spoke more than her words. Jack nodded his agreement.

"Well, if that's true, I've got a better deal than staying here. I've got a line shack on my property. Used to get more use when I was younger and we ran cattle up on the side of the mountain. But its cozy and it will put you right at the base tomorrow."

Katarina jumped at what sounded like an adventure. Soon the Ford was loaded with extra water, blankets, towels and some food as they learned the cabin had no drinking water but did have a hot spring for bathing.

Mrs. Dietrich drew a hasty map and retrieved the keys for the two locked gates they would need to enter to get to the property. It was dark when they pulled up to the cabin and Jack retrieved a flashlight so he could unlock the door.

Stepping inside, Katarina commented on the dusty smell which Jack explained that everything in the American West smelled dusty when closed up for any time. Exhausted from their flight and drive, they moved their belongings inside, brushed teeth and quickly fell asleep.

As Katarina drifted off, she realized this was their first time sleeping 'met kieren' since their reconciliation on the rock in Greece. *I don't even mind, I'm so tired,* she thought.

The smell of oatmeal cooking got her moving in the morning. Hot tea got her sitting upright in bed as Jack finished preparing breakfast. He made sandwiches and put fruit into a backpack they had borrowed from Mrs. Dietrich's closet. Soon, they were ready for their climb.

Jack had gotten driving directions the night before and the Ford rumbled down the gravel road. Turning toward the mountain, they reached the end of the gravel where Jack parked and climbed out. He grabbed the pack and threw it on his back.

Katarina had guessed that even with the sun, the late season hike would be chilly. And up high, snow lightly covered the summit. The lower level desert offered a visible trail toward the top. With a rough sketch of the route from Mrs. Dietrich, they quickly escaped the sage country and entered open ground laced with pine trees.

Limestone rock interspersed with soil made easy footing as they climbed higher. Katarina knew they had about a five-mile hike to the top with over a four-thousand foot elevation gain. A good workout for someone used to Holland's flat country.

The workouts that ice skating provided made short work of the initial climb. As Katarina stopped to remove her fleece top, Jack joined her, breathing heavy. Now in her long sleeve black top and nylon sorts, she led off toward the summit.

She looked back to see Jack remove his top and wrap it like her around his waist. Now in a T-shirt, Jack worked hard to catch up. After a bit, they gained the top of the ridge that led to the summit. New bristle cone pine trees fought for life in between the limestone wherever the soil allowed growth.

The ridge was solid limestone and dropped off on each side. Katarina slowed her ascent to make sure there were no accidents. A tumble up here would be serious, considering the remoteness of the mountain.

Mrs. Dietrich had described the wilderness area that had preserved the mountain. Even so, few people came to climb here as there was no surface water anywhere on the mountain. As they climbed higher, the bristlecone pines changed their demeanor. Now looking like skeletons of trees, the weather-beaten flora stood in a determined clutch to life in the harsh conditions.

"These trees are beautiful," Katarina said. "They remind me of bonsai trees."

"Ones in California are the oldest living things on earth," Jack added. "One has been measured at over five-thousand years old."

"For real?" Katarina said.

"The Los Angeles air pollution has been stressing them, though. Imagine surviving five thousand years to only die of asphyxiation."

"From my family's brief time in LA, I can believe it," Katarina said.

A few last steps gained the summit. The view extended for miles in all directions. Other mountains in the distance were white with snow, but the sun helped elevate the cool temperature. With no wind, the summit was rather pleasant.

Jack proposed that they eat lunch. Pulling on their fleece tops, they found a sheltered spot that faced south, absorbing the solar energy from the surrounding rocks. They sat and ate Jack's sandwiches with barely a word spoken. Just a few comments on how good food tasted after such a climb.

Finishing, Katarina moved slightly, placing herself between Jack's feet, sitting in front of him. Jack pulled her into his chest as she wrapped her arms around his bent knees. Feeling extra warm in their small cocoon, Jack slid his left hand up under Katarina's top along her bare skin. Reaching her left breast, he shoved the sports bra and shirt up under the fleece.

He found her nipple and ran his fingers around until it responded. With his right hand, he lay it flat on her stomach, then slid it down under her nylon shorts. Moving past her panties, he found her sweet spot.

Katarina's head rolled back as she talked softly to Jack. In between moans and requests for more, Jack moved his right hand lower and retrieved some gathering moisture. He resumed a more lubricated massage on

Katarina's tender spot. Her legs spread wider and Jack pushed her panties aside for more room.

Still fully clothed against the cool air, Jack worked both hands, his fingers eliciting a constant stream of Dutch from Katarina. The Dutch ended in a loud explosion of screams as Jack's fingers finished their work. She leaned back, enjoying the sensuous feeling and the spectacular view.

Standing up, Katarina turned around and helped Jack to his feet. Reaching down to his nylon sorts, she lowered them to release Jack's manhood. She massaged the area and then lowered herself to warm him up. Jack moaned and jerked as he too reached satisfaction.

The two sat afterward and let the last of the sun's energy keep them comfortable. But as the sun moved west and drifted toward the horizon, cold finally forced them to beat a hasty retreat. Again, Katarina kept a careful pace until they dropped below the narrow ridge. Then it was almost a sprint back to the truck. They arrived clutching their sore thighs, breathing hard.

They had seen the steaming hot spring when they left that morning and both knew the soothing effect would help with their sore leg muscles. A quick trip in the Ford through two locked gates took them to the cabin. They were soon running down the hill with towels.

The hot spring lay about two-hundred feet below the cabin. The steam rose up from an embankment, the small stream feeding the wet hillside. A horizontal pipe had been pounded into the ground to catch the hot water. The pipe led to a tiny bath house atop the bank. Moving a canvas screen aside revealed a claw-foot bathtub hanging precariously out over the hill.

Mrs. Dietrich had instructed that the water was too hot to sit in straight from the ground. The tub had to be filled and allowed to cool off until the right temperature was reached. Jack had run down in the morning and filled the tub, placing the pipe aside where it spilled through the loose floor boards.

Checking, Katarina announced that it was much too cool. Jack pulled the pipe and allowed the steamy water to cascade into the tub. The water overflowed and spilled down as Jack added hot water, displacing cooler water.

Again checking, Katarina announced that it was close enough. Stripping down, she hung her sweat-stained clothes and towel on a hook. She climbed in, lowered herself down, and announced it was just right. She spread her legs to make room and announce that Jack was welcome to join her.

Jack was soon naked and sitting opposite, facing his bath companion. Relaxing in the warm water, as the temperature continued slowly to drop, Jack would carefully add more hot water. After the first experience, they both learned to stand up so as to avoid getting scalded.

Once more settled in together, Katarina let her legs float up to the rim of the tub as she slid her chest lower into the water. Jack placed his hands under her and helped float her higher. With room below her now, Jack slide down to where his face was level with her vagina.

Dutch once again flowed in a rising crescendo until Katarina shook violently, spilling water over the small shack. Relaxing for a moment, Katarina reached for Jack once more but he gathered up both hands and pulled her around so they were facing the same direction, Katarina's back tight against Jack's chest.

Protesting slightly her inability to please him, Jack held his ground. He leaned close to her ear and whispered, "Just let me be gentle with you."

She relaxed as Jack played maestro on her body. With his dancing fingers under the hot eater, Katarina was soon shaking water from the tub. Her head thrust back as she tried to chew one of Jack's ears. He turned his head and kissed her hard while his hands stroked her body.

Toweling off briskly, Jack led Katarina back to the cabin where he lit a fire in the glass-fronted wood stove. Throwing some blankets on the floor, towels were discarded as the two lay down. Katarina pulled another blanket over them as she nestled into moving down Jack's stomach.

Jack diverted this attack and moved her over onto her stomach. As the fire warmed the cabin, the top blanket was soon dispensed with. With strong fingers, he massaged Katarina, starting with her legs. The soreness of the hike coupled with the hot water soak made the massage feel ecstatic. Jack worked the back of Katarina's legs to more moaning.

Reaching between her upper thighs, Katarina spread her legs and raised her bottom into the air. With free access, Jack worked the sensuous zone from one spot to another. Finally settling on the critical one, he rolled her onto her back, her legs spreading wide.

His head dove to its place as his tongue found its mark. With slow steady circles, Katarina found release again. Now exhausted by the day's activities, she struggled to reach for Jack to add to his pleasure. Once more, he would have none of it.

He went back to massaging Katarina, this time her upper body. With no protest, Jack moved her onto her stomach again. His fingers dug into muscle and ligaments as he worked each one. Rolling her over, he continued on her front.

With her breasts flattened against her, he delicately prodded each one until the nipples announced their interest. He slid his mouth down her stomach until he met the groove, finally stopping on the small bump. Katarina feigned protest at the attention between her legs, but Jack just slowly changed her mind. With finger prodding and tongue swirls, Katarina screamed out in very guttural Dutch as her head shook side to side.

Once more, after a slow recovery, she reached for Jack. He attempted to push her away once more but her protests in both Dutch and English convinced him she had had enough. He gently entered her as he kissed her. Their tongues danced together from mouth to mouth as Jack's hips slowly moved up and down. Just as Katarina grabbed Jack's backside to pull him in tight, Jack let go with a moan. The fire flickered as the two collapsed, spent.

The only sounds in the cabin for a long time was the crackle of pine wood burning. Two sleepy people lay under a blanket just snoozing and listening. Finally one spoke.

"Jack, I've never done that before," Katarina said.

"Which part?"

"All of it, I've never had such a passion-filled day, ever," Katarina said.

"As I said, I wanted to be gentle with you."

"You have no idea. Where has that been all this time?" Katarina asked. "It wasn't like that on the boat."

"Too many people," Jack answered. "I'm not much for listening to second-hand sex and I sure didn't want to provide it."

"But on the beaches, we were alone."

"I was still getting used to you," Jack offered. "I think I know you now."

"Like no one else," Katarina sighed as she said it.

"You mean no one has ever treated you like that?"

"Are you serious?" Katarina said. "I've been lucky to get an orgasm out of the whole thing. My experience has been fast and furious."

"Twenty-something males can be like that," Jack said. "So I take it multiple times hasn't happened before for you."

"Are you crazy, no," she said. "I had a girlfriend that mentioned having two one time. But six in a day, no way. That was unbelievable. It might be a Dutch national record."

"Well, I doubt that, but it was fun. We'll have to go for seven next time."

"But not now. I just want to sleep, I have such a glow. So don't bother me again."

153

"Met kieren, then," Jack joked.

He received an elbow in the ribs for his joke about sleeping with clothes on avoid any more trouble. The fire soon died down to embers but no one was awake to see. Two very tired hikers slept soundly through the night, without clothes.

Chapter 20

Preston, Nevada

"Are these pictures of your family?" Jack asked. He was standing in the Mrs. Dietrich's living room examining the numerous framed photos on the wall.

Katarina was in the bathroom showering as Mrs. Dietrich made breakfast. She and Jack had risen early, packed up their belongings and locked up the cabin. Arriving back at the main ranch, Mrs. Dietrich insisted on a good breakfast before heading into Ely.

Her car had finally been repaired and Jack had offered her a lift to town to retrieve it. After that errand, he and Katarina would continue their truck trip to Las Vegas. *It's about a four=hour drive,* Jack thought. *But there's something about this one photo that intrigues me.*

"Yes," Mrs. Dietrich answered. "That's my husband and my two sons."

But Jack was still concentrating on one particular photo. "Is this your son with the race car?"

"Yes, that was taken at Riverside International Raceway in California. He had just won the SCCA West Coast Open Division Championship. The track closed the next year."

Jack studied the picture and the car her son was standing next to. *A very nice car*, he thought.

"So, what is it your son does now? Jack asked.

"One son is a banker in Ely," Mrs. Dietrich said. There was a pause before she added. "My second son died fifteen years ago."

Jack felt embarrassed for asking. He hadn't intended to dig into the woman's past, especially if there was pain there.

"I'm sorry," he offered.

"That's OK, Jack," Mrs. Dietrich said. "He's been gone long enough. I still miss him every day. Especially when his brother comes around."

So there's more to the two-son story, Jack thought. He hesitated to open up any wounds she might have.

But Mrs. Dietrich's sudden presence with food for the table ended any reluctance on Jack's part. As the two sat down to eat, the story of her two sons flowed out.

She told of her disgust at her oldest son, the banker. Explaining the relationship they had as financial only, Mrs. Dietrich told of a son who looked at all things through their dollar value. When her husband had died, she had soon run into financial problems. The ranch was marginal at best and even less so when a ranch hand was needed to run the spread.

Without her husband to handle the ranch chores, expenses soon out-paced income. Her son had bailed her out but only by her signing over the deed to him. She retained the right to live at the ranch as long as she chose, but if she decided to move or if she died, he would have full control.

Everything had been included in the agreement, including her old 1948 Chevy. Only one thing remained of her old life that was still exclusively in her name. And the oldest son had been on her to sign off that to him also.

"But he'll never get that," she said, the anger rising.

Jack was clueless as to what this last item might be. But from the photo on the wall, he imagined what it might be. The two ate in silence, only to be broken by the arrival of their third member as Katarina stepped from the bathroom.

"Oh good, breakfast. I'm starving," Katarina said.

As she served herself, Katarina stopped as she became aware of the silence at the table. Reacting to the decided quiet in the room, she asked, "Did I miss something?" Then in German, she asked Mrs. Dietrich, "Alles in ordnung??

The older woman raised her gaze and looked at her German speaking guest. "Ja, ich denke, alles wird gut."

Jack sat and tried to absorb the foreign language lesson. He had caught a little of the brief conversation but didn't understand the entire context. He went back to his breakfast as he was stopped by a question.

"Jack, your old truck. You collect older vehicles?" Mrs. Dietrich asked.

"No, not really," Jack answered. "My brother is more the collector. He has some very special cars in his collection in Wyoming. He sort of encouraged me but I went for an old truck instead. Seems to fit my personality better."

Mrs. Dietrich seemed to think about that for some time. Katarina worked on her breakfast as Jack finished his. He cleared the dishes and placed them in the kitchen sink. Returning to the dining room table, Mrs. Dietrich was ready.

"My youngest son would be about your age, Jack, if he had lived. In fact, I would like to think that he would have grown up to be a lot like you."

New to the conversation, Katarina asked, "How did your son die?"

"He was killed in a race car he shouldn't have been driving," Mrs. Dietrich said. "After he won his SCCA Championship, another race team asked him to drive one of their cars in a race. His car was being rebuilt so he jumped at the chance. He wasn't familiar with its handling and crashed during the race." The table went quiet at the revelation.

Finally breaking the somber mood, Jack offered, "Mrs. Dietrich. your hospitality has been wonderful. But if we're to get you into Ely to pick up your car and make it to Las Vegas today, we really need to get going."

"Oh, yes," Mrs. Dietrich said. "Forgive an old woman's reminiscing. I'll get my things."

The thirty-minute drive into Ely was pleasant with Katarina describing the climb to the top of Currant Mountain. With the mountain looming out the left hand side of the truck, Mrs. Dietrich filled in with her tales on the mountain. Neither woman went into detail on anything that had happened on the climb,which relieved Jack.

Stopping at the mechanic's shop, Jack waited outside in the sunshine while Mrs. Dietrich conducted her business. The late fall day was brisk at Ely's elevation, but in the sun and against the shop's wall, it was pleasant. Katarina stood beside him as they waited.

"Jack, I made a decision last night about my one thing that still remains mine," Mrs. Dietrich explained when she emerged. "I wrote it all down in a letter and included the paperwork with it. I'm getting too old to live out on the ranch alone and decided awhile back to go live with my niece in Salt Lake City. I was just undecided on what to do with one thing and you two offered me an answer. I hope you accept the offer."

Jack opened the envelope and with Katarina looking over his shoulder, quickly realized what was being passed on to him. Reading over the letter, he smiled and gave Mrs. Dietrich a long hug.

"I'll follow your wishes," Jack offered. "You can trust me to honor your son."

Chapter 21

Las Vegas, Nevada

The lights of Las Vegas shown bright as Jack drove by downtown in the Ford flatbed. Katarina sat close beside him, staring out at the glitter.

"We're not staying?" she said as Jack continued down the I-15 freeway that passed close to the strip.

"Not tonight. LaMarcus is expecting us out in Henderson," Jack answered. "He has an old buddy out there that he's been staying with. Says there's plenty of room for us."

Jack glanced toward Katarina and saw the expression his comment produced. He added, "We can check it out tonight and then find a place in town maybe tomorrow."

The smile returned. Jack understood the allure of Vegas, not that it did much for him. *Lost Wages, that's what they really should call it,* he thought. His few trips to Las Vegas had cemented his opinion of the place. Old people on Social Security smoking cigarettes and pumping money into slot machines. *Stunned mullets, all of them, if you ask me,* Jack thought. It didn't appeal to him and he didn't even get Social Security yet. Just his police pension. And now royalties from his book. Neither of which he wanted to throw down the rat hole called Vegas.

Katarina read off the directions LaMarcus had sent. Jack watched the address numbers on the subdivision houses as they slowly drove up the correct street. In the low light, he only caught every other number.

"Here it is," Katarina announced.

Jack pulled into the empty driveway and shut down the diesel. He surveyed a setting of typical ten-year-old California-styled houses. Some were two story and some only had one, but the common factor of all of them was a two-car garage and a wide driveway. With water restrictions here in the desert, little green showed.

Knocking on the door, the two travelers waited. The door opened to a large African-American man with a wide smile.

"About time you showed up," LaMarcus said. "I thought I'd have to finish all the fun without you."

As he said it, he zeroed in on the woman standing beside his friend. Now barely noticing Jack, LaMarcus adjusted his conversation.

"But I totally understand the delay. Hi, I'm LaMarcus," he said as he stuck out his hand.

"Goedenavond, ben ik Katarina," she offered in her strongest Dutch.

LaMarcus's smile broadened and brushing past Jack, he took her elbow to escort her into the house. Jack fell in behind as they made their way to the family room at the back of the house. Gary, the home owner, rose to greet the new arrivals as he offered a seat to Katarina.

The two men were entranced by the Dutch woman sitting with them as Jack sat and let them carry on. Katarina switched to English to help in the conversation, but made sure her Dutch accent carried through. She even threw in a few Dutch words to keep the two men smiling.

Jack, frustrated, finally broke in. "Excuse me, but we do have your uncle to find."

Startled, the two other men looked at Jack as if he had just arrived. Katarina's smile grew and Jack was quickly forgotten as the conversation swirled around the lone woman. Jack sat back and waited. *Eventually we'll get to the uncle*, he thought. He was wrong, at least that evening.

At breakfast the next morning, LaMarcus finally filled Jack in on where he was in the missing uncle investigation. Jack made sure to keep the conversation on topic but Katarina's late arrival in the kitchen made that difficult.

"OK, back to your uncle," Jack said. "You said that you checked out as many woman working at the brothels as you could."

LaMarcus gave Jack a dirty look and then tossed his head toward Katarina. LaMarcus was indicating his displeasure at talking about prostitutes in front of his guest.

"LaMarcus, it's OK, she's from Amsterdam for God's sake," Jack said.

LaMarcus still held his frown at talking about his escapades in his investigation. Jack rolled his eyes.

"Obviously, you've never been to Amsterdam," Jack said. "The women sit in windows while their customers stand in the street and work out the arrangements. Tourists are walking by as this all happens. And there's a Porno Museum next to the main train station downtown. Never mind the hash smoking coffee shops everywhere."

Katarina laughed at the description of her hometown. Compared to Amsterdam, Las Vegas came off rated PG.

"OK, I get your point. Now let's drop it," LaMarcus said.

"So, where are you at, and how can I help?" Jack asked.

"We, don't forget, this is a team we have here," Katarina said.

LaMarcus and Gary both looked at the Dutch woman, then turned back to Jack for an answer.

"She's right. She and I agreed we work on this together if I'm involved," Jack said.

"That's fine, your choice," LaMarcus said. "But I did locate a brothel worker who might have known my uncle. She's in college right now, so I haven't been able to get an appointment like the other women."

"How do you propose approaching her then?" Jack asked.

A pause as LaMarcus seemed to be thinking. "If our Dutch spy wants to be part of the team, maybe she should be the one that does the work."

Jack began to protest but Katarina stopped him. She offered that meeting a college student didn't imply much danger and that Jack could be close by in case anything happened. Finally agreeing, LaMarcus laid out the arrangements.

From an ad in the community college newspaper, a woman had emailed LaMarcus that she might know the man in the ad photo. The email further asked for verification that the thousand dollar reward was legitimate.

"So, when is the meeting set for?" Jack asked.

"Tomorrow, noon, at the student union," LaMarcus said.

"Public place, lots of people around. She knows enough to be careful," Jack offered. "You really offered a thousand big ones? You still have that much left after your other costs here?"

LaMarcus gave Jack a dirty look and then smiled at his friend. Jack knew that his police pension was substantial with his retiring as a captain. *Hell, he's probably writing it all off as a business expense*, Jack thought.

"Which leaves the rest of the day for us tourists," Katarina announced. She looked at Jack and got a nod of agreement. They could be tourists for the day.

"Ah Jack," LaMarcus interrupted. "That truck you're driving. Since when did you become farmer Bob?"

"That is a classic 1947 Ford dually my friend."

"It didn't sound like a classic Ford last night when I heard it pull in the driveway," LaMarcus said. "You plan on blending in driving a classic truck."

Jack thought about LaMarcus's comment. The flat bed Ford definitely was unique and would be noticed. As Jack debated what he should do, LaMarcus smiled and held his car keys up.

"Take mine, it's in the garage," LaMarcus offered.

The Cadillac Escalade was quiet and smooth running all the way out to Hoover Dam. While the older Ford had its charms, carrying on a conversation wasn't one of them. The combination of old truck lacking insulation and diesel engine made a decidedly noisy ride.

Later that night, the Cadillac really shown as all four took a drive to the famous Las Vegas Strip. To be seen at night for the full effect, Jack had offered dinner at one of the nicer restaurants in the city. Katarina had jumped at the chance to finally dress up and Jack even borrowed a black suit from Gary who luckily was of similar build.

Avoiding a dress shirt and tie, Jack settled on one of LaMarcus' black T-shirts instead. Looking rather urbane, LaMarcus commented, "You know, you clean up good."

As the three men threw comments at each other on their evening clothes standard, Katarina emerged from the bedroom. Stepping confidently down the hallway, her high heels announced herself before she turned the corner into the family room.

Three men's mouths stopped talking. Katarina stopped in front of them and twisted her hips slightly. With both hands firmly planted on each side, she swiveled back and forth on her toes, looking at the men. The black dress clung to her shape while her tanned bare legs emerged just inches below her panties. The neckline was high enough that nothing of what was underneath was exposed. But the shape the tight black material took made it very obvious what lay beneath.

"How do I look boys?" Then in Dutch, "Is dit goed?"

The three men were speechless as they stared at their dinner companion. It was LaMarcus that spoke first.

"Jack, good luck with that."

Dinner went smoothly as the four enjoyed an evening out. Besides the long stares of each male customer as they entered, Katarina settled into being the subject of the three men's attention. Jack noticed a few times other men in the restaurant switching their gaze to their table. Some with dates received a stern look when they shifted their attention back.

The tab was picked up by Jack as Katarina asked if there was a place they could go to dance. Gary, the local, mentioned that Las Vegas certainly had nightclubs with dancing. Offering three of the more popular ones, Katarina asked which one was the most popular.

"Blue Jasmine, I think," Gary offered. "It's not one of my weekly hangouts, but from the television coverage, it seems to pop up the most."

"Can we, Jack?" she pleaded.

Night clubbing wasn't big on Jack's list. While Jackson Hole, Wyoming was a resort town and had some swinging places, none compared to what Las Vegas offered. And he seldom visited the ones in Jackson.

"Are you guys up for it?" Jack asked. Gary and LaMarcus nodded agreement while Gary announced that they could walk there.

A few blocks later, the line outside announced itself before the entrance to the Blue Jasmine came into view. Gary led the group up to the front door. A large bouncer stood by the door blocking entry.

"Hold on, the line forms back there," he said.

The three men stood looking at the long line as Katarina stepped around LaMarcus whose large frame had been blocking her from view. The bouncer noticed the change.

166

"Is er toch mijn vrienden en ik kan krijgen vanavond?" she asked, her Dutch startling the door attendant.

"I don't know what you just said, but you're more than welcome." He stepped aside and opened the entrance door. Groans from those waiting wafted over to them.

"But my friends," Katarina said, switching to heavily Dutch accented English.

Hesitating slightly, the bouncer relented as she tapped the others on the shoulder as if counting them as they passed. The grumbling of those still stuck in line increased.

Once inside, Jack heard none of the grumbling. The noise level amazed him as music pounded out from speakers somewhere deep inside the club, and precluded hearing most anything. He glanced at LaMarcus as his friend leaned over to his ear. Yelling to make himself heard, his friend said, "As I said, good luck with that."

Jack raised his eyebrows in response and they followed their black-dressed leader toward a table. The place was jammed with people and Jack felt lucky that they found a spot. LaMarcus didn't wait as he asked Katarina to dance right away. The two disappeared onto the pulsating dance floor.

Returning, Jack hadn't noticed the music stop at any point. Katarina grabbed his hand and led him out to the other gyrating couples. Jack did his best interpretation of dancing, assuming in the crushing melee that no one would notice his amateur standing. Katarina was all smiles to show that she didn't mind his attempt at dancing.

The music seemed to go on forever as the sweat grew and soon Jack's back was damp. *I'm not cut out for keeping up with twenty-somethings*, he thought. As he finished his thought, the music miraculously ended. He grabbed Katarina's hand and led her back to the table just as a new song blared out.

Collapsing in his seat, Katarina was whisked back onto the dance floor by LaMarcus after Gary feigned age and remained sitting at the table. He leaned over to Jack and explained he was much too old for this type of thing, but he was glad to sit and observe. Jack nodded acknowledgement. *I'm not sure that I'm that far off from where you are*, Jack thought.

That was when Gary jabbed Jack again, this time pointing out LaMarcus and Katarina on the dance floor. It appeared that a fellow dancer had tapped LaMarcus on the shoulder to break into his dance. Katarina was now dancing with a shorter man with a dark complexion. Long hair combed back on his head combined with a gold chain around his neck established to Jack the man's personality.

LaMarcus arrived back at the table and sat down. Not saying anything, he stared at the two dancing. Katarina's smile had disappeared as she politely continued her dance.

As the music seemed to end, Katarina started to leave, but the man took her hand stopping her. She pulled her hand away and turned to head back to her table. The man followed in her wake talking the whole time.

Jack took in the scene of the two on the dance floor, but his police antennae went to full alert as he noticed two large men on the edge of the dance floor. They were intently watching the exchange on the floor and when Katarina moved toward Jack, these two out-riders shifted their position with her.

Motioning to LaMarcus the two men interested in the happenings on the dance floor, his friend nodded in agreement. LaMarcus leaned back to inform Gary of the developing situation as all three retired cops watched carefully.

Katarina suddenly stopped, turned, and slapped the short man. Jack was out of his seat like a shot. Reaching Katarina, Jack pushed her behind him as he stepped in between the two. From his peripheral vision, he saw the two large men move onto the dance floor.

The shorter man said something but Jack didn't hear what was said as the music noise drowned out all communication. But when he turned a quick glance and saw Katarina now crying, he turned back to face the man. The dark complexion was offset by a very lascivious smile, his white teeth contrasted against his dark tan face.

Jack crushed the man's face with a head butt, his forehead meeting bone and gristle. The sickening sound carried over the dance music as the man staggered and dropped to one knee. The man lingered in a dazed state and Jack wound up to put him down. But as he turned to apply force, his arm was caught by one of the outriders.

Thrown off balance by the large body pulling him back, Jack swung around to attack his new antagonist. His vision caught the flash of a knife from the second man coming in fast toward his mid-section. Pushing against the man holding his right arm, Jack tried to increase the distance from the knife.

Then the knife was gone as LaMarcus swung his police baton down, crippling the man's wrist as the knife fell to the floor. The man screamed in pain but his voice was lost to the music. People around them were suddenly realizing something was happening and retreated, shoving other dancers in their wake.

Slowly a hole in the crowd formed where Jack now spun sideways, catching his captor by surprise. Now behind him, Jack lunged onto the back of the large man, placing a choke hold around the man's throat. With the man struggling to get Jack off him, his oxygen slowly ran out, stopping any fight.

Jack lowered the man onto the dance floor as he passed out from lack of oxygen. By now, the original man was up from his head-butt. Blood flowed down out of his crushed nose. Staggering slightly, his right hand swept behind him to the small of his back. Jack saw the chrome revolver emerge just as Katarina screamed.

Standing not five feet from the man, Jack reached quickly with his left hand to intercept the forward moving hand gun. His hand caught the revolver mid-way while the man brought the weapon forward.

Looking quickly at the hammer position of the revolver, Jack grabbed the cylinder of the gun and squeezed as hard as he could. The forward momentum of the man's hand brought the gun forward, now pointing toward Jack's crotch. The man's face contorted as he attempted to pull the trigger. Jack's grip on the cylinder never let up and the revolver refused to fire.

When the man looked down as to why his gun refused to discharge, Jack caught him with a massive right cross to the side of the head. The man folded, his grip on the gun forgotten. Jack yanked the gun out of his hand and scanned to see if the other two were still out of the fight.

Gary stood over the sleeping outrider while LaMarcus held the other with the threat of another baton swing. Jack looked around the club. The dancers had all stopped and screams now muffled the music.

Two bouncers suddenly appeared and Jack raised his hands in submission. *No need hurting innocent people*, he thought. More bouncers arrived as one took the gun out of Jack's hand. Another took LaMarcus's baton as they were escorted into an office.

Police soon arrived with an ambulance right behind. Jack and LaMarcus were handcuffed and taken to the police station. Katarina and Gary managed to plead that they were just innocent witnesses and other dancers confirmed their story.

That was when Gary heard who Katarina's dance partner had been. He took Katarina home and prepared her for bad news.

Chapter 22

The tropical weather continued with perfect sunny days. Being the winter season, the days were pleasant but still warm, the ocean breeze keeping the humidity away. The unusually dry conditions added to the lower humidity which made the nights enjoyable for sleeping.

L.C. sat on the beach under a large shade tree, the branches almost reaching across the beach to the waterline. The entire beach area was covered in the large trees whose leaves made sure the sand area was pleasant.

Sitting beside him, his friend and bungalow mate, Gunny. Both nursed a bottle of beer. They had gotten used to the local beer and while not up to the brews from back home, certainly helped the hot day pass.

One could only handle so much time floating in the warm sea water or sitting on the hot beach. A couple of beers made their excursion to the beach more enjoyable. Not that they wouldn't have enjoyed it without the beer.

Living where they did offered other inducements to lounging at the beach. And as they sipped their beer, two walked by, dressed in matching small triangles of cloth on their upper body and one small triangle on their lower front which was attached to strings running around their back side.

While they lived around retired men of various ages, they also lived around many young women, typically dressed very scantily. It was the main perk of living where they did. Being in an undeveloped country, women were available who worked cheap. *Or inexpensively, as management described it*, L.C. thought. *And luckily, it just wasn't eye candy.*

All of the young women were attached to the retired men. During the day, their job was to mingle throughout the area, just looking good. L.C. jabbed Gunny and nodded toward two more walking down the beach. The two former Marines smiled as two topless women came towards them, thong bottoms their only attempt at modesty.

"Looks like Pacman's former roommate," L.C. said. "I can't believe he wasn't satisfied with that. He had to go and sneak off into Haad Rin to do what?"

"Hell if I know," Gunny said. "Dumbshit wasn't happy with that lying next to him every night. He had to go try who knows what in the village. And now he's back in Frost Bite Falls, Minnesota, or wherever the hell he lived, cursing himself."

"Ain't it the truth Gunny," L.C. added. "Tell you what. If I ever get to itching that scratch, you just whomp me in the head with a two-by-four and set me straight."

"Same here brother," Gunny said. "We be taking care of each other, for sure."

"So, tell me again what happens at the end of the contract?" L. C. asked.

"I've told you this how many times?" Gunny replied.

"I know, but I just can't believe it," L.C. said. "We get to switch?"

"Once more," Gunny started. "If Maya wants out of our bungalow, she puts her name in the lottery. At the same time, all the other women who want to move put their names up for grabs."

Gunny's comment brought smiles to the two men's faces. *All up for grabs,* L.C. thought.

"Once all the women who want new roommates are set, then by seniority, each cabin starts the selection."

"But women don't have to go where they don't want?" L.C. asked.

"No, its not slavery. Its consenting adults working out a business arrangement."

"So if Maya wants out of our cabin and lets say Skinman has first pick, she doesn't have to move in with Skinman?" L.C. asked.

He had selected the consensus creep of the whole area. Skinman was an appropriate nickname that the man had chosen. And from the complaints from the women who got stuck with him each year, his reputation proceeded him. Even women who didn't live with him had complained about his excesses and he was currently on probation.

"No," Gunny said. "But if Skinman slides down the priority list, a woman may have to accept his offer if she wants to work here. That's what has happened over the last two years. He could only get a women that wasn't one of the good-lookers."

"Yeah, that last one was just glad for the job," L.C. said. "Things must be really tough out there for someone to put up with the likes of Skinman. Do you think he'll get thrown out?"

"He will if he does anything he's not supposed to," Gunny said. "The management has finally put him on a short leash. One screw-up, and its back to the good old United States of America."

"But I thought Skinman was French?"

"Is he? Well, c'est la vie, Mr. Frenchman then," Gunny said.

"Yeah, yeah. I fart in your general direction," L. C. added. The two cracked up at the Monty Python reference. While they had never watched the show in the States, with the British contingent around them, they had expanded their cultural experiences.

In fact, European men made up about half the retirees encamped with them. Heavily represented by German and English men, the rest of Europe was also well represented. On the Western Hemisphere front, Americans made up almost half the population with a sprinkling of Canadians. L.C. had run into a couple of men from Argentina and had learned that a small contingent of Latin American retirees were among them.

"So, Gunny, how come no Asian men? The Japanese businessmen are regulars at the brothels in Bangkok. How come not here?" L. C. asked.

"Management is a German company," Gunny explained. "They started out with brothels in Berlin. They expanded into the Amsterdam market before they opened their showcase place outside Las Vegas."

"That's where I found out about this place. Spent some nice time in their place there," L.C. said.

""Me too," Gunny said. "They'd just built their new place near Vegas when I discovered them. It seems they're more comfortable with Western tastes and mannerisms. The Japanese and Chinese markets are

175

different. I guess management is happy with the countries they service. Maybe down the road they'll open an Asian retirement center."

The two laughed. Many things made them break out laughing. And the one most often on the chuckles revue was when back home got mentioned. They were always cracking jokes about their friends back home who would be down at the local senior center for puzzle building. Then maybe a Meals on Wheels lunch out of a Styrofoam container followed by vigorous arm spinning while sitting in their chair. Food, entertainment and exercise, all courtesy of the city of your choice.

L.C. knew their recreation center offered old movies three nights a week. Hence the British men's selections of Monty Python. And the Germans got their pick one night a week. And there were communal meals put on by the management, but they were usually on the beach. *And as for exercise, well, back home just didn't compare to my options,* he thought.

"Ever miss home?" L.C. asked.

Gunny stopped laughing and looked straight at his friend. "No wonder you only a Lance Corporal. If you that dumb, you lucky to be that." He paused as his stare continued. "Miss home? Now, let me remember. Miss an ex-wife that called every other day complaining about something? Nope. Miss shoveling snow every Baltimore winter? Nope. Miss shit ass melting humid summers? Nope. Miss working my ass off to pick up some honey in a bar for a little carnal pleasure, just to find out in the morning that she wasn't so good looking and that at her age she should be home knitting? Nope."

"Come on, there must be something?" L.C. asked. He played this game on a regular basis. *With all the time sitting on the beach in between passing young female types, it passed the time. And it sure riled up Gunny,* he thought.

"Oh, and the taxes," Gunny added. "I sure miss them. And the car insurance costs, another sure miss. And sitting watching crap on television will I suck beer and peanuts. I sure miss the fifty pounds I lost coming here and living the way we do."

"Yeah, me too, I've dropped twenty so far and I've only been here four months," L. C. said.

"And you'll lose that entire gut before the year's out. It's amazing what fresh fruit and vegetables, outdoor living, and willing companionship does for you," Gunny said. "There's not a fat person among us if they've been here more than a year."

"That's a fact," L.C. agreed.

"And how many have dropped their blood pressure medicine after moving here? Never mind all the other drugs people showed up here with," Gunny said. "The medical center posts the stats on the bulletin board on how many of us have dropped taking that stuff. And we ain't keeled over yet."

"Don't forget Plunger, he could have used some heart medicine."

"I don't think it was his heart that gave out. The man was incredible," Gunny said.

"Yeah, I didn't know him long, but I could tell something was going to give. A man his age and he hires two women. It's amazing he lasted as long as he did," L.C. said.

"Yeah, that Plunger was something else. Fitting we named the swimming pool in his memory," Gunny offered. "Since the bodies all get cremated and sent home to the relatives, we couldn't have anything else."

L.C. sat and thought a long time before speaking. "You got someone for them to send you to? I mean, when the time comes?"

"Not really. My two kids left home after dropping out of high school. Never heard from them again. The nag would dump me down the Baltimore sewer if I arrived in an urn at her door," Gunny reflected. "Being in the Marines for twenty isn't beneficial on the family front. No, they just might as well sprinkle my ashes here on the beach. Let high tide take 'em out. How 'bout you?"

L.C. again stared at the ocean in front of him. He didn't even shift his stare to the three bikini clad lovelies walking in front of him.

"Yeah, I got someone," L.C. finally said. "A nephew, my older brother's kid. My brother left. He was no good. I raised his son like he was my own. Him, that's the only thing I miss."

The two former Marines drifted off in thought as the small waves lapped at the sandy beach. The sun moved across the tropical sky and the two old warriors sat mute, lost to other things.

Chapter 23

Las Vegas, Nevada

"I hope your uncle is worth this," Jack said.

"Hey, don't blame my uncle," LaMarcus shot back. "I didn't bring the Dutch treat to Las Vegas and then run her up and down the Strip."

Jack gave his friend a dirty look at the implication of Katarina's blame in their sitting in the Clark County Jail. So far, they had spent the night in lock-up awaiting arraignment in the morning. Their retired cop status had gone for naught with the Las Vegas Police Department. Even Jack's status as a Wyoming Deputy Sheriff for Teton County hadn't moved the locals.

"So, do you think Katarina will make her noon appointment if we don't get out of here?" LaMarcus asked.

"You're assuming she didn't get locked up, aren't you?" Jack asked. "We were a little busy last night."

"And she was sure in her 'I only know Dutch mode', had the police stymied there."

"I just hope she and Gary got home last night," Jack said. "And maybe they found a lawyer for our asses this morning."

"Wesley, Lewis, let's go," a jail attendant yelled.

Jack and LaMarcus stepped up to the barred door as the control was thrown, opening the holding cell. Directed toward the courtroom, each one tried to straighten their orange jail jumpsuits and comb their hair with their fingers.

After a circuitous route, they were finally led into the side door of a courtroom. The proceedings were already underway as the judge ran through the day's caseload. Katarina waved from the audience as the two sat down where they were told.

A man in a suit sat next to Katarina with Gary on the other side. They awaited the next case.

"State of Nevada versus Wesley and Lewis," the clerk called.

"Counsel for the defendants your honor," the man in the suit stood and addressed the court.

"Approach," the judge advised.

Joining Jack and LaMarcus at the table, the lawyer opened his briefcase and pulled out a file. He opened it and pulled out two sheets of paper. A brief conversation between the three ensued. Standing, he turned to the judge.

"Your honor, my clients plead not guilty. We ask that they be released on their own recognizance. They are both retired law enforcement and have very strong ties to their community. In fact, Mr. Wesley is currently a Deputy Sheriff in Teton County, Wyoming and is here on official business. Why the District Attorney is pursuing charges is beyond me."

The judge changed his focus to the man at the other table and zeroed in with his stare.

"Is that true?" the judge asked. "If Mr. Wesley is a duly-sworn Deputy Sheriff, why is he before me?"

"Your honor, it's our contention that Mr. Wesley was not on duty last night at the time of the altercation," The assistant DA said. "Further, we have witnesses that state that he started the events that put three men in the hospital, one near death. We further have witnesses that state they saw Mr. Wesley pull a gun, a gun that may well show involvement in other crimes."

"I see," the judge said. Shifting his gaze back to Jack's attorney he added, "It appears that there is sufficient evidence to hold open this case. I'll take the not guilty plea for the record and release you both on your own recognizance. Next case." The gavel marked the end of Jack and LaMarcus' time before the judge.

The attorney told them to go get processed and that he'd met them in the hallway. Turning in their jumpsuits and after getting dressed, the two soon emerged from processing. They walked over to where their friends waited. Katarina hugged Jack.

"Oh Jack, I'm sorry. It's all my fault," Katarina admitted.

"No it's not," Jack said. "It's some pig that started this. You just wanted to dance when he shoved his snout under the tent."

Gary jumped in, "I don't want to disillusion you, but that pig you mention has got a lot of juice in this town. Busting him and his two boys up won't go well."

LaMarcus was the first to get it out, "How connected are we talking?"

"As connected as you can get in Las Vegas," Gary added. "Remember, in the last few Presidential elections, after New York and Los Angeles, Las Vegas was a strong third in political campaign donations. Takes a lot for a city this size to beat out the likes of Chicago and Houston."

The lawyer finally chimed in, "He's right. Ernesto has been on the shady side of legality for many years in this town. He has greased a lot of palms and made a lot of friends. That you hit first won't be easy to get dismissed." Then turning to LaMarcus, he added, "And your baton is illegal to carry in this county. Your retired police status won't help you."

"But what about Jack's sheriff status?" Gary asked. "That will help him'"

"If his sheriff backs him up that he was on official duty," the lawyer said.

"He will," Jack said. He was confident that his sworn officer rank would be backed up.

"Well, you'll have time to work out all the details," the lawyer advised. "The courts are so backed up we won't see the inside of a courtroom for a month."

"A month. I can't sit here for a month waiting," LaMarcus said. "And neither can Jack."

"I'll see what I can do. I'll call you if anything changes. Otherwise, in my office in two days to start the process," the lawyer ordered. He walked off toward the elevator.

"Come on, we have to hurry, if we're going to make my noon appointment," Katarina said.

"That's right, I almost forgot," LaMarcus said. "Gary, can you take them out to the school while I go pay off the parking garage to get my Cadillac back?"

* * *

They drove west toward the College of Southern Nevada, Jack filled her in on extracting information from reluctant witnesses. But Jack's energy was wasted. Katarina had dressed for the meeting.

Meeting under the clock in the student union courtyard, Katarina spotted a woman who appeared to be scanning the crowd for someone.

Walking up to her, she asked, "Are you here about the thousand dollar reward?"

"Yeah, do you have it with you?" a woman about twenty-two asked. She looked around furtively.

"It's nearby. If you tell me what I need to know, I'll make the phone call and it will brought to you," Katarina asked. "So, have you seen this man?"

Katarina pulled a color photo of LaMarcus's uncle from her bag and held it out. She watched the woman's face for signs that Jack had told her about. Any person had tells over whether they were telling the truth or were lying. Katarina studied her subject.

"Yes, like I said in the email. Now where's my money?"

"Not so fast. A little more information please," Katarina said.

"How much more can you handle?"

"Where did you know him? Let's start there."

"I was working the Rising Sun Resort out in Pahrump. He came in once or twice at first. We hit it off and after that he asked for me each time," the woman said. "At least if I was working, he'd ask. Don't know if he came in other times."

"So how long did your little business arrangement last?" Katarina asked.

"Maybe two months, I forget. More than a tourist dropping in once or twice. But not so long as to get boring, if you know what I mean."

Katarina looked at the woman. She was a couple years younger than her but looked a few years older. Katarina had seen the same in Amsterdam. Young women coming in from Eastern Europe looking for money and passing themselves off as older so they could work the sex trade. The newspapers had frequent accounts of arrests made in brothels with underage women. *They all looked older to me*, she thought. *And I don't know what it takes to be bored with sex.*

"Do you know what happened to him? There are people who are worried about him."

"They shouldn't be," the woman said. "He's fine. He'd talk about his plans after we did it. He paid extra for me to linger. Easy money, laying there listening. Put up with a little grab ass or tit squeeze maybe."

"And what were those plans?"

"He bought in to the whole Rising Sun mantra. Life is good and we'll make sure it happens for you bullshit."

Katarina was confused. Her English was good but this woman was talking with too much American slang for her to get the meaning.

"Please, enlighten me. What bullshit are we talking?"

"They've got this whole thing going. Sign over everything you own to them and they make your life wonderful," the woman offered. "I don't trust the bastards. Germans running brothels in Nevada. How they ever got to come in here, I'll never know."

"So they're bad to their workers?" Katarina asked.

"No, its not that. In fact, they've been the best place I've worked. At least its not some dumpy single-wide trailer out on the desert acting like a real whorehouse or anything. I'll give it to them, they've brought class to sex around here."

"But you were saying where my friend went to," Katarina pressed.

"It's some voodoo crap they pull. One day your guy is happily screwing away here in Nevada, happy as can be. The next day he's never seen again."

"And you don't know where they go?" Katarina asked.

"Rumors only, but their money continues to roll into the bank in Pahrump. All those social security and pension checks plus annuities flowing in like water. Must be millions by now."

"What do the rumors say?"

"You're not the first, you know," the woman said.

"What do you mean?"

"Other girls have talked about people that have come looking for their loved ones. They all hit a stonewall. The Germans can prove their loved ones are still alive at a whim so the checks can't be stopped. But privacy rights keep them from admitting anything more. And I hear that the biggest law firm in Las Vegas helps to keep it that way. Nice and quiet."

"Again, no idea where they disappear to?"

185

"No, but all that stuff is in the main office. Very locked up. If you could get in there, you'd find your missing uncle."

The two women talked briefly before Katarina reached into her bag and pulled out a thick envelop. She handed it to the woman who discreetly scanned the contents, the ten one-hundred-dollar bills running quickly through her fingers.

"I got to get to class. Good luck finding who you're looking for."

Katarina watched her hustle off to class before leaving. She caught Jack on the other side of the courtyard where he had been watching the entire time. He hooked his arm under hers as they headed to the parking lot where Gary waited.

Chapter 24

The lottery was scheduled in a week. This was the time when all the contracts for the women in the enclosure came due. Once per year, all the residents had to scramble in a giant musical chairs of young women.

L.C. sat at breakfast waiting for Gunny to show up. The two of them had been having regular discussions on the upcoming lottery. While a certain part of the whole thing bothered him, he tried to accept the event at its face value.

As an African-American whose ancestors had endured slavery, the lottery smacked of involuntary servitude. Gunny had explained the whole process to him many times, but L.C. still couldn't put his mind around what was about to take place.

A tired Gunny opened his bedroom door, headed into the kitchen and grabbed the coffee pot that L.C. had brewed. He poured it thick and black and sat down, sensing what was coming. As the two men feigned interest sipping their coffee, a naked Maya flitted out of Gunny's room and disappeared into her room..She soon reappeared, now dressed in a bikini bottom and a tank top, her daily attire attracted the usual attention.

Both men followed her movements as she headed to the bathroom. They were still contemplating their coffee when she emerged and announced she was heading to the beach.

They knew that she had this morning off and that they were responsible for their own breakfast and lunch. She would return for an afternoon of either cleaning or laundry and always cooking supper, except on her one day off each week. She usually made enough of something to carry the two men over for that one day.

With her out of the house, the real discussion could begin. They had danced around the subject between them for a week now. It was time to decide.

"Gunny, what are we going to do?" L.C. asked.

"As we've discussed, what do you want to do?"

"The world is our oyster, so to speak. Do we take our chances or stay where we are?" L.C. asked.

"Don't know, my friend, but its sure wonderful having choices," Gunny replied.

The crux of their discussion had always been whether to offer Maya a new one-year contract and if they did, whether she would accept it or not. Or whether they would try their luck in the lottery. Management guaranteed a woman roommate, but didn't guarantee how young they would be, nor how good looking, nor how nice they would be to live with.

If they went the lottery route, they could end up with someone far worse than Maya. But in the same vein, they could end up with someone even better. The question was whether the chance was worth it of not.

"We could end up with a lot worse than Maya," L.C. said.

"Yes we could, and I've seen it. Guys get greedy and end up paying hell for a year," Gunny offered. "Look at Hermann. The German went for the big prize. That sweet young thing they brought in last year, the one who ended up with Jersey."

L.C. registered on the reference. So that's what had happened. Having only been in the bungalow a few months, he hadn't been through a lottery before. But he knew Jersey. Everyone did.

Jersey was the former offshore investment banker from the Channel Islands in the English Channel. A part of Great Britain, just off the French Coast, Jersey and Guernsey were famous for their cows. However, money was what really ran the Channel Islands with their special tax haven status. And the man they called Jersey knew how to manipulate the system so well, he was a local legend.

Generous with his knowledge, not only the retirees relied on his knowledge to establish offshore accounts, but he was known to help many of the women who wanted to invest their earnings. And rumor was that some of the women were doing very well. With their room and board covered by their employers, most women could put away the majority of their earnings.

With the tax-free compounding on investments offered by Jersey, L.C. figured some of the women working around him would have a better retirement that he had. And considering that their working age ended at about forty years of age, a twenty-year working career would leave them set for life outside the walls.

The two men sat with their coffee, once again stymied in what move they should make in the coming lottery. Gunny broke the silence first.

"You know, rumor has it that Jersey is sort of the odds maker on where the women will go. Maybe we should go talk to him."

L.C. jumped at the suggestion. They needed some sound advice, and not just on money issues.

They found Jersey holding court in his usual spot by the main pool, his young woman for the previous year lingering nearby. *She is a beauty,* L.C. thought. *If I could only. . .*

"Jersey, could we bother you for a minute?" Gunny asked.

Looking up from is reclined position on the lounge, he shaded his eyes to see who was asking him for help. Recognizing Gunny, he offered the two men a seat. Two young women scooted off their chairs nearby to make room.

The man has them coming out of his ears, L.C. thought. *He has to clear them out of the way.*

Gunny didn't take the seat offered but asked instead, "Jersey, we were hoping we could sort of talk in private, if it's not too much trouble?"

"Not at all, my fine American friends," Jersey said, his British accent noticeable. "Its almost time for my ocean swim anyway. Let's head down to the beach, we'll talk on the way."

Leaving his bevy of adoring fans, Jersey headed to the beach, Gunny and L.C. close behind. Once away from the crowded pool, Gunny broached the subject of the lottery.

"We need some advice on the lottery, Jersey. Rumor has it you are the odds maker on how it will play out."

Gunny was referencing the fact that Jersey, in spite of the supposed seniority system for selection, really had the top pick. As the more senior men would pick first, the more desirable women could decline the initial offers, holding out for a less senior man, but one offering a more lucrative contract. Since Jersey was the wealthiest retiree among them, by default, he had first choice.

Management didn't allow anything over the set price per woman in any of the contracts. They had established a six-hundred American dollars per month rate of pay for any woman and required the men to abide by that set amount. The German manager of the resort offered that a set rate made sure that prices wouldn't inflate over time as the wealthy bid up the price.

The men had worked a way around the set contract, though. Side deals were quietly made to entice the more desirable women to hold out in the lottery until the prearranged match was met. These side deals often included gifts for either the woman or her family. Since most of the women sent money back to their villages to support their families, the men upped the ante. A new roof here, a pig there, maybe a cow or even an entire hut was thrown in on the side deals. So far, management had looked the other way. But word had come down that management wasn't happy at the level the extra enticements had reached. Everyone wondered if they were about to set new rules to keep the lottery relevant.

191

Because of these side deals, everyone knew most of the top women would have already reached deals with the affluent men. Which left the ladder of seniority rather rungless. Gunny knew from the previous lottery that one had to check the top half of the men selecting to see who would be going with whom.

"Glad to help out, men," Jersey said. "What do you want to know?"

"We're having a difficult time deciding whether to work to keep our current employee, or go for someone new," Gunny said.

"Have you asked your woman yet? Because you may not have a choice?" Jersey asked.

We hadn't thought of that, L.C. thought. *Maybe Maya has already found a better deal and we don't even know it.* Gunny shook his head that they hadn't done that yet.

"Well, you need to start there, unless you're not happy with her," Jersey said.

"No, we're happy. She cooks real good, and keeps the bungalow clean," L.C. added.

"And the important thing, she good there?" Jersey asked.

"Oh yeah," Gunny and L.C. almost said in unison, with Gunny continuing, "She's fine in that detail."

"But just thinking that there might be something better out there, eh boys?" Jersey said.

"Doesn't hurt to think about it, but that's why we came to you," Gunny said. "Word is, you set the top mark and everything falls in line after that."

Jersey stopped and turned to the other two, "You flatter me. I think Hermann has something to say in all that. He's senior to me and has the money to attract the top talent, as we say."

L.C. knew that Jersey was being modest. *In a showdown, Hermann didn't have a chance compared to Jersey,* he thought. *I might have been here only a few months, but I've seen the two go head-to-head with Hermann coming up second fiddle every time.*

"But your opinion on what we should do, renegotiate or go for a new woman?" Gunny pressed.

They had reached the beach and Jersey dropped his towel in one of the chairs under an umbrella. A number of the working women were lounging nearby. He leaned in close to Gunny to ask, "Is your current woman nearby? If she is, point her out to me."

Gunny scanned the beach and spotted Maya. She was sitting with two other women a short distance away. He leaned toward Jersey's ear and described her to him. Jersey zeroed in on Maya and examined her closely. Gunny became nervous at the time he lingered in making his evaluation.

"So boys, you say she's a good cook and pleasant to be around," Jersey said.

"Yes, sir," L.C. said.

"She's young, looks to be mid-twenties, typical bust development for our women."

"Yes," both Gunny and L.C. offered.

"Would you say she's adequate or above average in the nighttime recreational activities?" Jersey asked.

L.C. was suddenly getting nervous at Jersey's questions. *Was he looking at our Maya to have her as his own*? he thought. He tapped discreetly on Gunny's arm to send him hopefully a message.

"Maybe a little above average. Willing, but lacks energy sometimes."

L.C. relaxed at Gunny's lie. Maya was a wild cat in bed to him and he knew Gunny had the same experiences. L.C. was suddenly getting antsy to get together and offer Maya a new contract. He had to wait until Jersey finished.

"Well, I'd advise holding pat," Jersey said. "I've seen the new models that management has brought in for this year and they are nothing like last year. I think that most of the men are tying up their current woman, if they can. I've already agreed in principal to my young woman continuing with me for another year."

"Thanks, Jersey," Gunny offered. "If there's anything we can do for you, just ask."

"No problems, and thanks for the offer," Jersey said. "And good luck with negotiations."

Chapter 25

Las Vegas, Nevada

Jack smiled to himself as he stepped out of LaMarcus's Cadillac and walked the short distance to the entrance. The large building looked more like a forlorn furniture warehouse lost in the desert. While the big box store was painted in browns and dull reds to match the surrounding desert motif, the entrance screamed otherwise.

Stopping to scan the outside surroundings, he was amazed at the community of Pahrump, Nevada. With legal prostitution as its sole reason for existing, Pahrump wasn't your typical western desert town.

Over to the east, Jack spied the other two brothels in town. But they were decidedly lackluster compared to the monster he was walking into. The other brothels were a step ahead of the single-wide mobile home set in the middle of a dust bowl he and Katarina had seen on their drive down form Ely, but not by much.

The two competitors were old single-story motels that had been spiffed up in a cheap tawdry way. Jack wasn't bothering to investigate them at LaMarcus's suggestion. His friend had worked his way through all the surrounding brothels and knew the answer to the missing uncle was in the big new one.

Jack opened the door and was met by a blast of cool air. The hot outside air mingled in the small space until Jack opened the second set of doors. His eyes struggled to adjust to the subdued light and he almost walked into a potted plant in the foyer.

A sharp-dressed man in a suit greeted him. "Welcome to Rising Sun Resort. Are you a member with us?"

As Jack's irises finally opened to allow his pupils to see properly, he shook the man's hand.

"No, not yet. But a friend who's a member set me up with your time share meeting."

"Yes, sir," the man said. "You're just in time. That session starts in fifteen minutes. A drink perhaps? Compliments of Rising Sun."

A little early for a stiff one, Jack thought. LaMarcus had made an appointment for the ten o'clock sales pitch. Being the first one of the day, Jack figured he'd have the rest of the day and evening to check the super-store of sex out properly.

The woman who Katarina interviewed had been a worker here when she had established LaMarcus's uncle as regular customer. An answer to his disappearance would have to be pried out of the resort somehow.

"Some water would be nice," Jack answered.

The man led Jack toward a small room off the lobby. After retrieving a bottled water for him, he excused himself and returned to his greeting duties. Jack was left with three other men of various ages. Taking a sip of his water bottle, Jack noticed that the other three all had hard drinks in their hands. *Way too early for that shit,* Jack thought. *But alcohol limbers up people and definitely loosens their wallets.*

196

To enjoy the pleasures held by the Rising Sun Resort, Jack had learned one had to be a member. And to avoid the one-hundred-dollar membership initiation fee, LaMarcus had learned that sitting through the sales pitch earned a certificate, good for one membership.

A well-tanned fit man entered the room and motioned for everyone to take a seat. He introduced himself and went around the room so people could introduce themselves to hear where everyone had traveled from. Surprised that two of the men were locals, Jack offered Oregon as his place of residence. *Partly true, I still had a pile of possessions in storage there,* he thought. The fourth man offered that he was from Germany.

With the introductions finished, the salesman began his spiel. Jack half-listened as he had no intention of buying a time-share at the resort. But the more the salesman talked, the more Jack became interested.

It became apparent that Rising Sun was not your typical resort. Watching the video tape of features offered by the resort, Jack decided the resort was unique. *And it wasn't your typical brothel either*, he thought.

As the salesman wrapped up his half-hour sales pitch, three new men in suits walked in ready to sign people to contracts. The main salesman grabbed Jack and escorted him to one of the many tables that lined the outside walls of the room. With his three cohorts working hard on making a sale, Jack listened to the talk.

"So, Mr. Wesley, I see from your application you're a retired policeman from Oregon. And a divorcee with kids all grown up. Ready to make the plunge to an exciting lifestyle right out your door step?" the man asked.

Jack was a little taken aback by the personal information just thrown at him and realized LaMarcus would have filled out the online application when making the reservation. Jack knew he had to play nice to get inside the resort.

"Just looking," Jack answered. "My friend sure likes it here. Can't say enough about the perks."

"Well, yes, we do have our perks," the sales man said. He smiled in a man-to-man kind of way. "Which perk is your friend most impressed with?"

The question sort of caught Jack off guard. He recovered quickly.

"You know, I haven't heard him zero in on just one. He seems to be enjoying the whole smorgasbord right now."

"I've heard that before many times. But to really get the entire experience, you really need to own a little piece of heaven yourself. Has your friend bought his piece yet?"

Jack knew the salesman was referring to the time share, not the other products offered. But he punted politely on any commitment to purchasing a time share. After about fifteen minutes of determined but pleasant sales job, the salesman knew he had a tire kicker on his hands.

"Well, Jack, you just want to see our resort with your own eyes. I'd be the same way. Watching videos and listening to me blab on just isn't convincing. Am I right?" the salesman asked. "But I'm confident that our product sells itself. So take your membership certificate and go check it out yourself. I think you'll agree. Here's my card. Call anytime when you've decided."

As the two men stood and shook hands, Jack finally had the chance to see the other three men. Each was busy signing papers, buying their little piece of Nevada heaven. He grabbed his water and headed to the front desk. Within minutes, he had his official Rising Sun smart card.

The front desk receptionist instructed Jack in the use of the card. The smart card held a computer chip built in and could be used throughout the resort. Charges would be recorded and he would receive a monthly bill.

Along with the smart card for billing, a coded wrist band was attached. The wrist band was for convenience while paying for things in the resort. Jack was advised to always wear the wrist band on his person, no matter where he might be. The device was water proof, so swimming in one of the pools was not a problem.

As he stepped away, Jack noticed the German man from his sales pitch just finish his paperwork. The German walked briskly over to Jack and extended his hand.

"You're the writer, aren't you? The one with the German book on the double killing?"

Jack was taken aback by his celebrity status raising its head here in Nevada. He stammered in answering.

The German didn't wait. "I thought I recognized you from the picture on your book. And then you said you were Jack form Oregon and I knew. Gunther Werk, from Dusseldorf. I'm glad to make your acquaintance."

Jack took the German's hand, "Glad to meet you Gunther. I'm afraid I'm still not used to my celebrity status."

"And to meet you here, of all places," Gunther said.

"Yes," Jack said. *Of all places,* he thought. *But this could be an opportunity.* "So, Gunther, it looks like you bought a time share."

"Ja, ja. This place is the best. Have you been coming here long?" Gunther asked.

"No, first time," Jack answered. "And you?"

"Fourth time since it opened. Sehr wunderbar," Gunther said, slipping into German. "Nothing like the places in Berlin or Amsterdam."

A pause followed as both men seemed lost for words. Then Gunther added, "But if you've never been here before, let me be your escort. I can show you how the place works."

The German grabbed Jack's elbow and escorted him toward a door marked 'Private, Members Only'. Stepping through, they were met by a scanner. Gunther passed his wrist band over the reader and then showed Jack how to log in.

"Your account is now being charged," Gunther advised. A slight pained look gave Jack away. Gunther responded, "Not to worry, it is a small cover charge. Compared to the other ones, it is nothing."

I'll see about that, Jack thought. *I need to read the stuff in the folder they gave me when I signed up. They said the rates were all listed there.*

But Gunther allowed no time for reading as he led Jack into the locker room. Showing how to use the locking steel cabinet, Gunther stripped down. He pulled out a Speedo styled swimsuit and stepped into it.

"Did you bring a suit?" Gunther asked.

"No, I didn't know I'd needed one," Jack answered.

"Not to worry, they sell them right over here. My treat, what color would you like?" Gunther passed on Jack's color request and again waved his computer chipped wrist band over the scanner. The attendant passed over the new swimsuit. Jack stripped, placing his clothes in a locker, pulled on his swimsuit and passed his wrist over the locker reader. He heard the lock close.

"OK, let's go party," Gunther announced.

LaMarcus had given Jack some insight over what he was about to step into so when the door opened to the noise of frolicking people at a pool, he wasn't totally surprised. But part of him was, and he stopped to look. He had been prepared for what he imagined was a brothel. Not that he had ever been in one, but he'd seen pictures and read descriptions.

This brothel looked more like a college campus apartment building, but one where a bunch of older guys had stumbled into. Young, good-looking women in various swimsuits were mingling with a wide range of men. Gunther grabbed Jack and led him to the fun.

"Not like any brothel, is it Jack? You were expecting sex in your face as soon as you walked in, didn't you?"

Gunther was right there, Jack thought. In spite of LaMarcus's talk, he had expected the typical women trolling a room setting up business arrangements, dressed in seductive attire. This pool was inside the two-story box store type structure. Trees and greenery lined one side of the pool with skylights filtering light in on the whole scene.

On both sides of the pool area, rows of rooms led off a balcony that overlooked the area. With a door and one window, it appeared more like a short Embassy Suite building then a whorehouse.

Grabbing a table, Gunther directed Jack to sit down. A woman with a serving tray stopped and asked for orders. Jack held up his water to motion he was fine. The German ordered beer and turned to Jack.

"The timeshares line the pool area. I have a second story unit so I can sit on the balcony and watch the fun. That's what this area is all about, looking."

"You mean none of these women are available?" Jack asked.

"No. Almost all are college students who get paid by the resort to be here and look sexy," Gunther explained. "The resort runs a shuttle bus between Las Vegas and here every two hours. The girls run out here between classes, make good money, have a little fun and head back to school."

Two young women approached their table and sat down. One was well-endowed while the other was small but perky. They asked if the men would buy them a drink. Gunther waved at the waitress for two more drinks and scanned his bracelet on the portable device the waitress carried.

The women sipped their drinks and chatted small pleasantries with Jack and Gunther. When they asked the two men to go swimming with them, Gunther begged off but said maybe later. The women moved on to another table

Alone again, Jack asked, "So did we just get charged for those two to sit here?"

"That's all part of the cover charge for being in this section of the resort. The drinks are charged but not the eye candy."

And there is plenty of eye candy, Jack thought. He estimated that there was about one woman for each man that he could see. Some men were fully engaged swimming with one of the workers or sitting in conversation. Drinks and food flowed out to tables as the men just relaxed around the good-looking women. *It all seems very innocent,* he thought. *That is if you ignore the age difference between most of the men and the women they were cavorting with.*

Then Jack thought of Katarina. He was lucky to find his own cute young thing due to both his writing celebrity and her subsequent discovery of his other adventures. That had been enough to attract her. But what did these men have? Not fame and certainly not an exciting past. *Just a little money to fill in for a lonesome life,* Jack thought. *That had always been prostitution's draw, lonely men looking for what? Pleasure, companionship, love? Why else would LaMarcus's uncle ask for the same woman each time? Familiarity leads to closeness. We're all looking for partners, even if you had to pay for it.*

"I can show you my timeshare, Jack. It'll just take a minute. Then we can have lunch before we venture to the other side."

Jack knew about the other side from LaMarcus. But the inside of one of the time shares had escaped his Marine friend.

The two men climbed the stairs and walked down the balcony past numbered doors. Below, the swimming pool scene continued in lusty fun. Gunther swiped his bracelet at one of the doors and the latch clicked. Stepping inside, Jack was taken aback by the basic nature of the room.

Fashioned as a standard hotel room, it had a bed, a table with two chairs, a love seat for two, a small counter holding a microwave, a tiny refrigerator, and a bar sink. A bathroom on the back wall completed the space.

"Not much, is it? But all the fun is outside, so who needs luxury?" Gunther said.

"Looks like a regular hotel room," Jack added.

"But it comes with maid service each day and it beats driving an hour from Las Vegas each day. And if you noticed, Pahrump doesn't exactly offer much in the way of accommodations."

Jack had noticed that the town around them was decidedly bleak. Everything it seemed was brought in from the nearby big city. Las Vegas could easily knock Pahrump off the map, but for one fact, prostitution was legal here and not over the nearby county line.

The two men were soon back at a table by the pool ordering lunch. Again, Gunther wouldn't allow Jack to pay.

"You're my guest," Gunther said. "At least on this side of the wall. This afternoon, you're all on your own."

Jack saw Gunther's eyes grow in carnal anticipation of the afternoon activities. Jack was a little nervous about moving on to the other parts of the Rising Sun Resort.

Chapter 26

The lottery went about as Jersey had predicted. The day before, management had trotted out the new women that would be working. Ready for a close examination, all the men were free to mingle with them and determine if their personalities and physical attributes met their pleasure.

L.C. and Gunny attended the event by the main pool more to satisfy their curiosity. After their talk with Jersey, they had sat down with Maya. After a brief discussion, the three reached a tentative agreement. Maya would remain in their bungalow for another year. Terms were similar to the previous contract except that the two men had decided to give her a fifty dollar bonus per month. Since management forbade her receiving any cash rewards above her normal pay, the money would be sent to her father back in her home village.

They knew that in the pecking order of all the women, a bonus of some sort was required to maintain status. A woman who was retained at the same rate without bonuses on her new contract was socially suspect. Her status with the other workers would be diminished with the subsequent trouble that would follow.

Gunny had remarked about how catty the women could be and once a woman lost status, the other women could be unmerciful in their behavior. Both men knew that management spent a lot of time resolving these disputes to keep harmony going through the community.

So, with their present worker on board for another year, they scoped out the new talent. As Jersey had said, it was a lackluster year. These new women would end up being selected in the bottom third of the lottery by men who were known as difficult.

Everyone knew who were the wrong men to work for. Some men just demanded too much attention, were never happy about their meals, or were just obstinate. Management worked with them to try to assure a smooth life for everyone, but some were very difficult.

Lately, though, the word was drifting around that the difficult ones needed to be careful. A waiting list had been started of retirees who had discovered the compound and wanted to become members. Management had hinted that with the limited housing, people may be asked to leave if they persisted in their complaints. The effect on the lottery was noticeable.

"Here goes Hermann," Gunny said quietly to L.C. The two friends sat in the shade at the back of the amphitheater as the official lottery took place.

They watched as the German walked over and placed a contract down on the front table. Management announced his selection and the woman came forward to sign. Everything had been worked out ahead of time and the two signed the papers.

Jersey looked over at them and smiled in acknowledgment. Almost all the senior men were staying with their current woman. The moderator announced that Skinman was next. The bald-headed man walked up and announced his selection.

The assembled crowd gasped as the woman's name floated out. L.C. saw the scowl immediately on Jersey's face as his woman's name was called. Skinman was making a power play for the best-looking woman available.

"No way," Gunny said.

"Shit, do you think he can pull it off?" L.C. said.

"No flipping way. Beat out Jersey? The Skinman is delusional. Too much sun on that bald head of his," Gunny added.

The two watched as the woman in question stood and walked forward. *Was she really going to do it?* L.C. thought. *I can't believe Skinman has that kind of juice.*

He watched as Jersey's face grew redder and redder the closer the woman got to the table. When she bent down and signed the contract, the silence of the gathering was complete. The top woman had just signed with Skinman, a retiree whose reputation was less than stellar. In the time L.C. had been there, Skinman's complaints had become legend. That she would chose to hook up with him for a year was inconceivable to everyone.

Suddenly L.C. was nervous. With Jersey's woman taken, what would the rich British retiree do? Gunny and L.C. soon found out as Jersey was next on the seniority list.

Standing up, Jersey scanned the crowd in what appeared to be a mind working hard. He had to select a woman who would keep him satisfied for a year. Walking to the front, he announced Maya's name.

As Gunny and L.C. slumped in defeat, Maya jumped up and ran to the front. The two quickly negotiated an agreement before they turned to sign the contract. With a huge smile on her face, Maya scooped Jersey's arm and accompanied him out of the amphitheater.

Five more men selected and then Gunny's name was called. Since they shared one woman, L.C. walked to the front with his roommate. They had been frantically whispering the entire time as they scrambled to find a suitable replacement. Looking over the available women, they lingered in discussion.

Management as well as the remaining retirees were aware that the selection process could linger a long time. Officially, each retiree had an hour to make a selection. While the first picks went fast, the second half was always slow. With surprise selections upsetting people's plans, there was considerable maneuvering involved.

Gunny looked over the choices carefully. While the truly beautiful ones had already been selected, there were some still available that held their own. Some of the women that were good-looking had already earned a reputation for being difficult. Hence, they still sat waiting.

Gunny passed them by as L.C. let the more senior man make the decision. L.C. would have to trust his friend to make the best of a deteriorating situation. With many of the new women still available, Gunny read over each woman's biography. Management provided a brief history of each woman: where they lived previously, any special training, and schooling.

After reviewing each new candidate, Gunny went back through the lot, carefully evaluating each one. He motioned one to stand up. She was short and petite. Her round face was outlined by dark straight hair. While good-looking, she wasn't a knock-out like Jersey's former partner was.

Speaking to her in a language that escaped L.C., Gunny carried on a brief conversation. He turned and took her by the hand to the front table.

"She'll do," he said to the moderator. The moderator announced Sho Lin had been selected as the three all signed the contract.

With the other remaining retirees looking, the two men escorted their new roommate back to their bungalow. On the way, before L.C. could ask Gunny what had tipped him to this woman, they ran into Jersey.

"Sorry mates, no hard feelings," Jersey said. Maya stood beside him, a triumphant look on her face. In the status of the working women, she had just been elevated to the top.

L.C. wanted to slap him for taking Maya away, but he held back. Whoever their new woman was, he knew nothing about her. Maya he knew and already he missed her tender nighttime diversions.

"No worries," Gunny said, a smile radiating from his face. "Another year in the books."

He's being much too casual about this, L.C. thought. *Sho Lin, as she called herself, was what? Who knows what we just signed up for? And a whole year 'til the next chance to pick.*

At the bungalow, Gunny carefully showed Sho Lin her living quarters. A tour of the cabin followed with an emphasis on the kitchen. They would show her the communal laundry building later. A few words in her language passed and she was instantly at work in the kitchen.

L.C. couldn't stand the suspense any longer. Grabbing Gunny's arm, he pulled him out onto the porch.

"So tell," he demanded. "Why her?"

"Slow down brother," Gunny said. "Don't tell anyone, but I think we hit the jackpot today."

"What? Why?"

"She's from the north. It seems she's a Chinese refugee that got scooped up by the Thai authorities. She's very happy to be here instead of being returned to China," Gunny said.

"And so? What's so special about that?" L.C. asked.

"Plenty. I was stationed at the U.S. Embassy in Beijing for three years. That's where I learned some Chinese. I also learned that Chinese women invented some of the most erotic moves in human history. And one more thing . . ."

But before Gunny could finish, Sho Lin interrupted him. The two men stepped back into the bungalow. The first course was already on the table as Sho Lin readied the second course in the wok.

As L. C. dug into the first serving, he noticed the difference from what they had been eating. Maya had been a good cook and made the local fare tolerable. But this was something else altogether.

Soon, the second course arrived as L.C. discovered what the one more thing that Chinese women were good at. He stuffed his mouth and the flavor exploded.

"And wait 'til she gets all the right ingredients. She's just working with what Maya had lying around now."

L.C. decided right then that he couldn't wait. As he watched her petite body move through her cooking motions, he wondered about Gunny's comments. He would have to wait to find out as Gunny was senior man in the cabin. He would have the first nighttime shift. L.C. would have to wait three days.

Chapter 27

Pahrump, Nevada

Jack's eyes grew big as he and Gunther stepped through the door dividing the titillating area from the serious side. They had finished their lunch while the melee of tight young bodies pranced around the pool. Lots of flesh and female body parts in scantily clad swim suits added to the eating experience. But as Gunther announced, it was time for the main event.

Swiping his bracelet, the green light indicated that the computer now knew that he was on the expensive side of the Rising Sun Resort. While sex was the main trade on this side of the wall, it wasn't required. As Gunther explained, some men just enjoyed the bawdy atmosphere that this area offered.

Once inside, another pool similar to the first was the center of activity. Two hot tubs near the pool were occupied as the two men made their way to a table.

Sitting down overlooking the pool, a naked waitress arrived to take their order. Jack moved up to a hard drink to join Gunther. Once again, Gunther swiped his bracelet for both of them, but reminded Jack that all his other selections were on Jack.

At the table next to them sat three men in swim suits. The large collection of empty beer bottles on their table spoke to the boisterous attitude the three displayed.

The waitress soon returned with drinks for Jack's table. On her large tray were three lunches.

She placed the tray down nearby and passed Jack and Gunther their drinks. Then she retrieved two of the burger platters for their neighbor's table. Walking over, she stopped, placed one foot on the empty fourth chair and bent over, placing the food on the table. Walking back, she retrieved the third burger platter and repeated the maneuver. Jack watched intently as her handy work serving food was only exceeded by her erotic female display.

The woman had her moves down, Jack thought. While men may be hungry for their meal, other things were placed close at hand to entice them further. She picked up the now-empty tray and disappeared into the kitchen.

"Hey buddy, did you see that?" one of the men at the next table said to Jack.

Jack focused on the man, a little startled, "You talking to me?"

"Yeah, you saw that waitress, didn't you?"

"Yes," Jack said.

"She practically had her pussy in our food," the man complained.

Well, duh, you're in a brothel, not Denny's, Jack thought. *What do you expect?* But Jack went along. "She did seem to be missing a hair net down there."

"Yeah, see? I told you," he said to his table mates. Then back to Jack, "Don't they have health inspectors in this state? There's some kind of law about that, isn't there?"

Boy is this guy as dumb as a post, Jack thought. But he decided to play along. "I think you should call the county and complain. They'll run right over and check it out. I'm sure pubic hair control is at the top of their list."

"I think I will. It just ain't right. Hey thanks, enjoy yourself." The man returned to his friends as he grabbed his hamburger and took a large bite.

Jack turned to Gunther who was wide-eyed at the exchange. Jack just shook his head and shrugged, the international sign for what can you do. Gunther smiled in return.

Jack sat back and scanned the other selections as they walked by for evaluation. As the two new arrivals, the working girls all swung by to make their products known. Some were topless while others were naked. Over in the pool, a loud man had three naked women in stitches, laughing at something. A man and a woman sat in one hot tub, content to hold each other.

"There's no sex out here. Strictly verboten," Gunther offered. "You have to make your arrangement with each individual woman. She has a scanner in her room to record the transaction before anything fun happens."

"And all the rest of this?" Jack asked.

"Your cover charge on entering meets the more explicit eye candy here. If you want, you can hang out here the whole time. Swim with naked women, soak with naked women, eat dinner with naked women. No additional charge."

"But head to one of the rooms and ka-ching," Jack offered. *I really need to read that rate sheet,* he thought. *This side must be expensive.*

Wanting to ask Gunther the going rate just to be at the pool, the German seemed to read his mind. "Works out to be about forty dollars an hour just to sit over here. Food and drinks are more, naturally."

"And to head to the rooms?" Jack asked. He was fascinated by the whole setup. His vision of brothels had been that one placed two hundred dollars down and fifteen minutes later left a happy man. *If that sort of thing satisfied you,* he thought. *But here stimulation, foreplay and sex were all on sale.*

Gunther was ready for the room fees. "Depends what you want. For the full measure, a couple of hundred. If you want tenderness and caring, add a few more. If kinky stuff is what you want, don't come here."

Jack looked at Gunther, not realizing there was limits to people's desires. Gunther jumped right in.

"Other brothels will accommodate most anything. It's really up to the women. They act as private contractors and pay a percentage to the house," Gunther explained.

"But if I want . . ." Jack started to ask.

"They actually run a fairly routine place here, as sex shops go. Like Las Vegas discovered when they toned things down for families, there's more money in mainstream."

"You're not saying . . ." Jack started to ask.

"No, nothing like that here. But the owners recognize the potential of all those baby boomers in your country. Many are lonely, divorced, frustrated but have a good retirement. Money talks and bullshit walks, as they say."

"So, missionary style and you're done?" Jack asked.

"No, my friend. It can get a lot more interesting than that. But if you plan on coming here after reading those popular S&M novels everyone seems to be hooked on, you'll be disappointed," Gunther answered, referring to the top selling novel trilogy of late.

"So no whips and chains. I get it." Jack offered.

"And no back door men allowed around here also," Gunther said.

Jack took the reference to those men that had a proclivity for packing. *Which seems to limit their clientele,* he thought.

"So, you've been here before. Do these limits seem to hurt their business? Won't the other brothels steal the rejected away?" Jack asked.

"Probably, but there seems to be plenty of others who appreciate the toned down atmosphere. Just good healthy sex with good-looking women," Gunther said. "They even have senior night."

"What?" Jack asked. His look of shock met Gunther's smile.

"That's right. Every Tuesday and Wednesday there's a twenty percent discount for the over fifty-five crowd. All resort features. And veterans on active duty always get ten percent off."

"Well, I'll be. So this Tuesday night I should come out and check it out? The over fifty-five crowd really swings?" Jack asked.

"You'll miss the fun," Gunther answered, a smile growing. "The resort runs shuttles from Vegas and pulls in a crowd. But it's a day time thing. Those seventy and eighty-year-olds fade out after eight, especially if they've been here since opening."

"Must be a sight. All those old timers having sex," Jack said.

"Word is, most don't. They just enjoy being dirty old men without getting yelled at. Most just sit here and ogle the naked woman. Some never get past the titillation pool next door," Gunther said. "In fact, the resort offers cuddling. Want to lay down with a young nubile woman? They can make it happen. Want clothes on? It's one price, scantily clad is another."

"And naked cuddling? Another price?" Jack asked.

"No naked cuddling price. The resort's attitude is, if you're lying down naked with a woman, something more is going to happen."

Gunther perked up as one young woman walked out onto the pool deck topless. Her long blonde hair hung down, partially obscuring her breasts. But they were still substantial enough to make their presence known.

"Oh, here's mine," Gunther said. "I remember her from last time. I was hoping she was working today."

Jack checked out his choice in women as she came toward them. Gunther raised his finger slightly as if to order a new drink. She recognized the sign and strolled over, sitting down opposite Jack. She threw her hair back, revealing her attributes.

Gunther began a negotiation as Jack sat and listened. The arrangements went fairly quickly as both were experienced with the process. She stood and started to walk toward one of the rooms that lined the pool area. Gunther was right behind, but turned to Jack as he left.

"Good luck finding your own."

Jack nodded his new German friend off to pleasure and sipped on his drink. The alcohol buzzed his head as he watched more desirable woman stroll by looking for a deal

Now alone, Jack focused on why he was there. He had Katarina back at the house who easily outshone anyone in front of him. That could wait, as he had to figure out how to find LaMarcus's lost uncle. He nursed his drink to avoid a second one. *I'm sure the local law enforcement hang just over the county line waiting to nab those returning to Vegas*, he thought. *Too much drink meant a big bill and hassles in the morning.*

After a short time sitting alone, Jack realized that the resort must have a policy that no man sits alone. A beautiful naked woman soon arrived at his table and asked if he'd buy her a drink. The naked waitress arrived with two more drinks, and Jack finally swiped his bracelet for his first purchase.

The woman engaged Jack in a conversation about his life asking personal questions. Jack punted on them as he let her talk. He realized she was attempting to socialize with him in order to overcome the paid sex part. *They've been taught how to break down people's unease with prostitution. Reeling in those baby boomers,* he thought.

Still nursing his first drink, Jack used his police detective skills to move the conversation where he wanted. He needed information about the uncle.

"So, I had a friend who was coming here on a regular basis," Jack said. "Couldn't say enough nice things about the whole place. Really liked the people that worked here. Said they really cared."

"We do," the woman said.

"But then I stopped hearing from him," Jack said. "When he stopped calling, I wrote by mail to him. His address was a P.O. Box in Pahrump. The Postal Service never returned any letters, but he never wrote back."

Jack watched as the woman's demeanor quickly changed. Her gaze flitted around the room as if looking for someone or something. She took a gulp of her drink and placed the empty glass down on the table.

Sliding his second drink very slowly over in front of her, she naturally took the glass and drank it down. She never looked down the entire time, fixated on scanning the pool area.

"I don't know nothing about that, mister," she said. She placed the second empty glass down, still surveying her surroundings.

"Sure is a strange one," Jack said.

"Look, are we going to have sex or something? If not, I need to move on."

Jack studied the person who couldn't look him in the eye. Her behavior was one of a trapped animal looking for a predator. He decided to take a chance.

"I'm told that there is cuddling available here."

The woman stopped searching and focused on a customer asking a question.

"Yeah, we do cuddling. But I'll have to throw some clothes on for that," she said.

Working out the rate for an hour of cuddling, scantily clad, he followed her to the side of the bar. From a gym bag she pulled out a bikini bottom and a top, throwing them on. She led Jack up the stairs and opened a room. A scanner was presented and Jack ran his bracelet over the machine. A green light announced the charge.

The woman was soon on the bed and as Jack laid down, the woman wrapped herself around Jack. She nestled her head on his shoulder and the two lay quiet.

"This is nice," Jack offered. His arm held her tight and he could feel her relaxing. The tension she showed at the table seemed to slip away as the time passed.

"Are you sure this is all you want?" she finally asked.

"Well, let me think." Jack then asked what a full frolic would be. Hearing the price, he offered a deal.

"I can't do that, mister."

"Are the walls bugged or something?" Jack whispered in her ear. She whispered back that she was pretty sure the room was safe, but what he was asking could get her in trouble.

When Jack offered that the shower would drown out any prying ears, she reluctantly agreed. Standing, the scanner was once more produced. The woman punched in the agreed amount and Jack's charge went through the machine.

The two stepped in the shower, still in their swim suits while Jack turned on the faucet full blast. With the noise of the water and a few vocal sound effects thrown in just in case, Jack continued his questions quietly.

"So, no idea what might have happened to my friend?" Jack said. He added a loud groan at the end for effect.

"Oh, oh, oh!" the woman said loudly. Then in a whisper she added, "Some of the girls have noticed some of the regulars disappear. Just when they are steady, then nothing."

"Oh yeah!" Jack said loudly. Again whispering, he asked, "Do you know where I can find an answer to where they might be?"

"Yes, yes, yes!" carried through the bathroom. Then quietly, "The main office on the second floor over the entry. I know all the records are kept there. There's an inner office. One of the girls that services the boss said there's a big safe. I suppose that would have all you need."

"More, more!" Jack moaned loudly. "How many people have access to the office?"

"Push it, push it!" the woman groaned. "There's the boss and his secretary. And Leonard, the accountant. I suppose he'd know most of what's going on."

"It's there, it's there!" Jack yelled. He had to be careful as he was getting excited. The closeness of the woman and her wet body rubbing his as they continued to talk dirty while whispering in each other ears was getting to him. Quietly he added. "Tell me about Leonard. Married? Live locally? Habits?"

"Kind of a creep, if you ask me," the woman offered. Then she remembered the act they were performing. "Oh yes, shove it!" Switching back to her low voice, "He takes perks with the women here, if you know what I mean. Has a wife and three kids in Las Vegas. And then acts all high and mighty."

Jack figured that was as good as he was going to get and thrashed around making a lot of extra noise followed by one last loud groan. The woman mimicked him as she added to the charade. They stepped out and turned off the shower.

"Was it good for you?" she asked.

"The best," he answered.

Chapter 28

Pahrump, Nevada

Toweling off, he headed to the locker room to retrieve his clothes. As he passed the pool, the naked crowd had grown and he saw his German friend sitting at a table. Seeing Jack emerge from one of the rooms, Gunther lifted his drink in salute as Jack waved acknowledgement back.

The drive from Pahrump to Henderson seemed to last a lifetime. While no local sheriff impeded his drive, the extra stimulation of his shower scene distracted him. His mind was on one thing and the sooner it happened, the better.

Reaching Gary's house, he slammed the Cadillac into park, turned off the ignition and stepped out onto the driveway. The front door opened before he was halfway up the driveway and Katarina stepped out on the front step.

"Jack, you're home early?" She said. "Everything go OK?"

Before she got an answer and as LaMarcus and Gary emerged into the foyer, Jack swept Katarina into his arms and directed her to their bedroom.

"Hey, what gives?" LaMarcus asked as the two disappeared around the corner.

An hour later, LaMarcus got his answer as Jack returned to the family room. Gary and LaMarcus looked up at their friend finally emerging.

"That good, was it?" LaMarcus joked.

"Katarina thought so, and she wasn't even there," Jack said.

"You some kind of guy if you held it in that long. You might have burst a vessel or something," LaMarcus said. "Never could do that myself."

"I did have someone here in Henderson, you know," Jack said.

"You've got me there, Marine. If that was waiting for me, I'm not sure what would happen," LaMarcus said. Gary nodded agreement.

After another hour, Katarina finally made an appearance. Freshly showered, she sat down and curled up on Jack's arm. Her purr could almost be heard across the room.

"You need to go investigate that resort more," she offered. The two men stared at Jack and smiled.

"Maybe so, but we do have some answers already. Answers that our previous detective seemed to have missed," Jack said.

"I was trying," LaMarcus pleaded. "Damn, you don't know how hard I was trying."

"Yeah, we'll compare resort bills when they arrive in the mail," Jack said. "But 'til then, I think we have an opening."

Jack related what the woman had revealed about the information being in the office. But the three retired cops were stumped as to how they could break into the office, crack a safe and escape undetected. Their arguments continued while Katarina half slept on Jack's arm.

Startling everyone, she announced, "I know how."

The three cops stopped and turned their attention to her. Waiting for an answer, Katarina let the moment sit. She seemed to be savoring the moment.

"I've outthought the three of you. I can't believe it," she said.

"Yes, we're very proud of you," Jack said.

"I can't believe I thought of the answer and you guys didn't, " she teased.

"We don't know that you've solved the dilemma until you tell us," Jack said. "So please enlighten us professional investigators."

"This is what it feels like, isn't it?" she teased. "To know the answer way before anyone else in the room. It's very empowering."

"OK, you win the prize," Jack offered. "Now, will you tell us?"

Katarina sat and continued the torment. Just as Jack was ready to turn to force, she relented.

"Fine, I'll tell. This Leonard guy I heard in the conversation."

"Yes, the accountant," Jack said.

"Yes, the accountant," Katarina repeated. "He's a little on the hypocritical side. A little sex at work with the help, then home for a little bit of love with his wife."

"Yes, the guys a dirt bag," LaMarcus said. "What's your point?"

"We set up a spider trap and catch him. Then we blackmail him to tell us what he knows," Katarina said.

"Oh sure, but I don't think Gary dressed in drag will do the trick," Jack said.

"I don't think so either, no offense Gary," Katarina agreed.

"Don't look at me, and LaMarcus would scare any but the most foolhardy off," Jack said.

"Come on boys, think a little outside the box," Katarina said. "Young, female, attractive and right here in your mitts."

"Oh no," Jack exclaimed. "You don't get to do entrapment work."

"Jack, she's right," LaMarcus offered. "From the sounds of it, he'll be easy to reel in and you can be right there, taking pictures."

Jack attempted more protests but the three others all agreed. Katarina was the best-looking spider they had and they needed to move on it. Too much time had passed already to work out breaking into the office. And that didn't include the risk a break-in involved.

As Jack tried to explain the risk that Katarina would be taking, again his concerns were drowned out.

Gary put the finish on the discussion with, "He's an accountant for God's sake. How much trouble could he cause?"

The rest of the evening was spent on how to spin the web. They had to entice their accountant close to their spider in order to get compromising photos. Jack continued his protest at the whole scheme but knew it was the best plan. He would make sure he was close at hand when it all happened, no matter what Gary's assessment of accountants was.

Chapter 29

Las Vegas, Nevada

Katarina made the phone call. Leonard was reached in Pahrump during work hours and Katarina started on her story. She was checking on a bill her father had received. Since she managed her father's accounts for him, she had some questions concerning the monthly charges that came through showing a lot of activity each Tuesday. Even with the twenty percent discount on the bill, the fees added up over the month.

Using her best Dutch-accented English, she asked if he could meet her in a bar on the Strip that night. They could go over the bill as he explained what the charges were for.

Meeting resistance at first, Katarina turned up the charm as she broke down slightly and reverted to more Dutch. Pleading that she was responsible for her father's affairs and she couldn't let him down and couldn't Leonard help her just thus once. He sounded like such a nice man and she had met so few of them in Las Vegas since she had moved from Holland.

The visions of naked Dutch girls in nothing but wooden shoes must have done the trick as Leonard agreed to meet Katarina after work that evening. A bar was selected that just happened to be part of a casino with a large hotel attached.

Gary had contributed a monthly bill. A fishing, drinking, football-watching buddy down the street had been a member of Rising Sun resort for some time. Gary complained that his friend was forever attempting to get Gary to join up and experience the pleasures available.

With the friend's last bill safely tucked in her handbag, Katarina sat at the bar waiting. She had on her sleek black dress and high heels as she scanned the room. Close by in a booth sat LaMarcus. He had a drink on the table and the day's newspaper for cover as he kept a watch on their spider. Jack waited, camera in hand, in a room in the hotel.

Katarina rolled her wrist and checked her watch. It was a little past six, which figuring Leonard's leaving work at five, an hour drive in from Pahrump, a few minutes to park that he should be arriving shortly. She shot a glance toward Lamarcus and saw he was busy reading the paper.

"Can I buy you a drink?" a man asked.

They had already pulled up a photo of Leonard after doing a background check for his last name. Gary knew a sergeant on the Las Vegas police force who was glad to do a favor for an old buddy from the Marine Corps.

"No, thanks, I'm waiting for someone," Katarina answered.

The man scanned the Dutch woman up and down before adding, "We'll if Mr. Lucky doesn't show, I'm sitting right over there."

Katarina watched him leave and sit down in a booth. That had been the fourth guy who had hit on her since she had sat down. *I wish he'd hurry up and get here,* Katarina thought.

The bartender drifted over on one of his numerous checks to see if his guest needed anything. He chatted briefly with Katarina, just friendly like.

"Excuse me, is this seat taken?" a voice to her right said.

Katarina turned from the bartender to the person who had spoken, recognizing Leonard.

"No, I've been holding it for you," Katarina said. "Are you Leonard?"

The man in the wire-rimmed glasses didn't answer right away, but his eyes took in the woman who had spoken. As his gaze moved up and down, Katarina kept her composure as she waited for his answer.

"You must be Katarina," Leonard finally said. "I'm happy to meet you."

He held out his hand and Katarina shook. But then she lingered in her grip, twisting her upper body around to offer more of a view. She watched as Leonard took the opportunity to explore her body even more. She leaned forward slightly and his gaze zeroed in on her now-exposed cleavage.

A shiver went up her spine at the blatant stare the man was taking. *Can he be more obvious?* she thought. *But then, I am pulling him into my web.*

"I owe you a drink. You are so kind to help me," she said. Katarina made a finger motion toward the bartender, who responded immediately. "What are you drinking?"

"Vodka martini, shaken, not stirred," Leonard replied.

"Make that two," Katarina added.

Turning slightly on her seat, Katarina made sure her right leg came in full contact to Leonard's leg. Leaning over, her right arm brushed against Leonard's arm. His reaction told Katarina that her fly was willingly settling into the web.

"So you said you were from Holland," Leonard inquired. "Living here in Las Vegas now?"

"No, I just drive over from LA twice a month to check on my father."

"He's lucky to have such a devoted daughter. And work lets you have the time to get to Vegas?" Leonard asked.

"I do modeling and the work usually comes in spurts. A photo shoot and then maybe a commercial," Katarina lied. "Plenty of time in between for a trip out to the desert."

"I see," Leonard said. His eyes again followed down from Katarina's neck to her voluptuous chest. She was half-turned his way and leaning toward the man, offering as much a view as possible. And the accountant was taking a long look.

She moved her right leg, increasing the pressure on his leg as she swiveled around and grabbed her bag. She pulled out the resort bill that would be her prop for the night. Unfolding and laying it on the bar, Leonard's gaze switched to the paper.

"Maybe we could go over my father's bill now?" she asked.

The accountant looked to focus on the charges as Katarina's hand moved toward each line. Her long fingers pointed out one charge.

"Ah yes, our massage center," Leonard said. "Your father took a one-hour massage on what looks to be the 16th of the month. We offer a full sauna beforehand to loosen the client up before our expert masseuse goes to work. Very therapeutic, I can assure you."

"Sounds wonderful," Katarina said, her voice shifting slightly. "I just love getting naked and having someone work me over."

She thought Leonard was going to spill his drink over her comment, so she increased the web.

"You know, it's getting so noisy in here. Maybe we could go to my room. I have a bottle of Tequila there. Do you like Tequila shooters?" Katarina asked.

It looked as though beads of sweat had appeared on Leonard's forehead. Adding to the enticement, she took his arm and pulled tight. He now was fully engulfed against her right breast as Katarina increased her lean forward.

With his arm squeeze from below and her angle, her breasts practically spilled out onto the bar surface. Leonard gave up any resistance.

"I guess that would be OK," he said, a slight croak in his voice. "It is rather noisy in here."

Katarina did not wait for a change of heart. She slid off the seat toward Leonard, being sure that the gap in her high-riding dress was directed at her mark. She saw his gaze take in the view between her legs before she pulled him with her. With one arm tightly wrapped under his arm, she escorted him toward the elevator. As she passed, Katarina saw LaMarcus pick up his cell phone, still staring down at his newspaper.

Reaching the fourth floor, Katarina led Leonard down the hotel hall. She stopped at one of the doors, produced a card and swiped the reader. The sound of the door unlatching would alert Jack that they had arrived. *At least I hope he's in here,* Katarina thought.

The room lights invited them in and Katarina let her prey free as the door swung closed behind her. She walked over to the small bar and picked up a bottle.

"A drink first?" she asked, looking over her shoulder.

Leonard nodded. In the mirror, she saw Leonard scan the room. There was a table with two easy chairs, a love seat, the bar with refrigerator and microwave and two end tables next to the king-size bed. It suddenly dawned on Katarina that they had not brought any luggage. A woman traveling from LA would have luggage in her room.

"You travel light," Leonard said. He turned to her with an inquisitive look showing.

Oh shit, think fast, she thought. *This deal could be blown right now.*

"It's still in my car," Katarina lied again. "I've been at my father's all day and just checked in before I went to the bar. Haven't had time to bring it up."

Leonard seemed to accept that explanation, she thought. Turning the seduction mode on to change the subject, she scooped up the two drinks and handed one to Leonard. Then taking his arm with the full breast squeeze, he led him to the love seat.

The two sat close as Katarina held up her shot glass. "Ready?" she asked. With Leonard holding up his glass, she threw her drink down. He followed with his shot.

"Warms you right up, doesn't it?" she purred. With a slight pause for effect, she leaned over and stuck her tongue into Leonard's ear. She undid his tie and pulled it off, tossing it on the table. She reached down and unbuttoned his sport coat, running her hand up and down his chest. Withdrawing her tongue, she offered in a low voice, "I think business before pleasure has it all wrong. I think we should get comfortable before we go over things, don't you?"

Leonard's answer was a hand to her breast as he massaged the wondrous flesh. He bent down and kissed the part spilling out of the top of her dress. Katarina slid her hand down to his belt and unfastened it, pulling on one end as she threw it next to the tie. She unbuttoned the top button of his pants and yanked on his zipper.

Leonard's hand moved to her leg and began to slide upward. Katarina stood up suddenly, pulling her entrapped victim with her. She finished with the fly and slid his pants down to his ankles while kissing him. His hands moved around to her ass as he pulled her tight against him. She gently pushed him away and stepped toward the bathroom.

"I need to use the lady's room first," she said. "Why don't you get comfortable and jump in bed. I'll only be a minute."

She retreated to the bathroom, closing the door, but left it slightly ajar. Leaving the light off so she could make sure her mark complied, she spied through the crack in the door jamb a quickly disrobing Leonard. As he pulled his clothes off, Katarina scanned the room as to where Jack

234

must be hiding. *I definitely hope he's in the room somewhere,* she thought. *Otherwise, the next few minutes will be decidedly interesting.*

She stepped out of her black dress and hung it on the hook on the back of the door. Standing in just her black strapless bra and black panties with her high heels, she took a deep breath. *This had better work*, she thought.

She glanced out the door once more and saw that Leonard had turned out the lights. Knowing that good pictures might require better lighting in spite of flashes, Katarina's first move as she emerged was to find the light switch.

A startled naked Leonard looked up as the light came back on. He reached slightly to cover his private parts on instinct. Katarina turned seductively toward Leonard.

"I like to see what I'm doing. Don't you want to see these?" she teased as her hands lifted both tits up and gently bounced them.

Leonard's already aroused state increased from Katarina's viewpoint. She slowly walked to the foot of the bed and placed one knee on it. She leaned forward onto her hands, now directly over Leonard's lower legs. He spread his legs in anticipation of the wondrous pleasures that were about to rack his body.

Suddenly a man with a camera was behind the object of his desire taking pictures. The flash added to the surprise as Leonard began to panic. The man continued to move around the woman, the digital camera firing away. Leonard moved to cover himself with his hands as

Katarina looked away from the camera but being careful that her upper body was fully in view.

"What the hell is this?" Leonard finally spit out.

As he said it, Katarina fell on top of him, still keeping her face away from the camera. Leonard had no option then to catch her, exposing himself in the process. The camera continued firing away.

Recovering, Leonard pushed Katarina off him and jumped out of bed. He started to move toward Jack but realized that his antagonist had four inches and fifty pounds on him. Thinking better and noticing Jack's scowl, Leonard grabbed his clothes. He looked first at the door to the hallway, but Jack moved to block an escape. Leonard headed to the bathroom.

Jack threw the bedspread to Katarina and she wrapped herself. They waited until a fully dressed Leonard emerged from the room. Jack pointed to one of the chairs at the table and Leonard sat down. Katarina disappeared into the bathroom to dress.

"What do you want?" Leonard asked.

"Right to the point, I like that," Jack said

"Who are you?"

"Not important. But be aware that I'm your worst nightmare if you don't do what we want. We know about your wife and three kids out in West Las Vegas who would be devastated to learn just what the man of the house did in his spare time."

"I don't have any money, if that's what this is about?" Leonard asked.

"We're after something more important." Jack looked up as Katarina reentered the room, sitting down on the love seat. Leonard turned and scowled at her.

"Like what?" he demanded.

"Information, that's all. Tell us what we need to know right now and we'll watch as you delete every photo off my camera," Jack offered.

Leonard's demeanor perked up at the news. He was being given a way out of his dilemma and the price seemed low.

"What kind of information? I'm just an accountant, what do I know?"

"We hope plenty, for your sake," Jack said. "So, first, tell us about Rising Sun Resort."

"So that what's this is about? You don't want to be messing with those people. They've had to play rough to get into the whole Las Vegas scene. Not easy for a foreigner to come into Nevada and beat the locals at their own game."

"Don't worry, we're not after your boss or his money," Jack said.

"Then what?"

"We want to know about the side deal," Jack said. "The one where men show up at Rising Sun, learn to enjoy the pleasures offered, and then disappear. Their money continues to flow but no one seems to ever see the person again."

"Oh, is that all?" Leonard asked. "Who are you looking for exactly?"

"Joe Lewis, disappeared about four months ago."

"That's it? I answer that question and the photos are erased?" Leonard asked.

"That's the deal."

"I had to get blue balls over just that, shit," Leonard complained.

The three in the room sat and stared at each other. The quiet anticipation was frustrating to Katarina. She had done things that didn't exactly feel right, but she wanted answers.

"So, what's the answer?" Katarina finally demanded. The two men were slightly startled by the intrusion in what had been their conversation.

"Mr. Lewis is one of our Platinum Members. As such, he has taken advantage of our offshore facility where things are run differently," Leonard said. "And he hasn't written anyone?"

"No, not a word," Jack said. "And where is this offshore location?"

"Thailand," Leonard answered. "And I'm not surprised that no one has heard from him. We've had other inquires from friends and relatives of members that have relocated there."

"Are they held incommunicado?" Jack asked. Katarina looked as if the English escaped her.

"Not at all. But they only have the post available to mail letters. No electronic communication is allowed from the resort there."

"And they're free to contact outside the resort?" Jack asked.

"Yes, but we notice that when our retirees reach the resort, they seem to take on a whole new life. Living an ex-pat life, most want to forget their past lives. They are limited in ever returning." Leonard didn't elaborate on that comment. Jack didn't press the issue.

When Leonard told them the location in Thailand, Jack handed him the camera. The pictures were quickly deleted. Leonard stood to leave.

"Am I free to go now?"

Jack motioned toward the door and Leonard made to leave, but stopped in front of Katarina. "I guess I should thank you for an interesting evening. We never did get to your father's bill."

Katarina looked down from the man's gaze. The guilt held her still and Leonard headed to the door. A short time after Leonard had left, LaMarcus stepped in holding his card. He surveyed his two partners sitting in the room.

"Did we get out answer?" LaMarcus asked.

"What are blue balls?" Katarina interjected.

Before Jack could enlighten her, LaMarcus interrupted.

"What have you two been up to?"

Chapter 30

Ko Pha-Ngan Island, Thailand

The Gulf of Thailand lay flat and serene in the late evening light. With no wind, the ocean surface was smooth, no swells hitting the nearby beach. A camp fire added its warm glow to the fading daylight as the flames flickered skyward.

The small secluded beach was rimmed by moderate cliffs. A trail had been chiseled in the rock that led down to the sand. Above, tropical growth rimmed the top of the cliffs in all directions. It was the most secluded spot at Haad Rin Resort. Located on the southeast quarter of Ko Pha-Ngan Island, the resort that catered to retired men sat in walled exclusion.

Enjoying the warm evening on the very secluded beach were two people. Sitting next to the fire on a blanket, the couple stared at the flames as the man placed another log on the fire. The flames slowly licked the new wood before it too caught, adding to the warmth and brightness.

L.C. placed his arm around Sho Lin as she moved closer. The past week had ben one of discovery for both he and Gunny. And for Sho Lin. All three individuals were still getting used to their new life together and this had been L.C.'s first opportunity to score the beach.

Unlike the main beach, this small secluded beach was reserved for romantic pursuits. Available by reservation only, the beach was split into three time slots.

Morning, afternoon and evening with the evening slot having the option of all night.

A gate at the top of the trail with reservation names posted assured they wouldn't be disturbed. L.C. reached behind and undid Sho Lin's swim suit top. She pulled it off and dropped it on the blanket. He scooped up her small breast in his hand and rubbed it gently. A slow moan came from the Chinese woman as she reached for his groin.

They had been intimate the previous week so the nervous first time was past. But they were still determining what each liked and L.C. figured an evening and night on the beach would leave plenty of time to find out.

L. C. slid his hand down and hooked Sho Lin's swim suit bottom. She raised off the blanket slightly as the suit slid down her legs. Once out of the way, L.C. leaned her onto her back and began the slow kissing down her body. Discovering the differences between Thai women and Chinese woman, L.C. was suddenly enjoying the difference.

The first had been the food. Sho Lin was creative in her use of the local fare in creating wonderful Chinese dishes. Already, L.C. had felt his pre-resort middle returning. His extra weight from forty years of middle class life in America had melted away over the time he had been in Thailand. He hadn't eaten as many fruits and vegetables in his entire life as he had the last few months.

And his waist line showed the result. Now, the lavish fare that Sho Lin offered each night were already telling on him. He and Gunny had already talked that they needed a chat with their new roommate.

But her other attributes had distracted them both. Wise in the techniques of keeping a man satisfied, Sho Lin had already made sure that Maya was long forgotten. *Let that Limey gentleman steal our woman away*, he thought. *We just need to keep what we got to ourselves.*

As his thought of keeping Sho Lin's abilities quiet, he groaned loudly as her small mouth wrapped itself around him. All other thoughts left him as he concentrated on just one thing. As things exploded, his only thought was, *Who needs any little blue pill?*

The beach activity continued as the unattended fire slowly died. Soon, L.C. was asleep in his Chinese woman's arms for the rest of the night, her caresses on his head adding to his slumber.

The heat of the morning sun on the blanket covering them broke the spell, Dressing quickly, they made their way up the cliff trail and back to their bungalow. Sho Lin disappeared into the bathroom while L.C. ambled into the kitchen, where a smiling Gunny sat, drinking coffee.

Once L.C. had his coffee, Gunny asked, "Pleasant evening?"

"Shit man, if you only knew," L.C. said. "I think I'm ready for a nap already."

The two men took sips of coffee. L.C. seemed to rise with the caffeine coursing through him. Their female companion emerged from the bathroom and disappeared out the front door. Her routine had quickly been established over the short time she had been with them. With each morning off, Gunny and L.C. had learned that there was one other Chinese woman in the resort. Because of the enmity shown to them by some of the Thai women, they sought each other out where they could speak in their language freely.

"Gunny, what are we going to do?" L.C. finally asked.

"'bout what?"

"Sho Lin. If word gets out, she'll be next year's top pick. One of the senior guys with money will snatch her in a minute."

"Simple, don't say nothin'," Gunny offered. "When people ask, be vague and non-committal. Offer that she's OK but that we miss Maya."

"Think they'll buy it?" L.C. asked.

"Why not? Only you and I know the truth."

"I guess you're right Gunny."

"Of course I'm right. Didn't I tell you at the lottery what I found? Gunny knows his Chinese women."

"That's for sure," L.C. said. "But what about the cooking? Shit, I can feel my middle coming back. If we gain weight, we'll lose her just for her culinary skills alone."

"Yeah, I know what you mean," Gunny said.

The two men both processed what had been said. There were those in the resort that looked for a woman who could cook. To them food was more important than sex. *Strange people if you ask me*, L.C. thought. *And we have one that can rock both your worlds.*

"We need to sit her down and make the excuse that her meals are too expensive," Gunny said. "Chinese are incredibly frugal, and if we say we need to lower our food budget, that will keep the amounts toned down. Should work."

"Good thinking, Gunny. Can we talk to her tonight?

"Don't see why not."

"Good, I'm going to take a nap now. Wake me for lunch," L.C. said.

"Sure thing Marine. We jarheads need to stick together. War is hell so go rest up for the next battle."

* * *

"So how soon do we fly to Thailand?" Katarina asked.

"Hold on, I'm not sure we includes you," Jack said, looking at Katarina. He received a frown in return.

"Well I can't go," LaMarcus said.

"You? Why not?" Jack asked.

"Before I knew you," LaMarcus answered, "I had a little problem when I was last in Bangkok. I was on leave from being stationed on board ship out of Japan. Like all good healthy men I took my ass to Bangkok for a little close-order drill."

"And you can't go back?"

"I'm not sure. I sort of left in a hurry. Seems one of the female companions I hooked up with wasn't exactly a working model. She was very connected with the upper crust and had been out on the town sort of being wild," LaMarcus said.

"She was slumming, you mean," Jack said.

244

"Well, yeah, but I was being a gentleman. But anyway, her family caught up to us in Chiang Mai and I thought the whole town was after me. They really got the locals all riled up, accusing me of deflowering their sweet young thing of a daughter," LaMarcus said.

"And you didn't do any deflowering?" Jack asked.

"Hell no, she was busy teaching me things. It sure as shit wasn't her first time," LaMarcus said.

"And you can't go back now?" Jack asked. "That complicates checking on your uncle then."

"No it doesn't," Katarina said. "Jack and I can fly out to Thailand and locate this resort. LaMarcus can make inquires to see if he's remembered after all these years."

"I suppose that could work. You don't mind, do you, Jack?" LaMarcus asked.

"I'm still not set on the Katarina part. I don't know what I'm stepping into."

"You heard our accountant," Katarina said. "He wasn't nervous about flipping on the resort at all. So it must be what he said it was. Where's the danger?"

"I just don't know. It was bad enough watching you seduce Leonard from the closet," Jack admitted.

"Well, I was just glad you showed up when you did. Mr. Blue Balls might have been hard to hold off," Katarina said.

As they sat in Gary's family room discussing the pros and cons of Katarina's further involvement, Gary finally joined in.

"May I remind you, Katarina is the only person who is free to travel out of the state. Besides myself." Gary smiled at Katarina as he said it. Her large grin lit the room.

"That's right, you two are under court order and due to answer charges," Katarina said. "So, I guess it will be Gary and I heading to the warm beaches of the South China Sea. Have your passport, Gary?"

"Always," he answered back.

"Shit, that's right," LaMarcus said. "Our little night club foray. We can't go anywhere until we're cleared of that."

"If that's the case then, excuse me," Jack said. He stood and headed to his bedroom. The others watched him leave and then looked at each other quizzically. It wouldn't be until the next day that they would learn why he had left.

The next afternoon found them sitting in their lawyer's office waiting for a phone call. Jack had done his work the night before and after a call first thing in the morning, had made arrangements to meet the lawyer in the afternoon. The phone on the lawyer's desk rang and he picked it up. A brief discussion ensued before hanging up.

"Well, that was the District Attorney," the lawyer said. He switched his gaze onto Jack and added, "It seems people in high places have gotten involved. Jack, all charges have been dropped and your weapon and identification are available for pick-up at the Clark County Courthouse."

"What the hell? How about me?" LaMarcus asked.

"Do you have friends in high places, Mr. Lewis?" the lawyer asked.

"What kind of high places?" LaMarcus asked.

The lawyer said, "Seems the Governor of Wyoming placed a call this morning to the Governor of Nevada. To make a short story even shorter, pressure was applied in sensitive areas for the Great State of Nevada to recognize the duly sworn law enforcement official from the Great State of Wyoming."

"And he's free, just like that? Shit," LaMarcus said.

"Not so fast," the lawyer added. "After the governor was done yanking the poor man's short hairs, the DA got a call from Washington. Seems the Senior Senator from Nevada was ballistic over the whole affair since the Junior Senator from Wyoming had just called and pulled his support of our senator's bill."

"Jesus, Jack. You got the juice going," LaMarcus said.

Jack looked at Katarina who was wide-eyed at the revelation of power politics, American style. He knew he would have to explain it all to her later. That he had dropped a call to his older brother last night had greased the wheels. And today those wheels were rolling over the opposition.

Ed Wesley had moved up, along with his political benefactor, to become Chief of Staff to the Junior U.S. Senator of Wyoming. As such, a quick call to Wyoming's Governor had gotten the first ball rolling. Having his boss change his committed vote got the second call flowing west to Las Vegas.

"So, any of that juice left for me?" LaMarcus asked.

"Not unless the Governor of the Great State of Massachusetts calls soon," the lawyer said.

"Commonwealth of Massachusetts. It's not officially a state," LaMarcus explained. "And no, the governor isn't my personal valet."

"Too bad," Jack teased. "I guess you'll have plenty of time to work out that Bangkok thing then."

LaMarcus scowled at his friend. Jack knew the thought of sitting in Clark County jail writing letters to the Thailand government wouldn't sit well with LaMarcus.

"Well, there seems to be a little residual juice for you, Mr. Lewis," the lawyer finally admitted. LaMarcus perked up, hoping for bette news.

"You mean I won't be stuck here?" LaMarcus asked.

"That will be up to you," the lawyer said. "They have made you an offer. Considering the time constraints with the search for your uncle and the risk of jail time in the alternative, it might be the best solution."

"What are they offering?" LaMarcus asked.

"They will drop the charge to a Class A Misdemeanor from the current Felony Assault. No jail time."

"OK, but where's the kicker?" LaMarcus asked. He had been a policeman for too many years to know that such a deal would still have pain to it.

"Ten thousand dollars in restitution to the man whose wrist you broke along with a one-thousand dollar fine to the court. You get probation for a year."

The room was quiet as LaMarcus considered his options. As they waited, Jack could see the blood pressure rise in his friend.

"And the guy I busted up, the one with a knife, no consideration for that?"

"Unfortunately, he claimed he'd never seen it before. The knife had been wiped clean by someone before the cops got there to secure things. Same with the gun, wiped clean," the lawyer said.

"How can that be?" Jack asked.

"I told you Ernesto has powerful friends in the state," the lawyer added. "Either someone at the dance did it or someone on the force helped out. The gun had been stolen the year before so nothing tied it to Ernesto."

"Question?" Gary spoke up for the first time. "If the gun technically wasn't involved in the fight and the knife was a non-factor, how come Jack isn't up on assault charges, law enforcement or not?"

Gary received a long stare by Jack at re-implicating him after he had pulled strings to get untangled. Being thrown back under the bus didn't appeal to Jack.

"Good question," the lawyer said. "With Jack getting powerful figures outside the state involved, the powers that be within the State of Nevada just want this to go away. No need for any outside interests digging deep on how the gun and knife dropped off the evidence rolls. Best to just clean it up so business as usual can continue."

"So I take it they'll probably let me do my probation anywhere I choose?" LaMarcus asked.

"The further from Nevada the better," the lawyer said. "And they'll even let you pay the restitution on the installment plan."

The others sat and waited LaMarcus' decision. Under the circumstances, it seemed to be the best deal he was going to get. He also realized it and so agreed to the deal.

"How soon can we settle?" LaMarcus asked.

"We can get a court date next week," the lawyer said.

LaMarcus turned to Jack and said, "Looks like you'll be there before me. You got recon, Marine."

"Oorah," Jack offered in support. He glanced over at the Dutch contingent of the team. The look he received said it all. Jack added "We vliegen."

"Really, we fly together?" Katarina asked, then added. "I can be good at recon."

The four men in the room all nodded in agreement.

Chapter 31

Bangkok, Thailand

The wide-bodied jet settled into its approach to Bangkok International Airport. Out the window of the lumbering plane, green fields spread out on the Chao Phraya River valley. The heat waves could almost be seen coming up off the farms and villages as the plane banked to adjust its approach.

The view now was straight down on one side of the plane and details loomed at the low elevation. Three-wheeled scooters with canopies for the sun putted along leaving a blue haze in their wake. Other roads showed farm trucks hauling material to sites around Bangkok.

Soon the closer density of the surrounding towns indicated the plane's nearness to the airport. One more small turn and the pilot lined up in the runway. Dropping down in the heavy humid air, the flaps adjusted once more in getting the big jet to settle onto the ground. The scenery changed to blank fields and no structures as they passed over a chain link fence surrounding the airport.

Almost immediately, the plane slowed and dropped onto the pavement, the tires squealing. Passengers were thrown forward as reverse thrust was applied and the wings opened to block air movement. The plane slowed as brakes shuddered and then went quiet.

The pilot put the engines back to forward as the plane idled onto a taxiway. The wings moved back to their closed position in readiness of parking at the terminal.

Inching forward, the plane performed one last bow as it stopped. The engines died along with the fresh air.

Immediately, Katarina felt the hot sun on the plane's fuselage. Staring out the window, the heat waves radiated off the tarmac, blurring distant objects. The temperature inside the cabin steadily rose as the passengers sat and waited.

"Why aren't we moving?" she asked.

Jack was busy digging two surgical masks out of his carry-on luggage. He handed one to Katarina. He tied one over his face, then turned to help his seat mate.

The flight from Los Angeles had been two days after getting a reprieve from the Las Vegas DA. Leaving LaMarcus to catch up later, the two had driven the old Ford to Los Angeles. Leaving the truck parked with one of Jack's friends in Pasadena, they caught a flight to Hong Kong. A three-hour layover there put them into Bangkok in the late afternoon, the hottest part of the day.

"Jack, what's going on? Everyone is just sitting," Katarina again asked.

Jack reached over and just held her knee. He patted it for patience. LaMarcus had warned him what to expect, and he didn't have long to wait.

A man in a white shirt with the epaulettes of a governmental official walked down the aisle with a mask on his face. In each hand he held an aerosol can that he was spraying throughout the cabin. As he walked by, the mist of the spray settled down over everyone.

"Oh my God, what is this?" Katarina demanded.

"DDT. Pesticide," Jack answered. "They spray each plane to stop any mosquitoes from coming into the country. Keeps diseases from spreading."

Katarina groaned as she inhaled the foul odor. Jack applied more pressure to his grip on her knee for support. They would have to sit and endure the process until the cabin doors were opened. The official returned down the other aisle continuing his spraying. The sun baked the outside of the plane as the passengers began to sweat profusely.

"How much longer. I can't breathe," Katarina said.

"Just hang on," Jack said. "There it is, they just opened the door."

Everyone stood as one as Jack and Katarina gathered their belongings. Jack led as they moved out into the aisle. Since most of the passengers had loaded in Hong Kong, Jack towered over the shorter Chinese and Japanese. Even Katarina was a giant compared to those around them.

But the jostling for escape had its downside besides hot foul air. As inhabitants of some of the most densely packed cites in the world, their fellow passengers were extremely aggressive at making space where none existed. In their endeavor, they swung their elbows, loaded with luggage.

Unfortunately for the taller individuals, the elbow swings came in at crotch level. Jack and Katarina were quickly covering up from repeated blows to sensitive areas. Jack, being more sensitive, grew tired of the abuse and used his size in compensation. Soon, Katarina had a clear path through to the exit.

Reaching the open door, the fourth torment hit them. Stepping out into the sunlight, they realized that they weren't at a gate at all, but were parked far from the terminal. A line of shuttles awaited as passengers descended the stairs.

Stepping out, Jack was hit by a wall of humidity. He turned to Katarina as she stepped out.

"Oh my God," Katarina muttered. Her shirt instantly turned wet as Jack felt his body compensate. Water dripped down his face as he descended the stairs. Stepping into one of the shuttle buses, the wet clothes became instant ice packs from the air conditioner turned to the maximum.

Arriving at the terminal finally, they followed the crowd toward the door and entered another frigid atmosphere after a brief sojourn back into the wet heat. Katarina followed Jack as they headed to the carousel to collect their luggage.

Standing back from the crush of passengers all eagerly awaiting the arrival of their bags, Jack stared straight ahead. That was when he noticed it. People were staring at him in large numbers. He focused and realized it was mostly men who were staring at him. Further focus revealed that the Asian men were not exactly staring at him, but at the person beside him.

He turned to Katarina and discovered the intense interest she held. Her shirt, soaked from the humidity, was now being attacked by the cold of the terminal air conditioner. The results were what attracted the interest. And he had to agree, the rigid nipples that were sticking out of the wet shirt surely competed with any bar room contest.

Katarina noticed Jack's stare and smile. A certain confused look came over her until she determined the angle of Jack's gaze. She quickly looked down.

"Shit, why didn't you tell me?"

She pulled on her shirt to uncling the material. Turning to Jack so as to block a direct view of those staring but to also hit Jack in the arm for his oversight, she made a face at him.

"What?" Jack pleaded. "You're the naturalist among us. You should be used to it."

"Not in a damn airport, thank you," she threw back at him. "Are they still staring?"

"No, the luggage is arriving so they're busy now," Jack said.

They returned to staring at the luggage as they waited for their bags to arrive. Katarina pulled her shirt constantly to keep the clinging factor to a minimum. Soon, Jack muscled his way forward and grabbed two bags. Receiving an elbow in the groin in return from a little Chinese woman, he cleared her out of the way with one bag as he used the other as a shield to further abuse.

Reaching the taxi line, Jack let the driver place the bags in the trunk. He climbed in beside Katarina as the humid air once again brought the sweat flowing.

"Miss Tum's Guest House near the Thieves Market," he instructed. The driver nodded understanding, shifted the taxi into gear and crawled away from the curb to join the melee of traffic attempting to leave the airport.

The drive into the city center was one of a slow crawl. With no air conditioner and windows lowered, the car acted as a sauna. The wet shirts became wetter as Jack and Katarina sat enduring the trip. Mixed in the traffic were buses spewing black smoke into their taxi to join the typical smoky air of a Third World county. Poor countries use wood for cooking and heating. While Bangkok enjoyed a warm climate so wood heating was unnecessary, cooking in the city was done mostly with wood. Added into the stew were farmers burning agricultural waste products.

"It's like taking a sauna in a road side ditch," exclaimed Katarina.

Jack agreed with her that Bangkok had its unpleasant side. He just hoped that LaMarcus was right on recommending Miss Tum's Guest House. He had checked on the internet and it still existed. Close to the main town center, it was just a block from the famous market. Wanting a full cultural experience, Katarina had agreed to the small guest house versus a big international hotel.

The driver wheeled the taxi onto a narrow side street and stopped at what appeared to be an alley way. Motioning that Miss Tum's was just down the alley, Jack climbed out to retrieve the bags, paid the fare and watched the taxi drive off.

Picking up both bags, he entered the narrow alleyway, not certain what lie ahead. Katarina's expression belied that she was reconsidering the cultural experience and that one of the large hotels was looking better all the time.

As they continued down the alley, a short distance ahead they saw an open gate. They walked under the gate and the world changed as they stepped into a shaded courtyard. A fountain in the center announced the cascading water which seemed to lower the temperature ten degrees.

Just ahead was a sign over an open door marking Miss Tum's Guest House. Other Westerners were lingering on chairs arrayed under the trees sipping drinks. Jack stepped into the small lobby.

"We have a reservation," he said. "Wesley is the name."

"Ah yes, Mr. Wesley," the older woman at the counter said. "So very nice to have you. Two in your party?"

Jack confirmed that there were two in his party and watched while the woman flipped through a box full of cards. Growing a little nervous at the length of time it was taking and whether their reservation had really made it, Jack was relieved when the woman finally arrived at a decision.

Pulling a card out of the box, she said, "So sorry for oversight, but the Guest House is totally full."

Realizing they were in a Third World country and that things didn't always flow smoothly, Jack started to turn to Katarina to discuss their next option. He was interrupted before he could speak.

"But we have most wonderful room in main house," the woman said. "It has own bathroom and locking door. No family intrusions on your stay."

"You mean we stay with your family?" Katarina asked, clarifying things.

"Oh yes, very nice room. Only special guests get to stay there. And my family not bother you."

Katarina looked at Jack and smiled. Their cultural experience was about to be expanded. Agreeing to stay with the family, they took the key and followed the woman up the stairs into the main house. Opening the door, a large room with windows overlooking the courtyard welcomed the two, the woman disappearing.

Shutting the door, Jack felt the cool air from the overhead fan circling. He stripped his wet shirt off after setting the bags down. Stepping out of his long pants in relief of the heat, Katarina joined him in stripping down to basics.

"I need the bathroom right away," Jack said.

"You first, I used the one at the airport," Katarina offered.

Walking through the open door into the bathroom, Jack froze. Where there should have been a toilet, there was only a hole in the floor. His sudden complaint drew Katarina's attention.

"It's a squatter, Jack," Katarina said.

"Great, our room comes with a squatter. I've heard about them, but never seen one."

"I've experienced them in Turkey on dive trips there," Katarina said. "Actually, they're very healthy for you. The act of squatting straightens out the colon so you don't have to strain like when you're on a western style toilet. Let me show you."

Katarina walked by Jack and stepped onto the porcelain fixture on the floor. More than just a hole in the floor, a squatter had all the plumbing associated with a regular toilet. Two imbedded foot prints denoted where one placed one's feet. Katarina stepped into the two porcelain foot outlines and then squatted down.

Jack liked the pose, even if she had her panties still on. His smile at her position earned him a rebuke.

"Jack, pay attention," she said. "You do your business, being careful with your aim. Be sure to hit the hole or you'll make a mess. And for men, no standing and trying to hit the hole. Everyone squats. When you're finished, take a scoop of water and pour it in the hole. The water that's sitting there already will flush like a regular toilet when the added water gets dumped in."

Katarina demonstrated after she stood up with a douse of water from the small tank next to the squatter. The fixture had a water trap like other toilets and when more water was added, it flushed like a regular toilet. The small tank refiled itself until once again it was full, ready for another dip of the scoop.

"OK, I've got it," Jack said. "Now, please excuse me, I'd like some privacy."

Katarina returned to the main room and Jack walked over to the toilet. His first problem was trying to line his feet up with the indents provided. No matter how he twisted and turned, he couldn't get both feet in the spots and still squat over the hole.

Smaller Asian bodies, he thought. *Western male bodies just couldn't fit the standard foot markings.* Placing both feet on the floor outside the marked spots, he could

259

finally fit over the target. He did his business with no more adventures. Using the scoop, he flushed.

Before he could leave the bathroom, however, a naked Katarina entered. She pulled the remaining clothes off Jack and announced they needed a good shower. A large ceramic-lined shower stood in the corner and Jack quickly agreed. They both realized no curtain or glass door confined the spray which just landed on the floor and flowed to a central drain.

Taking the soap, Jack lathered Katarina's back as she held her head under the flow. Moving down, soon more erogenous zones were being cleaned and massaged with warm soapy water. Katarina turned around and took the soap from Jack. She plied the soap over his body as they kissed and embraced.

A tile bench was built into the shower and Katarina turned and bent over, placing her hands on the flat surface. With water running down both of them, Jack slipped into what was being offered to him and pulled with both hands on her hips. He moved one hand around to further stimulate Katarina as she moaned with pleasure.

As their bodies thrashed in unison, water flew about the bathroom. Finally Katarina threw her head back in one final loud moan as Jack pulled tight on her body. A few final thrusts of his hips brought him to a finish.

Toweling off, they moved to the bed and collapsed. It had been a long day with a hot humid ending. The nighttime sky was visible through the trees outside the window as the two drifted off in each other's arms, still sweaty and sticky.

Chapter 32

Haad Rin, Thailand

The aftereffects of the lottery to determine the men's bungalow partners was still having its consequences. Jersey had been avoiding Gunny and L. C. since stealing Maya away from them. While it wasn't technically stealing, as no one owned anyone at the resort, L. C. considered it bad sport that someone would step in on a done deal.

But Gunny had changed the dynamics when he had discovered their diamond in the rough as they were calling Sho Lin. Knowing the attributes of Chinese women from his time serving in China, Gunny had made sure that he and L. C. would have a contented year. Sho Lin was turning out to be everything the two men wanted. Pleasant company even with no English skills, Gunny worked each day teaching her.

But the turmoil in the resort was now centered around Panzer. A German retiree, Panzer was the unofficial problem solver where the Thai women were concerned. And with limited entertainment among the four-hundred men and an equal number of women, little things like Panzer's punishment details were ripe for gossip.

"L. C., you ready yet?" Gunny asked.

"Be right there," L. C. yelled from the bathroom.

Pulling up his nylon shorts that were standard attire in the resort, L. C. quickly caught up to Gunny on the bungalow's porch.

"Tell me again, what are we doing this morning?" L. C. asked.

"Lance Corporal, I just can't get over how you made it past private in the Corp," Gunny grumbled. "We're catching the latest installment in Panzer rolling over the opposition."

"Oh, yeah, that," L.C. said. "Why's that important?"

"Because Panzer is the unofficial punishment detail for management," Gunny said, a little exasperated with his roommate. "Any of the women get out of line and they end up with Panzer for a year of retraining."

"That's right." L.C. seemed to finally understand. "At the lottery, he got that good-looker from last year."

"Yeah, but that good-looker turned out to be a big dud," Gunny offered. "Her retiree soon found out that looks aren't everything. She didn't clean or do the laundry. Her cooking was lazy and boring. And to hear tell, her nighttime work was uninspired if not boring."

"And a year with Panzer will straighten he rout?"

"Or she'll be gone. If Panzer can't get her on track, no one can," Gunny said.

"And management doesn't mind?" L. C. asked. He was reminded of the rules that the retirees had to follow in their treatment of the women. There was absolutely no physical abuse allowed. The women were to be treated as the valuable employees that they were and management allowed no deviation, except for Panzer.

Not that Panzer beat any of his charges. But his strict German attitude, combined with an intimidating demeanor, commanded obedience from all but the boldest women.

"Is it true that Panzer was German Special Forces, the KSK, I think they're called?" L. C. asked.

"That's what the other German retirees say. He sure acts like it," Gunny said. They had reached the main beach, site of Panzer's punishment this morning. The whole camp had been following Panzer's work at instilling the virtues of one particular woman focusing on her job.

They sat down in chairs arranged under the trees, joining a gaggle of retirees that were attempting to be nonchalant about observing Panzer at work. Nearby, a group of Thai women, off duty from their resort work, sat on the beach watching.

From down the beach came Panzer hard on the heels of a Thai woman. Both were running on the sand in their swim suits. Panzer blew his whistle and both plunged into he sea to continue running in thigh-deep water. Struggling was more a description versus running as the shorter woman pushed forward against the water, Panzer hard on her back yelling.

"Jesus," L. C. exclaimed. "Yesterday I saw them running the cliff trail near the secluded beach. Up and down all morning. This guy is brutal."

"But look at the other women," Gunny said. "They are very quiet and paying close attention. The message is getting through."

"They'll think twice about dogging it with Panzer on the job," L. C. said.

"Damn straight partner," Gunny said. "When this woman got away with slacking off on her duties, you remember how the other women started adjusting. Suddenly, the bungalows weren't as clean and the laundry started piling up."

"Even Maya," L. C. offered, "I noticed the night-time activities changed. Excuses followed excuses why things couldn't happen. It got bad there for a while."

"And that's why management lets Panzer get away with stuff the rest of us would be thrown out on," Gunny said. "We sign a contract for certain work to be performed. If the women get an idea that they control things, we're in trouble. But it is changing. Richter says the list of women seeking employment here is growing. Word is getting out that the working conditions here are good and the pay fair."

"That will help keep them focused," L. C. said.

As the Thai woman ran by with Panzer still on her for more effort, she yelled something in Thai to the other women watching. One of the women yelled back. Everyone turned to the retiree present that was the best Thai speaker.

"What did she say?" Gunny asked.

"She was complaining to the other women about how much she was hurting," the man offered. "And she tried to get them to support her by going to management."

"What did the other woman say back to her?" L. C. asked.

"Not good for her," the man continued. "She told her to shut up and do her job. Then she could join the others on the beach."

"So the other women aren't staging a revolt in support?" Gunny asked.

"Hardly, they can see how things are. They know how many women are trying to get jobs here," the man said. "But like everyone, they'll push the limits if their allowed to."

"And we have Panzer to keep them within those limits," L. C. said. "Gunny, maybe we need to buy the German a beer tonight at the pool."

"Good idea, he's doing a great job for all of us and needs to know we appreciate it," Gunny said.

* * *

Katarina awoke to the early morning coolness of the overhead fan's breeze. She pulled the top sheet up and spread it over herself and Jack. Moving slightly to the disturbance, Katarina wrapped her arm over her bed partner and went back to sleep. With it not quite light out yet, the darkened room slumbered on in a dreamy state.

Moving to her dream, Katarina rotated onto her back as her mind envisioned a warm tropical beach somewhere. A faceless man lay beside her as the ocean waves crashed nearby. In her mind, palm trees swayed over head as the sun dappled over her naked body, leaving frond patterns in their wake.

The dream continued as it grew more intense. The upper body of the man beside her moved away from her while his lower body moved closer. With her still on her back, the man's hips slipped under her bent legs as he twisted onto his side.

A sensuous feeling washed over her as her mind focused on a pleasant feeling down below. Or was it only

265

in her mind? Katarina's subconscious fought for clarity as the strong feeling between her legs grew in intensity. She felt her legs spread more as the warm flush feeling kept her mind fixated on her pleasure zone.

Things were tingling all over and her mind recorded each tingle. Her subconscious recorded that she had never had a dream like this before and wanted the pleasure to continue on forever. But a bump into her thigh jogged something in her conscious part of her brain. Her eyes twitched from the intrusion on her other feelings.

Another bump, stronger this time, brought her partially awake. Katarina struggled to stay in her dream as the pleasure continued. But the bumping only brought her more awake. At some point the subconscious gave up controlling the pleasure and the conscious took over. That's when Katarina realized it wasn't a dream.

Opening her eyes, she saw Jack lying on his left side, his hips bumping into her raised thighs. His eyes were shut while he slid back and forth inside her. Pulling her legs up higher exposed her more and Jack's thrusts went deeper.

Now awake to the love making, Katarina could fully enjoy the reality of the situation. She reached out to caress her partner just as things let go inside her. But the touch awoke Jack, who stammered at finding himself between her legs.

"What the . . ."

"Go ahead, you can say it," Katarina said softly. "You were asleep and you still found me."

Jack struggled to catch up with his dream as he slipped out of Katarina. He moved up to kiss her breast as his consciousness tried to catch up with the morning's activities. Katarina received the benefits of Jack's attention as he moved to make sure her dream was complete. They both rolled onto their backs with everything even.

"I can't believe I did it in my sleep," Jack finally said.

"You weren't the only one. You disturbed a very pleasant dream I was having, but I forgive you."

"How do you know it was really a dream?" Jack asked. "After all, my dream was stimulating your dream."

"Are you saying your dream started things and I only joined in after?" Katarina asked.

"I think that would be accurate," Jack teased.

"Whichever way it was, I've never done it in my sleep before. It was amazing. Think we can do it again?"

"In our sleep? I'm not sure we can control that," Jack said. "But I agree, it was surprising."

* * *

With a day to kill in Bangkok before their flight to Surat Thani, they were soon out of bed and showering. They had decided to see the city and the early morning held more appeal then the hot afternoon.

Eating a quick breakfast in the guest house dining room, the two organized their day. They would visit the famous stupas across the river before returning for the market nearby. Energized for a full day of sightseeing, the two headed out walking in the direction of the river.

Reaching the landing, they paid the attendant for a ferry ride across the Chao Phraya River. Long skiffs with car engines flew by as they made their way across. Some skiffs had V-8 engines attached to a swivel. The operator would lower the propeller that was attached to a long shaft into the water, much like a hand-held cake mixer. The spinning prop would explode the water, spraying everything behind the boat.

With the brown polluted water, Jack and Katarina worked to keep the aftereffects of the racing skiffs for landing on them. The river banks and nearby stagnant water told of the human waste and debris that was thrown into the river. Naked kids swam off house boats that lined the river banks, oblivious to the danger the water carried.

Jack helped Katarina climb the steep stairs up the Wat Arun Stupa, Temple of the Dawn, where the view over Bangkok revealed itself. They stood high on the monument looking out over the teeming city.

Walking over to a nearby stupa with its gold leaf-lined mantras, they observed the religious art with an added bonus that much of it depicted sexual images of gods in various states of pleasure.

Returning across the river, they made their way to the Thieves Market. Bangkok's outdoor market was one of the largest in the world. With Thai fighting kites overhead, Jack led Katarina into the maze of vendors. Walking through one section, Katarina marveled at al the cats and dogs in cages for sale.

"Look, Jack, the pet section," she said.

Jack looked around at the stacks of animals. A nearby ex-pat Westerner offered a clearer picture.

"Excuse me, but I just overheard you refer to these as pets," the man said. "I need to enlighten you, this is the food section. People buy these animals and then go home and cook them."

"Oh," Katarina blanched.

"Please, if I could show you. Just as one Westerner to another," the man offered. "I've been vacationing here for ten years now and still get amazed at the locals."

He took Katarina by the elbow and walked her through the market. Jack scrambled to keep up as his new tour guide twisted and turned around vendors. He stopped in front of a man with a large wok, hot oil smoking.

Next to the wok were stacked eggs in large square flats. The vendor, seeing a new potential customer, smiled and offered his wares. The guide motioned for two eggs and the proprietor dutifully selected two eggs.

The cook stirred the oil to make sure it was ready and with Katarina standing close by, cracked the first egg on the edge of the wok.

"I can handle fried eggs," she said. But she turned white at what came out instead.

Opening the shell, the cook dropped a baby chick into the hot oil to a sizzle sound. Soon a second chick was popped out of its shell and hit the oil.

Katarina backed up, holding her mouth as if to stop her from vomiting. Jack stepped forward and took the two hot chicks from the vendor and passed over the necessary baht in payment. He turned and gave his guide a dirty look. The guide took the two chicks and handed them to a local standing nearby. The man gulped them down quickly in one bite.

"Sorry about that. Just keeping the cultural experience flowing," the guide said. "I assumed you didn't want them."

"No thanks," Katarina barked.

"If you don't mind, I can show you a few other famous things of Thailand."

Jack hesitated since the cooked chicks routine hadn't been a big success. But Katarina was still game.

"No more cooked chicks though," she demanded.

"No, but remember, we drop live lobsters into boiling water. Seems pretty barbaric to a vegan don't you think?" the guide asked.

"OK, what's next on the list?" Jack asked. He wanted to move the fun along.

Again taking Katarina's elbow, he moved through the vendors until he found the right one. This one was outside the market, set up on the side of the street, a large mound of plant waste next to her stand. Small slices of yellow fruit sat on her table.

The guide motioned for Jack to pay for three slices as he took one in his hand. Jack and Katarina watched carefully as the man proceeded to pinch off his nose with his free hand and then toss the fruit onto his mouth with the other. He chewed and then swallowed before releasing his nose.

"Durian," he offered. "Go ahead and try it. You'll discover you'll want to hold your nose before biting."

Katarina carefully picked up a slice and raised it towards her nose. She backed away quickly, lowering the fruit.

"Mijn god, het stinkt," she said.

270

"It is a little ripe in the smell department," Jack added as he too sniffed carefully and withdrew.

"But a marvelous taste," the guide added. "Just close your nose."

Both rookies dutifully clamped their fingers onto their nostrils. Then in unison, they placed the fruit in their mouths. Smiles came up as the taste hit them. Releasing their grip, they both said together.

"Tastes good."

"See, just have to get past the other part."

Jack sniffed his hand that had held the fruit and moved his hand away. The lingering smell would need to be scrubbed off later. Katarina wrinkled her nose when her smelly hand came too close to her nose.

"Well, thank you for the tourist highlights," Katarina said. "I know we would have never experienced them on our own."

"Quite alright," the man said. "Have you been to Sukhumvit Street yet? You don't want to leave Bangkok without at least as troll down there."

"No, but is it appropriate for all ages. I've heard about some of the attributes of Bangkok," Jack said.

The guide turned to Katarina. "Your accent is Dutch if I'm right?"

Katarina acknowledged that she was from the Netherlands. She wondered what that had to do with Sukhumvit Street.

"Then if you spent any time in Amsterdam, you won't be shocked."

"I don't know, but . . .," Jack started to say.

"My good man, it's the noon hour. Things don't really get going 'til after dark. You'll get a flavor of the place without the blatant stuff the night brings," the guide said.

"It's OK Jack. I did grow up outside Amsterdam," Katarina said. "I'm sure there's not much that could shock me."

A short taxi ride took the two intrepid tourists to Sukhumvit Street. As Jack paid the driver, their guide pointed out the bars to Katarina. Both sides of the street were lined with glitzy garish lights announcing all that could be experienced inside. Bar girls in scanty outfits and high heels strolled the front of each establishment enticing the passerby to venture inside.

One bar girl walked up to their guide and called him by name. He reached down and grabbed her in privates in greeting as she giggled and grabbed his in return.

"See you later honey," he said, retrieving his hand. She glided her hand up his chest as he led Jack and Katarina further into the district.

"So, it seems you frequent here?" Jack asked.

"I take a two-month vacation here every winter. Gets me out of the snow and cold of Germany. And the women keep me entertained every night I'm here. My hotel room is just over there." The guide pointed at a hotel just off the main street. It lay an easy stroll away from all the bars.

Katarina knew she wasn't in Amsterdam anymore when she saw one bar girl standing on the street corner

272

with a sign. Katarina read the inscription and turned to her guide.

"Is that true?" Katarina asked. "Free with a drink purchase?"

"Oh yeah," their guide said. "In fact, you don't even have to leave the bar to get serviced. You just sit at the bar drinking while below you a curtain parts. Soon your pants are undone and a warm mouth finds its target. Hell of a country."

Katarina turned to Jack for an answer. Jack looked back but could offer none that were good.

"Katarina, supply and demand," Jack tried to explain. "In a poor country women have few options. Just like poor Eastern European women showing up in Amsterdam to work the sex trade. It's just here, its so cheap you get a freebie with a drink. Sort of like a happy meal."

He received a scowl in return for his attempted humor. Their guide noticed the displeasure his charge was displaying.

"Things have changed though," he offered. "As the factories for western goods moved in, the women have other choices. Now the bar girls tend to be Cambodians and Laotians. They come to the big city to earn money to send back to their families."

"See, they can work in factories," Jack repeated. He got more scowl in return.

"It's all over the world. Last year I was in Gambia," he said. "That's in west Africa. Long tall black women with warm weather, two fun ingredients to life."

273

"You take sex vacations around the world each winter?" Katarina asked.

"Yes," the guide said. "I've been to the Philippines, Brazil, Colombia, and Vietnam over the last few years."

Katarina turned to Jack and asked if they could go back to their hotel. They thanked their guide who quickly disappeared into one of the bars, grabbing three girls along the way. A taxi dropped them off at the head of the alley way and the two walked the short distance to the guest house in silence. Once inside their room, Katarina sat down on the bed.

"I've been around the brothels all my life in Holland," she said. "But that was just never so in-your-face as here."

Jack let her talk as she continued on about what they had seen on Sukhumvit Street. But it was when she started to get on her men-are-pigs rant when Jack stopped her.

"Katarina, not all men are pigs," Jack started. "Yes, some are. Sitting at a bar with people all around while some woman buries her head in your crotch isn't for me. Not a lot of tenderness involved."

"They're still pigs."

"Some, but most aren't," Jack said. "Most men are content to be at home with their wife when they really wish to be frolicking on a beach naked with five buxom blondes."

"What are trying to say?"

"I'm saying most men dream of lusty adventures with numerous partners, but settle for one woman, a home, and children," Jack offered.

"Is that what you think I'm about then?"

Jack didn't offer an answer. Their room was very quiet the rest of the day and into the evening. Both went to bed without furthering the conversation.

Chapter 33

Surat Thani, Thailand

The short flight from Bangkok down to Surat Thani Airport offered a stunning view of the South China Sea out the left side of the airplane. Jack sat on the aisle as Katarina stared out the plane's window the entire time.

They had left their guest house that morning with the pall of the stilted discussion on the finer points of the male libido. Nothing had been added to the conversation since yesterday. Only a few comments between the two travelers had passed, and those related solely to making their way to where LaMarcus's uncle waited.

Or at least where they hoped to find Joe Lewis. With the information provided by the Rising Sun accountant, they had located where they needed to be and the route to get there. One short plane flight followed by a taxi to the ferry that would take them to Ko Pha-Ngan Island.

Ko Pha-Ngan Island lay just past the more famous Ko Sumi Island which held numerous western-style resorts. World travelers flocked in to take in the warm weather and water as they made their way around the world. Coupled with European tourists flocking to Thailand for relief from cold weather, the area had numerous facilities for foreigners.

The taxi got them to the ferry with only a short wait for the next boat. Soon, Jack was hiring a three-wheeled vehicle called a jitney for the last leg of their journey. The driver shifted the jitney into gear and with a pall of blue smoke, the two were transported facing backwards under the small canvas canopy.

Jack had asked on the ferry of places to stay in Haad Rin. One of two women from Belgium traveling together offered that she had been on the island before and the place they were staying was the best around. Now following the two women in their own jitney, Jack twisted around to see the small village come into view.

The driver stopped at a motel-like looking building next to the water and switched off the engine. Helping his passengers out of the back, the driver scooped up the two bags and carried them into the office. Receiving his fare, he kicked the engine back to life and sped off behind his fellow jitney.

Having only talked to Jack onboard the ferry, the two young Belgians raised their eyebrows when they saw Jack's travel companion. Jack and Katarina waited while the two others checked in. Picking up the vibes when the two women walked by him on their way to their room, Jack determined that having dinner together probably wasn't going to happen.

A second-story room overlooking the sea was rented and Jack carried the bags to the room. Katarina walked closely behind, her silence continuing. With it still early in the day, Jack announced he was going for a walk. Katarina offered no protest.

Jack knew from Leonard the accountant that the Rising Sun's resort was nearby. He wanted to reconnoiter the site so that he could determine the best way to reach LaMarcus' uncle. As he headed out of the small village, the road heading north on the island offered the only other choice from the road they'd just arrived on.

No resort-looking property existed between Haad Rin and the ferry boat dock, so north was the next choice. Just outside the village, Jack spotted a side road leading into the heavy tropical forest. He veered onto the side road and soon ran into a building with a high fence heading off on both directions. The building wall was blank except for one entry door with a small covered porch attached. A larger closed gated entrance that could accommodate vehicles lay close by.

Jack examined the gravel and noticed that no vehicles had passed through the gate in a very long time. Then he noticed tire tracks to his right and followed them. Around the end of the building was a metal roll-up door hidden around the corner. Fresh tire marks indicated that many vehicles had recently found their way to this door.

Turning around, Jack walked back to the only entrance. He opened the door and stepped into a small lobby. A chair and another door were all that were in the lobby except for a pass-through window which was closed. Waiting to see what would happen, Jack scanned the empty room.

Hearing noises behind the screened pass-through, Jack readied his best story. An unlocking noise and the sliding door was shoved aside. A dark-haired man stood ready.

"Yes, may I help you?' the man asked.

"Hi," Jack started. "Say, I'm staying in a hotel in Haad Rin and I was walking by and saw this place. It looked like a resort and I was wondering if you had any rooms available?"

"No, I'm afraid not," the man said. "This is a private club, for members only."

"I'm sorry, my name's Jack. I didn't catch yours. Do you have any brochures? Might be a club I'd be interested in joining."

"My name is Richter, and we don't have any brochures and you would not be able to join anyway. We are quite exclusive."

"Well, Richter, I can be as exclusive as the next guy," Jack offered. "Say, do I detect a German accent in there somewhere?"

"Yes, and you are quite American in your talk. But please excuse me, I'm very busy."

Before Jack could get another word in, the slider slammed shut and the lock noise announced itself.

Well, be that way, Jack thought. *I'll just have to open up my own membership.* Stepping outside, Jack followed the fence to the north. The ten-foot-high chain-link fence was covered in plant growth from the tropical forest. But it was possible for Jack to stop and pull at the leaves to reveal the other side.

Making out mostly forest, in spots Jack could make out a cabin set in a clearing not too far away. He continued his march, always keeping the fence to his right. The fence line had been maintained and the walking was moderately easy as the fence continued on for a long distance. Hearing the ocean as he grew closer, Jack moved ahead cautiously. He stopped at the top of a cliff before plunging the one-hundred feet to the sea. The fence had a large half round attachment of razor wire to prevent anyone from sneaking around the end.

Jack turned around and headed back to the office. Reaching the building, he walked right past, heading south. He noticed that the sun was high in the sky as he pressed on in his scouting of the perimeter. Each time he stopped and pulled the leaves free, the same view of small cabins set in the forest was revealed.

The fence eventually started working itself downhill. The sound of the ocean rose up to him as he dropped down in elevation. Soon the sea was visible through the cleared fence line and Jack walked right up to the water. But unlike the other end, the fence ended on a sandy beach. Whoever constructed the fence had attempted to run the barrier out onto the beach but weather and surf had defeated the attempt.

While two large poles sat in the water that should have had fence attached, the chain link hung loose in a number of places. *Not that I couldn't have swum around the end anyway*, Jack thought. *I probably wouldn't even be over my head getting around the original fence.*

With the gaps created by a half collapsed barrier, he wouldn't even have to get his feet wet. *Strange that they haven't maintained their fence better,* Jack thought. *But with the resort open to the sea, they always would have security problems.*

The sun was now dropping toward the horizon and Jack hurried to get back to the road. By the time he reached his hotel, his stomach complained loudly from his all-day hike. Jack walked into the hotel courtyard to find Katarina and the two Belgian women sitting by the pool.

Walking over and sitting down after ordering something to eat, Jack noticed the cool reception he received from all three women. A waiter came over with bottled water to offset Jack's long hot walk. The three women carried on their conversation that they had been having before his arrival. Jack was just glad to sit for a while with his water.

"So, Katarina says that you saw the exploited women of Sukhumvit Street in Bangkok," one of the Belgians announced suddenly.

Jack sat up a little as the strongly worded statement seemed to be directed to him. "Yes, we met a German who took us over there."

"Those pig Germans," the woman barked. "Bringing their Euros and buying sex. Every winter the same thing. Germans and Frenchmen. As if the Japanese businessmen weren't bad enough, throwing their yen around. It's disgusting."

Jack knew enough to know where he should stay mum, and this was one of those times. In his policing days, as a detective he would run into the strident ones during his investigations. They were demagogues in their beliefs and no amount of discussion would persuade them they might be wrong.

And not that they were necessarily wrong about the fleshpots of Bangkok. Or anywhere else in the world. *Exploited women certainly were forced into the sex trade, but some women chose the profession all on their own,* Jack thought.

Given a choice between a life on a marginal farm, living a subsistence living or working in a sweat shop factory sewing running shoes for Westerners, some chose the oldest profession in the world. Prostitution, while not his cup of tea, put money in a woman's pocket. *Unless abused by men who stole the money*, Jack thought.

"So I suppose you came here for that kind of thing," the older, loud-mouthed Belgian accused Jack.

Jack looked at Katarina to see if she would respond. She sat passively next to the aggressive Belgian.

"No, actually I didn't," Jack said. "And up until a couple of days ago, I'd never even seen the inside of a brothel before."

"So now you're into that scene eh?" The Belgian woman looked sternly at Katarina. Again Jack saw no defense coming from his partner as the woman practically accused Katarina of being here with Jack for money.

"Actually, what I'm into is none of your business any more than what you're into is none of my business." Jack leered at both Belgians as intensely as he could. He saw the younger, quiet one blanch at the scrutiny.

Her partner came to her defense quickly, "What we do is our business, asshole. Come on." She stood up and grabbed the other Belgian by the hand. The two headed to their room.

Jack sipped his water and looked out on the lights reflected off the ocean. He took a deep breath to relax himself. He'd seen the type before.

"Jack, I'm sorry," Katarina finally said. "I should have said something. It's just we got to talking before you arrived and she was so forceful."

"Katarina, it's OK," Jack said. "Those types are everywhere. Busy bodies in everyone's business but shine a light on their lives and watch out. Like cockroaches in the kitchen when the lights come on, all of them."

"Can we go to bed now?" Katarina asked. "The past two days have been very upsetting to me. Could you just hold me close tonight? I need some tenderness?"

"Like I told you, let me be gentle with you." Jack grabbed his dinner plate with one hand and took her hand in the other as they walked up the stairs to their room.

Chapter 34

Henderson, Nevada

"I just heard from Jack," LaMarcus said as he walked into the family room to find Gary. "He's done his first reconnoiter of the place my uncle may be in. Says it won't be a problem getting inside."

Gary nodded at the good news his friend was offering. Events in Las Vegas were proceeding quicker than had been planned. With Jack's release from custody, LaMarcus's case for carrying an illegal weapon was moved up. Tomorrow LaMarcus and the attorney would meet with the Assistant DA to work out the final deal.

LaMarcus would plead guilty to a lesser charge and receive probation for a year. In addition, he would pay a fine as well as restitution to the victim of his illegal weapon. It still didn't sit right with LaMarcus, but time was moving on and he needed to determine whether he could get into Thailand without any past troubles coming back to haunt him.

Working through a private investigator in Bangkok that had been recommended, LaMarcus was waiting on news from Thailand. That Jack was ready for a full insertion to find his uncle made him even more antsy to get going.

Gary and LaMarcus met with the attorney in the courthouse the next morning. Standing in the hallway waiting for their court time, they were surprised to see Ernesto and his two body guards show up. Standing on the other end of the hallway, LaMarcus could see Ernesto's face bruised with is nose bandaged. One body guard had a cast on his arm from LaMarcus's baton swing while the choke hold sufferer seemed to have made a full recovery.

The Assistant DA walked by and nodded to LaMarcus's attorney. They followed him through the main doors into the court room with Ernesto and his team following. While LaMarcus moved to the front and sat down, Ernesto and the boys sat in the back.

"State of Nevada versus Lewis," the bailiff called.

"Defense is ready," LaMarcus' attorney offered.

"The people are ready, your honor."

"What do we have here?" the judge read the paperwork as he spoke. "An agreement has been worked out, I see."

"Yes your honor," the DA offered. "Mr. Lewis, in the consideration of justice, has agreed to the terms outlined before you."

"Very well, I shall . . .," the judge was interrupted.

"If I may speak, your honor?" Ernesto asked.

The judge looked over his glasses at the interruption. His look was not a happy one. "And you are . . .?"

"The victim in this. And this agreement is a travesty of justice, your honor," Ernesto pleaded.

Turning his attention to the DA, the judge asked, "Mr. Prosecutor, are you aware of this man's concerns?"

"Yes your honor, he has made his point very vocal to my office," the DA said. "But again, we have worked out an equitable settlement in this case. If the victims wish to seek damages in civil court, they are free to pursue those avenues."

"You bet your ass I'll pursue them. And everywhere else I can," Ernesto said. Before the judge could raise his gavel to rule his speech out of order, Ernesto threw in one more threat as the security personnel moved in his direction. "As they say, the only justice in the halls of justice is in the halls."

"I take that as a threat and rule you out of order. Bailiff, remove that man and his associates. And let the record show that a direct threat was just made in my presence," the judge ordered.

With Ernesto and his friends gone, the proceedings went smoothly. LaMarcus signed the document and posted his thousand-dollar fine. That hurt some but at least the ten thousand in restitution would be made in monthly installments. That took the bite out of things slightly. And his probation could be served anywhere in the country.

The next day, LaMarcus said goodbye to Gary and thanked him for all his help. Heading his Cadillac Escalade northeast out of Las Vegas, he would head back to Boston to serve out his probation. At least that's what he wanted everyone to believe. He hit the Utah State Line and the speed limit went up to eighty miles per hour. He pressed on the accelerator and the big Cadillac responded. *I might like it out west,* Lamarcus thought. *Yes, sir, more freedom out here.* The head wind hit the front of the car and the SUV shuddered.

* * *

Jack was up and moving before the sun broke the surface of the Gulf of Thailand. He moved quickly through the village as a few dogs made their presence known. But they were all firmly locked in pens so Jack paid them little mind.

He reached the path he'd found that would lead to the southern end of the fence line. Reaching the spot as the sun broke the sea's surface, he stepped cautiously under the gap onto the resort property. He moved slowly looking for cameras that would announce his intrusion. Seeing none at this obvious spot, Jack relaxed slightly. *If this didn't warrant a video feed for security, their whole resort must be loose about it,* he thought.

Climbing a rocky point, he stepped into the vegetation for cover. Jack moved ahead along the coast until he came to a large beach. Dropping down off the rocks, he kept to the trees as he worked his way along the beach.

Something up ahead moved, and Jack threw himself against a nearby tree. Watching the movement, he determined that it was a large man doing squat thrusts in the sand. Beside him, a petite Asian woman was trying to keep up. The man was counting out each set in what sounded like German.

Knowing he had to contact someone inside the resort for help in locating Joe Lewis, Jack moved away from the tree and headed for the couple. As he neared, the large man stopped, staring at Jack. The Asian woman stopped briefly but a bark from the big man got her moving again.

287

The man stood staring at the intruder on the beach for what seemed eternity to Jack. Then something clicked for the man as he walked to Jack and held out his hand, "Guten Morgen, Herr Wesley."

Stunned that the man knrew his name, Jack shook hands in bewilderment. *How does he know my name?* Jack thought.

"Sprechen sie English, mein freund?" Jack asked. He was suddenly wondering if he should have brought Katarina along.

"Ja, ich sprechie English," the man answered.

"What is your name?" Jack asked.

"Oh, my name is Panzer."

Strange name, Jack thought. *He might be built like a tank, but to be named after one is unusual.*

"Mr. Panzer, I'm looking for a person named Joe Lewis, an American," Jack started.

"No no, not Mr. Panzer, just Panzer," he said. In the background the Asian woman was flagging in her efforts. Panzer turned and told her to go sit for five. She complied immediately. "And no Joe Lewis here."

Jack looked perplexed, so Panzer tried a different approach. "But no one uses their real names here. We all take on a new name when we arrive. What does your friend look like?"

Jack started to describe LaMarcus's uncle when he remembered the picture he carried. He reached in his pocket and retrieved the photo of Joe.

"Oh, L.C.," Panzer beamed. "Sure, he lives here. Bungalow 44 I think."

"Could you take me there?" Jack asked.

"Of course. Come with me."

Panzer barked at the Asian woman who fell in behind the two men. A brisk walk off the beach, the trio passed a number of bungalows. Jack noticed everyone seemed to be still sleeping still as they passed no other people. As they wound their way through a heavily wooded section of the resort, a bungalow came into view. Sitting with four other cabins around a clearing, Panzer marched right up onto the porch of one and walked in the open doors. The German talked to someone inside the cabin and motioned Jack inside.

Without saying a word, Panzer turned and opened a closed door. He pointed for Jack to enter, closing the door after him. Jack was alone except for two sleeping bodies in the bed. *What do I do now?* he thought.

As he considered his next move, an Asian woman's face appeared from under a sheet. Her eyes got big seeing a stranger in the bedroom and she nudged the man next to her.

"What, not again?" the man said, still lying on his stomach. "You've plum wore me out tonight."

The woman was frozen in place with the sheet pulled up to her nose, staring at Jack. Not saying a word, neither one moved. Then she nudged the white-haired man next to her again, but more forcefully this time.

"I tell you I can't do it anymore. Just go do something and let me sleep."

But a further nudge got the man to flip half over. Before he said anything, he noticed the intense stare his bedmate held on something behind him. He snapped around, pulling the sheet protecting the woman away. She scrambled for modesty as her breasts were exposed.

"What the fu. . ." L. C. said loudly. "Who the hell are you?"

"Slow down Mr. Lewis. LaMarcus sent me to find you," Jack said.

L. C. stopped at the statement and Jack could see his mind turning. He looked over at the Asian woman who continued her stare at the stranger. Turning to his partner he said, "Go get some clothes on, honey, we got company."

As he said it, she crawled out fully from the sheet. L. C. slapped her bare ass as it passed by and she scooted by Jack out the door. Jack reached around and closed the door behind her.

"LaMarcus sent you, you don't say?" L. C. said.

Chapter 35

Haad Rin, Thailand

Katarina sipped her coffee by the pool as she watched the sun clear the horizon over the Gulf of Thailand. She had awoken to find Jack gone but the bed still warm. Assuming he wasn't too far ahead of her, she scrambled to get dressed and hopefully catch him at breakfast. But she had arrived in the dining area off the pool to no Jack.

Grabbing a coffee, she headed to the pool deck. The sun's warmth was missing and Katarina pulled her legs up onto her chest as she snuggled into a tight ball. She knew Jack would be inside the compound by now searching for LaMarcus's uncle. Waiting for an answer would require her patience.

"Goedenmorgen," the voice said.

Startled at her own language being spoken, Katarina looked up to see one of the Belgian women sitting down next to her. Luckily it was the quiet one. Katarina returned the greeting.

"I'm sorry, but my Dutch is a little rusty. Mind if we speak in English?" she asked.

"No, not at all. We didn't really meet yesterday, I'm Katarina."

I'm Uta, and my friend is Marche. It's a beautiful morning."

"Yes, it is," Katarina said. "Where is your friend?"

"Still sleeping. And your friend?" Uta asked.

"Out for a hike."

"I'm sorry about last night. Marche can be very opinionated."

"I noticed," Katarina said.

A quiet spell passed as each sipped their coffee and stared at the ocean view. The quiet soon grew tense as the two women seemed to be sizing each other up.

Uta spoke first. "I don't mean to pry, but you and your friend . . ."

"Jack," Katarina offered when Uta paused.

"Yes, Jack. I was just wondering . . "

At she stopped inquiry, Katarina jumped in. "How he and I got connected up, seeing as he's old enough to be my father?"

"It's none of my business, if you don't want to tell me," Uta said.

You're right, it's none of your business, Katarina thought. *But I have nothing to be ashamed of.*

"He's a gentle man who treats me special. What more could a woman want?" Katarina asked.

A break in the conversation ensued as both women paused. With the personal questions out on the table, Katarina shot back.

"So, you and Marche, you are a couple?" Katarina asked. Uta nodded her head in a less than enthusiastic manner. "And you are intimate?" Another nod in confirmation.

Katarina sipped her coffee and watched a local fishing boat motor by on its way out from the village, the subdued put-put sound of a single cylinder engine driving the craft. A flash of light of reflected sun off the boat's windshield hit her in the eyes causing her to turn away.

Opening her eyes, she stared right at Uta. Small tears were flowing down the Belgian's cheeks.

"What is it?" Katarina asked.

The tears continued as Uta sat immobile, not answering. Katarina reached over and took the young woman's hand in support.

"It's awful," Uta whispered. "I never thought someone could be so mean."

"Who?" Katarina asked.

Again, a long quiet spell as Uta looked around. Assured that no other ears were near, she answered.

"Marche."

"But how?" Katarina pressed.

The answer spilled out in a torrent. Uta had just graduated from high school when she and her boyfriend decided to take a trip together. They each had saved their money and, with graduation cash, they set off to hike in the Himalayas. They had stopped first in Goa for the sun and the beach. Uta described the wonderful time being with someone special to her.

"It was so romantic," she offered.

"But what happened?" Katarina asked.

The two had made their way by bus across India to Nepal. The trip had strained their relationship. Uta had picked up a bug that knocked her flat with Delhi belly. The boyfriend got tired fast taking care of her. After a few days in Kathmandu, he announced he had met some others who were heading out trekking and proceeded to leave her.

Alone and sick in Kathmandu, she was in a panic. Uta couldn't leave her room for the explosive diarrhea that hit her at any time. When she was at her most depressed,

Marche had shown up in the hotel room next door. Carefully nursing Uta back to health, Marche doted on her night and day.

Finally healthy, Uta was so grateful at the older woman's help that she accepted the offer to head to Thailand with her. That was where the confusion started as Marche made physical advances toward the younger Uta. Afraid to be left alone again, Uta had gone along.

"But I want to vomit after every time we're together," Uta said.

"You should leave," Katarina said.

"I tried in Bangkok after we got back from a visit to Chiang Mai," Uta said. "But Marche can be very forceful. You saw her the other night."

"She doesn't own you. You need to get away."

"I know, but I'm just not strong enough. And I'm all alone," Uta said.

"Is your airplane ticket still good for a return to Belgium?" Katarina asked.

"Yes, but I have to get back to Mumbai to use it. And now my money is low. Marche has been paying for things since Nepal. I don't know what to do."

"Don't worry about that," Katarina said. "I'll make sure you get home."

"You'd do that for me?" Uta asked, a certain suspicion in her voice.

Good, she's getting a little more wise in the world, Katarina thought. *Not that I'm that much older than she is.*

"I live in Amsterdam. I'll give you my address. You can pay me back when you get the money."

"Thank you," Uta said. "I'll pay you back first thing."

"OK, now we just need to plan your escape," Katarina said.

As the words came out, a voice barked from inside the dining area. Both women sitting on the deck froze.

"Uta, what are you doing up so early?" Marche demanded. "And why have you been crying?"

Katarina panicked as she glanced at Uta. The streaks down her face were visible in the bright sunlight.

"It's the sun," Katarina offered. She held her hand up over her eyes to shade them from the sun for emphasis. "Uta, move over here so the sun isn't right in your eyes."

Uta dutifully scooted around the table so the sun was now at her back. Marche sat down opposite Katarina.

"That's better," Uta said.

The older Belgian looked at Katarina in a threatening stare. Processing the sun information, she relaxed as the sun hit her on the side of her face, the glare bothering her one eye.

"I guess it is a little bright," Marche said. Then turning to Katarina, "So where's Mr. Wonderful?"

"Out hiking," Katarina offered.

"And he didn't take you? How inconsiderate," Marche said.

Katarina let the comment lie. She was busy thinking of an escape plan for the poor younger woman who was trapped. Sitting next to the mouthy one only made Katarina more determined to snatch her companion away from her.

"So, what are you two up to today?" Katarina changed the subject.

"We've heard that there's a resort nearby that exploits local women into the sex trade," Marche said. "I'm a member of the Sex Workers Freedom Movement. We go around the world spotlighting women who are forced into the sex business. By putting the media on the men who make this sickening trade possible, we are freeing women everywhere from demeaning themselves."

"And how is your movement doing?" Katarina asked.

"You said you're Dutch," Marche offered. "We've held demonstrations on the streets outside the brothels in Amsterdam. We hand out flyers that show the results of the sex trade worldwide. The incidence of disease these women suffer. The drug abuse associated with prostitution. Women who are kidnapped into the sex trade against their will. It's criminal that the male-dominated media refuses to fully cover any of it."

"So do you include the pretty-boys in your crusade?" Katarina was referring to the male prostitutes she and Jack had seen in Bangkok. She knew they existed in Amsterdam but with less visibility than the women. "They seem to be as exploited as the women."

Marche gave Katarina a long sour look. "Not our problem. We're concerned with the women. Men have always been the dominant ones in our perverse patriarchal society. Serves all of them right, bent over getting the shaft for a change."

Marche smiled at her little metaphor. The other two women stared back at her in quiet rage. Katarina knew now more then ever she would help Uta escape. Marche seemed to sense the mood at the table and changed the subject.

"So, do you or your friend know anything about this sex resort?"

"No, 'fraid not," Katarina lied.

"That's fine. I'm sure the locals know all about it," Marche said. "Can't hide something like that."

"Yes, I'm sure they do," Katarina said. "Well, have fun with your search. I'm headed to the beach."

Katarina stood up and looked at Uta. With Marche looking around for some locals to go harangue, Uta slipped a look back to Katarina that pleaded for help. Katarina winked and smiled at her in return. *Things would have to wait for right now,* Katarina thought. She headed down to the beach with her bag and grabbed an umbrella. Pulling out her paperback book, she settled in for Jack's return.

* * *.

The snow on the highway leading into Boston was building. LaMarcus had been lucky all the way across the country in having clear roads. His Cadillac Escalade flew east, although at a considerable slower pace than Utah had allowed. His order of business was checking with his probation officer and getting right with the Nevada justice system.

Once he was on the official probation list, he then needed to decide what to do next. His friend Jack held that answer and as soon as he heard from Thailand, LaMarcus would know which route he would take.

Parking in his single car garage, LaMarcus grabbed his bag and headed to his apartment. He checked his email as soon as he walked in the door and noticed two messages sitting in his inbox. Dropping his bag, he sat down and opened the first one.

The email was tagged from Gary's neighbor in Henderson. After their day fishing Lake Mead, the three had made plans to try their hand at more livelier streams in Montana. Each enjoyed the camaraderie of time spent with friends fishing, talking and maybe drinking a beer or two. The neighbor's message had LaMarcus moving to pour himself a stiff drink. His future plans had just changed.

Chapter 36

Haad Rin, Thailand

"Man, I'd never thought I'd see someone from back home," L. C. said. "You're that Marine buddy LaMarcus talked about so much, aren't you?"

"I guess that would be me. Jack's the name."

"They call me L.C. here, short for Lance Corporal. The guy in the kitchen is Gunny, also from the Corps. Don't know his real name. And you met Sho Lin a minute ago."

"Sorry to barge in on you like this," Jack offered. "But the big German was on a mission as soon as I showed him your picture. Don't think I'd have gotten far asking for Joe Lewis."

"That's for sure," L. C. said. "And they don't call him Panzer for nothing."

"So, any problem with me sneaking in here? I tried to ask at the front gate yesterday but they weren't very cooperative."

"Don't know," L. C. said. "Don't think anyone has ever slinked in here. Plenty have snuck out and I do know management don't like that one bit."

"What about security? I didn't see much of anything by the fence line where it hits the sea," Jack said.

"Well, we'll know in a minute. Panzer is head of our security. He's German Special Forces, retired. He and a couple of other German ex-military are in charge of keeping us safe."

Jack scanned out the window to see if the big German and his pals were arriving armed to the teeth. The walkway outside was quiet as the resort slumbered on.

"Since we may not have much time I need to ask, are you OK? LaMarcus has been worried about you."

"Shit, I know I should have written him to explain," L. C. said. "But I've been adjusting to my new life and then I felt guilty because I hadn't written. You know how it is?"

Jack let L.C. suffer some from his lack of consideration to his nephew. As LaMarcus' friend, Jack understood the fragile link with family that often supported us in life. That L. C. had abused that connection didn't sit right.

"So, there's no one forcing you to stay here?" Jack asked.

"Forcing me? Hell no, son. I just wish I'd learned about this place sooner."

"And they aren't stealing your money back in Nevada?"

"Shit no," L. C. said. "I set up my retirement checks for automatic deposit in the bank in Pahrump and the Rising Sun managers take their expenses and their percentage. Then they send the rest over to me. We all have an account with the local bank here."

A creak in the floor boards on the front porch from a large body stepping on them startled the two men. L. C. jumped out of bed and pulled on some shorts just before a faint knock announced itself on the bedroom door.

Opening the door carefully to see who was on the other side, Jack confronted a smiling Panzer. He pulled the door open and L. C. stepped between the two men.

"What's up, Panzer?" L.C. asked. "Any problems?"

Jack held his breath. He had the vital information he needed to pass on to LaMarcus, but the place intrigued him and he wasn't ready to leave yet.

"Nein, no problems," Panzer said. He swung his large arm around from behind and raised it up in front of Jack. In his hand, Panzer held a copy of Jack's book. "Bitte, you could sign this for me?"

L. C. turned to Jack and caught a smile. Still not grasping what was happening, L. C. stepped back.

"What is this?" he asked. "You didn't tell me you were an author."

"A best-selling author in Germany," Panzer added. "I just finished it. My sister in Frankfurt sent it to me. That's how I knew who you were on the beach."

Panzer flipped the book over to Jack's picture on the back cover. He smiled as he pointed Jack out. *The man is sharp if he connected those dots that fast,* Jack thought. *Now, did he inform whoever of me being here?*

Panzer produced a pen from his other hand and Jack looked around for a flat surface so he could write. L. C. motioned him to the kitchen table where Gunny still sat in disbelief. L. C. introduced his roommate and Gunny offered Jack a cup of coffee.

"Would you have any tea?" Jack asked. Before anyone could even answer, a small young Chinese woman appeared in the kitchen. She immediately put water on and grabbed a jar with tea leaves in them.

"You said the magic words to someone anyway," Gunny said.

Jack looked over the woman they had called Sho Lin. Now fully clothed, she bowed slightly toward Jack as he returned the bow. She came over and directed Jack to sit at the table while things were prepared. Soon eggs were being prepared and thrown in a pan to cook. Jack went to work on signing his book for Panzer.

As the German read over the inscription and nodded at the sentiment written, Sho Lin delivered plates of food to the four men. The smell reminded Jack that he hadn't eaten that morning and his stomach was protesting the lack of food.

Taking a bite, Jack stopped in wonderment. The three other men looked at him in amusement. Gunny was the first to say anything.

"Good, eh?"

"These are the best," Jack said. He took several more bites as the hot peppers did their work. Tea arrived but not before Jack was asking for water. Gunny and L. C. both had big grins at their guest's response.

"All our meals are like this," L. C. said. "At least the ones Sho Lin cooks. We usually get our own breakfasts and lunches but I guess she knows today is special."

"All the women are a little more energetic lately," Gunny added. "All the men are reporting that their woman is more cooperative. Must be that they see what Panzer is doing to one of their slackers."

"Ja, ja. Slackers. We don't need no slackers here," Panzer said.

"The woman on the beach when I arrived?" Jack asked. He had seen the Thai woman working hard on the beach while the rest of the resort slept.

"Yes, Panzer is our one-man re-education detail," L. C. said. "They either get with the program or management replaces them."

"And do most get with the program?" Jack asked.

"Always," Gunny added. "The reality of life outside these walls for the women is much worse. We have a waiting list of women who want to come work here."

"So, fill me in on how the resort works," Jack said.

Gunny explained the yearly lottery that set the work contracts for the year. Explaining the duties that each woman took on under that contract, Gunny went through the list. Jack's interest rose with each item.

"So, you two share Sho Lin?" Jack asked.

"Totally," L. C. said. "Gunny has his days of nighttime companionship and then it's my turn. The day time chores are in addition to the nighttime duties."

"Can I ask how much does this all cost?" Jack asked.

"Sho Lin is paid the same as every other woman in the resort," Gunny said. "Six hundred a month plus room and board. For us, that's three hundred apiece. Add in rent on the bungalow of three hundred apiece which also covers the resort fees. Then we split about three hundred in food costs per month."

"And yeah, we've even cut that back from our previous cook. With Sho Lin's cooking we were putting weight on so we cut back a bit," L. C. said.

"Finally, incidentals like clothes and stuff add about another one hundred dollars per month," Gunny added.

"From the looks of things, you don't need much for clothes," Jack said.

"That's a fact. A couple of local shirts and shorts along with flip flops, and you're dressed for success here," Gunny said.

"So I got about seventeen hundred a month split two ways for you," Jack said.

"About right," L. C. said. "Add in the twenty-percent handling fee that Rising Sun takes out of our monthly checks and we're just at a thousand for the month."

"And with both our retirement checks almost double that, our bank account here in Thailand grows each month," Gunny offered.

"Tell him about Jersey," L. C. said.

"Oh yeah," Gunny said. "Actually things are even better than that. Ex-pats don't pay Uncle Sam's taxes if you're under ninety-five thousand a year in income and Thailand has very low taxes if you don't own any property, which we don't. So our extra money gets invested by Jersey, who used to run an offshore investment company in the Channel Islands. Everyone on the resort has accounts that he helps us with."

"The women too," L. C. added. "I think all the woman have accounts. With their room and board covered, they can save a lot each month. Depends how much they have to send back to their families. But the other money, Jersey knows how to keep it offshore and away from taxation so everyone does real well."

Jack was amazed at the entire enterprise. But somethings still bothered him.

"You said the women can't leave?"

"No, it's part of the disease control. Beaker and Gurkha run a tight ship here to keep us free from you know what," Gunny said.

"Short arm patrol?" Jack asked.

"Spoken like a Marine," Gunny answered. "There's a lot of AIDS in Thailand. If you came through Bangkok you might have seen how lose it is up there. The Japanese businessmen come in here on a quick sex holiday and spread all sorts of disease around."

"And who are Beaker and Gurkha exactly?" Jack asked.

"Beaker is a retired British Health Inspector," Gunny answered. "Gurkha spent twenty years in the British Army as a doctor before moving on to work in London. On retirement, they both landed here. They're our medial team, so to speak."

"So, everyone gets quarantined for two weeks before they're allowed entry to the resort, retirees and the women," L. C. explained. "If a retiree sneaks outside the walls, he's dismissed. Same as any of the women."

"So once inside, no one can leave?" Jack asked. *Seems a bit draconian to me,* he thought.

"Everyone gets two excused chances to leave," Gunny said. "The first time they have to sit out the two

305

week quarantine again. If they leave a second time, it's a thirty day quarantine. A third time outside and they don't come back."

"But why would anyone leave?" L. C. asked. "Food, shelter, water, warm weather, good friends and regular sex, what more can a man want?"

LaMarcus' uncle had Jack on that one. *Opposed to what: high taxes, snow, bitchy wives offering no sex with expensive tastes sucking one's retirement dry. There was no comparison,* Jack thought. *And here, you get to change sex partners once each year as a bonus.*

"And only six hundred a month?" Jack reiterated the monthly charge for female companionship. "I suppose you could have one all your own if you could afford it?"

"You can have two if you're so inclined," Gunny said.

"How many of you share?" Jack asked.

"About a third of us share one woman," Gunny said. "The rest all are solo couples. Except we still have a few triple couples, three men sharing one woman."

"But management isn't accepting any more of them," L. C. said. "We have a waiting list of retirees to get in here so management is being more selective now. The existing triples can stay but no new ones."

"This is so successful that management is building another resort just up the coast from us. It's already half subscribed to," Gunny said. "We can talk to Richter if you're interested."

Panzer finally joined in the conversation, "Ja, Richter, he do what I say. You want into the new resort, I speak to him for you."

"Well boys, I'm good right now, but I'll keep it in mind," Jack said. "I think right now I need to head back to Haad Rin so I can tell LaMarcus that you're alive and well. I also need to check on my companion. She probably needs some attention."

At the mention of a female being attached to Jack, all three men implored him to return and to bring his friend with him. Pressing why the interest, the retirees said that they had only seen Asian woman for a long time and while very pleasant, seeing a western woman had been missed.

"I'll ask her," Jack said, not sure what he would be getting her into.

"Good, we'll organize a picnic on the beach in both your honor," Gunny said.

"Management won't mind two outsiders sneaking in then?" Jack asked.

"I told you, Richter does what I tell him," Panzer growled. "You bring your friend, we have a party."

Chapter 37

The winter temperatures on the frozen lake were fitting for the ice fishermen as they sat in their warming huts scattered around the lake. On the eastern shoreline, Canobie Lake Park's amusement rides sat snow-covered and quiet. The summertime screams that would echo out across the lake were long silenced as the bitter cold stifled any noise.

The crunch of heavy boots announced an intruder to the small three-sided shelter protecting the fishermen. A thumb and a half-wave indicated it was time to put fishing gear away and head to the nearby warm cabin. Actually, more of a house, about half the houses on the lake held year-round residents.

The one the two men walked to was a summer place set by itself on the north side of the lake. That the two men were living in it was an act of extra work since the access road wasn't plowed to the house. Everything had to be brought in by sled the remaining three-hundred yards of snow-covered dirt road.

The cabin offered seclusion and that was what LaMarcus was looking for right now. Along with a fellow retired Cambridge cop, they had arrived yesterday. After the email LaMarcus had received, a new plan had been designed.

Stripping out of his extra heavy camouflage jump suit, LaMarcus was sweating from the effort in the warm living rom. A roaring wood fire had the cabin almost too warm and his friend shut down the damper to reduce the fire. He would open it back up upon his return, but first, he had a delivery.

Driving LaMarcus's Cadillac to nearby Manchester, LaMarcus thanked his friend and headed into the bus station. Carrying only a small bag with a change of clothes and a guitar case, LaMarcus paid cash for a one-way ticket to Boston where he would catch Amtrak to Phoenix.

After a short wait in South Station, the train pulled in. Stepping onto the train, LaMarcus settled in for a three day endurance ride west. *At least I can get out of these heavy clothes*, he thought. Phoenix had been in the eighties the day before when he had checked the train schedule. But he'd have to wait some before the shorts came out.

It had been Gary's neighbor's message that had forced his trip west. Gary had been killed in a shoot-out in his home. Luckily, the ex-Marine had managed to kill three of the perpetrators before succumbing himself. A bad guy had presumably survived as the home was soon engulfed in flames as someone attempted to hide the evidence.

Quick work by the Henderson Fire Department meant the crime scene still offered enough clues as to how it all had happened. When LaMarcus heard the identity of one of the dead suspects, LaMarcus knew he had unfinished business in Las Vegas.

Knowing his parole officer from thirty years on the police force, he also knew that the guy was a little bent. Always in debt from his women activities, LaMarcus knew that a little money could cover his quiet trip to Nevada. He would be covered in his absence while his friend at the remote New Hampshire cabin gave him an alibi. Any law enforcement looking into the whereabouts after the fact would hear that LaMarcus had been ice fishing the entire time.

For what needed to be done, LaMarcus figured he wouldn't be gone that long. Three days on the train each way combined with maybe a week in Vegas, he'd be back in under two weeks. That was if Jack could catch up with him. He'd placed the Skype call to his friend in the Thailand hotel and explained what had happened. Jack said he'd meet LaMarcus in Phoenix in three days.

LaMarcus pulled out Jack's book and opened it to the first page. He hadn't had time to start reading it and the train ride offered plenty of time.

* * *

The call had come in the middle of the night in Thailand. Jack had his laptop and the hotel had Wi-Fi service. Leaving the computer running in case of such an event, Jack wasn't prepared for the news.

Katarina sat pensively on the edge of the bed listening to a one-sided conversation. With his headphones on, she only caught Jack's infrequent replies in between the caller's long talks. Knowing that good news doesn't come in the middle of the night, she was ready when Jack pulled off the headphones and closed the computer.

"Gary is dead," was all Katarina heard as she buried her face in her hands and began sobbing. Jack took her in his arms and held her tight.

"How? Why?" she demanded.

Jack told her the story as LaMarcus had relayed it to him. She sat straight up when he mentioned who had been identified among the bodies in the burnt house.

"You mean Ernesto is behind it?" she asked.

"Seems like he's taking his threat to LaMarcus to whomever he can find," Jack said.

"So you and LaMarcus will show up in Las Vegas and he can eliminate you two," Katarina said.

"Maybe."

"You're going, aren't you?" Katarina asked.

"LaMarcus is already on his way from Boston. I have to scramble to catch up," Jack offered.

"That would be we remember. We're in this together," Katarina said.

"No way," Jack said. "That little arrangement was when we were searching for LaMarcus's uncle. Well, we found him. Our deal is done."

"Look here Jack Wesley, I knew Gary as long as you did. He saved me from the same man in the night club that night. I owe him." Katarina said it like the Marines that Jack had heard before.

Jack looked at the young Dutch woman with different eyes. He studied her long stare that she gave him with her defiance showing.

"Ok, you can make the trip," Jake said. "But contingent on what LaMarcus and I decide to do will determine how involved you are. Agreed?"

"Agreed," the Dutch woman said.

They got busy on the computer making travel reservations. There were no seats on any flight out of Surat Thani the next day but they did secure space on the first flight the following day. From Bangkok, Jack made reservations to Mexico City with a connector flight to Cabo San Lucas.

Next, he pulled his head phones back on and clicked on the Skype icon on his computer. He searched for a name and selected it. Katarina sat and listened again as Jack made further arrangements. It would be tight, but if all the connections worked as planned, they would make their date in Phoenix.

By the time they were done, the morning glow on the ocean announced a new day. Katarina suddenly remembered her commitment to Uta. She instructed Jack to get back on line and book a third seat out of Surat Thani airport to Bangkok with a connection to Mumbai, India. When Jack hesitated slightly, Katarina filled him in on what name the seat should be reserved.

Which left them in Haad Rin for the day. They planned on taking the last ferry off the island that afternoon and staying the night near the airport. They would catch a taxi and be ready for the early morning flight.

Tea and coffee were collected as soon as the kitchen had things set out in the dining area. Another warm day was in store as the two took a table by the pool. Uta soon arrived, coffee in hand.

"Uta, we leave tonight," Katarina said. "We've booked you with us on the flight to Bangkok where you'll catch your flight to India. Just be ready about four this afternoon."

"I don't know if I can do it," Uta said.

"Just have your things ready," Jack said. "We'll make sure you get away."

"But Marche will be so mad. I just can't risk it."

"If you don't go now, you'll never get away," Katarina said. "Is that what you want? You told me how being with her makes you feel."

"It's terrible, I just don't know what I should do," Uta said.

"Stand up for yourself," Jack said. "Don't ever let anyone control you or make you do something you don't want. Even if she represents the Sexual Workers Freedom Alliance."

Katarina looked at Jack. She had told him of her conversation with Marche the previous morning. Now he was backing her up in helping Uta.

"Well, isn't this a cozy confab," the heavy voice of Marche announced itself.

Uta immediately began shaking as the older Belgian sat down at the table. She looked at her partner.

"Uta, you should run up to your room and grab something to put on, you're shivering," Katarina offered.

Uta took the suggestion and sprinted back into the hotel. Marche looked suspiciously at her two remaining table mates.

Katarina quickly changed the focus, "So, locate that sex resort you were looking for?"

"I'm surprised, none of the locals know anything," Marche said. "I found a resort right up the road here but the man that answered at the entrance didn't offer anything. I tried to look through the fence but the vegetation was to thick too see much."

"That's too bad," Katarina lied. Jack looked in her direction and got the raised eyebrow glance in return.

Marche was staring out at the rising sun as it lifted itself out of the ocean, its rays growing in intensity each second.

"Yeah, I can't figure," Marche said. "You'd think they'd know about such things. And if they did, they'd want our help in eradicating such a disgusting thing."

"Why?" Jack asked.

Marche turned a jaundiced eye toward the male at the table. "Why what?" she asked.

"Why would they want your help in shutting down a resort that offers sex, among other things?" Jack asked. "You don't want them exploiting gardeners that work to make the resort beautiful. Or farmers who work in hot fields with poisonous snakes growing food to sell to the resort. You don't want those people exploited, and I see from walking by them, some are women out in the fields risking their lives."

"Are you flipping serious?" Marche asked. "You're comparing honest women farmers to sex workers? You're out of your mind."

"But the sex workers don't risk death every day like the women in the fields," Jack offered. "One bite of a red-headed krait snake and they might walk ten feet before dropping over dead."

"What about AIDS? That's a death sentence," Marche almost screamed.

"Easily avoided with precautions," Jack countered. "A well-run organization would protect its chief assets."

"Their women, your damn right about that."

"Not only the women, but more importantly, the paying customers. If the men all contract diseases, they would no longer be with us to purchase more product," Jack said. "Seems simple to me. Keep everyone healthy and the money keeps flowing."

"I can't believe I'm having this conversation," March muttered. "You're a male so you can't understand the suffering these women go through. Man after man clawing at them all day and night. It's disgusting."

"Maybe in some places it's like that," Jack said. "But lets suppose a place exists where the men and women live together as couples. Good medical staff keep disease at bay even with semi-monogamous relationships going on. The women provide a needed service of companionship, care, cleaning and cooking."

"And sex. Naked old men groping young innocent girls, all for money," Marche said.

Katarina looked directly at her as Marche realized what she had just said. She began to backtrack slightly but Jack was right there.

"And is there something wrong with older people finding companionship with younger people? If both are consenting adults, who's to say where love and caring spring from?"

"But it's the patriarchal suppression of women that keep women subservient to men. Cleaning and cooking and spreading their legs, all for the mighty male," Marche said.

"So, should we have Uta come down here so we can ask her about the matriarchal dominance that seems to be springing forth all around the world?" Jack shot back. "Do you think she would agree with you about the goodness and light that women hold for their fellow women."

Jack saw Katarina's expression at his bringing Uta into the discussion. He skewered on.

"And would she claim that all men are pigs while all women are saints?"

Marche stammered as her anger rose faster than her mouth. Red-faced, she opened her mouth to respond, spittle flying out.

"You're a real asshole. Take your shitty male attitude and shove it." And she was gone, headed to the hotel room.

Two remained at the table, sitting in silence for a long pause. Finally Katarina said, "Jack, you shouldn't have gotten Uta involved. We have to get her away this afternoon and we don't need Marche intimidating Uta into staying."

"You let me worry about our dominatrix. Let's go pack, you're invited to a picnic. Maybe Uta would like to go too?" Jack asked. Jack stopped on the way to their room to settle their bill.

Reaching their room, they quickly packed and stepped into the hallway. Yelling could be heard a short distance down the hall where a loud voice was berating someone.

Noting the door not fully closed, Jack pushed his way into the room. Marche turned on him like a viper.

"Get out now," Marche demanded.

Ignoring the older woman completely, Jack addressed the younger one. "Which bag is yours? We've had a change of plans, we're leaving now."

A stunned Uta pointed at her bag. With the contents spilling, Jack shoved Uta's things into the bag and grabbed the handles. Uta quickly grabbed the few remaining items she could see that belonged to her as Katarina helped her. The two women left the room as Jack blocked the way for Marche.

"I'll call the cops," Marche screamed. She made a move to step into the hallway to grab Uta. Jack blocked the move with Uta's bag and Marche fell backwards onto the bed.

Jack stepped into the hallway and slammed the door shut. He got the two women moving out of the hotel. A screaming crazy woman sprinted out of her room aimed squarely at Uta. Reaching them, Jack swung Uta's bag, again knocking the Belgium onto her back side. The three ran out of the hotel and headed north on the dirt road.

Jack looked behind and saw their tormentor rise up and gather herself. She took up a chase after them, but Jack knew his way and directed the two women into the forest. Moving quickly down the short hill, they found the fence line and followed it to the beach. Jack kept them moving under the crippled chain link fence into the resort.

If what he knew might be ahead, they would be safe. He turned to see Marche gaining as she slipped through the fence gap. But up ahead was his relief. The big German was working his Thai charge hard running toward them on the beach. Recognizing Jack, Panzer smiled and waved, redoubling his speed forward.

With Jack pointing out the charging woman behind them, Panzer recognized the threat immediately. Stopping Katarina and Uta from any further attempt at escape, he turned to watch.

"Halt!" the big German yelled.

Marche continued her sprint toward Uta, ignoring the large man in her way.

"Halt, ist verboten." His voice boomed over the beach and Marche suddenly realized what was about to happen. But her momentum was too much as she ran up to where the German stood.

Panzer lunged as Marche tried to reverse direction. He dropped her onto the sand on her stomach and shoved one knee into her back. Grabbing one hand, he yanked it backwards. Marche let out a scream which only made two more large Germans appear from no where.

One of the new arrivals produced a snap tie and handed it to Panzer. He lashed her two hands behind her and yanked her upright.

"You can't do this to me, Marche yelled. "I'll call the Belgium Embassy. You're in big trouble."

The second German security guard produced a cloth that Panzer wrapped around Marche's mouth. She struggled to free herself and kicked Panzer in the leg. She was summarily dropped hard, her face driven into the sand. Another snap tie around her ankles stopped any leg flailing. But still Marche persisted.

Now yelling through the gag, or attempting to yell, and struggling with her wrist and ankles bound, a third snap tie bound the woman's legs and arms together. With one German on each side, they grabbed her ankles and carried her as a deer on a stick is carried by hunters.

"Panzer, thank you," Jack said.

"Kein problem, Herr Mr. Wesley. As you can see, we do control undesirables from entering our resort," Panzer said.

"What will you do with her? We leave tonight and if you could hold her 'til tomorrow, that would help," Jack said.

"You don't know how things work around here then," Panzer offered. "The resort spends plenty of money in the local economy. We have farms that supply our food, fisherman that sell us their catch of fish, workers we hire for building our new resort up the road. We are very much appreciated by the local authorities. Many of our woman are daughters of locals. The money they earn here goes to support the entire family."

"So we can assume she'll be out of our way for the next day?" Jack asked.

"I'm afraid that she has stepped into more than she realized," Panzer said. "The last intruder got six months hard labor in the district jail. And that one didn't resist anything like your friend today. I think we can guarantee a year for her, especially since the resort will pay the cost of her upkeep. You can be sure of a year with no trouble from that one."

Uta smiled weakly at the news as Katarina held the young Belgian. Jack shook Panzer's hand, thanking the German.

"I'll see you at the picnic, but now I need to meet the local officials and get our intruder squared away," Panzer said.

Jack led the two women on up the beach while the Thai woman that had been Panzer's focus drifted over. She bowed to Jack numerous times, smiled broadly and joined them as they headed off the beach toward L. C.'s bungalow.

Chapter 38

Haad Rin, Thailand

By the time they had reached L. C.'s bungalow, Jack and the three women had gathered a following. Word spread rapidly through the resort that Western women were on the premises. Rumors from the previous day that two guests were being feted for lunch had the men excited.

While they enjoyed the company of their Asian companions thoroughly, some had not seen a Western woman in a few years. That one would be their guest was special. That two had shown up this morning was unbelievable. Jack led the entourage along the gravel walkway until it reached L. C.'s.

Standing on the porch were Gunny and L. C. who commented to everyone on respecting the privacy of their guests. The retirees grudgingly dispersed knowing they had to prepare a picnic.

"We're quite the celebrities," Jack commented.

Gunny looked longingly over the two young women standing at the bottom of his steps. He motioned them welcome to the cabin.

"Come in," Gunny offered. "I don't know about you, but these two lovely ladies are certainly celebrity status around here."

"Goed, dank u," Katarina said. "You must be Gunny. You're just as Jack described you." Then turning to L. C. she added, "And you must be Uncle Joe. LaMarcus has told me so much about you."

Feeling like family, L. C. took the opportunity to give Katarina a long embracing hug followed by a kiss on the cheek. Seeing the younger Belgian standing alone, L. C. gave her a similar welcome.

"Wow, merci," Uta said. "I feel part of the family now."

Inviting them in for breakfast, Gunny led everyone to the kitchen where Sho Lin was busy cooking for her guests. When Jack walked in, Sho Lin turned and bowed to him several times. She immediately handed him an English Breakfast Tea just a she liked it.

"Boy, some one around here receives special treatment," Katarina said.

Jack jumped to explain, "Yesterday when I sort of turned my nose up at the green tea I was offered, Gunny passed on that I only drank English Breakfast Tea. A quick trip next door to their British neighbors produced the right stuff."

"I don't see anyone else being handed tea when they walk into the room," Katarina said. Her sarcasm carried with a smile. "And the bows, what's with that?"

"Just Asian hospitality," Jack offered, hoping the conversation would move on.

Food on plates soon appeared along with coffee. The women, realizing the small table had limited space, offered to take breakfast out on the deck. Along with Panzer's Thai woman, Katarina and Uta walked outside. They pulled three chairs together on the porch and sat down to enjoy Sho Lin's cooking.

"I can see why these men enjoy it here so much," Katarina said. "This food is wonderful."

The Belgian looked at Katarina and smiled. She didn't know what type of place they were in, just that she was away from her tormentor. That the resort staff had spirited Marche away with assurances that she would not see the light of day for a long time added to her relaxed state.

But the Thai woman understood the comment. "Oh yes, men here very much like good cooking."

Startled, the two Europeans looked at her. Learning that her name was Soraya, Katarina had numerous questions looking for answers.

"Soraya, your English is very good," Katarina said. "How long have you been here?"

"I new girl last year," Soraya answered. "I was very bad. Panzer teach me how to be best girl. Now I know how to take care of my man."

"Did he beat you?" Katarina asked.

"Oh no, Panzer make me work very hard," Soraya said. "Make up for all work I no do last year. I lucky I still working here."

"You enjoy working here with all that you have ot do?" Katarina asked.

"No so much work. I have most mornings off, then an hour cleaning and an hour cooking. Two, maybe three hours a day not much," Soraya explained. "If I'm back in my village I work eight hours in fields. Then have duties around house, cooking, sewing, weaving, cleaning, taking care of kids."

"But they have work for women in the cities," Uta said.

"Oh, very hard," Soraya offered. "Sew running shoes twelve hours a day, go back to cramped apartment and cook and sleep. Share room with five other women working in factory. Then maybe factory catch fire and burn all women alive. Very bad."

"But you have to sleep with the men here. And do, you know . . ." Katarina said.

"Bang bang with old men. No problem," Soraya matter-of-fact stated. "Most time just sleep. Once per week, maybe have bang bang time. One hour of work, rest sleep time. Unless I get two men to take care of, then bang bang two times in week."

"You have to have sex with these men?" Uta asked, finally realizing what type of resort she was on.

"Oh yes, sex is fine," Soraya answered. "If your man really old, not even bang bang in month. They happy just holding in bed, no bang bang. Even easier work then. But younger ones, can be plenty busy. But that OK too."

"You like bang bang?" Uta asked.

"Sure thing. You no like bang bang?"

Uta looked away a little embarrassed at the question. As they talked, Katarina noticed some of the men quietly filtering back into the clearing in front of the cabin. With three other cabins circling L. C.'s cabin, they were joining the neighbors in a respectful observation of the two European women. Far enough away to provide some privacy but close enough to see.

"Well you're very beautiful. Surely you could get a job other than here," Uta said.

"But I have bad attitude, Panzer told me," Soraya said. "I not work hard to make my man happy last year.

Now I have to work extra hard. Still more easy than any other job I know of for Thai woman."

"But to get paid for having sex, that's not right," Uta said.

"What not right?" Soraya asked. "You have sex, make bang bang?" The Thai woman looked at Uta, waiting for an answer. Uta nodded that she had sex.

"You get paid for it, or you give it away for free?" Soraya pressed.

"But sex shouldn't be for sale," Uta offered.

"Why not? Everything else in world for sale. Why can't I make money off what I do well?" Soraya asked.

"But the diseases."

"No diseases here. Beaker and Gurkha very smart," Soraya answered. "All girls very healthy. Men too. No drip drip problem here. Not like Bangkok girls."

"How do you not have diseases if you bang bang all the time?" Uta asked.

"I get checked by Gurkha two times each month. Men too. I stay very clean," Soraya said. "My man, only bang bang with me. No other girls allowed with my man. And no rear bang bang."

The two other women looked and tried to translate what rear bang bang meant. Their answer came from Gunny, L.C. and Jack stepping out onto the porch. They looked up with a quizzical look.

Gunny offered an answer, "That's right. Gurkha says the poop shut is off limits. And no one messes with the doc. You break the health rules and you're history."

"I've heard of the no fudge packing rule before at their resort in Nevada," Jack said.

325

L.C.'s face lit up in recognition, "Why didn't we think of that? I bet that's why Pacman got kicked out for going over the wall. He was heading into the village for a little rear-door action."

"Pacman?" Jack asked. "It fits his name."

"It sure do, now that you mention it," Gunny said.

"So this is the sex resort my friend was looking for," Uta said.

"Well, we're a hell of lot more than a sex resort," Gunny said. "First, there is companionship. Most of these retirees were divorced or single back in the country they came from. Companionship was hit or miss unless they were lucky. We've eliminated the luck factor here because every man is guaranteed a woman's companionship."

"But at what price?" Uta asked.

"Fairly reasonable as a matter of fact," Gunny continued. "There are some here that are wealthy, but the majority are like me and L. C.. We have a good retirement but nothing that would attract a lot of feminine interest back home."

"But paying for sex, it's not right," Uta said.

"You're young and have some lessons to learn yet," Gunny said. "Trust me, my marriage cost me plenty every month so I could get sex. And the longer it went on, I experienced less return on my expenses. That former Beatle found out the hard way how expensive sex is when his lovely bride divorced him after four years and took him to the cleaners."

"But marriage is a union of two people that love each other," Uta said.

"Maybe at first, but give it time and it soon becomes a struggle of money and sex," Gunny said.

Jack offered his insight. "I read an article by a famed psychologist whose argument was that marriage is an unfair trade-off. She mentioned that the majority of women dream of a husband, a home and children. Men dream of lying naked on a tropic beach with multiple naked women. Now, which one of the two gets to follow their dream? She concluded that men deserve tremendous credit for giving up their dream so a woman could fulfill hers."

"Hear, hear," L. C. added. "Gunny, we get to fulfill our dreams every day here."

"But at the expense of the local Thai women," Uta said.

"We don't hear too many complaints," Gunny said. "In fact, management says we have a waiting list of women who want to work here."

"Only because they have no other options."

"Well, until they do, I guess we're in business," Gunny said.

* * *

Jack noticed Katarina avoiding the discussion while staring off toward nothing in particular. He reached down and pulled her out of chair and took her off into the forest.

"What's bothering you?" Jack asked.

"All the talk of marriage just got me to thinking, that's all," she answered.

"About yours in particular?"

"I don't have a marriage. These women working this resort have more of marriage than I do. When I see the joy in Sho Lin's face just in bringing you tea. And talking to Soraya, she understands what it takes to keep her man happy after Panzer's education."

"And you don't have that?"

"I know how to make a man happy, you taught me that. Along with what makes me happy," Katarina said. "But I'm married to a boy. He doesn't understand anything but his own lust and where he can put it."

"And it doesn't include you?"

"Thank god, no. Let him bang bang all those groupies that are attached to him day and night."

Jack let the moment linger before asking, "So, we haven't talked about it for some time, but have you decided to do something?"

"Would you like me to do something about it?" Katarina asked.

Jack hesitated again. "Katarina, what you do about your marriage is between you and your husband. That is a very personal decision that only you can decide. I've been through it myself without much of a choice. My wife left me for another man. I understand why she left, but that still didn't help the pain much."

She's looking for more, Jack thought. The age difference held him back. Katarina deserved a life with a man her own age who truly loved her. They needed to have a family and live a life together raising that family.

I'd be seventy-five when any child I had graduated from high school, Jack thought. *And Katarina would be forty-two. She would be in the prime of her life taking care of an old man.*

The conversation drifted to silence as each one wanted to avoid further discussion. They headed back to join the others where Gunny was ready to start the festivities. More of the retirees had gathered outside the cabin as Jack and Katarina walked into the discussion.

"We've decided, we're all going to take a jaunt on the beach and then a dip in the ocean. You do have swim suits, don't you?" Gunny asked.

Jack answered that a run and dip sounded delightful while Katarina smiled her answer. They motioned to Uta that she was invited too as they grabbed their luggage and disappeared into a bedroom to change.

"Will this one do?" Katarina asked.

Jack was pulling on his Big Dog nylon shorts and looked up. Katarina was standing naked holding one of her two suits. It was the more conservative one since it was larger than a handkerchief.

"No, I think the boys need a thrill," Jack offered.

"I should go naked then?" she asked.

"Spoken like a born naturalist, but no, I think the shock might be too much for some of the old timers," Jack said.

"OK, this one." Katarina slipped into her thong bikini bottom. Straightening out the skimpy top, she put her arms through the straps, got each breast covered slightly and hooked the front clasp.

Jack stood and admired the result. "Yes, that should stir something. Should be a lot of bang bang going on tonight."

They stepped into the hallway as Uta emerged from the other bedroom. She had a partial thong bottom and a similar skimpy top. Lacking the full figure of Katarina, she still filled out her top in a respectable manner.

As the three waited for their hosts, Gunny, L. C. and Sho Lin finally stepped out of the third bedroom. While the two former Marines had similar shorts to Jack, Sho Lin's petite body was covered by the smallest bikini that Jack figured he'd ever seen on a grown woman.

Word had spread quickly and by the time they reached the beach, the entire resort community was waiting. With close to eight-hundred men and women, Jack was stunned when he realized how many people called the resort home.

"Mr. Wesley, let me introduce you to our manager, Richter," Panzer offered.

"Jack please. And let me thank you for your generosity allowing us the privilege of visiting. I know you don't have many visitors."

"None to be exact,''" Richter said. "You are our first since we opened."

Beaker and Gurkha were introduced and Gurkha got right to the point as he looked over the three guests.

"Gunny tells me you've already heard about our strict disease control that we practice here," Gurkha said.

"Yes, my compliments on no STD's. The outside world could learn a thing or two from you," Jack offered.

"It's in the vein of that outside world that I need to mention something," Gurkha said. "As our first ever outsiders, I have to ask if any of you intend to have sex with any of our occupants, male or female? This may seem like a rather personal question, but as described, we take disease control very seriously."

Jack looked at two startled women beside him and prodded them for a response. Each one shook their head no.

"No, I think we're good. We will refrain from any sexual activity while on the premises. You have our word," Jack said.

"Good, let's get some exercise then," Richter said. "We try to get everyone moving every day. But I've never seen a turn out like this."

Richter turned to Katarina and Uta to ask if they would lead the procession at a slow pace. The two European women led off in a slow jog down the beach. Jack fell in with Richter behind them but off to the side. The other four-hundred or so men all attempted to jog right behind the two leading woman. The beach was about a mile long, and about half way to the end, Katarina turned to Jack.

"The pace fine?" she asked.

"Looks good," Jack said as he turned to look at the parade.

The younger men were keeping up but as the age and infirmities grew, men lagged further behind. Jack figured most were the regulars at the pool side chair sitting exercise that Richter had just been describing. But the added treat of the guests had brought everyone to the beach.

Worrying that some would expire at the effort, Jack was glad when they reached the end of the beach. Turning around, now the two women would be running straight at the entire male troupe. Most just stopped in their spot to admire the view as it came bouncing toward them. Jack watched as they passed each one who would stare with mouth wide open before turning to stare at the rear view.

Soon, everyone was back at the start ready for the dip. The local women had been setting up for the picnic with chairs and umbrellas all around. Food was being brought from the cabins and placed on tables.

Some of the women joined in the swim and Soraya was right next to Jack splashing. He noticed Katarina become aware of where Jack was and made her way through her adoring fans to Jack.

"Having fun over here?" she asked.

"It's hard to get near you from all the adoring fans you have," Jack offered.

"Yes, I have been offered a place to stay if I wanted to join the resort."

"Only one? I'm disappointed," Jack teased.

"Uta told me she's had five offers so far. Seems the boys all recognize that you and I are sort of attached already."

"Might do her some good working here for a year. Help her grow up and realize the important things in life," Jack said.

"You mean it's not all about bang bang?" Katarina said,.

"Well, whatever the other side calls it, she found out from Marche that those who swing the other way don't have all goodness and love for their partners. Maybe what the men here have is just as worthy or more so."

"How?" Katarina asked.

"Talking to Richter as we ran he said the women are instructed to report any man abusing them in any way, verbal or physical. Besides no rear bang bang, there's no bondage or other off the charts sex play. The women are not allowed to have sex with anyone other than their partner. So any man offering money for a neighbor's woman is in trouble. At the time of the contract the men can hire more than one woman if that's what they want. But no sneaking out."

"So Soraya's talk of Panzer's treatment fits how?"

"Panzer is responsible for training any woman that doesn't understand their role here. And he only works them hard. No hitting. But his verbal can get strong sometimes. But he's the only one."

Uta made her way over to the two of them as most of the men drifted out of the water. They seemed to discover that the view was more relaxing sitting and watching. The three outsiders found themselves alone.

"So, Uta, you going to take up an offer to stay?" Jack asked. He was only giving her a hard time and never expected her answer.

"I'm thinking about it," Uta replied.

"Are you serious?" Katarina asked.

"Richter was one of the ones asking. He isn't so old," Uta said.

Jack looked at Richter and figured him to be about fifty. Younger than the over fifty-five crowd the resort required for membership. That she was considering the offer set him back.

"But you know what the duties are, right?" Katarina asked.

"As Soraya said, I give it away now, and look where it got me," Uta said. "Tropical beach, two hours a day working, room and board are covered and I pocket six hundred a month free and clear. Some guy named Jersey even offered to set me up with an off-shore account and teach me the fine points of investing."

"You could learn a lot here," Jack offered.

"I agree," Uta said. "What's back in Belgium? No work, university too expensive and everyone my age on the dole. All they want to do is get high and get laid. If I can learn a career here and I only have to spread my legs once a week, doesn't sound too bad."

"You might get more interest than that from Richter," Jack advised.

"So, more is fine. I mean, look at you two. The age thing doesn't seem to hold you back," Uta said.

The comment stifled further conversation as both Jack and Katarina realized what they looked like to an impressionable eighteen-year old. Katarina was only a few years older than her and Jack definitely had a few years on Richter. The silence grew as the three stood in the warm sea water.

"I'm sorry if I said something I shouldn't have," Uta finally said. "It's just you two helped me so much. And then to see this place and how happy everyone seems to be. Do you know how many of my friends have either herpes or chlamydia? Neither one ever goes away. Just having sex and not worrying about that is a plus."

"You realize that you have to go through a two-week isolation before you can join everyone. And once inside, you can't really leave."

"That's fine. If I can study with this guy Jersey, I don't need to go outside. I figure it's as good as a four year-university degree. And I'm getting paid," Uta said.

"And you'll be the only western woman here. Do you think the local woman will like that?" Jack said. "They can't say much if you're with management, but they might shun you."

"Yeah, I hadn't thought of that," Uta said. "I'll talk it over with Soraya."

Uta swam off toward the beach. Jack noticed eight-hundred eyeballs following her every stroke. *At least the ones that could see that far*, he thought.

"Well, that's a shock," Jack said.

Katarina moved in close and wrapped her arms around him, kissing him. She tipped her head slightly so her mouth was next to his ear and whispered.

"Maybe we should see if we can join?" she said. "Someone mentioned they have a secluded beach that's reserved for one couple at a time. Now, what do you suppose goes on there?"

"If you forgot, we have a job to do back in Las Vegas. After that, we can discus all options," Jack said.

At the mention of Las Vegas and their friend that had died a violent death, both grew quiet. Katarina took Jack's hand and led him toward the beach. They needed to finish their visit. A plane tomorrow would take them back to reality. A reality that shouted out for retribution.

Chapter 39

Cabo San Lucas, Mexico

Uta had decided that staying in Thailand outweighed returning to Europe. When Jack reached Bangkok, he had the time to cancel her ticket to India and get a credit. But the plane seat to Bangkok had been lost. *Oh well, my contribution to L. C.'s generous hospitality*, Jack thought. *Who knows, maybe someday I'll want to join them.*

Before he and Katarina had left, Richter gave a full tour. They had seen the hospice cabin where the dying members got round-the-clock care by two Thai nurses the resort employed. Richter explained that some of the older women when they reached the retirement age for being a companion sometimes hooked up with an older retiree. If they got married, they had to leave the resort. But management, with the wealthier members contributing, had built a small group of cabins near a village on the other side of the island where they could live out their days together.

Those that stayed would be cared for until their death. Their bodies would be cremated and shipped back to any family member on record. Lacking that, the ashes were scattered in the ocean off the beach.

Jack and Katarina discussed Uta's choice through the entire flight from Bangkok to Amsterdam. With a short stop and a transfer in Paris, their long flight landed in Mexico City. Jack had booked them the long way around to avoid landing in the United States. He wanted to avoid their official entrance until the correct time.

Jack had worked out a basic plan with LaMarcus after the call about Gary's death. It required a delicate entrance into the United States and to accomplish that, Jack had called a friend. With their flight from Mexico City to Cabo San Lucas, he was about to discover if the second part of the plan was going to work.

Clearing Customs, Jack grabbed a cab and threw their two bags in the trunk. Katarina climbed in the back seat as Jack told the driver the destination, a hotel by the boat marina reserved from Bangkok.

Jack figured they had about two days to wait for their ride north. He knew the ride was on its way from the email he had received announcing that the Mexican border had been crossed. A message from LaMarcus announced that he was crossing Texas and that all lights were green. The first part of the plan was proceeding on time.

Two days later, Jack spied what they had been waiting for while sitting by the pool overlooking the boat harbor. A catamaran sailboat lowered its sail as it motored into the harbor. Tapping a lounging Katarina to announce that relax time was over, Jack got them moving.

With bags in hand, the two passengers walked out on the dock as a Mexican Customs official passed them heading toward land. Reaching the catamaran tied up on the outside of the dock, he hailed the captain. A familiar face appeared out of the bridge cabin.

"Marta, I'm glad you could help us out," Jack greeted his old friend. Marta had been the boat captain when Jack had to race across the Pacific Ocean to find a kidnap victim.

"Jack, you always call me needing something," Marta said. "You could just stop by for a beer sometime, you know."

"I know," Jack said. "I could be a better friend. But I appreciate the help."

As Katarina walked up, Jack introduced the two women. They sized each other up before speaking.

"Welcome aboard," Marta said. "And just to set the record straight, Jack and I have never."

"Thanks for the commentary Marta," Jack offered. "But Katarina is familiar with my past."

"Nice to meet you. Thanks for helping out," Katarina said.

Jack noticed her checking the boat captain over a little more sternly. He knew he would need to defuse any more idle talk.

"I'll grab the lines and we can head out," Jack said.

"Doesn't a girl even get to step foot on land? A cold beer would be nice," Marta complained.

"No time I'm afraid. LaMarcus is probably already in Phoenix waiting. We've got some sailing to do," Jack said.

"You didn't say this was a Jack-and-LaMarcus deal," Marta complained.

"I'm sure this is the last time," Jack said as he shoved the boat away from the dock.

Marta had started the engine and as he jumped on board, the big cat moved ahead. Marta swung the wheel over and aimed for the tip of the Baja. As she motored around the last bit of Baja California Sur, Jack helped raise the sails. With the engine shut down, the quiet groan of the mast took over as the catamaran sliced through the water heading north.

With two hulls holding separate cabins, Jack and Katarina had their own stateroom and head. Marta occupied the opposite hull. In between, a cabin stretched between the hulls on a bridge over the ocean. This held the common area with a galley, salon, chart table and an inside helm. Safely out of the weather, the boat could easily be operated from inside except for sail changes.

Jack settled down on a settee with a glass of red wine. Marta sat at the helm checking that the auto-pilot was doing its job.

"Thanks again for the ride," Jack said. "It won't be a problem taking us back in about two weeks, will it?"

"No, I love sailing up and down Baja with illegals sneaking in and out of the States," Marta said.

"For what we have to do, having a cover in Mexico will be handy."

"And LaMarcus?"

"He's got a cover in New Hampshire. He's ice fishing and out of touch," Jack offered.

"You two will be the death of me yet. And does Katarina know what she's getting into with you to?" Marta asked.

"Does Katarina know what?" Katarina asked as she climbed the short ladder from the hull into the main cabin.

"Marta has suspicions as to why we're sneaking into Los Angeles without the proper paper trail," Jack said.

"Probably for the same reason you sneaked into Holland without border checks," Katarina answered.

The salon went deathly quiet except for the whoosh sound of seawater passing underneath. The two stared at Katarina.

"You certainly couldn't announce yourselves in Loosdrecht, now could you?" Katarina asked.

The answer would remain unanswered. The retribution Jack had sought in Loosdrecht was an unsolved murder. Somehow, Katarina was stumbling into the truth. Marta looked carefully at Jack as to what was to happen next.

"Katarina, you suppose you know the answer to Loosdrecht," Jack said. "You've put two and two together and think you have reached four. But it's a question that needs to lie silent. What happened there is done. What we are about to do is a whole new issue."

"I understand," Katarina said. "It won't come up again."

The trip north was moderately routine after that. Each took turns standing watch as the three hours on, six hours off routine took over. It left Jack time with Katarina but it also left him time alone to think.

The important part was getting done. When Gary's neighbor had called LaMarcus with the news, the neighbor had suspected what would happen. Being retired Army Special Forces, the neighbor let slip that he could do the recon on his friend's suspected killer.

Since LaMarcus had joined the neighborhood friends for a fishing trip to Lake Mead while he awaited his court date, the two men knew each other. But both knew that any action taken would be best left unsaid between them. The neighbor would supply information and then go back to his life in Henderson. When terrible news hit the local airwaves, it would be a surprise to the neighbor like everyone else.

Reaching reliable cell service as they approached San Diego, Jack checked his email. LaMarcus reported from Phoenix. Jack replied that they were close and shut things down.

Another day's sail and Marta aimed the sailboat toward Catalina Island, the lights of the ballroom on the point a visible marker to the harbor entrance. Before they reached the breakwater, Jack and Katarina lowered the dinghy from the stern. Jack unclipped the davits while he cinched the line holding the small boat to the catamaran.

As Marta lowered the sails and got the engine running, Katarina climbed down into the dinghy. Jack pulled to start the outboard. As soon as it was running, he reached around and slipped the line holding them to the big boat.

Jack set a course outside the breakwater where they waited for Marta to make her moorage. The harbormaster radioed instructions for her to pick up a buoy on the south side of the harbor. As she disappeared around the rock breakwater, Jack swung the small boat toward the north. They would land at the dinghy dock on the north end of the harbor. They could tie up, walk over to the ferry terminal and catch the last ferry to Long Beach.

Marta would return to work the next day teaching windsurfing at Marina Del Ray. She would be walking for a brief time since Jack was borrowing Marta's Subaru Forester after taking the bus north from Long Beach.

Jack reached under the car's seat and retrieved a thick envelope. He checked the large wad of cash it contained before placing it back under the seat.

Driving all night to Phoenix, they caught up to the rest of the team. LaMarcus waited in the lobby when they pulled into the motel in Sun City, north of Phoenix.

"'Bout time you two showed up," LaMarcus said.

"Hey, you travel half-way around the world and then sneak into the country. I'd like to see how long it would take you," Jack said.

"So what's the plan?"

"Sleep. Everything else can wait," Jack said. As he and Katarina started toward their room, he turned back to his friend, "Oh, and your uncle says hi."

Chapter 40

Sun City, Arizona

A call early the next morning from Gary's neighbor set the planning session in gear. While Katarina slept, Jack and LaMarcus met in the other motel room and went through their options. The neighbor, being retired Army, knew how to recon a target without being seen. The information he had gathered allowed a plan to be formulated.

By the time Katarina had shown up, the two men were ready. Needing supplies, Jack and Katarina headed to Home Depot in the Subaru to go shopping. As she pushed the cart, Jack selected the things they would need.

"A barbecue? Jack, really, a barbecue?" Katarina said.

Ignoring Katarina's questions, Jack pulled out a large box holding a disassembled grill. He slid it into the cart and walked ahead. Finding the aisle he needed, he grabbed a five-gallon plastic gas container. As Katarina caught up to him with the cart, she stopped and he placed the container in the cart. He thought for a moment, then grabbed a second container.

Katarina remained quiet after the non-response she had gotten on the barbecue question. Jack headed off toward check-out with the cart following.

"Excuse me, but where can I get my propane tank filled?" Jack asked the check-out attendant.

The man took Jack's cash payment and, after making change, told Jack that about a mile east on W.

Thunderbird Rd. there was a filling station that sold propane. Jack thanked him and motioned Katarina to head out to the car with their purchases.

Before he left though, Jack remembered one more thing. "I need to find a health food store nearby. My daughter only eats tofu, so I need to find some for the barbie."

"You'll pass Natural Foods Wholesale just before that filling station. They should have what you need," the clerk said.

Jack noticed him check out Katarina's backside as she pushed the cart out of the store. *That's right, just a father and daughter out buying party supplies, if any one comes asking*, Jack thought.

They discovered what they needed at Natural Foods Wholesale and loaded the two boxes in the back of the Subaru. Locating the filling station just past the natural food store, Jack got the attendant to fill the propane tank that came in the unassembled barbecue grill set.

Back at the motel, they unloaded the two boxes from the food store, leaving the remaining purchases in the car. Once in LaMarcus's room, Jack opened one of the boxes and pulled out the organic apple juice. The one-gallon glass container was summarily emptied into the bathroom sink and the now-empty container placed back in the box.

Katarina sat and watched the operation as Jack repeated the process, placing the now-emptied glass bottles back in the boxes. As he worked, he looked over at Katarina and recognized the quizzical stare.

"Did you want to drink some before I throw it all away?" he asked.

"No thank you," she offered.

Jack continued his work until all the juice was on its way to the sewer. He shoved the boxes over to the door and sat down on the bed. He looked at LaMarcus who had been busily studying the topographical map that he had purchased. An outdoor store located across the street from the motel provided his purchase. Noticing a guitar case shoved in LaMarcus's closet, Jack perked up.

"Since when did you take up playing the guitar?" Jack asked.

"Since I had to ride the train out here from Boston," he answered. He grabbed the case and placed it on the bed. Unbuckling the strap he had placed around it for added security, he unsnapped the latches. "And I didn't need anyone knowing I was carrying this."

LaMarcus flipped the lid open revealing something besides a musical instrument. Jack and Katarina both stared at the contents. A long narrow object wrapped in an old pair of sweatpants with Northeastern University stenciled down the leg filled the space.

"I can see why you couldn't fly, besides wanting to keep the myth that you're still in Boston," Jack said.

Jack reached in the case and unwrapped the object. He pulled the rifle out of one of the pant legs and held it to his shoulder. Aiming down the length of it while ignoring the scope mounted on the rail, Jack took a bead on an imaginary object.

"Yes, this will do nicely," Jack offered. ".308 caliber, AR-10, semiautomatic with a twenty-round mag."

He lowered the weapon down as he sat. With the rifle across his lap, he examined the scope. "Burris Red Dot sight backed up by a PVS14 3rd generation night vision. Yes, this will do very nicely. You bring ammunition for it?"

"Do bears shit in the woods?" LaMarcus asked. "Of course, both kinds."

"I know I'm a rookie at this and you two are the veterans, but can you tell me a little what's going to happen?" Katarina asked.

"The shit storm is about to hit Ernesto. Payback time for our friend Gary," LaMarcus said.

Jack didn't offer anything more and Katarina sat quiet. *At least she knows her place in all this,* Jack thought. *She's not pressing, that's good. There may be some things she doesn't need to know for her own sake.*

Jack and LaMarcus had already discussed their Dutch contingent to the operation. She might know more than they wanted about their past life, but the two men weren't totally on board with having her in on this operation. Going to war was serious business and it had always been a male pursuit for a reason. And Jack wanted to keep it that way unless they really needed her help.

Until they heard again from Gary's neighbor, Katarina was an alternate warrior for the team. And they expected that call in two days. Between now and then, they would reconnoiter their killing ground.

Checking out of the motel the next morning, they loaded everything in the Subaru. LaMarcus grabbed the back seat while Jack drove. Leaving Sun City, Jack turned north on Highway 93, headed for Las Vegas.

As they crossed the Colorado River, LaMarcus went to work with his topographical map. While he studied it and watched for the turnoff, Jack drove along like any other tourist with California plates. The Las Vegas area was full of California plates as the LA area fed gamblers in droves. One more California car just melted in with the locals.

Seeing a turn-off, LaMarcus told Jack to take a left. The gravel road headed off through the scrub brush and disappeared over a rise a mile away. From the rise, the three could see off to the right the top of the canyon that held the Colorado River. On this side of the main highway, it was backed up behind Hoover Dam.

LaMarcus's Marine Corps training as a sniper guided him to the spot that Gary's neighbor had described. The two former military men knew map coordinates and LaMarcus guided Jack to the spot they needed. Turning off the main gravel road, Jack headed cross-country toward Lake Mead.

Maneuvering around the intermittent brush clods, he weaved his way southeast. Patches of solid rock appeared as they drew closer to the top of Black Canyon. LaMarcus was busy with his map as Jack stopped the car. Rock outcroppings blocked any further progress and they would have to walk from here.

"It should be just ahead," LaMarcus said. He took out his compass and set the map down on a flat rock away from the car. Aligning his compass with the compass rose on the map, he bent down and took a reading on a large hill to the west. Moving himself to the other side of the rock, he bent down and took a reading on a peak to the northeast.

"We good?" Jack asked.

"Should be just over there." LaMarcus pointed to the southeast.

Katarina grabbed a small backpack and placed three water bottles in it. She threw it on her back just as Jack looked at her.

"I'll take that. You need to watch the car. Too many valuable things in it to have them stolen now," Jack said.

Leaving a disappointed looking Dutch guard with the car, the two men headed toward the cliff-top. It was a short half-mile scramble over rimrock to reach the break. Standing atop the cliff, the two looked down into a finger of the main lake.

The neighbor had been shadowing Ernesto since Gary's killing and as the neighbor had described things, Ernesto and his friends came out frequently on a houseboat to this spot. They would hang out and do whatever it was they did out here. Sometimes women would accompany them and sometimes women would show up the next day. But they generally anchored at this spot all weekend before returning on Sunday afternoon.

"Well, it all depends where they anchor," Jack said.

"Supposedly it's too deep on the other side, so they'll be on this side," LaMarcus said.

Jack looked up and down the canyon. It was a side canyon off the main lake with towering walls on both sides. No more than one hundred yards across at this point, the canyon curved and twisted around bends with only a short section visible from where they stood.

Satisfied that they had the right spot, they hiked quickly back to the car. Jack started the engine as Katarina climbed in the passenger door. He fiddled with the GPS on the dashboard attempting to set their location. It would be invaluable in returning to the same spot in the dark. His feeble attempts at programming drew Katarina's interest.

"Here, I can at least help with that," she offered. Jack sat back and let her take over. "Some things are best left to youth."

"Good thing you brought her," LaMarcus teased.

Jack didn't offer a rebuttal but shoved the car into gear when Katarina gave him the OK. The spot had been locked in the GPS and when the time came, should lead them back to the spot.

They weaved their way through the scrub once again and found the gravel road. Jack stopped and got out with a piece of yellow construction zone tape. He tied it on a bush just off the opposite side of the road. He climbed back in and drove off.

"What was that?" Katarina asked.

"A low-tech way to find our way back," Jack said. LaMarcus laughed loudly from the backseat.

Chapter 41

Henderson, Nevada

They had picked a nondescript motel on the outskirts of Henderson to await the phone call. All the equipment had been stored in LaMarcus's room. Final preparations were made as Jack ran to Las Vegas to find a filling station. The two plastic gas containers were soon filled with clear gas.

Jack had requested airplane gas for its lack of ethanol. Ethanol burnt at a lower temperature than real gasoline and Jack wanted as much heat as possible. The attendant didn't question the purchase as everyone used clear gas in their motorboats. With Lake Mead nearby, the station sold a lot of clear gas.

Jack then found a secluded spot west of Las Vegas where an empty road lead to an even emptier side road. He stopped in a wide spot and opened the back of the car. He placed the two gas containers outside and grabbed the first of the glass bottles. He filled each one carefully before returning it to the cardboard box.

With eight full glass bottles, he dumped the remaining gas into the Subaru's tank. Not wanting empty gas containers in the car, he placed the two plastic ones beside the road and placed a large rock on them to keep them from blowing away. He figured some off-road enthusiast would spot them and add them to their inventory.

Expecting the call at any time, the team was ready. The three waited in the motel room drinking water and grabbing something to eat from the sandwich shop across the street. Each was dressed in black with boots on, ready for the rough hike they had to do.

At seven that evening, LaMarcus's cell phone rang. He flipped open the disposable phone he had purchased in Phoenix. He listened without saying much and then hung up.

"Let's go, they're at the marina now," LaMarcus said.

"Everything set?" Jack asked.

"Ernesto and three body guards, laughing and carrying on and about to have a fun time on their houseboat."

"And no female guests?" Jack asked. He noticed Katarina's flash of concern.

"We're good," LaMarcus answered.

Katarina sat in a pensive state. As the two men loaded up the gear, she waited in her place. As Jack reached for the door knob, he turned to her.

"Come on, its payback time. Are you sure you want to be part of this?"

"OK, Jack. Just tell me what you want me to do," Katarina said.

"You grab LaMarcus's guitar. We'll need that tonight."

Katarina dutifully snatched the case and carefully carried it out to the car. She started to get in the back, when Jack pointed to the front passenger seat.

"We may need expertise on the GPS," Jack said.

"And that shit isn't coming from me," LaMarcus offered as he sat down in the back seat. "Kinda strong gas smell in here. Your friend going to appreciate her car back with volatiles wafting through it?"

"We'll drive it back to LA with the windows down. Might clear it all out," Jack said.

The nervous chatter over, the rest of the trip south was quiet. The task at hand was front and center on each one's mind as the city was left behind. The Subaru rolled on into the desert with light traffic around them.

Spotting the turn, Jack swung across the highway and accelerated up the gravel road. He watched the odometer and when it got close to the distance he had remembered from the other day, he slowed. The yellow ribbon fluttered in the slight desert breeze and the car turned off the road.

The headlights caught the tire tracks they had left and Jack swung the steering wheel to follow the twisted path to the rimrock. Not wishing any sign of them on the cliff top that could be seen in the canyon, Jack turned off the lights completely as he stopped the car.

Jack detached the night scope from the rifle and slipped it into the head strap accessory. Now acting as a monocular, Jack's one eye made out the desert track. Shifting into gear, they slowly moved ahead.

Reaching the rock obstruction, Jack turned off the engine. Jack had already disabled the dome light as they quietly opened and closed the car doors. In darkness, they gathered their weapons.

The starlight offered enough definition to see the rocks they had to cross so Jack reattached the night scope to the rifle. LaMarcus slung the gun over Katarina's shoulder, moving the gun so it hung down her front. Then he and Jack each grabbed one of the boxes full of bottled gasoline. With four gallons in each box, they carefully carried them forward as falling and breaking the contents wasn't an option. They slowly inched forward.

Katarina walked slowly behind them with the rifle. Reaching a spot just back from the top of the cliff face, the two men lowered their loads. Jack took the rifle from Katarina. Motioning Katarina to wait, the two men dropped and crawled over to the edge.

Sliding over the top of the cliff, just below sat a forty-foot houseboat. Jack estimated it to be about thirty feet out from the cliff. Looking up and down the canyon for neighbors, he saw nothing but blank water. *Ernesto likes solitude*, he thought.

Both men pushed back from the cliff until they could stand-up without a chance of being seen. LaMarcus headed back to the car while Jack pulled out the glass jugs. Lining them up just back from the cliff. He then made sure the rifle was loaded by checking the magazine. He pulled back on the slide to chamber a round.

LaMarcus soon returned carrying the propane tank. He placed it next to the eight glass bottles. Jack looked in the dark at Katarina sitting patiently. He leaned into her ear and whispered.

"Are you ready?"

"Yes, I think I feel Gary here with us," Katarina whispered back.

"That's what we all feel about our fallen," Jack said. "It's time to engage the enemy. You watch our back for anything unusual. And it's going to get very loud soon so put these in."

Jack handed her two foam rubber ear protectors and helped her set them. He placed protection in his own ears and turned to LaMarcus. Jack gave him the thumbs up.

The lights of the houseboat illuminated the canyon in weak light. Inside, laughing could be heard as Ernesto and his buddies were doing something they found amusing. Jack slid forward with the rifle cradled in his elbows. The rock bit into his arms and legs, but Marine Corps training blocked all distractions.

Reaching the edge, Jack moved the rifle into firing position. Taking aim at the houseboat, the residual light of the interior lights glared in the night scope. He would have to try to blank that out so he could see his target.

Jack glanced up at LaMarcus as the bigger man picked up the first gasoline filled glass bottle. LaMarcus began to swing the bottle back and forth with his right arm, getting the heft of the bottle. Jack turned back to his target. From his peripheral vision he saw LaMarcus let fling the bottle.

Catching sight of the falling object in the night scope, Jack watched the bomb fall. Missing the houseboat, a large splash of white announced the oversight. LaMarcus already had the second bottle in motion before the first one had hit and this one was soon falling.

A white splash marked the short. Already a commotion could be heard on the boat as four men scrambled to determine what had caused the noises outside. The third bottle of gasoline hit the stern of the houseboat just as two bodies appeared out the sliding glass doors on the front.

Before they could react to the breaking glass sound behind them, Jack fired. A red tracer round hit the spilled glass in an explosive burst. LaMarcus had the fourth bottle airborne as the flames consumed the rear of the house boat. Hitting amidships, the gasoline immediately burst in an explosion of flames.

Now, one after another of the remaining four gasoline bottles landed on or near the house boat, LaMarcus's aim wavering on the last two. Jack removed the now useless night scope and lined the red dot up on the added targets. One after another, the four floating bottles were hit with tracer rounds, engulfing the water round the boat.

Trapped by the flames on deck, the four men had disappeared into the inferno. LaMarcus readied the final prize for the thugs below. Jack told Katarina to step over for the finale. As she reached the cliff edge, she finally saw the burning inferno below.

Grasping the propane tank, LaMarcus began to swing the bottle back and forth, adjusting his swing by his judgment on the eight previous tosses.

"That one is for Gary," LaMarcus said as he let go.

Just as the tank was released, a moving body suddenly appeared in the flames, twisting and turning. No sound was heard but the fire tearing through the boat: the human being continued his death spiral.

As the propane tank floated down toward the flames, Jack took aim. Timing it perfectly, he shot just as the propane tank reached the uppermost flame. The red tracer hit the propane tank. The massive fireball that erupted crushed the boat and raced up the cliff face. Jack ducked as LaMarcus swept Katarina back quickly. As the explosion passed, Jack stood up and pulled Katarina forward.

"You always want to see your enemy die," Jack said. "It's part of the ethos, a soldier's creed."

From hundreds of feet above the site, the heat reached up and licked at them. Then it was all done. The flames settled into a few floating pieces of debris. The house boat was gone.

Jack used the night scope to carefully scan the area for any signs of life that might have escaped. He saw none.

"Never seen that before," LaMarcus said finally.

"Seen what?" Jack asked. They had been on plenty of missions that led to their enemy's death before so he was stumped as to his friend's statement.

"A fuel air explosion, that's what. Where'd you learn such a thing?" LaMarcus asked. A fuel air explosion was the closest thing to a nuclear blast that the military had developed. As a formal weapon, propane was placed in a bomb or missile. When deployed, the container holding the propane would rupture near the target releasing the fuel. As it dispersed its designed distance, a spark would ignite the propane. The resulting explosion was devastating to anything in the near vicinity. The military had used fuel air explosives for such things as minefield clearing and sinking large ships.

"I guess I just picked it up somewhere along the way," Jack said.

"Well, it sure did the job. Not that forty gallons of gasoline wouldn't have done the trick," LaMarcus said.

"You saying it was overkill?" Jack asked.

"Excuse me, can we conduct the post-action commentary back at the motel?" Katarina interrupted. "I think we should get out of here."

Agreeing, Jack slung the rifle over his shoulder as LaMarcus and Katarina each grabbed one of the empty cardboard boxes. They slowly made their way to the car. The rifle was wrapped back in its sweatpants and returned to the guitar case. The boxes were crushed for recycling.

The night scope, back on Jack's head, led them back to the gravel road. Jack stopped to retrieve his yellow ribbon. Turning on the car's headlights, Jack headed toward the main highway. As they reached the main road, they were hit by a torrential downpour. Jack slowed the car as the windshield wipers failed to clear the deluge. Finally stopped, they waited as the downpour continued. After fifteen intense minutes, the rain slowed to manageable levels and Jack resumed driving. Reaching the main highway, Jack turned left and accelerated into the night headed toward Phoenix.

"That rain was lucky for us," Jack offered. Any tracks we just left out to that spot will be gone after that rain."

"Yeah, lucky," came a weak response from Katarina.

In the morning, LaMarcus was on an Amtrak train east without his guitar case. He had left the case and contents with Jack with the excuse that risking its discovery crossing the country once was enough for him. The cardboard was deposited in a recycling bin behind a convenience store.

357

The new unassembled barbecue still in the back, the Subaru turned west and headed toward Los Angeles with its windows down. Reaching Pasadena in the middle of the night, Jack stopped and deposited the guitar case in his old Ford flatbed's metal box on the bed. He made sure the lock was tight before he jumped down. They caught up with Marta in the morning as she prepared her class for their windsurfing lesson.

Jack and Katarina settled onto the catamaran for their return trip to Cabo San Lucas. They left that night with a fair wind. It would be a five day sail south followed by a run into the harbor in the motorized dinghy while Marta was checked by Customs. Once ashore, Marta would return to Los Angeles alone while Jack and Katarina made a formal entry into Los Angeles International Airport.

Chapter 42

Salt Lake City, Utah

Officially in the United States, Jack and Katarina went about their normal existence. They took a shuttle out to the 1947 Ford truck and headed toward Utah. Breezing through Las Vegas, the couple made sure they didn't stop. The Utah border increased the speed limit but Jack kept the diesel steady at seventy miles per hour. Reaching Salt Lake City, the Ford took the exit and was soon pulling up outside Roger's shop.

"Everything ready?" Jack asked as he stepped into the office.

"Just as you instructed," Roger said. "The guys are going to be sad to see it go. It isn't every day they get to work on a car like yours."

"And no problem locating an enclosed car hauler?" Jack asked.

"No, found a used one in nice shape. It's all loaded and ready to go."

Katarina was listening with interest at the conversation. Jack knew that she had no idea what Mrs. Dietrich had entrusted with them. No matter what happened between them, one thing would always tie them together. It had been her German conversation combined with Jack's restored Ford that had swung her. That, and a need to keep something away from her eldest son. One thing he would never get his hands on, she had said.

The mechanics took a break as they watched Jack and Roger get the car hauler connected to the Ford's receiver hitch. Lights were attached and checked as everything was made ready for the trip to Wyoming. Jack paid the final bill and he and Katarina said goodbye.

Jack had placed a call to his brother the day they hit Los Angeles and convinced him he needed a break. Now on his way to Jackson, the two brothers would meet up at Ed's house. Katarina sat quiet as the miles of northern Utah desert turned into miles of eastern Idaho desert. She perked up as the Tetons came into view with its forests of pine trees.

Once over Teton Pass, the Ford labored dropping down into Jackson Hole. Jack continued through town and headed toward the small community of Moose. He turned up Ditch Creek Road and the Ford labored to reach the ridge.

Ed's house sat on a ridge overlooking the Teton Mountains and Jackson Hole. With the owner in Washington D.C. or campaigning around Wyoming most of year, Jack had become the de facto main resident of the house.

Turning into the circular driveway, Jack swung the trailer around and stopped. To his right, a large shop sat with one garage door closed for the weather. Being early December, he had lucked out on getting back to Jackson without any storm interference. The cold struck both of them as they stepped down from the truck's cab and stretched.

Ed came out of the house pulling on his down vest. The two brothers met in the driveway as Katarina held back. Jack motioned her to come over and meet this brother. They exchanged greetings and then Ed turned to Jack's restored Ford.

"Looks good, brother," Ed said.

"Runs great with the diesel," Jack offered. "No problem pulling the trailer over Teton Pass."

"Yeah, what's with the trailer?" Ed asked. "You didn't mention you were pulling a car hauler when you called. Anything interesting inside?"

Jack knew his brother's interests were peaking. The Ford flatbed dually was forgotten as Ed focused on what might be hidden behind it.

"Now, I've dreamed of this moment all my life," Jack said. "I've purchased these for this occasion."

He pulled out two red bandanas from his back pocket and stepped behind Katarina and Ed. He twisted them into a blindfold and tied one on each.

"Be patient while I open the car hauler." Jack stepped to the back of the trailer swung the doors open. Fitting ramps to the back he climbed inside the trailer and undid the straps that secured the load. Then he walked around to the small door at the front left side and stepped inside. Reaching under, he undid the front straps.

Climbing in the car, Jack settled into the contoured bucket seat. He released the parking brake and pushed in the clutch. The car rolled down the slight incline out of the trailer before he touched the brakes to stop. Jack crossed his fingers that the car would start.

With a roar only a large V-8 could make, the car sprang to life. Jack watched his brother's reaction as he raced the motor and then backed it off, the exhaust's throaty roar noticeable. The rumble of the exhaust was too much for Ed. He ripped off the blindfold and yelled. Katarina, concerned, pulled off her own blindfold.

"You've got to be kidding me!" Ed yelled over the car's rumble. "You came up with one of the most valuable cars in existence. How?"

"Not just me, Katarina owns half," Jack said. He climbed out of the driver's seat as his brother ran and gave him a bear hug. Once back on the ground, Jack gathered up Katarina as they stood watching Ed climb into the driver's seat

"But a Ford GT40?" Ed yelled. "It's a million dollar car."

"It is?" Katarina asked. It was the first time she had seen it, and the first she knew that she owned half. "What do we do with a million-dollar car?"

Ed turned to his brother with the same question. "What are you going to do?"

"Park it among your collection, I suppose," Jack offered.

"I don't think so. A car like this needs its own very secure garage with climate control," Ed offered. "Come spring, we'll get right on it."

"Thanks, brother, but the car has a mission," Jack offered. "The woman who gave us the car wanted two things to happen. One was to keep it out of her son's hands. The second was to celebrate her dead son's memory."

"How do we do that?" Katarina asked.

"Something like make a wish," Jack said. "She wants us to take kids out who are experiencing tough times. Take the GT40 to race tracks and meet up with kids to give them a thrill on the track."

"Sounds like something you'd love doing," Ed said. "I'll try and get away to join you. Driving a car like this anytime is special."

"But from the looks of the weather over the Grand Teton, we better make room for it in the shop before it gets snowed on," Jack said.

Ed agreed. He climbed out of the driver's seat and opened the shop's main door. He began making room among his other cars as Jack took Katarina up to the house where it was warmer. The GT40 was safely under cover when the snow hit.

"I fly back tomorrow, so you two will have the run of the place," Ed said. "And because of my early flight, I'll head to bed now."

Jack and Katarina were left sitting before the wood fire in Ed's living room watching the snow blow. The Teton Range had disappeared into a whiteout as dinner was served. Now relaxing, Jack opened the wood stove and added another log. The flames licked the dry pine log and the pitch crackled intensely.

Jack noticed Katarina shuddered at the sight. He knew she was back on the rim of the canyon watching four men meet their deaths. Jack also knew that even bad men dying forced guilt in good people.

"Katarina, they deserved to die."

"I know, but it was so horrible. That one man twisting in flames."

"And don't forget Gary. Gunned down in his own home and then set on fire," Jack said.

"I know, but I didn't have to watch that."

"I wanted you to watch, not to torment you, but so you'd understand," Jack explained. "You've brought up the time I stopped the school shooter. You seemed to take a certain prurient interest in what I had done in my past. I wanted you to get a real picture of the results."

"I know. Maybe I should have minded my own business," Katarina admitted.

"Too late now," Jack reminded. "You've crossed the line into warrior territory. You may try to lead a simple life from here on out, but inside, you've been to war."

"Could we go to bed now?" Katarina asked. "I just need someone to hold me."

The next week was one of turmoil for Katarina as she attempted to deal with the houseboat fire and explosion. Jack knew she was having a difficult time taking on the warrior status and he kicked himself for allowing her to be part of the whole thing.

* * *

LaMarcus made it back to New Hampshire undiscovered. Picking up his Cadillac, he headed to Boston to report in on his regular probation day. As he walked into the office, he noticed two Boston detectives waiting by the counter. One stepped over as he reported to the receptionists.

"You LaMarcus Lewis?"

"Yes, what's up?" LaMarcus asked.

"We need to ask you a few questions. Your probation officer has loaned us his office."

Once inside the office, the questions flowed. "Where were you on the night of November 29th?" one of the detectives asked.

"That would be easy," LaMarcus said. "I've been ice fishing in New Hampshire the last month. Since my last probation check."

"And can anyone verify your presence there?"

"One of your retired brother officers," LaMarcus said as he added the officer's name. He smiled inside at it all. Friends for thirty years with a Cambridge police detective, now that same detective would be covering his ass for his quick trip to Nevada. The wall of blue as it was refereed to.

"Oh, we didn't know."

"I can get him on the phone if you need to ask him," LaMarcus added.

"Not necessary," one said. "This is just routine. A request to check on the whereabouts of one LaMarcus Lewis."

"Who made the request?" LaMarcus asked.

"Clark County Sheriff's Office. That's in Las Vegas."

"I'm aware of Clark County. That would be my reason for reporting here today. Contrary to what they advertise, everything that happens in Vegas, doesn't always stay in Vegas." LaMarcus said. The two detectives smiled at LaMarcus's attempt at humor.

"It seems that the person you were convicted of assaulting died in a house boat explosion a week ago. The Sheriff is just covering all the bases," the Boston detective said.

"Do they expect foul play?" LaMarcus asked.

"No, it looks like the boat's propane tank exploded. They've had divers onsite and they found the remains of an exploded propane tank."

"So, why me?" LaMarcus asked.

"The boat owner's son is claiming it was murder. Claims you might have something to do with it, seeing as you had a run-in with the victim before."

"Well, I guess freezing my ass off on the lake solved something. Kept me out of harm's way in Nevada, sounds like," LaMarcus said.

"Yeah. We'll pass on that we verified you here in New England the entire time. Sorry to bother you."

"Not a bother, anytime for my brothers in blue," LaMarcus said.

As the two detectives left the office, LaMarcus's probation officer stepped in. Taking his seat behind his desk, he asked, "Everything OK?"

Having known the man for the last thirty years, LaMarcus knew he could trust the man. At least to a point. LaMarcus also knew his friend had financial problems from his third divorce and his search for number four. *The man just can't pick women.* LaMarcus thought.

"Seems to be. But the guy I was paying restitution just turned up dead," LaMarcus said. "I guess I can stop my monthly tribute to the Nevada law enforcement."

"Yea, lucky break there," the probation officer said.

LaMarcus wanted to discuss something with his friend and suggested that since it was near the noon hour, he would buy his friend lunch. Eager for a free lunch, he and LaMarcus headed to a nearby cafe. Once inside, LaMarcus made his pitch.

"You wouldn't have too much trouble covering for me for the rest of my probation, would you?" LaMarcus asked.

His friend was a little taken aback. "What's up?"

"I've decided to take a long vacation and I can't tell anyone where I'm going. If you can keep me good on the law side for the rest of the year, I can help you out right now."

LaMarcus noticed his friend's demeanor change at the mention of help. Reaching into his jacket pocket, LaMarcus pulled out a small manila envelope. He slid the thick packet across to his friend.

"Where I'm going, I don't need any of that. I've already signed the title to my Cadillac. I figure you know someone that can liquidate it for you."

His friend took the envelope before anyone noticed it and slipped it into his pocket. He nodded that he could dispose of the SUV with no questions asked.

"I figure it's good for at least thirty thousand," LaMarcus added. "Also, the key to my apartment is in there. You can liquidate everything in there for what you can get. The rent is paid for the rest of the year."

"LaMarcus. I appreciate the help and covering for you won't be a problem. But what are you going to do?"

"Retire. For real this time," LaMarcus answered. "The title for my boat is in there also. That should add another ten-thousand. And if you will, the deed to my Maine property. Pass that on to my kids for me."

"Sure I will."

"And next time, don't get married," LaMarcus quipped.

The two friends laughed at the man's situation as they finished lunch. As his friend got up to leave, a lot richer than before he sat down, a warning bell went off in the back of LaMarcus's brain. From the corner of his eye, someone was sitting and watching them intently.

Pulling on his coat, LaMarcus stepped out into the cold and headed toward the subway station. His Cadillac was safely parked at his apartment ready for his friend to sell it. He had planned his getaway long before this meeting.

Out on the street, he stopped to look in a store window. The man from the restaurant was behind and feigned interest in a newspaper box on the curb. Without turning around, LaMarcus continued his hike the two blocks to the subway.

Turning to his left to drop down the stairs, LaMarcus again spied the man following him. He dropped his token in the turnstile and clicked through the barrier. As soon as he did, he sprinted for the opposite train from the one that would have taken him home. *If the man knows where I live, he would assume I'm heading home now,* LaMarcus thought.

Turning a corner, LaMarcus waited where he could see the entrance to the other subway line. Blocked by a post and a newspaper stand, he waited. Soon, the man ran past and headed down the stairs to catch LaMarcus's regular train. Quickly heading up the stairs to street level, LaMarcus held up his hand and grabbed a cab.

"South Station," he said. Amtrak trains left South Station headed west. LaMarcus figured he needed to leave town right now. *I can pick up some luggage somewhere so I look like a tourist* he thought. With a wad of cash in his pocket and his son's borrowed credit card, he would head west before catching a flight. But first, he had to make a phone call. Someone needed to be warned.

Chapter 43

Moose, Wyoming

Jack was a little nervous. Actually, he was a lot nervous. The last he had heard from LaMarcus was the day before his probation meeting. Expecting a call to say he was in the clear back in Boston, the call had yet to arrive.

Added to that anxiety was Katarina. As the time passed since their encounter with Ernesto and his pals, she had grown more distant and uncommunicative. Jack really kicked himself for allowing her to be part of the hit. But the deed was done, and and now he attempted damage control.

Standing in the kitchen making breakfast for both of them, Jack stared out the window at the white wonderland outside. The Teton Range shown brilliantly against the bright blue sky with the results of three days of snow. Katarina walked in, dressed for travel.

"What's going on?"Jack asked.

"I've decided to head home," Katarina said. "I've made a reservation for early afternoon. Can you give me a ride to the airport?"

"You know I will. But why the sudden decision?" Jack asked.

"Christmas is next week and I've never been away from home for Christmas," Katarina said. "I'm just missing my family right about now."

"I understand. But is there more?" Jack asked.

"I've been thinking a lot since Thailand about my marriage. I think it's time to end the charade."

"I agree and support you in that decision," Jack said.

The two grew quiet as each considered what to say next. Jack turned off the burner and scooped the scrambled eggs out on plates. He placed the fry pan in the sink and went to Katarina. He took her arm and guided her to the living room.

As she sat her down, he joined her on the couch. "A lot has happened the last couple of months," Jack said. "Some very nice and some pretty awful. I hope you dwell on the pleasant memories when you're back in Holland."

"I will, Jack. I've learned a lot being with you. I guess my starry-eyed view of the James Bond life you seem to lead ran into a wall."

Jack held her tight as she lowered her head. She rested her head on his shoulder as both of them sat in silence.

"Michael will be glad to see you back," Jack offered.

"Why do you say that?"

"Because Michael thinks the world of you. He told me how much he cares about you on Roland's boat."

"He is a dear friend," Katrina said. "He's always been there for me."

"Long relationships have started with less," Jack offered.

A long spell lingered as the two sat quietly. Then Jack added. "We'll always have a race car together. No one can separate us on that."

"Yes, we do have that." Katarina's stunning smile broke out for Jack one last time.

Breakfast was forgotten as the two just held each other the rest of the morning. Soon it was time for Jack to borrow his brother's SUV to get down the hill to the airport. The road had been plowed the day before and Ed's neighbor had plowed the driveway. Parking at Jackson Airport, Jack helped Katarina out of the vehicle and pulled her bag out of the back seat.

"Please don't come in," Katarina said. "I'd rather not have to do this in front of a lot of people."

Jackson Airport wasn't exactly thronging with hordes but Jack understood the request. Things were ending between them and emotions were running high. He gave her a long hug and a warm kiss before she took her bag and disappeared into the terminal. He climbed in the SUV and drove home alone.

His cell phone went off as he walked into his brother's house. Not recognizing the number, Jack hit the answer button.

"Jack, I've been waiting to call you."

Recognizing LaMarcus's panicked voice, Jack asked, "Where have you been? I expected a call before now."

"We have trouble," LaMarcus said and went on to explain his interview by the Boston detectives. The statement that Ernesto's son was seeking revenge against LaMarcus got Jack's attention. Then LaMarcus told Jack of being followed out of his probation meeting and ditching the tail.

"Where are you now?" Jack asked.

"St. Louis. I arrived by train last night. I have a flight in an hour out of here."

Not clicking on where he would be flying to, Jack was more concerned about his probation.

"It's covered. No problems there. But if Ernesto's son is after me, they could be looking for you. Watch yourself," LaMarcus said.

"And you too," Jack offered. The call went dead.

Jack thought for a while before he remembered. He headed down the stairs to the garage under the house. Parked beside his brother's SUV was his old Ford flatbed. Climbing onto the bed, Jack unlocked the metal storage box and pulled out the guitar case.

In the rush of delivering the GT40 and Katarina leaving, he had forgotten his friend's rifle. He carried it over to the workbench and pulled down the cleaning supplies. The rifle was unloaded but hadn't been cleaned since Nevada.

He ran the cleaning rod down the barrel and wiped out the residue from the five shots he had taken. Tracer rounds were extra nasty in that they left extra residue in the barrel before they lit up on their way to the target.

With a clean gun, he dropped the tracer rounds out of the magazine. Two extra magazines and two boxes of ammunition lay wrapped in a cloth in the guitar case. He loaded the magazines, slipping two into his pants pocket and one into the AR-10. He slid the bolt back to load one round in the chamber. He pushed the safety forward as he climbed the stairs to the main house.

Jack turned out all the lights of the house. With the nighttime darkness lessened slightly by the white snow,

Jack headed into his brother's bedroom using the night vision scope to find what he needed. Dressing in his brother's outdoor survival gear, Jack readied for the cold nighttime air as his Marine cold-weather training kicked in.

Ed's house had a crawl space under half of it with a floor hatch in the bedroom. Jack pulled the hatch as he scrunched on his hat. He stepped down into the four-foot space and dropped to the ground. He closed the hatch before he crawled over to an access half door that opened into a storage section. He carefully opened the small door and scanned the room with the rifle ready.

Dropping into the store room, he walked over to the outside door. He rolled the deadbolt and opened it slightly. The snow was piled up against it and Jack was careful not to knock any into the door jamb. Stepping out into the cold, he pulled the door shut and locked it with a key.

Jack lowered himself down and looked through the night scope at the surrounding property. Seeing no threat, he stepped in the snow as he headed toward high ground. His feet sunk into the soft new snow up to his thighs. The snow was light and fluffy, typical Rocky Mountain powder, but still resisted his hike to the south.

This might be crazy to be out here, Jack thought. *But the way LaMarcus had panicked, I can't be too careful.*

The cold night air worked in all the seams of his suit as he moved forward, his skin catching sharp tingles. All that was out of his mind as he reached a high spot just on the edge of the trees. A clearing led all the way back to the house with a clear view of the driveway down to the county road.

Using his scope to observe movement, Jack swept the area in front of him for any threats. He settled into his small hole in the snow and waited. If someone was coming, they would be along early in the morning. He sat and waited, the house below him dark. *Anyone will wait for me to fall asleep before making their move*, Jack thought.

As he sat, Jack noticed that only his toes felt the cold. He wiggled them constantly to keep the circulation flowing. His right hand only had a fingerless glove on and was buried in his down jacket's pocket. Sufficiently warm, it was ready to take the trigger. His other hand held the rifle with a heavy wool mitten on it for warmth. Every few minutes he pulled his warm hand out and tried the trigger. The cold metal bit his bare fingers before he slipped them back into his pocket

An hour passed and Jack began to think he was being extra paranoid. Just because LaMarcus had someone following him didn't mean someone had made their way to Wyoming. After the second hour Jack was really doubting his decision to sit out in the cold. His feet were still struggling for warmth while his legs were now stiffening in the cold.

I better not have to run anyone down, he thought. *But, on second thought, running right now would get me warmed up.*

As his mind focused on running and warmth, his eyes spotted movement. Or was it movement? He lifted the night scope and scanned where he thought he'd seen someone.

There, by the mailbox. Something moved again, he thought. Holding steady on the driveway entrance, two figures appeared in the scope. They stepped off the road and began a slow deliberate walk up the driveway. Jack followed them in the scope as they drew nearer the house.

Stopping in front of the house, one motioned the other to circle around to the other side. The second followed as they walked around the far side of the house, Jack losing sight of them.

From his vantage point, he could not see the back of the house. Jack moved slowly to the west while his cold legs complained. Crouching low in the snow, he circled around to where he could see the deck that looked toward the Tetons. With two sets of French doors, Jack knew that they would be the most vulnerable to a break-in. And if these two were who he thought they were, opening a locked door wouldn't be a problem.

Jack observed the two figures slowly and carefully climb the steps onto the deck. Stopping at the first set of French doors they checked the door knob. Finding it locked, they moved on to the doors leading to the bedroom. Jack kept them in his sights the entire time.

Reaching the windowed door overlooking the bedroom, they carefully checked the knob. Finding this one also locked, each one reached under their jacket and produced something in their hands. By the way they were holding it, Jack assumed a hand gun was now aimed at the bed.

A quiet thump-thump noise sneaked out as the glass in the door shattered. Emptying their silenced semi-auto hand guns into the Jack's target of pillows covered by blankets, they moved to enter through the now-broken door.

The first one's head exploded as he reached for the inside door lock. Before the second one could react to his friend's head disappearing, a second shoot took out his right leg. He dropped where he stood, screaming in pain, holding his shattered leg.

Leaving his cover, Jack wallowed through the snow to the deck, keeping the wounded man in his sights. The deck on Jack's end of the house was only a couple feet off the ground and Jack grabbed the handrail and lifted himself over.

"You shot me you son of a bitch!" the wounded man yelled.

Stepping over to him, Jack picked up both handguns and threw them aside. He frisked the wounded man's jacket for a back-up but found none. He slid down his leg and discovered an ankle holster with a snub nosed . 38 revolver jammed in it. Jack retrieved the revolver and aimed it at the man's head.

"Who sent you?" Jack asked.

The man continued to swear at Jack about being shot but offered no answer. Jack stepped on the man's leg where he'd been shot. He pressed down hard. The man screamed louder.

"I'll repeat, who sent you?"

"You crazy son of a bitch shot me!" the man screamed.

"And I'll let you bleed out if you don't tell me who sent you." Again Jack pressed on the man's shattered leg.

"Stop, stop, I'll talk!" the man yelled. But then nothing.

"I'm getting impatient. Talk now. I already know Ernesto's kid sent you," Jack said.

"How did you know?" the wide-eyed man asked. "Yes, we are part of Ernesto's organization. His son, Daniel has taken over. He wants you and that big black bastard both dead. He'll never rest until you both pay for what you did."

"From what I hear, his old man died in a terrible boating accident. Why blame us?" Jack asked.

"He can't prove it, but he knows it was you two. And now you're dead," the man said.

Jack aimed the revolver at the man's forehead and pulled the trigger. The would-be assassin flopped over in the snow. Jack stepped over the body and kicked the man's semi-automatic pistol back to where it lay by the man's hand.

The plywood leaned on the shattered glass door ready to be screwed into the wood before the Teton County Sheriff arrived. Right behind were two other police cars carrying more deputies. Teton County didn't have many killings and the entire force was out. Waiting at the front door as the sheriff walked up, Jack opened the door.

"Jack, what the hell is going on?"

Jack led the sheriff through to the bedroom, past the shot up bed and opened the shattered door. Two bodies lay with a slight covering of wind-drifted snow. By the light from the house, they almost looked serene laying in the snow, as long as their heads weren't included in the view.

"Ah shit, Jack," the sheriff started. "It's bad enough when you step in this shit out there in the world, but now it's following you back to Jackson."

Jack took the reprimand in as the sheriff directed his deputies in their investigation. Taking a statement, the sheriff wrote notes as Jack described what had happened.

"Look, Jack, let's take it down to the office and let these guys do their work. It looks like a clear case of self-defense but I need to do it right."

"I know, let me call my neighbor. He can babysit the house to make sure nothing more happens," Jack said. After a quick call, Jack grabbed his coat to follow the sheriff into Jackson.

By late morning, the deputies had returned to the office. The bodies had been transported to the county morgue and endless questions about what it was all about had been answered. Jack left out any mention of involvement in Ernesto's death on his boat.

"OK, Jack, I think we're done," the sheriff said. "But I have to tell you, . . "

"Stop Sheriff, I'll save you the trouble," Jack said. "I'll be down this afternoon with my Teton County badge and weapon along with my ID. I don't expect you to keep me on now."

"It's just all those calls I get from other jurisdictions," the sheriff said.

"You don't have to explain. You've been great at covering my back," Jack said. Jack knew the sheriff was in a tight spot. Jack had gotten his deputy sheriff credentials only because his brother was now chief-of-staff to one of Wyoming's U.S. Senators. *I've put the poor man on the spot too many times*, Jack thought.

"What are your plans now?"

"Don't worry, they don't include Jackson," Jack answered. "I'll be gone before Christmas."

The two law enforcement people stood and shook hands. Jack thanked the sheriff for all he had done for him and then he left. His Teton County official gear was in his office that afternoon as Jack caught a ride with the neighbor to the airport.

* * *

Shooter sat on the deck off the main room and watched the palm trees sway. He was still adjusting to the heat and humidity that announced itself each day. Yesterday had seen rain all day which made the air heavy with moisture this morning.

He had just finished his oatmeal with fresh squeezed orange juice. Shooter wasn't sure where the fresh juice came from each day but he was happy to be around so much tropical fruit. It was beginning to catch up with him and he was sort of glad that he was required to stay in his room for the duration. The toilet was close at hand as his body adjusted to his new cuisine.

As he pondered what life had given him, the door to the outside world opened and a man walked in, a familiar face of an old friend.

"Jack, holy shit, it's you," Shooter said.

"Its Cowboy now, LaMarcus. We go by our new names. I hear you took Shooter," Jack said.

"But how? Where's the Dutch treat?" Shooter asked.

"Safely back home and not in the cross hairs of our Las Vegas friends," Cowboy said. He told of the late night visitors he had dispatched in Wyoming and the subsequent loss of his police status.

"So it was Ernesto's son," Shooter said. "But why come here, and how?"

"Same as you. Followed right in your foot steps, I think," Cowboy said. "Flight to Singapore from Wyoming then an all-day bus ride to the same village on the border you discovered. I hired the same fisherman to drop me on the beach out front."

"And they're taking you in?"

"Hell, I'm the guy that got the manager his hot teenage European sex partner for a year. You don't think he'd deny me," Cowboy said. "How'd you convince them to let your sorry ass in here?"

"Charm," Shooter offered. "Works every time. But how you working the money? You didn't go through the bank in Pahrump did you?"

"I set up an account in Singapore to funnel my retirement through. I'll pay the resort fees on this end. Richter said some of the retirees have local accounts only. And you?"

"Same, an account in Singapore," Shooter said.

"So, at least we have company for our two-week quarantine," Cowboy said.

"I'll be out three days ahead of you, though."

"So, have they said who you'd have for a woman partner yet?"

"No, but I guess one of the old guys just died. Seems I can take over his bungalow with all that it held. Don't know what she looks like yet, though," Shooter said.

"Like you would care," Cowboy offered.

"Hey, how about you? You've been here before. Who'd they set you up with?"

Funny thing," Cowboy said. "When I stepped onto the beach, Panzer was doing his punishment routine with one of the women who hadn't worked hard enough. As soon as he saw me, he knew I'd come to stay. He turned to the woman he was retraining to ask if she would like to be my partner. Her smile could have lit up Broadway as Soraya jumped at the opportunity."

"Who the hell is Panzer?" Shooter asked, but his broad smile for his friend gave him away. *Whoever Panzer was, it would all be good now* Shooter thought.

The End

Acknowledgements

First I would thank Timothy Johns, my tireless editor. Though he works hard that my writing is presentable, place no blame on him for the final product. That all rests with me.

My proofreaders offer valuable feedback at different phases as my draft is put together. Dick Martin, Jeanne Crownover, Marsha Wiles, Larry Stoddard, Tiffany Martin, Barbara Foster, John Briggs and Rod Gravelly have all kept me from straying too far off on tangents.

John Ewing was an early supporter who didn't get to see the final product. His wife Bertha Ewing was invaluable as a listener as I read my work out loud.

Finding Morwenna Rakestraw to do the cover layout was a relief.

Mitch Press of World Book has offered his wisdom from his family's years in the book business. While not all encouraging, his guidance as publishing transforms in the digital age has been invaluable.

Lastly, my wife, Agnes, deserves recognition for tolerating my swerve into being an author. I'm a lucky guy and she is my proof..

Dear Reader,

Thank you for your selection of reading material. I hope this book measured up to your expectations. The most critical part for a new author is getting the word out to other readers.

I would appreciate your help in spreading the word. There are three important things you can do. You need to understand the importance of the first one to my becoming a successful writer. If you do anything, go to Amazon.com and write a review.

1.   Go to Amazon.com and leave a review
2.   Tell a friend about this book
3.   Tell you your social network about this book.

Positive reviews made in various places will help readers find me.

Again, thanks for your support.

W.B. Martin

Read an excerpt of the exciting new Jack Wesley
adventure from W.B. Martin:

Be Prepared To Bleed
#9 in the Jack Wesley Thriller Series

Be Prepared To Bleed

Chapter 1

Missoula, Montana

The warmth of the Fall sun brought some relief to the Bitterroot Valley of Montana. The high mountains to the west still held the early white dusting that had arrived yesterday to announce that winter would soon come to Missoula. Classes at the university were in full swing as students with their backpacks walked by on their way to campus a few blocks away.

The leaves of the trees along the quiet residential street still held on but their color change portended their eminent fall to earth. The light breeze coming up the Clark Fork River rustled the dry leaves and would soon bring leaf piles coupled with the delight of children jumping into them. But for now the last visages of summer held on while the Craftsman style homes lining the street awaited the harsh Montana winter.

One soul fought for warmth on his front deck reading. He would take every opportunity to sit and enjoy the end of the outdoor season even if it meant being wrapped in polar fleece for comfort. To him every moment outdoors was to be cherished before being forced into the confines of artificially heated houses. He had lived through a number of Rocky Mountain winters now, and while they beat the rainy winters of the Pacific Northwest that he had endured for most of his life, he still wasn't content with the long dark winters.

Jack Wesley had settled into life in Missoula because of one reason, his grandchildren. Actually four reasons as he included his son and daughter-in-law in that equation. But being near J.J. and C.J. were reason enough. Now aged 5 and 2 they had enough personality to keep Jack happy for extended periods. That happened frequently since they lived next door to Jack.

Jack glanced over to his right at similar house for activity. Stacey would be leaving soon to pick up J.J. from his all day Kindergarten, C.J. strapped in his car seat in the back of the Pathfinder. But all was quiet. Jack scanned the street for the daily return of the local school kids from the neighborhood grade school two blocks away. But with no sign of school having been released Jack knew he had a few more minutes to relax.

Today was the day he would watch his two grandkids while Stacey went shopping. He enjoyed at least three weekdays with C.J. as Stacey had a part time job and Jack was glad to have C.J. time as he called it. He went to day care one day each week and today was Stacey's day off.

He found his place in his crime novel and continued reading. But his attention was distracted by the high whine of a car engine. The noise barely registered but Jack had heard it before and he knew what was coming. It happened too often on his quiet street or at least what should have been a quiet street.

Lined with 1930 style bungalow houses, his street was three blocks from the University of Montana campus. The Craftsman houses were all similar with a covered front porch, hip style roof and a single car driveway leading to a garage just off the back of the house. With three bedrooms down one side of the house, the other side held the living room in the front with the kitchen/dining room toward the back. One bathroom squeezed on the back finished off the 1200 square foot house.

The style dominated the street with slight variations as individual personalities had altered each one over the decades. Jack liked the intimate feeling the houses offered and during the summer the front porches provided families a neighborly feel as people watched their kids play on the tree lined sidewalks. And with each house having a long single driveway, cars didn't dominate the scene as in so many American neighborhoods with their large overwhelming two car garages and driveways up front. At least all but one house on his street held the pattern. His next door neighbor to the left had what Jack estimated to be a 1970's style house with the garage up front with two bays. A fire had consumed the original house Jack had learned and the two story more modern house stuck out noticeably.

But all that was forgotten as the whine of a high revving engine took on a more noticeable sound. Jack had seen the fast and furious wannabe before and had even called the police to report the danger it presented. But nothing seemed to have been done to slow the Japanese rice burner down.

Jack Wesley, retired police detective, put his book down and picked up his phone. If the police hadn't done anything over the three weeks this had been going on he decided that maybe a video on his phone might persuade the authorities to do something.

He clicked on his camera and aimed it down the street toward the growing noise. He could hear the gear changes as the car built up speed through the thickly settled neighborhood and then the down shifts as the car reached the corner onto his street. Accelerating quickly the engine hit extreme revs with the custom exhaust blaring out. Jack caught a glimpse through the trees of the lowered Honda Accord as it hit third gear. Jack had reported the driver typically went by his house at least fifty miles and hour and today was no exception.

The Honda flashed by parked cars and continued its acceleration. From the corner of his eye Jack saw something. Holding the camera on the moving car he shifted his eyes slightly to a large truck tire that was rolling down his neighbors driveway. The heavy metal wheel added mass and as the tire hit the flat sidewalk it bounced slightly over the driveway ramp off the street. Hitting the street pavement it bounced again with perfect timing just as the Honda reached the same spot. The lowered front end caught the wheel mid-hood which knocked the tire from vertical to horizontal. Now acting as a fling disk it smashed through the car's windshield jamming the glass into the passenger compartment.

The car continued down the street but the driver was no longer in control as he was pinned to his headrest by the heavy weighted wheel. Airbags deployed and saved the driver's life as the exploding bags directed the tire up toward the roof liner thus saving the driver from being decapitated. But with the driver incapacitated his jerking movement caused the Honda to swerve and slam into a tree across from Jack's house. The car crumpled while the energy released by the crash flipped the car to the right as it tried to twist itself apart.

Jack lowered his camera and dialed 911. Neighbors came running out of their houses from the crash noise and as one man reached the wreck he leaned into the car. Jack stood up as he talked to the

911 dispatcher and soon sirens were heard form the emergency response. As he hung up the first police car arrived followed quickly by an ambulance and fire truck. Letting the paramedics do their job, Jack walked to the end of his driveway and put his phone away. Standing and watching the scene, a man walked up beside him.

"Hell of a thing," the man said.

Jack turned to the voice and recognized his next door neighbor. "Sure is."

"Good thing there weren't any kids out in the street playing."

"Yes, good thing," Jack responded.

Jack had meet the man when he had moved in a little over a month ago. Jack also was new to the neighborhood and had gone over to say hi. But no other conversation had taken place and Jack now wished he'd been a bit more neighborly. But the man seemed to be a quiet type so Jack hadn't pushed. All in due time he had thought.

"I'm bloody amazed the authorizes hadn't done anything before this." the man offered.

"Yeah, I've called the police a number of times and nothing. It just continued. And with all the little kids around here too."

"No respect. Young people today have no respect."

Jack turned to face the man and held out his hand. "I'm sorry I haven't been more neighborly. I'm

Jack Wesley. We meet the day you moved. Greg isn't it?"

"Greg Roberts," the man replied. "And no Jack, I should have been more neighborly, Just with unpacking and getting sorted out time just flew by."

The paramedics were carefully pulling the driver out the car door. The firemen had had to force the door open and were now working on the passenger's door. A short back brace had been slipped in behind the driver and his head and upper body strapped to the brace. As the driver came out the paramedics laid him gently on the ground were a full body brace had been placed. His entire body was now strapped down to protect any potential spinal injuries.

As they examined the driver two emergency personnel were working on the man's girlfriend. She screamed as the men checked her for injuries. An inflatable leg splint was placed on her left leg after her door was forced open. The two were placed into the ambulance and driven to the hospital. One police officer stepped over and looked into the car. With his leather gloves for protection from the sharp metal and broken glass he yanked on a large object. Two firemen moved to help as the large truck wheel and tire were extracted from the car. Two of them rolled it onto the sidewalk and let it fall, the tire slamming the concrete with a bang causing some of the on lookers to jump.

An officer with sergeant strips stepped over the tire and asked, "Anyone see what happened?"

The people in the crowd all offered that no one had witnessed the accident.

"Who called 911 then?"

The sergeant looked around as a number of people held up their hands. He started going from one to another asking if they had witnessed anything or had just called after the accident.

Jack stood and watched the sergeant work through the hand raisers. Finished, the sergeant turned. "Anyone else call?"

Jack raised his arm slowly. The sergeant swiveled around the crowd and finally noticed Jack's arm raised. He walked across the street flipping his notebook to a fresh page.

"Name?"

"Jack Wesley."

"And you called it in?"

Jack nodded that he had.

"Did you witness the accident?"

Jack hesitated slightly. Things were getting complicated real fast. The truck tire that had caused the mayhem had come from the driveway of the man standing next to him. While the punk that had terrorized his neighborhood certainly needed to be put out of commission, Jack wasn't sure a truck tire though the windshield was the right answer. But he did like the neighbor's style if he had caused it. Jack had dealt with punks all his life as a policeman in Eugene, Oregon. And after retirement he had dealt with more of them. Bad boys deserved to put down and Jack was inclined to provide the force to put them down. So he hesitated to step to far into being a witness. The sergeant stared at him for an answer.

"Sort of," Jack said.

"Sort of what? Did you witness the accident or didn't you?" The police sergeant showing his irritation.

"I saw the crash when he hit the tree. I was coming out my front door just as the Honda hit the tree." Jack lied. He glanced slightly to the left. His neighbor had a stone face showing. The sergeant noticed the head movement.

"Who are you?" the sergeant asked, looking at Greg.

"I'm the neighbor. I live right there."

"You a witness?"

"No officer. I was in the house when I heard the crash."

"OK. Then Mr. Wesley, can you tell me what you saw."

Jack described the car hitting the tree and coming to rest lying across the street. The officer wrote his notes as Jack talked.

"Any idea how that truck tire got into the front seat?"

Jack hesitated again, then lied again. "No idea."

Jack saw the look he got from Greg but tried to conceal any sign that he sure as hell knew where the truck tire had come from. The sergeant looked at Jack and then at Greg.

"You positive about that mister?"

"Asked and answered sergeant," Jack said.

"You a wise guy?" the sergeant asked. One of the patrolman walked up to the group.

"From the black marks on the hood it sure looks like they hit that truck tire. If they were going as fast as some have said that could have killed them both. Like having a deer come through the windshield doing seventy," the patrolman said.

The sergeant turned back to Jack. "So no idea how a tire came to be in the middle of the road mister smart ass?"

"How do you know how fast they were going? I don't see any skid marks," Jack asked.

"The other people offered that this kid drove doing fifty through their neighborhood regularly. From the impact to the tree and damage we can estimate his speed. And no skid marks because he never hit the brakes since he had a truck tire on top of him."

"Well I called about this punk a number of times and you never did anything about it," Jack said. "I have grandkids living right here and this asshole zooming down the street didn't make things very safe. And you not doing anything about it didn't help."

"So you take things into your own hands then. Roll a tire out into the street?"

"You won't find my fingerprints on it. I didn't roll any truck tire out but if the punk had been going the required speed on this street I guess he could have avoided it. And if you have any other questions it will be in my lawyer's office."

"Got something to hide then."

"No, thirty years on the force. I know cops aren't your friends." Jack pulled out his wallet and flipped open to show his retired law enforcement card.

The sergeant eyed the credentials and then the person holding them. "I'll do that if we have any more questions."

"Excuse me sergeant." Greg interrupted. "How badly injured were they?"

"They'll live. The driver was lucky."

Greg continued "So will the driver be cited or something?"

"You English or something? The way you talk I was thinking."

"British actually. From Wales, part of the British union. Just interested how you Yanks handle law and order here. I'm new here."

"Well don't you worry about any citations."

"Considering the bad job you did stopping this driver before this happened then asking about citations is a reasonable question sergeant." Jack interjected.

"I'm not liking you one bit, retired law enforcement or not. So just mind your own business."

"This street is where I live so this is my business. What if my grandkids had been crossing the street and were now pinned under the car dead. Not my business?" Jack was getting worked up.

The Missoula police sergeant fixed a stare at the two of them before he turned and walked back to the accident scene. The patrolman followed behind.

"Are all your police like him?" Greg asked.

"Some. I guess. Pointing out how they didn't do anything before hand about this street racer doesn't sit well. No one likes their screw-ups pointed out" Jack offered.

The crowd dispersed as the wrecker hauled the Honda away, the truck tire still sitting on the side walk. The police had left so the tire seemed to be abandoned to the neighborhood. Jack and Greg stood on the side walk as the wrecker turned the corner and disappeared.

"Can we go to your house Greg?"

Greg acknowledged the request and led Jack up his driveway and through the garage into the house. They passed a vintage Mini obviously being worked on in the garage, a newer Toyota parked next to it.

"Project car?" Jack asked when he was seated on a bar stool in the kitchen. Greg offered Jack coffee and when Jack mentioned English Breakfast tea, Greg's eyes lit up. As he brewed tea a short dark man walked into the kitchen.

"Oh, Karma Somda, I'd like you to meet our neighbor, Jack Wesley."

Jack shook hands with Karma as the man returned a slight bow.

"And yes Jack, the Mini project is mine. Keeps my retirement interesting getting parts for it here in America,"

Jack wasn't sure how to approach the subject but he felt that he needed to. He pulled out his phone and brought his picture file up. Holding it up to Greg he hit the play button. Greg and Karma both watched as the video caught the tire rolling down the driveway and smashing into the car, the car slamming into the tree.

Greg stood in the kitchen and calmly sipped his tea. Karma made no facial expression to indicate what he was thinking. Two very cool characters Jack thought.

"Well Jack, you have your evidence right there that you certainly didn't roll the tire down the driveway on that bad boy." Greg said. Karma stood eight inches shorter then the Welshman but showed no emotion. Jack was getting more suspicious of these two as the minutes clicked by. He knew the tire had come from Greg's garage so one of the them was the culprit.

"You claimed you were in the housE when the accident occurred." Jack said.

"True. And Karma can be my witness. But remember that the garage counts as part of the house." Greg said.

"Technically yes." Jack said.

"But you didn't offer the video to the police or mention its existence. Being former law enforcement aren't you sworn to uphold the law?" Greg asked.

That was the issue Jack was focusing on. While he had evidence of a crime he wasn't all that concerned about implicating his neighbor. The fast and furious driver and his girlfriend had been dealt a lesson in life and Jack wasn't sure that anyone needed to know who had provided the lesson.

He looked once more at the video of the accident and then hit the delete button. He held up his smart phone so Greg and Karma could attest that the video no longer existed. Both smiled back at Jack as Greg picked up the tea pot.

"Another cup Jack?"

Chapter 2

Phoenix, Arizona

"Do we know anything yet?" the man asked. As the head of a criminal organization, the man expected answers. When none were offered by the other men around the table the leader exploded.

"I want some answers. This shit head who killed my father has lived too long already. He dodged us in Wyoming and then disappeared. Now we have information he has been spotted in Montana."

A short dark man with a black mustache ventured into to the tirade. "But boss, we have our spy across the street and he is sending in information."

"To slow. I want this man dead in a week. Do you hear me, a week. And I won't accept any failure this time."

The eight men around the table nodded agreement. It would happen in a week, this they knew. Daniel Vasquez knew how to get what he wanted. As the son of Ernesto, they knew the ruthlessness and brutality bred into his body. Most had worked for the family since Ernesto had risen to control his own organization in Las Vegas. That they had not prevented the boss from being violently murdered had set the wraith of the son on them.

A hit team that had gone to Wyoming in the dead of winter and had been killed just raised the stakes. And when the target had disappeared seemingly from the face of the Earth that had been the clincher. For a year the man had vanished only to finally re-appear in Missoula, Montana sitting quietly in his house. Already a team had been organized and was on its way from Las Vegas. All the while their money making business of drug running, prostitution and loan sharking was suffering. The boss turned his intense gaze onto Alfonso. The underling squirmed in his seat at the glare.

"Tell me it is done."

Alfonso swallowed hard. Making the boss unhappy could prove fatal. He carefully weighed his words. "Boss, I have a two man hit team leaving Las Vegas as we speak. It will be over in three days, I swear."

"You had better swear. A year is too long for that pig to live. And do we know the where-abouts of the black bastard. He dies too."

Alfonso blanched at the mention of the black man. No sign of him had surfaced and that would only enrage the boss more. "No sign of him boss. We have every resource on it. But nothing."

"And you have told our team to try to find an answer to that question before they kill in Montana?" Daniel asked.

"They have been told. And as per your instructions they need to videotape it all. And if possible that are to make it slow and painful," Alfonso offered.

"The slower and more painful the better. They will be paid extra if they impress me. You told them that right?"

"Si." Alfonso added.

"Good, good. Now when are we with bringing in our next shipment from Sonora?"

* * *

At that moment Jack Wesley was standing at the alter of the Air Force Academy Chapel besides his daughter Inez. The minister looked over the gathering and asked, "Who gives this bride away?"

"We do," Jack answered as he stepped back and sat down next to his ex-wife. She smiled slightly at the response.

But Jack had noticed the broad smile on his daughter's face at what he had just said. They had discussed the response before hand and Jack had offered an olive branch to say 'we do' instead of the more traditional 'I do'. Jack knew the traditional father giving away the bride had been replaced by a more politically correct version of inclusiveness. If it had been up to him he would have screwed with the inclusiveness but he knew it was important to Inez.

The daughter that had left long ago with the ex-wife in the divorce was back in his life. And Jack would suffer any indignities to keep it that way. Even including his ex-wife in the formal proceedings. Even sitting next to her while Inez married her love. And he would even suffer sitting in church next to the ex-wife while her boyfriend sat on the opposite side of her. Jack took a big breath and tried to relax. It would be a long day.

But he was ecstatic at his daughters choice. Eric was a major in the U. S. Air Force and was stationed at the Air Force Academy in an instructor position. Jack hadn't known Eric long and didn't know his life history. Only that he was from Wisconsin and had flown C-131 transport planes for his regular job in the air force. Beyond that, Jack hadn't been told much.

Sitting behind him was his son Carl, Carl's wife and one grandchild. The oldest grandchild, J.J., was in a miniature tuxedo standing behind Eric holding a pillow with two rings on it. Standing with Eric was a brother officer as best man. Having lived in Colorado Springs her adult life, Inez had a local friend standing with her. Neither of them had wanted a big wedding so no other attendants were present except for someone's young daughter being flower girl. *I think the matron of honor's daughter* Jack thought.

Jack was just glad his daughter, at age 34, was finally getting married. *And married to what seemed to be a great guy. Not like some of the drips she brought home* Jack thought. Soon the couple kissed and turned to greet the applauding crowd. Jack turned as sixteen fellow air force officers lined both sides of the aisle beside him. At the command, each drew their sword and held them aloft. The happy couple walked arm and arm under the swords followed by the attendants. Jack winked at J.J. as he passed trying not to hold the flower girls hand.

The officers sheathed their swords and marched out of the chapel. Two officers soon returned to release the guests one row at a time. Jack reached down and picked up C.J. as Carl and Stacey fell in behind, his ex-wife trailing behind with the boyfriend. Everyone headed to the reception located next to the chapel.

At the reception hall Jack noticed that his name was on one table place marker. He strolled around the round table and realized his ex-wife would not be with him.That brought a smile to Jack. Carl and Stacey came over and took their spots next to Jack at the same table, C.J. and J.J. taking their place with them. The ex-wife was seated closer to the groom's family which suited Jack. Jack looked over and saw her approaching.

"Hi Mom," Carl said. He gave his mom a kiss. The two grandkids gave their grandmother a hug as Stacey kissed her cheek.

"A nice wedding don't you think Jack?" the ex-wife looked at Jack as she asked her question.

"Yes, very beautiful," Jack offered.

"We raised a great daughter."

Jack noticed the consolatory attitude in the phrase 'we' and nodded his head. He had been a career minded policeman bent on advancement. That meant getting a college degree to supplement his Marine Corp veteran status that had got him onto the force. To make detective meant a degree and lots of overtime. He knew he had sacrificed his family too much in striving for the gold shield. And when his wife left for Colorado with his daughter he knew he had to make things right.

Carl, two years older, had stayed in Eugene and Jack went to work to mend the relationship. It took a lot of angry outbursts in martial arts training between the two to get back his son. That they both earned their black belt in the process was a bonus. And then the years spending time with Inez to earn his way into her life. Although mostly long distance with her in Colorado, Jack felt good about their relationship now.

"Yes, we raised a beautiful daughter together." Jack finally answered. And he meant it. He would always have resentment toward his ex for walking out on their marriage. But it had been enough years so he could put most of it aside. Especially on such a special day. The ex turned and walked back to her boyfriend and her table.

A tug on his arm caught Jack's attention. Inez and Eric stood next to him as the band started to play.

"This is Eric and my dance together. Dad daughter dance comes next. Are you ready?" Inez asked.

"Aways and forever." Jack answered which was always his response to his children whenever they asked.

"And parents have a dance coming up too, don't forget. So play nice."

"When have you ever known me not to play nice?" Jack lied.

The parents soon joined the bridal couple on the dance floor. It was a little stiff between Jack and his ex-wife not only for the past but also because Jack was not a smooth dancer. The two kept a proper distance between them and Jack avoided stepping on any toes, at least physical ones. He did manage to step in it when he asked about the boyfriend.

"So your boyfriend enjoying himself?" Jack looked over toward where he sat at the table, a scowl emanating.

"You know his name his Larry, so please use his name." The response came back.

"Sorry," though he didn't really mean it. "Is Larry having a good time?"

"He is being supportive which is a damn sight better then you did most of our marriage."

Jack decided he would let things go so that Inez could have her day. His answer was brief.

"Good man then." Jack lied and tried a little swirl on the dance floor. His ex, startled by the sudden change in rhythm, attempted to keep up.

"Been practicing have we?"

"Just getting better in my old age. Retirement has a way of bringing out new skills I never thought I was interested in."

"Or just trying to keep up with those younger women?"

Jack settled back to the slow dance and took the comment in stride. His ex had certainly seen him with at least one younger woman. Did she know about the others? Had Inez found out from Carl and passed that information on? And did the ex know that he had eventually been married again? A marriage that still existed in name only, as Jack's wife had chosen to leave him. The only reason it wasn't a second failed marriage was he hadn't been served papers for a divorce. So maybe somewhere out there he still had a chance.

The thought of two failed marriages kept Jack quiet the rest of the dance. He looked up as the music stopped and his ex-wife withdrew from his arms.

Jack retreated off the dance floor as the next honorees got ready for their turn with the bride and groom.

Sitting down at his table, Jack pushed his chair back away from the crowd. His thoughts were elsewhere and he was enjoying a quiet moment alone with his thoughts. The grandkids were with Stacey's parents at another table while Carl and Stacey danced, leaving the table empty. The solitude suited Jack's frame of mind.

Jack's thoughts focused on his second wife. A wife who seemed to attract trouble. They had met after she had killed someone who had attacked her. That it had been ruled self defense didn't help the psychological damage that Jack had witnessed. An intense relationship had eventually won through the scars. But that initial intense time had ended with them both going separate ways.

A reunion of sorts took place when the woman's sister needed help. That had rekindled the spark for a brief time. But it was Carl and Stacey's wedding when things had come together for the two of them and they had finally been married.

But trouble soon followed for his new wife and Jack had to rescue her once again. The compounded scars had been too much and she had disappeared on him. His pain continued as Jack missed her. The music continued as the happy couple swirled past. *If only I had another chance* he thought. *I could make it right between us.* A melancholy mood swept over him as he stared out over the hall, gazing at nothing.

"Penny for your thoughts," a voice beside him said.

Startled out of his trance, Jack turned to find his daughter sitting down next to him.

"Oh, hi honey. Don't mind me. Just an old man sitting here with his thoughts. Go back to your party."

"Come on, it's time for the garter toss."

"I'm married, remember." Jack said.

There was a notably lull in the conversation at his statement. Inez knew Jack's wife from Carl's wedding and a brief encounter in Colorado. But Inez hadn't been involved in all the troubles that seemed to come between Jack and his wife.

Jack perked up. "But Larry isn't. I'll come watch and see if he gets lucky."

"Now Dad, remember what I told you. And I suppose you want me to hit Mom with the bouquet too."

"It has been a lot of years that they've been shacked up together. It might spur them on to do the right thing."

Inez grabbed her Dad's arm and pulled him to his feet. Together they stormed to the head table where Eric waited patiently. As they reached the chair provided for the garter removal, Inez let go of her father's arm, but not before whispering in Jack's ear, "Jack Wesley, you are a trouble maker."

* * *

"He isn't there." Alfonso rushed into his boss's office.

"Who?" Daniel asked but already knew the answer from the sweat on Alfonso's face.

"Jack Wesley. He's gone. Our source called to say he left two days ago and they just figured it out."

"Permanently gone. Or just visiting? It is the holiday season." Daniel said, although he didn't pay too much attention to the holiday season. Just more tourists coming to Vegas to extract money from.

"Temporary it seems. The source talked to a neighborhood kid. Seems he was hired to keep the walkways shoveled. So they will be back. I haven't been able to get ahold of our team there yet."

Daniel glared at his underling from the news he was being told. He couldn't do anything about the man leaving and Alfonso had been on top of things. He would let him live another day.

"Check with me when you know more." Daniel said and went back to checking his accounting books. Alfonso knew when he was dismissed and quietly withdrew.